Praise for the w...

A Moment in Time

"Five stars! A scorcher! Totally entrancing! Every woman will be wanting to have Cole Morrison for herself. A story filled with characters you will fall in love with . . . a truly must-buy." —*Scribes World*

"Deb Stover has created a story that blends love, laughter, and miracles. Don't miss it!" —*Huntress Reviews*

"Will have you sitting on the edge wondering how this story can end happily. This has the greatest twist at the end you will love. Five Bells!" —*Bell, Book & Candle*

"Deb Stover continually reinvents the genre with her fresh and original novels. This is an author who has made her mark and continues to captivate. She should be on every reader's keep shelf." —*Romantic Times*

A Willing Spirit

"Sit back, hold on and enjoy the romance that will sweep you away! Ms. Stover writes with a wry wit. *A Willing Spirit* is delicious, titillating. Fine writing, a fantastic romantic tale." —*The Literary Times*

"Creativity, thy name is Deb Stover. Five gold stars!" —*Heartland Critiques*

continued . . .

Mulligan Stew

Deb Stover

JOVE BOOKS, NEW YORK

This is a work of fiction. Names, characters, places, and incidents either are the product of the author's imagination or are used fictitiously, and any resemblance to actual persons, living or dead, business establishments, events, or locales is entirely coincidental.

MULLIGAN STEW

A Jove Book / published by arrangement with the author

PRINTING HISTORY
Jove edition / June 2002

Copyright © 2002 by Debra S. Stover.
Cover art by Bruce Emmet.

Visit our website at
www.penguinputnam.com

ISBN: 0-515-13309-4

A JOVE BOOK®
Jove Books are published by The Berkley Publishing Group,
a division of Penguin Putnam Inc.,
375 Hudson Street, New York, New York 10014.
JOVE and the "J" design
are trademarks belonging to Penguin Putnam Inc.

PRINTED IN THE UNITED STATES OF AMERICA

10 9 8 7 6 5 4 3 2 1

Without the support, encouragement, and a timely kick in the seat of the pants from the talented Karen Harbaugh, this book never would have happened.

Kemberlee Shortland of *www.all-ireland.com* should be nominated for sainthood after her tireless research assistance—especially since she graciously insisted that no question was too stupid. No matter how many times it was asked. . . .

As always, thank you to my Wyrd Sisters—the world's best critique group—and to my ever-patient and loving family.

Annelise Robey and Gail Fortune simply rock! Bless you both.

Bridget's Bodacious Mulligan Stew

4–5 lbs. stew meat
¼ cup drippings (bacon works best)
1 cup of sourdough starter
¼ cup of flour (seasoned with salt and pepper)
6 russet potatoes, cut into ¾–1-inch pieces
2 large onions, cut into ½-inch pieces
1 humongous head of garlic, peeled and chopped
4–6 cups water
1 cup of chopped, fresh okra for thickening
1 cup of cooked pearl barley
3 Tbsp of fresh parsley
¼ cup of chopped celery
3 Tbsp salt
4 Tbsp fresh black pepper (more if you like it hot
    and nasty)

Cut the meat into pieces approximately ¾–1 inch in size, removing any excess fat (or use stew meat). Put into a bowl and dredge in sourdough, then coat with seasoned flour. Into a preheated pot, add the drippings and when melted and very hot, add the meat. Brown the meat quickly. When brown, add the onion, garlic, parsley, and celery. Cook for 2 minutes, stirring often. Reduce the heat, add water and reduce heat to low. Cook about 1½ hours, then add the potatoes, precooked barley, and okra. Place all in Crock-Pot for entire day, or cook 1–2 hours on stove top. Adjust seasonings as desired. Serve with warm corn bread.

Prologue

Perched high atop a craggy cliff, the black castle loomed over the rocks and shore below with an imperious air. It seemed almost human, some claimed, though most God-fearing souls believed whatever force troubled those halls descended not from this earth, but from the shadows of darkness. Indeed, within the boundaries of cold, forbidding stone, something sinister surely lurked.

Something evil.

Along the passageways and battlements of the forsaken tower, in the dank shadows of haze-veiled belfries, time-less injustice, tragedy, and passion clung like mist to the forsaken walls. Fog, turned bloodred by the distant sun, shrouded the parapet, issuing a silent warning to any who dared approach. The massive doors remained closed, and no hint of welcoming light shone from the leaded windows.

A lone figure stood in the long shadow cast by the tower as the sun sank into the sea beyond. The breeze whipped his shaggy dark hair about his shoulders, revealing a face square of jaw and nearly as complex as the decaying castle. He cocked his head at an angle, his expression so intent it seemed he strained to hear the voices of the past.

As if part of the land itself, a magnificent black horse stepped up to his side and nuzzled his shoulder. The man's face softened as he stroked the exquisite animal and a ghost of a smile tugged at his full lips.

With a longing glance at the castle, he gave an emphatic nod. In one fluid movement, he swung himself onto the beast's bare back and urged it into a reckless gallop.

Like the wind, man and horse vanished into the ripening shadows of dusk, leaving *Caisleán Dubh* alone again with its secrets.

For now.

One

Thunder boomed in the distance—undoubtedly Granny Frye kicking open the pearly gates. If St. Peter knew what was good for him, he'd take his coffee break about now.

Standing beside the open grave at the Eternal Peace Cemetery, Bridget Colleen Mulligan glanced down at her dark-haired, six-year-old son and gave his hand a reassuring squeeze. Even with Granny gone, she wasn't completely alone. She had Jacob.

But poor Granny was definitely dead. The old woman had never even seen the truck that hit her as she'd chased General Lee—dear departed Grandpa's deaf and senile coon hound—across the highway.

Unfortunately, General Lee didn't possess enough integrity to have thrown himself beneath the screaming tires along with his benefactress. Now that stupid old dog was sprawled out on Granny's bed, waiting for someone—namely, Bridget—to come home and feed him. Didn't seem right for that dog to outlive both Granny and Grandpa.

Danged unfair to Bridget, too.

She turned her attention back to the funeral service, trying not to grieve over Granny's death or the dog's insatiable appetite. Granny had been saying for years that she was ready to go on to her reward.

Lord, y'all best play bingo every Friday night in heaven or there will be hell to pay.

Grateful no one could read her mind, Bridget glanced around the sparse gathering and adjusted the umbrella over her son's head. She suppressed a shiver as the damp March wind whipped through the threadbare fabric of her old coat and the black dress she'd bought at the church rummage sale.

Brother Marvin's nasal voice droned on and the biting wind blew even harder. Though she knew it was irreverent, Bridget wished the service would end so they could all go home.

Granny would've cursed the sun for not shining on her funeral, and she wouldn't have been very happy about the low-budget coffin and lack of flowers, either. Of course, the old woman hadn't exactly been a realist. Her life insurance policy had devalued to the point where it didn't even cover the cost of this service, let alone anything more extravagant. Bridget had been forced to ask for an advance on her wages to make up the difference.

Money—there was never enough. She had a child to feed and bills to pay, but at least Granny's rundown old trailer was paid for. It was the only home Jacob had ever known, and the only one Bridget could remember.

Now all she had to pay to keep a roof—such as it was—over their heads were the taxes and lot rent. She could handle that. Since Granny had spent every Social Security check the minute she received it, Bridget had been paying the bills anyway. Barely. She hadn't been forced to accept food stamps in order to feed her son yet. However, if it came to that, she would swallow her pride and do what needed doing. Jacob came first—even before her pride and dignity.

Pity General Lee wasn't a hog or a cow. . . . She bit the inside of her cheek in self-chastisement.

Fortunately, Bridget's employers were generous. Cleaning house for the only lawyer in town and his wife had its advantages. They didn't mind her bringing Jacob along, and meals were included in her salary. Hers and Jacob's. Plus, Mr. Larabee had agreed to go over Granny's will and transfer the deed on the trailer without charging Bridget for his services.

The service ended, and Bridget forced her attention back to the present. Mourners filed past to pay their respects, such as they were. The Widow Harbaugh reminded Bridget that Granny had borrowed her red patent leather handbag in 1967 and never returned it. Bridget promised to look for it right away. Mrs. Poole asked for Granny's raw apple cake recipe, and Bridget made yet another promise.

Of course, most of the good women of First Southern Baptist Church had brought casseroles, pies, and cakes by the trailer. Bridget had frozen as much as possible to make the sudden windfall last, and thanked them all profusely, grateful the mourners would not gather at the home of the deceased as custom dictated. Their trailer couldn't hold more than six adults, plus Jacob and General Lee. For once, she was grateful for the minuscule size of her home, because entertaining folks this afternoon would've exhausted the very last of her tact.

The truth was, these people had scorned and belittled Bridget all her life—a legacy handed down from her parents, who'd married during high school after Bridget was conceived in the backseat of Daddy's old Chevy. When Bridget herself had eloped with a handsome stranger with a beguiling accent and more charm than the law should allow, that had clinched her reputation.

Momma and Daddy were both dead and gone now, but these people still looked down their high and mighty noses at their love child twenty-eight years later. Well, Bridget had done all right without Reedville folks, and she only tolerated them now out of respect for Granny. Once the thank-you notes were sent and the Tupperware returned, they need never darken her door again. And vice versa.

Soon, the only people left in the cemetery were Bridget, Jacob, and the men from the funeral home. Even Brother Marvin beat a hasty retreat the moment he could. Who could blame him? March in Tennessee could be as fickle as a forty-year-old spinster.

Right now, Bridget wondered if they'd ever feel warm again. With a sigh, she gazed down at Granny's coffin. "Well," she said, clutching her son's hand and swallowing the lump in her throat. "I'm not going to say good-bye, because you'll always be in my heart."

She'd always loved that wise old woman, even though Granny had dipped snuff and cursed like a marine. If not for her grandparents, Bridget would have been lost and alone after her parents' deaths. Granny and Grandpa hadn't thought twice about bringing their only grandchild into their home.

And now Bridget and Jacob were the end of the line. Except for General Lee, of course.

Bridget's eyes stung and she sniffled, willing herself not to cry. Jacob squeezed her hand and she glanced down at his large green eyes. Granny's eyes. Yes, the old woman would live through both of them. Bridget would see to it.

"Let's go, Jacob," she whispered.

"All right."

She walked down the tree-lined street to the edge of town, where her employers' grand home stood. The brick house was three stories high with white shutters and a broad expanse of porch that would've made Scarlett O'Hara proud.

Bridget had promised Mrs. Larabee she'd stop by on her way home and she always made every effort to keep her word, no matter what. Of course, she suspected the real reason her employer had asked her to stop by was to make sure Jacob had a decent meal. The Larabees were good folks and she never let a day go by when she didn't thank God for her job and being able to keep a roof over her son's head and food in his belly.

Once upon a time she'd nurtured dreams of going to cooking school to become a famous chef, and maybe even teaching folks the forgotten art of down-home cooking. She'd never be a Martha Stewart—not that she couldn't carve butter into flowers if she wanted—but maybe folks would like learning about good old-fashioned home cooking. Comfort food. If there was one thing Granny had taught Bridget, it was how to fix the world's finest comfort food.

Instead of fame and fortune, fate had given Bridget a beautiful little boy. Her eyes blurred with tears of pride as she glanced down at him, walking quietly at her side. Her breath hitched and she had to bite her lower lip to keep from blubbering right there in public. Then what would Jacob think of his momma?

She always wanted him to think well of her. The worst thing in the world would be to have her own flesh and blood ashamed of her. Bridget couldn't bear the thought, let alone the reality. It would destroy her.

So, by God, she wouldn't allow it.

Regaining her composure, she led Jacob through the garden gate and along the cobblestone path through Mrs. Larabee's prized rosebushes. There would soon be a profusion of fragrant blossoms, but now only twisted, thorny vines lined the path.

Bridget and Jacob were tired and cold and hungry by the time they slipped through the back door into the warm, spacious kitchen. She immediately removed her son's damp coat and hung it from a hook on the back porch, putting her coat next to it.

"I'm going to put some soup on to heat while I see what Mrs. Larabee needs me to do today."

"Mmm, chicken noodle?" Jacob asked, and she ruffled his almost black curls.

Bridget opened the cabinet door and removed the fa-

miliar red-and-white can. "Chicken noodle it is." She
opened the can, mixed in the required amount of water,
placed the dish in the microwave, and punched a few buttons. "Granny would've loved having one of these for her
instant cocoa."

"Yep. The kind with them little marshmallows." Jacob
opened a drawer near the pantry door and removed the
coloring books and crayons Mrs. Larabee had bought for
him, then sat at the table.

"You're a good boy, Jacob Samuel Mulligan." Bridget's heart swelled with love for her son. She had no regrets for those few nights in her husband's arms. None at
all. "Sometimes you look just like your father."

She never referred to the man who'd married her then
left her alone and pregnant as Jacob's "daddy," because he
never had been. Sowing his seed didn't make a man a
daddy.

But it sure as heck made a woman look the fool.

No, she didn't mean that. She had loved him in her own
way. If not for that hurried trip to the justice of the peace
and a honeymoon at the Super 8 out on the highway, Bridget wouldn't have Jacob. Besides, someday her son would
want to know about his father, then she'd have to find the
man.

She sure hoped someday didn't come too soon.

She'd chosen to keep her married name after the di-
vorce, especially once she learned she was expecting.
Culley Mulligan hadn't seen fit to respond to Mr.
Larabee's letters or even acknowledge the divorce papers.
Eventually, the law allowed the divorce decree to be fi-
nalized without his cooperation. Or child support. . . .

Jacob flashed her one of his best smiles and she melted
inside. She'd do anything for her son. Anything at all.
Even look up that no-account father of his when the time
came, and she reckoned it would. Kids were naturally curious about things. She just hoped Jacob took his sweet
time about getting around to curious.

She blew her son a kiss and said, "I'll be right back, darlin'. Stay put."

"I will, Momma."

And she knew he would. She slipped through the swinging doors and passed through the dining room before she heard voices coming from the study. Mr. Larabee was home, too. They'd offered to attend Granny's funeral, but Bridget had asked them not to. She couldn't bear for them to see how skimpy the funeral had been, despite their generosity. With a sigh, she lifted her hand and knocked on the heavy paneled door.

"Come in, Bridget," Mrs. Larabee said, swinging open the door. "It's a dreadful day, but I suppose that's only appropriate. Considering."

"Yes'm." Bridget didn't bother to explain that Granny would've preferred a sunny day for her laying to rest, because her wishing it wouldn't change the weather. Besides, it was too late.

"Having a seat, Bridget," Mr. Larabee said, rising from his massive leather chair behind his equally daunting oak desk.

She swallowed the lump in her throat and willed her hands to cease their infernal trembling. Was she in trouble? Had she forgotten to do a chore she'd been asked to perform? No, never. If anything could be said of Bridget Mulligan, it was that she excelled at being conscientious.

Her knees turned to the consistency of that wretched green gelatin Granny'd loved as Bridget sat gingerly on a dark burgundy wingback chair across from Mr. Larabee. Mrs. Larabee stood beside her husband, and when he returned to his seat, she perched on the arm of his chair, her hand resting on his shoulder. They both looked solemn and Bridget gulped.

"I've been going over your grandmother's estate," Mr. Larabee said.

"Estate?" Bridget coughed and shook her head. "I don't hardly think we can call a trailer house older than me an estate."

"No, but with her insurance and such, everything together is her estate . . . for legal purposes." Mr. Larabee drew a deep breath and folded his hands on his desk in front of him, his eyes gentle as he stared straight at her. "Did you have any idea about your grandmother's gambling problem?"

"Gambling?" She shook her head, searching Mrs. Larabee's sympathetic expression. "Granny liked her Friday night bingo. Is that what you mean?"

"Yes, and I'm afraid she was betting on the ponies at the fairgrounds, too." Mr. Larabee bit his lower lip, then reached up to pat his wife's hand where it still rested on his shoulder. "However, the situation isn't all bad."

The flesh around Bridget's mouth went numb and her blood turned colder than the rain that had pervaded Granny's funeral. "Exactly what do you mean, Mr. Larabee? I have a right to know."

"Yes. Yes, you do," Mrs. Larabee said in her soothing way. "No matter what you decide, though, I want you to know you always have a position here, as long as you want it. Don't worry about that. And a room if you ever need it."

Thank heavens. Bridget slumped back in her chair, her breath releasing in ragged spasms as she tried to make sense of nonsense. Girding her resolve, she pinned Mr. Larabee with a look she hoped would get to the bottom of this in short order. "Give it to me straight, sir. Please?"

"Fair enough." He leaned forward and leafed through a stack of papers on his desk. "After your grandfather died, you grandmother gambled away his life insurance money, then took out a loan from a finance company in Marysville."

"Oh, dear Lord." Bridget's heart thudded louder with every breath she took. "The trailer. She gambled away the trailer."

Mr. Larabee closed his eyes for a split second, then nodded. "In all honesty, the finance company never should've loaned her so much. I doubt the trailer's worth half of what she owed on it."

"How much?"

Mr. Larabee looked up at his wife, then faced Bridget again. "It was already in foreclosure before the accident. I'm sorry, Bridget, but it's no longer a matter of how much. There's a court order to vacate the premises by the end of this month."

"Granny knew?" She forced herself to breathe slowly. "But . . . she didn't know that truck would run her down."

"Of course she didn't," Mrs. Larabee said in a gentle voice. "Bridget, we both know your grandmother was a dreamer. She probably thought—*believed*—the next time she would win enough to pay everything."

"Yes, I'm certain of it." Mr. Larabee cleared his throat. "I'm sorry. I know this is hard, but—"

"Hard? It's all I have—all I *had*." Bridget clenched her hands together in her lap, determined to maintain her dignity, no matter what.

"Not all, child," Mrs. Larabee said quietly. "Tell her the other, Donald."

"Other?" A nervous laugh came from Bridget's mouth, though that hardly seemed possible. "She had other debts?"

"No, except for her Sears card, but the balance on that was small. It's been taken care of."

Mr. Larabee made a motion of dismissal with his hand, and Bridget knew he had paid off Granny's Sears card. They were good folks, but she dearly hated taking charity.

Then she remembered her little boy coloring in the kitchen. Right now, she didn't have any choice but to take charity. Jacob came first.

"Thank you," she said steadily, though she felt anything but steady. "You'll both go to heaven for your generous hearts."

Mrs. Larabee moved away from her husband. "I'll entertain Jacob. Is he in the kitchen?"

"Yes'm. We were heating soup in the microwave."

"I'll dish it up and we'll have a nice chat." She paused at the door. "I bought some more of those little oyster crackers he loves." Her lower lip trembled and she bit it, then drew a shaky breath. "Chin up, Bridget. Everything's going to turn out fine. You'll see." She cast her husband another glance and left the room.

Bridget waited until the door clicked shut, then she faced the man again. *I told Granny she'd live on in my heart, but I didn't know it would be heartburn.* Guilt pressed down on her. No. No, I don't mean that.

"I hope you won't be angry with me," Mr. Larabee said.

She looked up at her employer. "Why in tarnation would I be angry with you, sir? This isn't your fault."

Mr. Larabee's cheeks reddened. "I've kept something from you."

A chill permeated her bones, her heart, her soul. "Tell me everything, please," Bridget urged, eager to end this nightmare so she could determine where they would go once the trailer was gone. "What did you keep from me?"

"I finally heard from Culley Mulligan's family, but I . . . I postponed telling you until after the funeral."

She straightened, tilting her head to one side and holding Mr. Larabee's gaze. "So the scallywag decided to surface at last, did he?"

"Bridget . . ." Mr. Larabee's expression grew very sober. "Your ex-husband is dead."

"Oh." No other sound escaped her as she turned icy cold. Though she'd tried desperately to convince herself to hate the man who'd married and abandoned her within seventy-two hours, she'd never completely let go of the fantasy that Culley might return for her one day. Now she knew one day would never be. His wicked grin and roguish charm would remain forever silent.

"Dead." An odd tingling sensation spread across her face and down her throat. "How? When?"

Mr. Larabee drew a slow breath and pushed his glasses

farther up on the bridge of his nose. "The same day you last saw him."

"What?" Disbelief thundered through Bridget. "How? What happened? He was healthy as a horse the night before." Fire flamed in her cheeks as the words left her mouth and the vivid memory of her brief but fertile honeymoon flooded her mind.

Mr. Larabee cleared his throat and she noticed the redness in his cheeks. He was too much of a gentleman to comment on her unladylike remark.

Avoiding her gaze, he said, "Car accident right outside of Marysville."

She nodded slowly. "He . . . he said he had some business over there."

"As far as the highway patrol was concerned, his identification indicated they had a dead Irish citizen on their hands in a rented car." Mr. Larabee shrugged and shook his head. "They had no way of knowing about your marriage or that you should've been contacted." He arched a brow. "You didn't notify the police about his disappearance. Remember?"

Scalding tears filled her eyes. "We . . . we had a fight that morning about what his family would think about me not being Catholic." Though she'd been more worried about it than he had. "I thought . . ."

Mr. Larabee sighed. "So you thought he changed his mind about being married?"

She nodded vigorously, unable to speak. After clearing her throat, she dabbed her eyes dry and lifted her chin. "So they sent him back to Ireland?"

"He's buried in Marysville, but his possessions were returned to his family in Ireland."

"He told me about his momma, a sister, and a brother. And his granny." Bridget's eyes burned and her throat clogged with unshed tears. "All these years I've raved at the man for leaving me . . . and he was dead. All this time. I can't believe it."

"I know."

"It's like losing him all over again." A thought made her breath catch. "What should I tell Jacob?"

"I'm not sure. He never knew his father." Mr. Larabee lifted one shoulder. "It depends on what you decide to do. Maybe it would be best to tell him nothing at all."

"And let him grow up believing his father—his daddy—abandoned him?" Bridget shook her head and lifted her chin a notch. "I'll tell him the truth. I've done the man wrong by believing the worst. I owe him this."

"Whatever you think best." A gentle and bewildering smile curved Mr. Larabee's lips. "You know I sent the divorce papers on to his last known address in Ireland."

"Yes, I remember."

"They've been hidden until now."

"Hidden?"

Mr. Larabee lifted an envelope with an unusual looking stamp. "According to this letter from Culley's mother, she found the envelope containing the divorce papers among her late mother-in-law's personal belongings."

"She hid them?" Perplexed, Bridget furrowed her brow. "Why?"

"Mrs. Mulligan said her mother-in-law probably thought it best the family believed her grandson died unmarried, rather than married to a woman who would, uh, 'stoop' to divorce."

Liquid fire suffused Bridget's cheeks. "That's hogwash. She didn't know what—"

"Of course she didn't know, but that's past now," Mr. Larabee continued. "I received this letter the day after your grandmother died, and I wanted to wait until everything was settled."

"What's there to settle?" Her throat turned drier than August dog days. "I've lost my home, my granny, and learned my husband died instead of abandoning me. Mercy, what a lucky break." Bitterness edged her voice and her hands trembled.

"Don't you see, Bridget?"

"See what?"

"You and Jacob have family. In-laws." A shock of white hair fell across Mr. Larabee's forehead and he shoved it back with slender fingers. "And there's property."

Swallowing the lump in her throat, she wiped her sweaty palms and reached for the letter. "Property? I don't understand."

"Mrs. Mulligan believes you have a right to your share, especially since you weren't notified of your husband's death."

Culley's momma . . . ? "Is the property valuable? Can I sell it?"

Mr. Larabee smiled. "Being unfamiliar with Irish real estate, I can't—"

"*Irish*? Of course, it's Irish. I wasn't thinking." Bridget leaned forward. "So Culley's property is in Ireland."

"Yes. Culley Mulligan didn't own anything in the States."

Except my heart. "I know." She shook her head. "If I had a brain . . ."

"You have an excellent brain, and don't ever forget that." He placed both palms flat on the surface of his desk and leaned forward. "Your husband's family owns a farm in County Clare. That's on the west coast of Ireland."

"What do I have to do?" Property for her son? But in *Ireland*? Of course, once upon a time, she'd believed she would go home with Culley. . . .

"It's a fairly large farm by Irish standards, and it includes the original keep."

"Keep?"

One corner of Mr. Larabee's mouth turned upward. "A castle, Bridget."

"A *castle?*" Crazed laughter erupted from her throat. Here she'd been fretting the loss of an old trailer, only to learn her dead husband had owned a castle. After a moment, she wiped her eyes dry and cleared her throat.

Culley had never mentioned a castle, though she remembered him talking about his family with love. He'd described his home so vividly, she'd laughingly accused him of painting pictures with words. Except for the castle. . . .

She really had loved the man. A shaky sigh escaped her parted lips. *He's dead.* She would have to visit his grave to convince herself of that fact.

"The property—there has to be a catch," she said, bringing herself back to the present.

"It's part of his family's estate." Mr. Larabee flipped through the papers on his desk and removed one. "This is a printout of the microfiche file from Dublin."

With trembling fingers, Bridget took the document.

"As you can see, the family has clear deed to the land, but it's an entailed estate. You can't take your share and sell it unless the rest of the family agrees. In writing."

No sense getting greedy at this late date. "Right. His family." A family full of Irish folks she'd never met sounded like more trouble than General Lee that time Mrs. Baldwin's poodle went into heat.

But Jacob would have a granny, an aunt, and an uncle. In fact, he might even have little Irish cousins near his own age. Children were what made a family a family. She'd never had brothers, sisters, or cousins to play with. Until this moment, she hadn't realized how much she wanted that for her son.

"What do you think about all this?" Mr. Larabee asked gently.

"Not only is this written in legal mumbo jumbo, but there are words here I'm pretty sure aren't even English. Do you know what it *really* says, Mr. Larabee? The bottom line, sir, if you please?"

Mr. Larabee returned the document to the folder and removed another. "Read this letter from Fiona Mulligan instead. It might make more sense."

She took the letter and removed it from its envelope. Neat handwriting on crisp white paper leapt out at her. It was brief but friendly. "She wants to meet me."

Mr. Larabee nodded, his expression compassionate.

"That makes perfect sense. Her son died and left a wife behind she's just now learned about."

"Yes, I reckon she's curious."

"When I spoke with her on the phone, I got the impression she's a lot more than just curious."

Realization made the flesh around Bridget's mouth tingle again and she had to swallow several times before she could speak. "You . . . you told her about Jacob."

Mr. Larabee's cheeks reddened. "It should have come from you, but . . . the divorce settlement Culley never received did mention child support. I'm sorry."

"And . . . ?"

A huge grin split Mr. Larabee's face and his eyes twinkled behind his spectacles. "She said, 'I want to hold me boy's flesh and blood in me arms, and see the lad's face with me own two eyes.'"

Bridget had to laugh at Mr. Larabee's attempt at an Irish accent, though nothing about this was humorous. The man she'd married was dead, and his momma wanted to meet his son. Bridget owed Culley that. "I understand." She leaned closer, sliding the letter across the desk's smooth surface.

"I'll be blunt, Bridget," Mr. Larabee sobered again. "Mrs. Mulligan indicated to me that her older son—Riley, I think she said—believes you might try to con the family out of their land."

"Con?" Silently seething, she tried to quell her rising indignation. And failed. *"Con?"*

"Mrs. Mulligan also said that Riley will want proof."

She stiffened. "I don't need to *prove* anything to anybody. I know the truth."

Mr. Larabee cleared his throat. "Your mother-in-law had just the opposite reaction, however. She can't wait to meet you *and* Jacob. In fact, she reminds me of you."

That's what Culley said. Her heart stuttered and she warmed from within, realizing with a start that she could now give herself permission to have loved Culley Mulligan. "Culley's momma wants us to come for a visit?"

Mr. Larabee nodded. "More than a visit, Bridget. She wants you to bring her grandson home. Her words."

"Home?"

"Where he belongs, according to her."

An odd tremor of fear and excitement coalesced and pulsed through Bridget. Her cheeks grew warm and she clutched the fabric of her skirt in both fists. "He *belongs* with *me.*"

Mr. Larabee pulled off his glasses and leveled his gaze on her. "Mrs. Mulligan's said her late husband's will was pretty specific."

"Specific?" She knew it was too good to be true. There was probably some catch to all this that would keep Jacob from receiving his inheritance.

"I mentioned earlier, this is what's called an entailed estate. One family member can't sell any portion without the permission of them all."

"I remember."

"Your son will be entitled to an inheritance when he reaches his majority."

"That's good. Culley would've wanted that."

Mr. Larabee sighed. "They may require proof of paternity since the marriage was sudden and secret—"

"I'm not the one who kept it secret."

"I know, but they can probably prevent Jacob from inheriting anything, or at least drag it out for many years." Mr. Larabee met her gaze. "Going there will show good faith, and—let's face facts—you have nothing here except your job with us. You have nothing here except your job with us."

Bridget reminded herself of the eviction notice. She had a child to feed, and that child's daddy might finally come through with some support. Remembering Culley's laughing eyes, tears welled in her own. She'd much rather have had Culley with her all along than have his property now without him.

In fact, she owed it to Culley to make sure his son took his rightful place in the Mulligan family. Pride made her lift her chin and square her shoulders. A slow, determined smile pulled at the corners of her mouth. "Then I reckon I'll take my son to meet his daddy's family."

"That's the spirit." Mr. Larabee returned her smile. "When shall I tell Mrs. Mulligan to expect you?"

A sinking sensation struck Bridget. The final blow. Her mouth went dry and her eyes burned. "Never." She held her hands out, palms up. "I don't have the money for the trip." Her breath came out in a whoosh and she fell back against the chair. Defeated. "I guess that's the end of—"

"No. It's just the beginning." Mr. Larabee smiled again and handed another envelope to Bridget. "Open it."

Shaking from the inside out, she leaned forward and took the envelope and looked inside. "It's full of cash."

Mr. Larabee nodded. "Mrs. Mulligan wired the money for you and Jacob to use for plane fare."

"I see." Bridget stared at the money in amazement. "And she trusts me enough to believe I won't use this for something else?"

"She said if you don't bring Jacob to Ireland, she'll assume you lied about his paternity."

Bridget's pride reared its offended head and she rose, her knees quaking beneath her. "I never lie."

Mr. Larabee rose as well and gave her a satisfied nod. "I know."

After several deep breaths, she trusted herself to meet his gaze again. His eyes twinkled approvingly.

"Now what do I do?" She held the envelope against her chest, afraid it might vanish as magically as it had appeared. "I don't even have a passport. And what about General Lee?"

"We'll walk you through the process, but it will take a few weeks," Mr. Larabee promised. He rolled his eyes heavenward and chuckled. "And, heaven help me, we'll take care of General Lee."

She laughed along with him, and a strange new emotion filled and empowered her. A feeling she'd rarely known in her twenty-eight years.

Hope.

"Is there enough here to buy plane tickets *and* repay you and Mrs. Larabee for your generosity?"

"That's not ne—"

"Yes, it *is* necessary." She met his gaze and he nodded.

"Very well. I'm sure there's plenty."

A huge grin spread across her face and she hugged the envelope close. "A real castle, Mr. Larabee?"

He nodded, smiling. *"Caisleán Dubh."* He pronounced it *Cash-Lawn Doov.* "At least, that's how Mrs. Mulligan pronounced it."

"Doov?" Bridget echoed. "I wonder what it means."

"Mrs. Larabee said you'd want to know, so she looked it up on the Internet. We think it means black."

"Black? So '*Caisleán Dubh*' must mean 'Castle Black.'"

"Or Black Castle, I suppose." He folded his arms across his lean abdomen, his expression paternal. "We're going to miss you, but I think you're about to embark on an adventure."

"Lord, yes." Bridget stared out the window at the soft drizzle. "An adventure."

"I think I'm jealous."

She smiled. "You're just going to miss my biscuits and red-eye gravy."

The man blushed to his ears and gave an emphatic nod. "And everything else you cook."

"I'll leave recipes."

"Much obliged."

She released a long sigh and grinned. "By golly, that finance company can have the trailer with my blessing."

"Good for you."

"After all," she hugged herself to make sure she was awake, "who needs a rundown old trailer when they have a castle?"

TWO

Flying was both the greatest thrill and the most bone-chilling fear Bridget had ever known. All across the Atlantic, she'd prayed for their safety, while maintaining a false front of calm for her son's benefit. The last thing she wanted was to frighten Jacob.

However, Jacob was engrossed with the entire experience. He pressed his nose to the window to gaze down at the white caps and fluffy clouds. Every time the plane bounced through rough air, Jacob said, "Whee!"

Bridget stopped breathing.

If—no, *when*—the plane landed safely at Shannon Airport, she vowed never to fly again. When the time came for them to return home, she intended to book passage on a nice, slow boat.

Of course, the *Titanic* had set sail from Ireland. . . .

"Look, Momma," Jacob said, standing to peer out the window. "It sure is green."

Tentatively, Bridget unbuckled her seat belt and slid closer, holding her breath as she peered over her son's shoulder. "Well, I'll be."

"Is that where we're going?"

"I reckon that must be Ireland," Bridget whispered,

banishing her fear as the plane eased through more air turbulence. *Lord, have mercy.* Even after the flight attendant had told her to think of the turbulence as similar to a speed bump or a pothole, Bridget still hated it. After all, she could *see* speed bumps and potholes.

"What's that?" Jacob pressed his finger against the badly smudged window. His full face print was smeared onto the glass in several places.

Bridget saw sheer cliffs along the coast. "I remember reading about those." She'd done her homework before leaving Tennessee. The local library had contained more information about Ireland than she ever would have guessed. "Those are the Cliffs of Moher," she said, hoping she had the pronunciation right.

The man with the aisle seat next to them broke his silence and cleared his throat. "Aye, and what a grand place 'tis, too."

Bridget met his gentle gaze. His blue eyes twinkled amid a web of wrinkles and bushy white brows. "You've been there?"

"Aye, many times." The man sighed.

Bridget settled back and refastened her seat belt. "You're Irish, aren't you?" The man's accent was enchanting, reminding her of Culley. That persistent pang of guilt returned. If only she could undo the years of believing the worst of her poor dead husband.

"Aye, though I've been in the States with my daughter's family these past eleven years." He smiled, his face glowing. "But 'tis what I'm needing now, this homecoming." He held out his right hand. "I'm Brady, and I grew up right down the coast, in Ballybronagh."

Bridget shook the man's hand. "I'm Bridget, and this is my son, Jacob. Mr., uh . . . ?"

"Just call me Brady, lass."

Brady had kept his nose buried in a book the whole trip up until now. Since he felt like talking, she decided to pick his brain for information. "So you're from County Clare?"

"Aye, and proud of it I am."

Jacob withdrew himself from the window and turned his attention to the man. "Have you seen our castle?"

"A castle is it, now?" Brady's eyes twinkled. "There be many castles in Ireland, though I fear most are crumbling away."

Bridget had explained to her son that she'd learned his father—no, his *daddy*—was dead, and that they were going to Ireland to meet Jacob's grandmother. She patted her son's hand now, grateful she'd found the guts to tell him the truth.

"Momma, how do you say our castle's name again?" Jacob asked, studying her intently.

"It isn't ours, Jacob. It belongs to your daddy's kin." Her cheeks warmed and she feared she would butcher the pronunciation. "I believe it's *Caisleán Dubh*," she said carefully, glancing at Brady for approval.

The old man's eyes widened and his lips parted in obvious surprise. "*Dubh*, you say?" He shook his head. "That one's a sight to be sure." He looked at Bridget curiously.

"What kinda sight, sir?" Jacob asked, the way only a child could—directly, without subterfuge. "Is it really black?"

"Aye, 'tis very dark, and there isn't another anywhere I've heard tell of with its design." He gave them a sheepish grin. "At least, not in Ireland."

"Unique how?" Bridget asked, tickled to meet someone who knew about *Caisleán Dubh*. Maybe he even knew the family . . .

"*Caisleán Dubh* is a square castle with a round tower keep to one side." Brady stroked his chin and squinted, obviously trying to remember. "Most castles are one or t'other—not both."

"It sounds interesting." Bridget chewed her lower lip. "It's very large, then?"

"Aye." He half-turned toward her, obviously warming to his subject. "*Caisleán Dubh* is built on a cliff, overlooking the Atlantic."

"A cliff?" Jacob leaned forward. "Way high, like the ones we just seen?"

"Saw," Bridget corrected, smiling at her son.

"Saw." Jacob made a face at her that warmed her heart.

Brady chuckled and nodded his approval. "As a teacher, lad, I can tell you how fortunate you are to have a mum who cares enough to make sure you learn to use proper grammar." He winked at Bridget. "Even if 'tis American grammar."

Bridget liked this man, and she smiled. "So there's a large castle and a tower. The stones are black." She sighed, trying to picture it. "Does it have a drawbridge?"

"No," Brady said. "They positioned the castle close enough to the sea not to need one. The windows are high enough to prevent attackers from scaling the walls. From the land and sea, it appears inaccessible until you're right in front of it. At one time, there was a drawbridge that opened to the land through a wall built around the fortress, but only a few crumbling stones remain. It opened to the ground level, beneath the main hall."

"Oh, I can't wait to see the inside of it." Goose bumps popped out on Bridget's arms as she tried to picture *Caisleán Dubh*.

"The *inside*, is it? That would be a treat." Brady's brow furrowed and his expression grew solemn.

"I want to go inside, too," Jacob said. "Can we?"

"Well, lad . . . with the curse and all, I doubt you'll be seein' the inside of *Caisleán Dubh*."

An icy wave washed through Bridget. "Curse?" she echoed in a small voice.

"A real curse? Wow!" Jacob stretched half across Bridget to get closer to Brady. "What kinda curse? Is there a dungeon? Is it haunted? Is there a pit and a pen . . . pen . . . you know, like that movie?"

"Jacob." Bridget's cheeks flamed even hotter now and she placed a firm but gentle hand on her son's shoulder. "Don't bombard the poor man with questions."

The boy's face fell and he slumped back in his seat. "Sorry."

"'Tis all right," Brady said. "I'm the one who should be apologizin'. Perhaps 'curse' isn't quite the right word."

Bridget sighed in open relief. "I certainly hope it isn't cursed." She gave a nervous laugh.

"*Caisleán Dubh* is owned by the Mulligans," Brady said, watching her very closely. "So, I'm guessin' your husband must be a Mulligan." His brow furrowed and he stroked his chin with thumb and forefinger.

"Yes, sir." Bridget squared her shoulders. Now was the time for her to become comfortable with being Culley Mulligan's widow. "Culley Mulligan was my husband."

"Ah, Culley, was it? I remember hearing about his passing from my granddaughter," he said quietly. "I recall young Culley as being a fine lad. I taught school for twenty-six years and he was one of my finest pupils. 'Tis a tragedy."

Tears burned her eyes, but she blinked them away. "Yes, he was a good man." *And I'll see to it his memory is good and pure, Lord.*

Brady leaned forward and directed his question at Jacob. "So Culley Mulligan was your da, lad?"

Jacob shot Bridget a questioning glance and she nodded, hoping she could undo some of the damage her doubts about Culley had created in her son's mind and heart. Though she hadn't raved about Culley within her son's hearing, how could he not have picked up on her resentment all these years?

"Yes, sir." Jacob's eyes widened and he inched closer. "Do . . . do I look like him?"

Though she'd already told the boy at least a hundred times how much he looked like his daddy, Bridget recognized Jacob's need for confirmation. She bit the inside of her cheek, praying.

"Why, you're the image of young Culley. Aye, lad, you favor your da."

Thank you, Lord.

"And your uncle Riley, as well."

"He's my daddy's brother." Jacob bit his lower lip, obviously struggling to remember all the names. "And my aunt's name is . . ."

"Aye, an aunt it is." Brady smiled. "I'll not be rememberin' her name now, as she was but a wee lass when I left for the States."

"Mary Margaret," Bridget said quietly, stroking the curls that framed her son's face. "Culley called her Maggie, though."

"Ah, a fine name to be sure." The older man studied Bridget with renewed interest. "For that matter, Bridget is a fine Irish name in its own right."

She smiled, remembering her grandpa's stories about their ancestors fleeing Ireland during the Potato Famine. Of course, he hadn't been alive then, but the tales were passed down from generation to generation. And now she was returning to the scene of the crime. So to speak.

"Yes, Bridget Colleen Frye is my maiden name."

"Irish as can be." Brady's smile spread from ear to ear.

The old man's obvious pleasure at hearing about her Irish roots delighted her for some reason, and she returned his smile. "My grandpa claims I was named after my great-granny, though I never knew her."

"'Tis a fine thing to name children after those who came before them." A distant expression entered Brady's eyes, but he quickly resumed smiling. "There's somethin' about the name Frye I should be rememberin'." He tapped his chin thoughtfully. "It'll come to me later, to be sure."

"Tell us about the curse," Jacob said, leaning across Bridget's lap.

"Jacob," Bridget said warningly. She really didn't want to hear about a curse. She'd faced enough of those in real life without dealing with a make-believe one, too.

Brady exchanged glances with Bridget and seemed to sense her reluctance. He shrugged and flashed Jacob a cockeyed grin. "I might've stretched the truth a wee bit, lad."

"No curse?" Jacob's disappointment was downright palpable.

"Well, there was a tragedy at *Caisleán Dubh,* to be sure," the old man said. "Do you know the story of *Romeo and Juliet,* Jacob?"

Jacob shook his head and Bridget gave him an indulgent smile. "I don't reckon they teach Shakespeare in kindergarten," she said.

"Well, what happened at *Caisleán Dubh* is somethin' akin to that tale," Brady continued, shaking his head solemnly. "You ask your mum to read the story to you. A lad is never too young to be learning."

Bridget sighed and whispered, "Thank you."

"Besides," the Irishman said with an emphatic nod, "I believe you'll be hearin' all about the curse of *Caisleán Dubh* soon enough."

Riley Mulligan shoved a stubborn shock of black hair out of his face and unfolded himself from his mum's car. He despised crowds, and the nature of his mission today made his belly burn and his temples throb.

Fiona Mulligan was beside herself, because she had badly wanted to make the trip. However, an attack of gout had different ideas. The poor woman wouldn't be able to venture farther than her rocking chair for at least two days. And Maggie was too young to send alone to Shannon, though she'd been driving for over a year now. Besides, she had school today.

Riley sighed and made his way across the carpark and into the terminal. A quick glance at his watch confirmed that he should reach customs in plenty of time to meet the woman.

He'd rather drink a watered-down pint. Jaysus, he'd even rather eat Maggie's pitiful excuse for soda bread—a shudder rippled through him at the thought of his sister's most recent effort in that regard. Truth be told, given his druthers, he'd choose to be doing anything but this.

But a promise had been made, and keep it he would.

Mum's tears and pleading had done him in, just as she'd
known. He'd never been a man to deny a weeping woman
anything, so long as it made her stop. A weakness among
the Mulligan males, it was, handed down from generation
to generation. Alas, Riley Francis Mulligan was no exception.

And now, Jaysus help him, he was at the airport to
fetch the woman who claimed to have married Culley and
borne his son.

Renewed anger vibrated through Riley. Soon he would
see the liar's face for himself, and he'd be having nothing
less than the truth. Culley wasn't here to defend himself,
so it fell to his brother to do it for him. And do it he would.

Clenching his fists, he paused before a monitor and
checked the flight number and gate. "On time," he muttered, shoving his unruly hair out of his face again. He
glanced at his watch, and moved to the area where pas-
sengers would emerge after going through customs.

They didn't have so much as a photograph of the
woman or the lad, though the attorney to whom Mum had
spoken had provided a description. Bridget Mulligan was,
so Mum had informed Riley, an attractive young woman
with wavy brown hair, above average in height, and slender. The boy was said to have nearly black curls.

Like Culley's . . . and his? By the saints, he didn't want
to ponder any of this. The woman was a fraud and he
would prove it. Any resemblance would be pure coincidence.

Armed with this certainty, he stood staring as passen-
gers emerged from customs. He'd refused to hold the sign
his sister had made bearing the woman's name. She could
find him on her own or turn around and go back to the
States where she belonged.

His heart thudded louder as each passenger filed past
with no sign of a woman meeting her description, and not
a single dark-haired lad. *Well, fine, then.* He swallowed
the burning bile in his throat and shoved his hands in his
pockets, prepared to leave. Though Mum and Maggie

would be disappointed, this was for the best. The woman would've brought them nothing but misery, and Jaysus knew the Mulligans had seen more than their fair share of that.

Just as he retrieved his keys from his pocket and clenched his fist about them, they appeared—a woman in her late twenties with brown hair curling about her shoulders, and a lad with a head full of nearly black curls. Riley's breath froze as his gaze shifted from the child to the mother.

The woman stared at him, her eyes wide and her lips slightly parted. Her already fair skin paled further and he thought she might even have swayed a bit. Was it because he resembled Culley? Even so, just because the woman knew what Culley had looked like didn't mean she'd married the man and given birth to his son.

Something compelled Riley to look at the boy again. The lad was the image of Culley at the same age. *No, it's pure coincidence, Mulligan, and don't be forgetting that again.* They started toward him and Riley cleared his throat, returning his keys to his pocket. The lad really did have a Mulligan look about him. *Listen to yourself.* The world was crawling with dark-haired children.

He released a ragged sigh as they came nearer. She was a beauty, to be sure, and Culley had always appreciated a comely face. Riley's gaze lowered and he noticed the way her breasts filled out her green jumper. Aye, Culley could easily have fallen for her charms, but married her . . . ? No, Culley would never have married a woman he barely knew—not with a local lass waiting for him to come home and marry *her.* Besides, there was the church to consider.

This American woman was a scab—after money or the farm, but certainly not Culley's widow. *Keep it straight, you bloody caffler.* Girding himself, Riley straightened and squared his shoulders as the pair stopped directly in front of him.

No one spoke as they stood staring at each other. He

grew uncomfortable with her scrutiny and shoved his infernal hair out of his face again.

"You're Riley Mulligan," she said quietly, her voice quavering a bit.

"Aye." He gave a curt nod, not bothering with the formalities. He didn't want this woman and her son here, and he wasn't about to pretend otherwise.

"Forgive me for staring, but . . ." She drew a shaky breath and a nervous laugh followed. "You look so much like . . ."

Riley nodded again, not wanting to admit that the woman had recognized him because of the familial resemblance. The explanation was simple—she'd seen a photo of him, or at least of Culley. Any *gobshite* with eyes could see the resemblance.

He glanced down at the lad again. His eyes were green like his mother's—not Mulligan blue. Somewhat relieved, Riley allowed himself this one small victory, though he knew the battle ahead would be long and bloody. Something told him this woman would not give up easily.

Nor would he.

"You my uncle Riley?" the lad asked, his head tilted back so he could stare into Riley's eyes.

Heat crept up from Riley's collar and he bit the inside of his cheek to silence his thoughts before he said something unsuitable for a youngster's ears. Any youngster. Even this one. "I'm Riley Mulligan," he said instead.

The child released his mum's hand and shoved his right one toward Riley. "I'm Jacob Samuel Mulligan, and I'm right pleased to meet you, sir."

A rehearsed speech if ever he'd heard one, but Riley couldn't suppress the grin that tugged at his lips. The lad's accent screamed American hillbilly, like those Country and Western singers they sometimes heard on the radio. He squirmed inwardly, not wanting to like the woman or her son. Even so, there was nothing to do but shake the lad's hand, so he did.

Unfortunately, the woman seemed to have recovered

from her initial shock and thrust her hand forward, too. "Seems my son's got better manners than his momma." Her smile made her entire face glow. "I'm Bridget Colleen Mulligan."

Hearing the Mulligan name leave her lips tensed every nerve in Riley's body, but he reluctantly shook her hand. He tried, and failed, not to notice how small and delicate hers felt in his calloused farmer's paw. His face warmed and his throat tightened. Aye, Culley would've been attracted to this siren.

Could she be his brother's widow? *Enough of this.*

"We'd best be about finding your bags," he said, struggling to ignore the battling voices in his head. "Did they give you a pass in customs?"

"Yes, but not without stealing all my herbs."

"Herbs?" He blinked.

"Homegrown, and now they're gone." She released a long sigh. "I packed enough to last for months, too."

The foolish woman had packed fresh herbs, and from the sound of it, enough to open her own market. Didn't she think they had food in Ireland?

"Your momma didn't come?" she asked.

"She's down with a bit of gout." Guilt reared its ugly puss. Mum had asked him to pass along her regrets at not being able to come herself. He sighed and muttered, "'Tis sorry she is for not being able to fetch you and the lad herself." There, he'd done his duty and could now revert to his natural charm.

"Gout?" She made a tsking sound with her tongue and shook her head. "Grandpa used to get gout and the only thing that helped were cherries."

"Cherries?" Riley echoed, arching a brow in disbelief. "What'd he do? Stomp on them to make wine?"

She blinked and gave him such an innocent look, he decided then and there she had to be either the world's greatest actress or genuinely naive.

Finally she giggled. "Oh, a joke. I'm sorry." After a few moments, she shook her head. "No, he ate the cher-

ries for the gout and they always fixed him right up." She
tilted her head closer and whispered, "Kept him regular,
too, which always improved his spirits."

Riley's first instinct was to throw his head back and
roar with laughter, but he managed to save himself by
summoning a scowl instead. The woman had perfected
the art of playing the fool, but he didn't buy it for a
minute. This was all part of her evil ruse, of course.

But he saw right through her. Life had thrown him
plenty of hard knocks—enough to train him to recognize
deceit on any level. A nasty smile spread across his face
as he turned and started walking. After a moment, he
glanced back and saw the pair of them struggling with
their backpacks and carry-on items. *Aye, charm, Mulligan. That's you.*

Cursing under his breath, he swaggered back and
hefted the largest bag onto his shoulder, inclining his head
to indicate they should follow. Without another word, he
started down the crowded corridor.

Finally, they were on the road home and would be
lucky to reach it before dark. Mum would be worried, and
as much as he resented Bridget and Jacob's presence, he
would tolerate almost anything to avoid upsetting Mum.

Bridget chattered endlessly about every little thing as
they drove west. Riley didn't need to talk—she kept the
silence filled quite thoroughly. Not that he'd have minded
a bit of silence about now.

Barely saving himself from growling aloud, he glanced
in the rearview mirror and saw the lad had fallen asleep.
With his eyes closed he looked even more like Culley.

By the time Riley turned onto the narrow lane that led
to the cottage, Bridget had blathered on about cooking,
gardening, her granny, grandpa, and the Larabees, and
someone named General Lee who'd killed her granny.
And what was this "y'all" business, anyway?

Confident he'd heard her entire family history, he
breathed a sigh of relief when the whitewashed cottage
came into view. It was shortly after five o'clock and in

early May that meant they had a bit of daylight left to this very long day.

"Are we there yet?" a small voice asked from the backseat.

"I don't know," the lad's mother said.

Riley felt her gaze on him and he resented it all over again. She was an intruder on his land and in his life, and the last thing in the world his family needed was more trouble. The saints knew the Mulligans had known enough in this lifetime and generations past.

"Aye, we're there yet," he snapped, regretting his harsh tone immediately. After all, hadn't he promised Mum he'd behave himself and mind his manners . . . such as they were? "Almost."

"Oh, it's beautiful." Bridget looked out the open window and Riley glanced over at her.

As she strained to see the cottage in the distance, her breasts thrust forward, her nipples clearly outlined against her jumper. His gut pressed upward against his heart and his blood heated and thickened. She had a right nice pair of breasts. Once upon a time, he and Culley would've called them diddies. He shocked even himself by growing hard before he could draw his next breath.

Jaysus, what's come over you, Mulligan? He dragged his hands through his hair. A breeze wafted through the open window and the salty scent of the sea calmed him and soothed his sudden lust.

"Momma, look!"

Both adults turned to stare at the lad, who pointed toward something, his eyes round and dark. "Is that it?" he asked.

A chill washed over Riley and his mouth went dry. He knew without looking what the lad saw. "That'll be *Caisleán Dubh*," he said stonily, staring straight ahead.

Bridget leaned toward him, ducking her head to see through the window on his side of the car. The scent of something spicy drifted up from her glossy brown curls, but he caught himself before he could draw a second appreciative sniff.

The *cailleach*—witch—had cast a spell over him. That was it. Had she done the same to Culley with her false innocence and lush body? He glanced at her lovely face and swallowed hard. Aye, it could've happened. There was no denying her appeal.

"Is it really cursed?" Jacob asked, shattering the silence.

The castle's curse was Riley's least favorite subject, but he'd rather talk about that than dwell on the fierce attraction he felt for this woman. Even a curse was safer than whatever magic Bridget possessed.

"Aye, there is a curse." He steered up the winding lane toward his home.

"Do you live there?" the lad persisted.

Pressure commenced in Riley's gut and he wished he had remembered to bring his antacids along. "No one has lived in *Caisleán Dubh* for over a hundred years."

"Why?"

If there was one thing Riley Mulligan didn't want to discuss, it was *Caisleán Dubh*. Being Americans, he supposed they couldn't help themselves, though the woman was uncommonly quiet. Thank heaven.

"Why doesn't anyone live there?" the lad asked again.

Riley gnashed his teeth and released a slow breath. "Because it's old," he finally said.

"But—".

Bridget straightened and turned toward her son. "Don't ask so many questions, Jacob," she said quietly.

Riley glanced at her again. Her features seemed pinched, her tone strained. The castle had that effect on some.

Like him.

"I just wanna know why," Jacob said, his tone taking on a whining quality that sliced right through a man.

Gripping the steering wheel so tightly his arms trembled, Riley held his breath. He counted to himself, willing his heart to slow and his head to cease its infernal pounding. He should've torn that castle down stone by bloody stone right after—

"Can we go in there?" Jacob asked. "I wanna see inside."

"No." Groaning, Riley shoved his wayward hair back from his face again. He wouldn't lose control. The iron door at the back of his mind squeaked open, allowing the memories to creep closer to the surface. Threatening. *Not now. Not now, please.*

"Stop whining, Jacob," Bridget said. "Just let it be. Maybe you can go see the castle later."

"Never," Riley said, still staring straight ahead.

The lad said, "Why c—"

Rage whipped through Riley and he slammed on the brake, whirling around to face the cowering child.

"No one goes there. Not now. Not *ever.*"

Three

"Begging your pardon," Bridget said stonily, struggling against her rising anger, "but you don't have the right or reason to speak to my son in that tone."

Riley's knuckles whitened against the steering wheel, then he gave a curt nod and glanced in his mirror. "'Tis sorry I am for snapping at you, Jacob." Without another word, he continued the short drive to the cottage.

Bridget gave her now silent son an encouraging smile, then turned her attention to the countryside again. She didn't like starting off this way with Culley's brother, but she wasn't about to let him verbally abuse her child, either. Drawing a deep breath, she looked out at the lush green fields, huge rocks along the shore, the ocean glistening just beyond, and nary a tree in sight, save a few near the cottage. It looked like something out of a storybook.

Her gaze returned to the castle and her breath froze. A cold sweat sprang from her pores and she shivered. Granny would've said someone had walked across her grave.

You're being silly, she told herself and drew a steadying breath, turning her attention away from the castle and back to the beautiful farm. Yes, the Mulligans' farm was like a fairy-tale place—a magical kingdom complete with a castle. And a curse. She shot Riley a sidelong glance. *No handsome prince, though.*

Oh, he was handsome enough, but it was downright difficult to see beyond that shaggy mop of hair and persistent scowl. Still, he was Culley's brother and she would grant Riley the same tolerance she would have given her own brother if she'd had one.

As long as he didn't mistreat Jacob again. *That* she would tolerate from no one—kin or not.

A tall auburn-haired woman stood on the porch of the cottage, leaning heavily on a cane. She shaded her eyes and waved as the car approached.

Bridget swallowed hard. A pity her husband wasn't the man bringing her home to meet his family. Grief welled within her, sudden and fierce, but she swallowed her tears and drew a shaky breath. "Is that . . . Culley's momma?" Bridget asked.

"Aye, and mine," Riley reminded her, his tone curt.

Fuming in silence, Bridget gnashed her teeth as he swung the car around and parked it beneath the lone shade tree before the cottage. A profusion of spring flowers distracted her from her dark mood and she counted to ten, banishing thoughts of strangling Riley Mulligan. The flowers bloomed around the base of the porch, bordered by a neat row of rocks that ended at the steps and a worn dirt path.

Mrs. Mulligan came down the steps with the aid of her cane. A tall, redheaded girl followed. She looked so much like her mother, she had to be Mary Margaret, Culley's sister. They paused at the base of the steps, waiting.

Bridget drew another steadying breath and reached for the door handle. Riley jumped out of the vehicle as if it were on fire, racing around to open the door before she had a chance. *So he's minding his manners in front of his momma.* She couldn't prevent the smile that tugged at her lips. A man willing to please his momma couldn't be all bad, no matter what he wanted her to think.

Odd, but she was suddenly certain that Riley had been deliberately baiting her, and now he was putting on a show for his momma. *Fine, let him.* He didn't want her to like him or to feel welcome here when no one was watching. She had no idea what his motives were for either sort of behavior, but Granny would've said to watch for the true color of his stripes.

Dismissing Riley for now, she remembered the women waiting to meet her and Jacob. Bridget climbed out and took her son's hand as he scrambled from the backseat. "Let's go meet your granny Mulligan and aunt Maggie."

Riley made a snorting sound, muttered something Bridget couldn't understand, and slammed the car door. He went to the trunk to fetch their suitcases, leaving Bridget to introduce herself and Jacob. *Well, fine, you ornery old so-and-so.*

Squaring her shoulders, she gave Jacob's hand a squeeze and started toward the woman and girl. "Mrs. Mulligan?" Bridget asked, pausing before them. "I'm Bridget and this here's my son, Jacob."

The woman smiled, her blue-gray eyes twinkling. She reached out and patted Bridget's shoulder. "'Tis glad I am you've come," she said, and turned her attention to Jacob. Her eyes widened and her lower lip trembled. She held one hand to her throat. "Jaysus, Mary and Joseph, if you aren't the image of me Culley at the same age." She bent forward and enveloped Jacob in a one-armed hug. "Welcome, young Jacob. Welcome home."

"I'm Maggie." The redhead thrust out her hand and shook Bridget's in a very matter-of-fact way. "Welcome to Ireland, Mrs. Mulligan."

"Here, now, we'll be having none of that nonsense," Mrs. Mulligan said, straightening but still smiling. "You'll be callin' me Fiona and you're Bridget in this house. 'Mrs. Mulligan,' indeed." She turned her brilliant smile on Jacob again, who blushed to his earlobes. "And you, young man, will call me *mamó*. It means granny. I've always wanted grandchildren, Jacob. You're a dream come true to this old heart."

Granny. Mamó. Thank you, Lord. Bridget smiled and released a long-held sigh.

"'Tis almost like having me Culley . . ." Fiona bit her lower lip and drew a shaky breath. "Thank you, Bridget, for bringin' Culley's son home to us. Thank you, lass."

Overcome by the woman's enthusiasm and affection, Bridget blinked back the tears threatening to spill from her eyes. She felt Riley's accusing and perplexing glare on her back, but she'd be danged if she would let him see her cry. She had her pride, after all, and for more years than she could remember, that was about all she'd had.

"Thank you for inviting us, Mrs. . . . er, Fiona," Bridget said, smiling. On closer inspection, Bridget realized the woman's hair had once been as fiery red as her daughter's, but streaks of gray now dulled its brilliance.

"You're quite welcome, lass." She shook her head and her smile faded. "'Tis sorry I am not to have met you at the airport, but this gout misery plagues me something awful from time to time."

"Have you tried eating cherries?"

Fiona tilted her head to one side. "Cherries, is it? No, I can't say I have, but if you think it'll help, I'll send Maggie here to market tomorrow morning to fetch a basket." She pointed her cane toward the cottage. "You must be tired and half starved. Come in, let us be showin' you and Jacob your rooms."

The house was cozy and filled with antiques. A coat of arms on the wall bore the Mulligan crest. Back in Tennessee, the "cottage" would've been considered a rambling farmhouse. It seemed far too large to call a cottage, though Bridget had already discovered many differences between Tennessee and Ireland.

After a barely edible dinner—though both Bridget and Jacob had pretended to enjoy it—Fiona bid them all to gather near the hearth, where a low and welcome fire burned.

Jacob settled near Fiona's rocker and asked, "What's that weird smell?"

"Ah, 'tis the peat you're smelling, Jacob," Maggie explained. "Even in spring, we often have a fire come evenin'."

"Back in Tennessee," Bridget explained, "we burn hickory or oak."

"And how many trees did you count drivin' across our island?" Fiona smiled, obviously not expecting an answer.

"What's peat?" Jacob's brow furrowed as he stared at the glowing fire.

"Decomposed vegetation, sort of." Maggie ruffled Jacob's hair, then dropped to the floor and stretched her long legs out in front of her. "A peat fire will last much longer than wood, too."

Bridget liked Maggie almost as much as she liked Fiona. Why couldn't Riley be more like the female members of his family? Well, she didn't really care what he thought of her, but she did care what he thought of Jacob.

Seated before the fire in her rocking chair with her ailing foot propped on pillows, Fiona said, "Riley, fetch me the picture albums, please."

Bridget saw his reluctance. His gaze drifted from his momma to her, and she saw a flash of something indefinable in his expression before he looked at Fiona again and nodded. A moment later, he dropped three huge albums onto the coffee table.

"Give me the red one there," Fiona said, pointing at the largest one. Riley placed it gently in his mother's lap, and she motioned for Bridget and Jacob to come closer.

Standing behind the older woman's chair, Bridget noticed the faint scent of rose water wafting up from her hair. She was a tidy woman, with her hair pinned into a neat bun at her nape and her simple cotton dress meticulously pressed. Fiona leafed through several pages of baby pictures, then paused, staring down at a black-and-white photo of a boy who appeared to be near Jacob's age.

"Is that Culley?" Bridget asked, bending forward to touch the corner of the print. "Look, Jacob."

"Aye, that'll be Culley at seven." Fiona reached up and patted Jacob's cheek. "There's your da, lad." She looked over her shoulder and smiled at Bridget. "Do you see it? The resemblance?"

Bridget's eyes burned and she blinked. The only photo she had of Culley was the Polaroid the lady at the motel had taken of them when they'd checked in for their honeymoon. Bridget hadn't looked at that photo in years, but now she smiled in remembrance. She really had loved Culley Mulligan, and now she regretted the years of resenting him. Of course, she'd had no way of knowing about his accident. Even so, she should've known somehow that he wouldn't have simply abandoned her. *Hindsight is cheap, Bridget.*

Clearing her throat, she said, "Jacob looks just like him."

"Aye, the spittin' image," Fiona said with a sigh. The older woman looked across the room at her son. "Do you see it, too, Riley?"

He glanced up from the fire, his hand resting on the mantel near an antique clock. His only response was a slight lift to his shoulder, then he turned his gaze back to the fire.

Maggie gave a short laugh. "He'll not be admitting a thing, Mum, and you know it."

"A body can't deny what's right in front of his face," Fiona said, returning her attention to the album.

Bridget remembered that Mr. Larabee had said Riley refused to believe she'd married Culley and given birth to his son. The mere notion that anyone would believe she could lie about such a thing made her bristle like a porcupine, but she bit her cheek to silence her comments. Instead, she placed a protective hand on her son's shoulder and looked down at the album in her mother-in-law's lap.

Riley Mulligan's opinion didn't really matter.

Fiona's did.

As long as Bridget kept that straight in her mind, she could handle anything Riley threw her way. She glanced up at him again, studying his profile as he scowled down at the fire. And somehow, she knew he would do everything in his power to make her feel unwelcome and untrusted. Strangely, the lack of trust hurt most—like cutting your finger with a dull paring knife.

She noticed Fiona lingering over a photo of a boy and man standing in the meadow with the black castle looming in the background. "Is that Culley and his daddy?" Bridget asked.

"No, that'll be Riley and his da." Fiona touched the man's image with the tip of her finger and didn't move for several minutes. "Just before—"

"Don't, Maggie," Riley whispered without looking at them. "Please."

"Riley, you can't keep pretendin' it never happened." Fiona closed the album and released a long, slow breath. "Then again, as stubborn as you be, maybe you can."

Oh, I don't think there's any doubt about that. Bridget drew a deep breath and gripped her fists so tightly her nails cut half-moons into her palms. She should not and would not allow Riley Mulligan to spoil this for her. She glanced at her son. For them . . .

Hours later, after they'd looked through all the albums, Riley still stood staring at the fire, and Bridget felt she knew their entire family history since moving into the cottage. Whatever happened before, when the Mulligans had lived in the castle, remained a mystery.

After Riley's whispered plea, Fiona had also circled around the time and subject of Patrick Mulligan's death. Even so, Bridget could determine the approximate time of that tragedy, based on when the photos of him stopped. How sad for little boys to grow up without a daddy.

Listen to yourself. Wasn't *she* doing a decent job of raising a boy without a daddy?

Jacob had warmed to Fiona and Maggie, and Bridget smiled. She wanted this for her son—the family life she'd never really known. Pity his only uncle resented the boy's presence. An uncle could help fill the gap left by a daddy. Most uncles. Not this one.

"Why don't you live in the castle?" Jacob asked hesitantly, earning a scowl from Riley and a moment of stunned silence from Fiona and Maggie. Jacob glanced nervously at his uncle and Bridget silently dared the man to snap at her son again in front of his momma.

Fiona took Jacob's hand and gazed up into his eyes. "Bad things happened to the Mulligans when they lived there," she said. "Once they moved into this cottage and sealed the castle, the bad things stopped. Of course, that was long before any of us were born."

"My . . . my daddy died," Jacob said as if testing the word on his lips. "That was bad."

"Aye, very bad." A catch sounded in Fiona's voice and Bridget let her hand rest on her mother-in-law's shoulder. "But sometimes accidents happen, Jacob. The things the Mulligans suffered while livin' in *Caisleán Dubh* were constant and terrible. The castle was like . . . bad luck, I suppose. Is that makin' any sense?"

Jacob appeared thoughtful, but finally nodded. A huge yawn split his face a moment later and Bridget laughed quietly. "I reckon this world traveler is ready for bed."

The open fondness shining in Fiona's eyes when she looked back at her made Bridget warm and happy all over. She felt welcomed and wanted, and her heart swelled with affection for the older woman. "Thank you," she whispered, and Fiona smiled with a gentle nod.

They understood each other. They'd both loved Culley—one as a momma and the other as a wife. And they both loved his son now. An invisible and sacred bond drew them together. Bridget had shared a similar bond with Granny—God rest her soul. Women needed this sense of family and belonging.

"Come along, Jacob," Maggie said, rising. "I'll take you up to your room."

Jacob bent down and placed a kiss on Fiona's cheek, much the same way he'd done his great-granny's back in Tennessee. "'Night, *Mamó*," he said.

"Good night, lad." Fiona patted her grandson's cheek.

"I'll be up to tuck you in directly," Bridget said, earning a smile and a wave, even as the boy cast his uncle a wary glance.

Maggie also seemed to sense her nephew's fear of Riley and, when her brother looked her way, the girl tossed her head as if daring him to comment. She took Jacob's hand and they headed toward the stairs.

Riley's gaze returned to Bridget after his sister and Jacob were gone. He shook his head very slowly and arched one dark brow as if asking a question.

Bridget stared intently into his blue, blue eyes. She wanted him to welcome her and to believe her as his momma and sister had. After all, he was Culley's brother. Her brother-in-law. Jacob's only uncle.

Remembering what Mr. Larabee had said about Riley, she lifted her chin a notch, refusing to give an inch. The man had been rude to her, but he hadn't stated his suspicions or resentments outright. Until he did, she refused to confront him about them.

When it came to stubborn pride, Riley Mulligan had met his match.

Bridget tucked the patchwork quilt around her son's narrow shoulders. They had the entire attic to themselves—a small alcove with a narrow bed for Jacob and the main room with a high four-poster, a small iron stove in the corner near the window, and a rocking chair. They even had their own bathroom with an old claw-footed tub beneath a nice window.

Luxury. Pure luxury.

She washed her face and slipped into her worn flannel nightgown, then climbed into the bed, snuggling into—of all things—a feather bed. She had a vague memory of visiting her great-granny's cabin in the hills and sleeping in a feather bed once, and she'd thought then that it was the greatest thing in the world. She'd been right.

Thanking God for bringing them here to Culley's family, tears stung her eyes and she blinked. They'd come so close to being homeless, and now they not only had a home—at least for a while—but a family. A *real* family.

Her heart warmed all over again as she remembered the way Fiona Mulligan had welcomed and embraced them. Jacob had a real granny again, an aunt, and an uncle—well, sort of an uncle. Fiona and Maggie's warmth helped make up for Riley's aloofness. Surely he would realize how ridiculous it was to deny Jacob's relationship. The family resemblance was uncanny. Any fool could see it.

"Thank you, Lord," she whispered on a sigh.

Smiling, she turned on her side and clicked off the lamp. She folded her arms across her chest and stared into the dark for what seemed like hours. Sleep eluded her and she turned to her other side, staring at the patch of moonlight on the bedroom floor.

What time was it in Tennessee right now? She was exhausted, yet she couldn't sleep. Too much excitement, no doubt. She rose and padded barefoot to the long narrow window, welcoming the stove's radiant heat and the moonlight that bathed her face. The night was clear and cool. Mrs. Mulligan had said at dinner that the weather was fair for this time of year. Considering how incredibly green Ireland was, Bridget suspected rain was more common than sunshine.

Her gaze followed a streak of moonlight across the field toward the sea, but something tall, dark, and foreboding thrust upward from the earth to block her visual journey. *Caisleán Dubh.*

A tremor raced through her and she bit her lower lip. There was no such thing as a curse, yet something about that castle called out to her yet gave her the creeps at the same time.

A warning . . . or a welcome?

Oh, stop it, Bridget. With a sigh, she pressed her forehead against the cool glass and watched a lone figure stride through the moonlight. Her heart pressed upward against her throat. The figure paused and turned toward the cottage, and she had the undeniable feeling that he could see her standing there.

He was too far away to identify, but she knew somehow that the man was Riley Mulligan. Who else could he be? The land between the cottage and the castle all belonged to the Mulligans, and Riley was the only man in the family besides young Jacob.

He stood there unmoving, staring—so she imagined—right at her. After a few moments, he turned and continued on across the meadow. She released a shaky breath that fogged the windowpane. Rubbing the back of her neck, she went to peer at her sleeping son and smiled. At least one of them could rest.

A huge yawn tugged at her mouth and she decided she might try again, too. After all, tomorrow would be their first full day in Ireland, and she wanted to greet it fresh and rested.

The room was cool despite the stove, and she welcomed the weight of the patchwork quilt, tugging its softness up around her chin. As she had every night since learning her husband hadn't abandoned her, she pictured Culley's shy grin as he'd looked at their wedding, then later after they'd consummated their union. She reminded herself that their son had been conceived in love.

Her body warmed and relaxed. Her husband had been her first—and, so far, only—lover. She remembered as if it had been only yesterday.

He'd been so gentle, showing her how to please and be pleased. That first time had hurt some, but later . . . She sighed and a sad smile curved her lips. All those years of denying her love for Culley were past. Now she could remember him fondly and grieve for him.

And forgive herself for the years of doubt and suspicion . . .

Gradually, the image of Culley faded and another replaced it. This man was older, his hair long and shaggy, falling in dark waves to impossibly broad shoulders. His skin was bronzed from the sun, and his lips didn't display even the ghost of a smile. In fact, he scowled. Dark and brooding, Riley Mulligan's image filled her mind just as sleep finally overtook her.

And she dreamed.

The corner of the bed dipped from his weight and she felt his warmth before he touched her. He stroked her shoulder gently, trailing his fingertips to the slope of her throat, then along the neckline of her nightgown.

She wanted to touch him, too, and reached out to place her palms flat against his chest. Brazenly, she inched her hands lower to his ribs, marveling at the tautness of his abdomen. Reminding herself she was dreaming, she explored his body, outlining the slight indentation at his navel with the tip of her finger. Suspicion niggled at her just before his erection brushed against her hip.

He was naked.

So it was that kind of dream. But it was a dream, so the forbidden was allowed. A thrill shot through her and she didn't resist when her faceless lover eased her gown from her shoulders and slipped it down to her waist, baring her breasts to the cool night air. Her nipples tightened and puckered against the chill and a shiver skated down her spine.

Pressing her back against the soft bed, he hovered over her, his hard body burning her without touching. Then his lips sought hers, gentle at first, coaxing her mouth into a more pliant line. He traced the seam of her lips with his tongue and she opened to him, welcoming his hot, wet kiss as he buried his fingers in her hair.

Her nipples thrust upward and her breasts grew heavy. The crisp hair of his chest brushed against her taut peaks and a fire ignited her blood. No longer cold, she stared through the darkness without seeing his face at all.

She wanted him. Needed him.

He left her mouth and kissed her jaw, her throat, the curve of her shoulder. Her breath came rapidly now, her body suffused with liquid fire. No trace of chill remained as he blazed a trail along her collarbone, inching his way lower.

When at long last he cupped the weight of her breasts in both hands, she watched the dark shape of his head lower. Anticipation soared through her, but she resisted the impulse to link her hands behind his neck and drag him to her. She wanted his hot, wet mouth on her breast. God, what had come over her? She was out of her mind with desire. Hunger. Need.

He outlined her nipple with his tongue, lapping nearer the peak with each revolution. Finally, he covered one nipple with his lips and drew her deeply into his mouth as he massaged the other with his thumb.

She was on fire. So hot. She'd never felt this way before. He shared himself equally between her breasts and she finally surrendered to the urge to clutch him to her, pressing her bare flesh more fully into the heat of his mouth.

He eased one hand along the curve of her hip, pressing his rigid length against her bare thigh. He was so large, so hard, so ready. Something deep in her core tightened around an unbearable emptiness—a void she knew without a doubt that he could fill. And then some.

She murmured something shameless, though she wasn't sure of her words. All she knew was the wanting, the needing, the burning.

Then he left her breasts and hovered over her, poised between her thighs. A momentary panic stole through her, but she reminded herself yet again that this was a dream. Only a dream. She'd never had such an explicitly erotic

dream before, but she figured as dreams went this one was
a humdinger.

All right. She placed her hands on his slim hips, felt the
muscles rippling in his buttocks. Any moment now, he
would take the next step. She held her breath.

He muttered something in a husky voice and waited.

"What?" she asked, wondering what language he
spoke. Just her luck to conjure up a dream lover who
didn't speak English.

He remained poised above her for endless moments,
and she felt his stare boring into her. What the devil was
he waiting for, anyway? She knew he wanted her as much
as she wanted him.

He repeated the strange words, and she realized from
his tone that he was asking her a question. She shook her
head, trying to see his face through the darkness, but there
was nothing.

A mist swirled about her and her dream lover van-
ished.

Bridget bolted upright in her bed, clutching the high
collar of her nightgown with both fists. Gasping for breath,
she clawed the tightness away from her throat until her
lungs filled with sweet air. Sweat dripped down her face
and neck, trickling between her aching breasts.

"A dream," she whispered, shoving her hair back from
her face as she swung her feet to the cold floor. Her heart
thundered at an alarming rate as she grabbed for the glass
of water on her nightstand and drained it.

Slowly, her breathing eased and her body cooled. She
walked to the window again. The moon was higher now,
shining across the field but not through her window any
longer.

The man was there again, staring toward the house.

Toward her.

The castle loomed ominously in the background and
she thought for a moment what a great poster it would

make for a Stephen King movie or a Gothic romance. The brooding Irishman, the dark castle, the silvery moonlight.

And the damsel in distress?

She laughed quietly at her own foolishness. She sure as heck wasn't a damsel, nor was she in distress. Exactly. A yawn gripped her and she stretched, closing her eyes for only a moment. Reopening them, she looked outside again.

The man was gone.

Four

Riley gave up on sleep shortly before dawn. What little rest he'd managed to find had been disturbed by dreams hot enough to make a man ache. He couldn't remember dreams so vivid since adolescence. He and Culley had kidded around about—

Riley gritted his teeth. For a few blessed moments, he'd almost forgotten about the intruder and her child. Shirtless and barefoot, he stood over the kitchen stove, waiting for the kettle to boil, and squeezed his eyes shut. The lad was but a pawn in his mother's deceit, and it was wrong to blame young Jacob for any of this.

With sigh, Riley raked his fingers through his hair, then grabbed the hot pad and kettle. He inhaled the rich steam as he wet the leaves. The whole pot might help him feel human again. Jaysus knew too little sleep and too bloody much gnawing in his groin made Riley grumpy as a stallion at gelding.

A shudder rippled through him at the thought. Well, perhaps not *that* grumpy. Aye, but the dreams didn't help matters. He'd thought himself well rid of those in recent years. Alas, they had returned last night with a vengeance.

Since puberty, Riley had been plagued with dreams of

another time. The setting for these erotic dreams was an
archaic bedchamber he'd never seem. A shiver sliced
through him and he sipped his tea before it had cooled,
scalding his tongue. *"Eejit!"*

The hairs on the back of his neck stood on end and he
shivered. It was her. He felt her before he saw her, and the
sensation was powerful enough to render him silent.
Sweeping his scalded tongue against the back of his teeth,
he looked toward the archway where she stood.

Sunlight flowed through the window at her back, outlining the slender shape of her through her worn, white
nightdress. Small blue flowers on the fabric had faded
until they were practically invisible, and the gown left her
feet and ankles bare to the morning chill. The female certainly played her role of poverty well. He'd give her that.
But nothing more.

"Oh." She paused, her eyes widening. "Good morning," she said, smiling nervously. Her hair was mussed
from sleep, her voice smooth like cream. "I don't own a
robe. I . . . I didn't know anyone would be up and about
this early." She gathered the ruffled collar of her nightdress closer.

She's bogus. Don't be forgetting that, Mulligan. However, no amount of reasoning or self-admonition could
prevent his immediate physical response to the woman.
His body sprang into an expectant state that rivaled even
those infernal dreams.

*Jaysus, you'd think I was still a lad just discovering I
can get hard.*

Heat flooded him and he cleared his throat. "Tea," he
said, as if that explained why he was up even earlier than
usual. "There's more in the pot, if you've a mind. Give a
care. It's hot as . . ."

Mind your tongue, Riley. If he wasn't at least civil to
the woman, Mum would likely take a switch to him,
grown or not. And he'd let her, too, being the respectful
son he was. A smile threatened to curve the corners of his
mouth, but he caught himself.

"You don't drink much coffee in Ireland," she stated, rather than asked. "I read about some of y'all's customs before our trip."

Ya'll again. "Some drink coffee, but we don't."

"I don't drink it myself, though I do like iced tea."

"Iced tea is for Yanks." Maybe bickering with her would distract him from the way her glossy brown hair swung about her shoulders when she shook her head.

"I've developed an unsociable habit—so Granny said—of drinking soda pop in the morning."

She laughed and the sound skittered through his bones and settled right between his legs. One thing was for damned sure. He wasn't about to let her see how she affected him. Wincing, Riley sat at the table, wrapping both hands around his cup and concentrating on his breathing.

"Maggie has some cola in the icebox," he said, and she immediately crossed the room and opened the humming appliance in the corner.

Jaysus help him, but he shouldn't have chosen that moment to look at her. The shape of her bum was clearly outlined through the thin fabric. And a fine bum it was, too. *More's the pity.*

"Ah, this is perfect. Thank you." She opened the cupboard and stretched to reach the top shelf, her breasts straining against the threadbare nightdress.

Was she so ignorant not to realize she was flaunting herself? Well, bloody hell, wasn't he sitting here without a shirt? Mum certainly wouldn't approve of her son's appearance, especially at her table.

He narrowed his eyes as Bridget joined him there, pouring the foaming brown liquid into her glass. She lifted it to her full pink lips, then hesitated and held it out toward him instead. "Cheers."

The last thing in the world Riley wanted was to toast this woman. She was an intruder. The enemy. Even if she did light a fire in a man's blood.

Finally, he lifted his cup and said, *"Fírinne."* He smiled to himself at her look of confusion.

"What does that mean?" She sipped her cola, peering at him with large green eyes.

"Truth." He drained his cup and refilled it, carefully avoiding her gaze. She cleared her throat, obviously wanting him to look at her. He took his sweet time about it, draining his second cup before facing her again. "And speaking of the truth . . . ," she said, her voice trailing away.

Her luscious lips were pressed into a thin line now, her delicate nostrils flaring slightly, and her arms folded beneath her breasts, raising them to greater prominence.

Why'd she have to do that*?*

Maintaining a good hot head of anger with a woman he wanted to strip naked and take right here on his mum's kitchen table was wearing on a man. *Disgraceful, Riley.* Aye, but want her he did. Her nightdress was so thin he could actually see the shape of her dark nipples peering back at him.

Jaysus. He reached for the pot again, hoping his hands didn't tremble. If she had something to say, she'd best be doing it, or she'd be talking to his empty chair. He had a full day's work ahead.

And more than one kind of steam to burn off.

"Mr. Mulligan," she began.

"Riley," he corrected. "Mum won't be having it any other way."

"Riley, then."

She drew a deep breath, taunting him with her magnificent breasts. He swallowed hard, forcing his gaze back to her slightly flushed cheeks and flashing eyes.

Aye, he could see how Culley might have fallen for the wench, but married her? Not with Katie Rearden here at home waiting for him. Besides, Culley wouldn't have married without the church. Would he have?

No, Riley wasn't buying any of that nonsense. Though, he had to admit, his randy younger brother might have— Riley looked at her again—probably *had* bedded the comely Bridget. What healthy Irishman wouldn't, given the opportunity? And she had, undoubtedly, provided that opportunity.

"I've chores." He set his cup aside and rose, suddenly needing fresh air.

"Please, wait."

She rose, standing so near that the warmth of her closed the *very* inadequate distance between them. The room suddenly seemed smaller, the temperature scorching, and the air incredibly thick.

He ached with longing for this deceitful bit of skirt. What had come over him? The same thing that had come over Culley, no doubt. Riley drew a shaky breath, trying not to think about the insistent throbbing between his legs.

"What do you want?" he asked, trying to keep his voice impassive.

"Why do you hate me?"

He made the mistake of allowing her to capture his gaze. The emerald depths seized him by the throat and held him prisoner. He couldn't breathe. He couldn't move. He couldn't think.

Shite. He needed a woman, but not this one. No, the one who'd ignited the flame would not be the one to extinguish it. She may have seduced one Mulligan male, and that was one too many.

"Why do you hate me?" she prodded.

"Hate is a strong word." He managed to free his gaze from hers and stared beyond her at the windowsill lined with varicolored glass bottles Mum had collected.

"What would you call it, then?" She placed a hand on his arm.

Riley flinched as if burned, but he didn't pull away. He was so drawn, so imprisoned by this woman that he couldn't have brushed her aside right now if his life depended on it. Was this how Culley had felt?

"Are you a *cailleach*?" he finally asked, glancing down at her hand on his bare arm.

"What's a—what you said?"

"A witch." Rage built within him as he thought of his

younger brother. Culley should be here now, married to
Katie, as he'd promised. "Is that how you do it? How you
did it to Culley, *cailleach*?" His voice fell to a ragged
whisper as he struggled between rage and lust.

Her brows pulled together and she drew a sharp breath.
"I didn't do anything to Culley except . . . except love
him." Her voice fell to a ragged whisper and she looked
down, dropping her hand to her side.

Something wet landed on his bare toe. Riley looked
down in time to watch a succession of small droplets land
on and near his bare feet. Realization nearly unmanned
him.

She was crying.

He tightened his hands into fists, struggling against the
sudden, powerful urge to reach out to her. He was a sap.
Swallowing hard, he lifted his hand and reached toward
her shoulder.

"Good morning," Maggie said, marching into the room
and straight toward the icebox. She stopped midway
across the room and stared, obviously noticing that her
brother wasn't alone.

Riley dropped his guilty hand to his side and silently
cursed himself as his sister's gaze went from Bridget's
bowed head to Riley, shooting him an accusing glare.

"Riley Francis Mulligan, what have you done?" Maggie rushed to Bridget and slipped an arm around her waist,
guiding her back to her chair. "There, now, Bridget. Maggie won't let big, bad Riley hurt you," his sister cooed.

Jaysus. How the devil had *he* become the villain in this
nightmare? He raked his fingers through his hair and
looked up at the ceiling.

"He . . . he . . ." Bridget hiccuped, playing her role to
the hilt.

"You brute." Maggie stroked Bridget's hair.

Helpless, Riley shook his head and held his hands out
to his sides. Bridget had manipulated this somehow.
Maybe she'd known exactly what time Maggie would
come downstairs.

The voice of logic protested from the back of his mind, but he banished it. "I've chores," he said, stomping toward the back door.

He wrenched open the door and slammed it behind him, shivering on the stoop in the early morning fog. "You bloody *eejit*," he muttered, glancing down at his bare torso and feet. How was a man to save face in this house filled with conniving women? The whole lot of them were ganging up on him.

Nevertheless, a farmer couldn't put in a fair day's work without his boots. With a sigh, Riley opened the door and reentered the warm kitchen. Both Maggie and Bridget sat staring at him, as if they'd been waiting for him to return for his shirt and boots.

Head held high, Riley strolled past them to the back staircase, refusing even to acknowledge them. A man had his pride, after all.

Halfway up the worn wooden steps, he allowed himself to breathe. From now on, he would keep a safe distance from Bridget. With any luck, she would pack up and take her son back to the States where they belonged.

On the next step, something sharp and burning impaled his toe. "Ow!"

Female twittering drifted up the narrow staircase. Gnashing his teeth, Riley sat on the step and yanked the offensive splinter out of the soft underside of his big toe, then continued up the steps. They were laughing at him. Well, let them.

The sooner he set about his work, the sooner he could put Bridget *Not*-Mulligan out of his mind. The woman was a *cailleach* and a temptress. A siren. Aye, and a dangerously appealing one at that.

Even though he didn't believe her innocent hillbilly ruse, or her claim of having married Culley, he couldn't prevent himself from lusting heartily after the woman. He burned for her with a fierceness he had never known, except in those wretched dreams.

That thought shot through him like a flaming arrow,

setting his gut—and other more aggravating regions—on fire. Aye, he wanted the woman with an intensity very familiar to those relentless dreams. Why? His breath caught as he remembered the way she moved, the fall of hair over her shoulder, the silk of her voice.

What was it about her? Who was she, really? *What* was she?

And why did he suddenly feel trapped?

He was so distracted, he walked right into the low beam at the top of the steps. "Ow!"

Bridget took several deep breaths, forcing her tears to cease. She listened while Maggie made excuses for her brother's behavior. Though Riley *had* upset her, he hadn't made her cry. All those years of hating Culley had made her cry—not his brother. She would never be free of the guilt she bore over her late husband. If only she'd known. If only she could undo all the days of resenting him.

But that was past. Culley was dead and buried, but she was here with his son and the rest of his kin now. She would make up for thinking ill of him. She would. Otherwise, the confounded guilt would destroy her.

She sniffled, vowing to be strong. She didn't want Jacob coming down to catch his momma carrying on so. Hearing Riley's second "ow" did the trick, and Bridget soon found herself giggling along with Maggie.

When Maggie rose to fetch her soda, Bridget pondered the memory of how Riley had looked when she'd first walked into the kitchen this morning. She'd never seen such broad shoulders, or muscles so well defined. Heat suffused her all over again and her pulse did a square dance along her veins.

Mercy. The only time Bridget could remember feeling so physically drawn to a man was when she'd first met Culley. Sex appeal obviously ran in the family, though she'd already had her quota of Mulligan men.

Still, a girl was allowed to admire the scenery. Wasn't she?

Warmth settled low in her belly and she squirmed, crossing her legs as if that would banish her sinful thoughts and urges. Of course, this was mild compared to that dream she'd had last night. Erotically frustrating. Wasn't that what one of those fancy women's magazines at miss Daisy's Clip and Curl would've called it? She couldn't have chosen a worse moment to awaken from that dream than if she'd actually planned to torture herself.

Torture.

That pretty much described that dream *and* Riley Mulligan.

Forget Riley. Best forget the dream, too.

Dabbing her eyes dry with the edges of her sleeves, Bridget drew a deep, cleansing breath. "Thank you, Maggie," she said on a sigh, patting her sister-in-law's hand when she returned to the table.

"For saving you from that big brute?" Maggie directed a glower toward the stairs. "'Twas my pleasure."

Bridget smiled sadly. "No, I can handle the likes of him."

"Then why were you crying?" Maggie asked.

"Remembering Culley."

"Mum told me how you just learned about his accident." Maggie gave her hand a squeeze. "It must've been hard on you raising Jacob alone and not knowing."

Bridget nodded. "I believed the worst of my husband. That's what I regret most."

"Aye, but wouldn't Culley be first to forgive you?"

The tone of Maggie's voice gave Bridget pause. She met the younger woman's gaze and recognized the warmth of it in her own heart. "You're right. He would." And, as Granny would've insisted, that was all that really mattered. "Thank you."

"I didn't do anything." Maggie lifted a shoulder. "It's glad I am that you're here."

"I'm glad, too." Bridget rested the flat of her palms against the scarred old table. How many of these scratches had been committed by Culley as a boy? Dragging herself back to the present, she said, "I aim to earn my way, too."

"Nonsense, you're company." Maggie dismissed Bridget's words too easily.

"No." Bridget waited for Maggie to look at her again, then added, "I don't want to be just company. For Jacob's sake. And for his daddy's."

Maggie stared for several minutes. "I understand. You're family, and you should be treated as family. Both of you. Culley would've wanted it that way."

Bridget swallowed the lump in her throat and sniffled. "I aim to be worthy." She pushed away from the table. "And if I really am family, then I'll be doing my share of chores. Where should I start?"

Maggie's blue eyes widened and she leaned closer conspiratorially, looking toward the stairs. "Can you cook?"

Pride filled Bridget. "That's one thing I do pretty darn well, if I do say so myself." She glanced heavenward, adding, "Thanks to Granny."

"It's joyous I am to hear you say that." Maggie rolled her eyes. "With Mum laid up with the gout, I've been trying to do the cooking, but . . ." She grinned and shrugged. "Well, you tasted supper last night."

Bridget chewed her lower lip, forbidding herself from asking exactly *what* the main course had been. She'd eaten as much as was humanly possible, and was relieved now to learn her mother-in-law had not been responsible.

"Ah, well, you needn't pretend, Bridget." Maggie laughed quietly. "I'm a terrible cook, and don't I know it? Riley reminds me often enough."

"Can *he* cook?"

Maggie's eyes widened and she made a choking sound. "Oh, now that would be something to behold." She released a long sigh. "Riley Mulligan? *Cook?*"

"Well, then I don't reckon he has business judging *your* cooking." Bridget flinched as the front door slammed.

"Himself, sneaking out the front door so we won't laugh at him again."

They both laughed anyway, though Bridget tried very hard to resist. Still, snickering at Riley with his sister was safer than dwelling on the crazy things he'd made her think and feel earlier.

"He'll be back for breakfast after he sees to the stock, and Mum should be down shortly." Maggie looked toward the stove. "I don't have school today. Will you teach me to fix a breakfast that won't give everyone indigestion?"

"We'll rustle up something that'll even put a smile on grouchy old Riley's face."

Maggie sighed, her expression solemn. "I'm afraid that will take more than good food."

"If you mean because he hates me, he's made that clear as springwater." She shook her head. "But he'll come around once he learns that Bridget Mulligan doesn't lie."

"It isn't just you." Maggie rose, staring past Bridget. "When Da died, so did the happy, carefree lad who was Riley Mulligan."

Shivering, Bridget followed her sister-in-law's gaze to the window and beyond. Morning sunlight shone above the ground-hugging fog outside, and a dark, intrusive spire jutted heavenward from the bowels of the smokelike moisture.

Caisleánn Dubh.

Half-starved, Riley's belly button was making love to his backbone by the time he wiped his muddy boots and opened the back door. A plethora of heavenly scents drifted to his nostrils as he stepped into the kitchen's warmth and found Jacob sitting alone at the table.

No one else was there, though someone had definitely started cooking. Judging from the wonderful aroma, Mum must have been up and about this morning. Saints knew Maggie couldn't have prepared anything like this.

"Mornin', Uncle Riley," the lad said, looking up from his activity.

"Good morning." Riley didn't want to encourage Jacob's penchant for addressing him improperly, nor could he bring himself to correct the lad. *Sap.* With a sigh, he washed his hands at the sink and glanced over at the stove. All the kettles and frying pans were covered. Something wonderful was baking in the oven as well—definitely *not* Maggie's soda bread.

Praise the saints and the Almighty. Real food! He discreetly crossed himself for good measure, and poured tea before joining Jacob at the table. He glanced down at the lad's doodling and bit back a curse.

"Like my picture?" Jacob asked, thrusting the paper under Riley's nose. "It's your castle."

My castle . . . Resentment churned inside Riley, but he swallowed it. He squeezed his eyes closed for a moment, then forced himself to admire Jacob's drawing. *"Caisleán Dubh,"* he said, keeping his tone light. The curse wasn't the lad's fault, nor was his mother's subterfuge. "You've a good eye for detail, Jacob." *Right down to the sinister look of the place.*

The lad's smile dominated his too-small face, and his green eyes practically glowed beneath that pitiful scrap of praise. "Thank you, Uncle Riley." Jacob fidgeted, pride and eagerness practically flying out of him.

If only there were some way to stop Jacob from calling him "uncle." Each time Riley heard that title, it set his teeth on edge. Alas, he couldn't think of any way to stop the lad without hurting him. Another thought shot through Riley and he froze.

Bridget must have lied to the lad as well. Otherwise, how could an innocent play his role so convincingly? The woman's deceit knew no bounds. Riley clenched his fists in his lap and drew a deep breath. What sort of woman would stoop to lying to her own child?

His stomach churned and grumbled, jerking him back to more immediate, if less important, matters—his belly. He glanced back at the stove and sighed. Someone had turned all the flames to the lowest setting. "Where is everyone?"

"Gettin' dressed," Jacob said, not looking up from his artwork. "They said to tell you we'll eat soon, and not to touch anything."

Well, it couldn't be soon enough for Riley. A working-man needed to keep up his strength, after all. He looked longingly at the stove again. "Don't touch anything, eh?" Aye, and didn't Mum know he'd be doing just that any minute now?

"Ah, there you be," Mum said, hobbling into the room with her cane.

Concern edged through Riley. He hated seeing Mum in pain. He hurried to her side and kissed her cheek, pulling out one chair for her and another for her foot. Her toe still appeared angry and swollen.

"You shouldn't have been up and about cooking this morning," he scolded. "I could've done it myself."

She smiled up at him and patted his forearm. "Don't you be worryin' yourself about that now. Our Maggie and Bridget wouldn't let me lift a finger. Would they, Jacob?"

"Nope."

Maggie and Bridget hurried into the room before Riley had a chance to gripe about his sister's past culinary efforts. They went straight to the stove and cupboards. Bridget removed a pan from the oven and placed food into serving bowls and plates while Maggie set the table. Within a few minutes, the table was filled with fragrant, steaming dishes. Riley stared, stunned to silence. His sister, the worst cook this side of Dublin, had done *this*? His mouth watered in anticipation. No, Maggie couldn't have prepared this food.

Mum bowed her head and gave the blessing. Jacob tried to cross himself, but did it backward. Bridget's cheeks pinkened, but Mum simply showed the lad the correct way of doing things.

A moment later, Jacob dove for one of the scones. He split it open, then scooped up a ladle full of gravy, the likes of which Riley had never seen or smelled. In fact, everything looked unusual but tempting.

He shot Maggie a questioning look, but she merely grinned. He glanced at Bridget, who imitated her son's actions, as did Mum and Maggie. Riley took a scone, testing its weight in his hand. Light as a feather. Imitating Jacob, Riley covered it with thick gravy, then took a rasher of bacon and placed it on his plate as well. He looked around the table for black pudding, but there was none. Still, to be spared another of Maggie's attempts was worth the sacrifice.

He speared the gravy-covered scone with his fork and took a bite. Pausing, he savored the flavor for several moments, then added two fried eggs to his plate, and tucked into the unexpectedly pleasant task of satisfying his hunger.

Jacob took another scone, but this time he spread jam on it. With a shrug, Riley decided that wasn't a bad idea and split open another steaming scone. The outside of it was golden brown, but the inside was light and fluffy.

Mum held one in her hand. "They're so light. What do you call these?" Mum asked.

"Bridget calls them biscuits," Maggie said, a worried frown creasing her brow. "I showed her our tin of biscuits in the cupboard, but she said those are what they call cookies back in Tennessee."

Bridget said, "At home I would've used buttermilk and sourdough. I hope they're all right."

"They're delicious, but like nothin' I've tasted before." Mum took another bite and chewed, nodding. "I like the lightness. Quite tasty."

"Thank you." Bridget fidgeted with pleasure, much like her son had done earlier.

Riley swallowed with difficulty. He looked around the table, and down at Jacob, who ate with the abandonment only a lad his age could muster.

Despite Riley's dislike and mistrust of the woman, hadn't he seen evidence of her love for the child? Satisfied that the food was safe—not to mention tasty—Riley resumed eating what Bridget called a biscuit.

Riley examined the scone again, then covered it with jam and took a bite. *Delicious, indeed.* He took another bite, then decided he preferred these odd biscuits with the gravy, rather than jam, and prepared himself another serving.

"Men always go for the gravy," Bridget said, smiling. "Grandpa ate biscuits and gravy every mornin', and he was healthy as could be. Until he got shot, that is."

"Shot?" Maggie paused, fork in midair. "Someone shot your granddad?"

Bridget shook her head and sighed. "No, I'm afraid he shot himself."

Mum gasped and crossed herself. Maggie stared, eyes wide. Even Riley couldn't believe what the crazy woman had just said, especially in front of the lad.

Bridget looked around the gathering, seeming to recognize her blunder. Then she did the strangest thing. She started laughing.

"I see nothing amusing about suicide," Riley said, his voice hushed as he reached for his tea. "And it's unseemly to mention it." He captured Bridget's gaze and directed his own toward Jacob. Surely the foolish woman would see the error of her ways.

"Great-grandpa didn't shoot hisself on purpose, silly," the lad said, chuckling along with his crazy mum.

Mum and Maggie exchanged worried glances and Riley shook his head. The lad shouldn't even have known what the word "suicide" meant.

"He didn't?" Maggie asked, turning to Bridget.

"Lord, no." Bridget dried her eyes and sniffled. "Ned Lynn, one of Grandpa's oldest friends, had a penchant for corn liquor. In fact," she looked around the table and lowered her voice, "he even had his own still in the woods out behind his house."

"Corn liquor?" Maggie asked, looking at Riley. "Is that like whiskey?"

Riley lifted a shoulder and rolled his eyes. He glanced at Mum, who was listening with rapt attention. *Amazing.* The Fiona Mulligan he'd known and adored all his life was listening to a tale of illegal liquor and guns.

"What happened?" Mum urged, leaning toward Bridget.

"They drank too much while they were out coon hunting." Bridget sighed dramatically. "Poor Grandpa fell and his gun went off."

"Shot him in the head," Jacob added, still eating.

Riley narrowed his eyes. "Is that what they call breakfast conversation back in Tennessee?"

"Oh . . . I'm sorry." Bridget looked around the table, her face flushed and her eyes wide. "I wasn't thinking."

Maggie cleared her throat and said, "Don't worry about it, Bridget."

"And isn't it so very Irish of her to speak of family, even after they're gone?" Mum asked.

Riley recognized the warning in Mum's voice. He was expected to grant their "guest" dispensation for ill manners, and—apparently—insanity.

Bridget's expression grew solemn. "Jacob was just a baby then. I wish he'd been able to know his great-grandpa."

"We had Granny." Jacob seemed completely unconcerned about the topic of discussion and spooned another glob of jam onto yet another biscuit. "Nobody could out-cuss my great-granny."

Mum gasped, her eyes widening even more. Riley knew from the movement of her lips that she was praying. Her well-worn rosary beads would be in her apron pocket, as always.

Maybe now they would all see Bridget for the conniving *cailleach* she really was. With a smug feeling, he took a sip of tea, watching the stunned expression on Maggie's face as Mum crossed herself.

Mum sighed and reached over to pat Jacob's head. "There, now, Jacob," she said, "he doesn't do it often, but just wait until your uncle Riley staggers back from Gilhooley's some Saturday night singin' one of his bawdy songs."

Riley choked on his tea as his sister—the traitor—burst into laughter. He made the mistake of looking across the table at Bridget, whose eyes twinkled mischievously. Knowingly.

She'd manipulated things in her favor again. Just when she should have fallen from grace with his mum and sister, she'd pulled forth another victory. She was a sly one.

Her green eyes darkened to a smoky shade as he continued to stare. Pity she was beautiful. It made her all the more powerful.

He looked around the table. Jaysus, and she could cook, too. His gaze settled on her again, noticing the pink flush that had crept into her cheeks, setting her eyes ablaze.

The woman was dangerous. *Cailleach.*

Five

Bridget noticed the longing in her son's eyes as Riley excused himself and returned to his chores. Her heart broke right there in Fiona Mulligan's kitchen. Fresh air and physical activity were just what a growing boy needed.

And an uncle to help make up for the daddy he'd lost?

The ache in her heart was almost more than she could bear. Riley's treatment of her hurt enough, but his rejection of his own nephew awakened every protective maternal instinct Bridget possessed. How dare he deny his own flesh and blood his rightful place in the family?

How dare he break a little boy's heart . . . ?

"Maggie is goin' into Ballybronagh to buy some cherries for this misery of mine," Fiona said on a sigh.

Bridget blinked, forcing her attention away from the infuriating Riley and back to her mother-in-law. "I remember how much that nasty old gout pained Grandpa, but the cherries should help." She glanced over at Maggie, who had refused Bridget's offer of assistance with the dishes. "He ate a few cherries or drank cherry juice every day, once he learned they really made a difference."

"And did they keep the gout from comin' back?" Fiona's eyes widened with blatant hope.

Bridget lifted a shoulder. "He believed they did, and I reckon he didn't seem as bothered with the gout the last few years of his life."

Fiona nodded. "Then I'll believe it, too, if it will keep this misery from comin' back."

Maggie dried her hands, then stood behind her momma and rubbed the older woman's shoulders. "There's a bit of sun comin' in the front window, Mum," she said. "Would you like to catch it?"

"Aye, that I would." Fiona lowered her swollen foot to the floor, wincing as she pushed to her feet. "And won't I be finishin' all the mendin' in me basket by the time this toe stops painin' me?"

Maggie laughed and shook her head. "You know Riley will keep your mending basket full."

Fiona paused and glanced down at Jacob. "And what about you, lad?"

"What?" Jacob looked up at his new granny, finally distracted from pining after his uncle.

"Will you be keepin' *Mamó*'s mendin' basket full, too?"

Jacob grinned, though he still seemed distracted. "Momma says I wear out socks faster than anybody."

"You sure do." Bridget was determined to find a way to keep him busy. "Do you think your aunt Maggie will mind if we tag along to town?"

"And wasn't I counting on just that?" Maggie said, smiling. She helped her mother into the front room and placed some pillows under the older woman's ailing foot.

Bridget and Jacob helped situate Fiona's mending close enough that she wouldn't have to move from her chair for a good long while. They refilled her teacup as well.

"There," Bridget said. "If you're anything like Grandpa, that toe will start behaving itself again in a couple of days."

"Ah, I am lookin' forward to that." Fiona smiled and

gave her grandson a squeeze that made him giggle and blush.

Bridget's heart swelled with love for her son and for the woman who'd brought them into her home and welcomed them into her family. "Thank you," she whispered.

Fiona looked up at her with a gentle smile and blue eyes filled with love and acceptance. Despite the blunder Bridget had made at breakfast telling the story of Grandpa's demise, Fiona still wanted them here. She had to ensure that didn't change, for Jacob's sake.

Relieved, Bridget placed a kiss on the woman's cheek, then led her son back through the kitchen with Maggie. "Are my jeans all right?" she asked.

Maggie glanced down at her own jeans, holding her hands out to her sides in a questioning gesture. Laughing, Bridget nodded in understanding, though she wished hers didn't have a patch on one knee, and that they didn't droop from her hips. Shopping at rummage sales and thrift stores didn't provide much of a selection. She was lucky to have clothes at all, the way things had been these last few years.

But that was past. She drew a deep breath and squeezed Jacob's hand. "Will we need jackets?" she asked, as unfamiliar with Irish weather as she was with Irish people. All she knew was that it rained a lot, which, of course, accounted for the beautiful green she'd noticed yesterday.

"Oh, just a jumper will do," Maggie said, grabbing herself one from a peg near the back door. "'Tis a bright day."

"Jumper?" Bridget looked at Jacob, who appeared just as confused as she. "A little girl's dress?"

Maggie laughed. "Sorry. A jumper is a sweater."

"Oh." Bridget left Jacob with his aunt and rushed up to their attic room, pausing at the window to gaze out at the fluffy clouds sailing across the blue sky. She could see the ocean now, glistening in the sunlight just beyond—

Her breath caught at the sight of *Caisleán Dubh*'s majestic tower. Amazingly, it still looked dark and forebod-

ing even in full daylight. Yesterday, she'd thought her reaction to the castle was mere surprise at its size. After all,
she'd never seen a castle before, though she had seen
Graceland and thought it every bit as grand. Until now.

Today, the sight of the castle chilled her. A shiver
chased itself down her spine and she forced herself to look
away, tugging her cardigan over her shoulders. She
grabbed Jacob's Elvis sweatshirt and hurried back down
the stairs, determined not to think about that ugly old castle.

But it wasn't ugly. Not really. In fact, it was breathtak-
ingly beautiful, though in a mysterious way. She wondered if the stone had always been dark, or if age and
weather had changed it. "Listen to yourself think, silly,"
she said, smiling. At least Jacob had come by his curiosity about the castle honestly.

The back door stood ajar and she heard Maggie and
Jacob talking outside. Bridget stepped onto the porch and
pulled the door shut behind her. She didn't want her
mother-in-law to catch a chill if the wind picked up while
they were gone.

"Here you go." She tossed the sweatshirt to Jacob, who
pulled it on over his head, his face popping out through
the hood like a turtle's. He grinned at her, displaying the
gap where he'd lost a tooth last week. "You're growing up
too doggoned fast."

"Mum says the Blessed Virgin probably said the same
thing about her Son." Maggie took one of Jacob's hands
while Bridget took the other. "I'll graduate this year, but
Mum claims it was only yesterday I was still in nappies."

"Nappies?" Jacob echoed.

"Diapers." Maggie grinned at her nephew. "Are you
ready to escort two ladies to market, sir?"

Jacob giggled and the sound crawled into a special
cranny of Bridget's soul—one reserved just for her little
boy. She gave his hand a squeeze and they followed Maggie's lead toward the narrow lane that led to the main
road.

She didn't even pause as they passed the car, still parked where Riley had left it yesterday. "The village is close, then?" Bridget asked. She didn't mind the walk, but she was curious.

"Aye, on the far side of *Caisleán Dubh.*"

Bridget froze midstep and Jacob tugged on her hand, then stopped to stare at her. "What's wrong, Momma?" He stepped closer, his large green eyes filled with concern.

"Nothing," she said, forcing a smile. She struggled for a deep breath and looked at Maggie, who had also paused to stare at Bridget. "We'll be walking right by the castle, then?" She had to . . . prepare herself.

If only she knew why.

"Aye," Maggie said, and took a step toward Bridget. "The road curves 'round the spit of land where the castle sits, then back inland a bit to the village."

Bridget very slowly released the breath she'd been holding. "Okay," she said. "Let's go."

"*Caisleán Dubh* has a strange effect on some." Maggie's brow creased. "I try to ignore it, mostly."

Bridget had to laugh at that. "It's kind of big to ignore."

Jacob laughed, too, then they all continued down the lane. Bridget's heart thudded louder and her breath grew shallower as the road curved toward the castle. The closer they came, the larger it loomed. Some of the boulders along its foundation were even larger than the red sports car Mr. Larabee had given Mrs. Larabee on her last birthday.

Maggie paused near the castle and Jacob tilted his head back and said, "Cool."

His aunt laughed. "'Tis huge. I always wondered why they needed such a high tower."

"To keep watch," Bridget said without thinking. Realizing what she'd said, she blinked and added, "I reckon."

Maggie gave her a questioning look, then nodded, her expression solemn now. "And isn't that just what Riley's always said, too?"

For some reason, knowing Riley had the same thought

she had about *Caisleán Dubh* made a lump form in Bridget's throat. Shaking her head at her own foolishness, she couldn't prevent the surge of relief that swelled within her as Maggie started toward town again.

"Does our castle have a story?" Jacob asked as they walked away from the structure.

"It isn't *our* castle, Jacob," Bridget corrected in a gentle tone.

"Aye, it is in part," Maggie said. "After all, it's all Mulligan land, and you're both Mulligans."

Bridget nodded, blinking the moisture from her eyes. *You're both Mulligans . . .* She drew a deep breath and concentrated on the soft earth beneath her old tennies as they cut across a field.

At least *Caisleán Dubh* was behind them now. She breathed a sigh of relief, determined to regain control of her overactive imagination and unfounded fear of a pile of rocks.

"Does it have a story?" Jacob repeated after a few minutes, craning his neck to look back over his shoulder at the tower.

"Aye, more than one, I'm afraid." Maggie's voice softened, but her expression did just the opposite. "I think your *mamó* is the best person to tell you those stories. Ask her, Jacob, and I'm sure she'll share them all in due time."

"Okay." Seeming content with that explanation, Jacob faced forward and fell silent.

"Is this part of your farm, too?" Bridget asked, still unable to think of any of this as hers or Jacob's. She could hope, but not expect. Never that. After all, she'd expected to inherit Granny's trailer, and look what that had reaped.

Homelessness, if not for the miracle of finding Culley's family after all this time.

"Aye." Maggie paused, bringing the others to a halt beside her. She lifted her free hand and pointed across the field. "All that, too."

Bridget shaded her eyes with one hand and gazed out across the field. A hedge of riotous flowers lined one side of the field, and a man drove a tractor alongside it. She squinted, trying to see him more clearly.

A breeze wafted in off the ocean, lifting the man's shaggy, dark hair off his shoulders. He chose that moment to swing the tractor back toward them. Maggie waved, but he kept on driving.

"Grouchy old Riley," she muttered, continuing toward town.

Bridget felt something warm on her back, but she knew it wasn't the sun, which shone brightly in their faces. Keeping pace with Maggie and Jacob, she stole a glance back over her shoulder and saw that the tractor had stopped.

And the man sat there, staring.

A wave of heat—almost as if he'd touched her—washed through her. Riley Mulligan disturbed Bridget almost as much as *Caisleán Dubh.*

A demanding tightening low in her belly brought another surge of heat hurtling through her. Her breasts felt swollen and achy, her nipples hard and erect enough to make her tug her sweater away from her body self-consciously.

No. The man disturbed her far more than the castle.

Or the curse.

He released the laces, slipping the thin muslin from her shoulders. Slowly. The delay almost killed him, but he wanted to savor every moment, every glimpse of newly exposed flesh. He stood back a moment, admiring the way the fabric caught on the peaks of her breasts, as if waiting for a signal from him.

Aye, and he was weary of waiting. He met her gaze, watching the flames of desire leap in her eyes. She stood before the hearth, and the warmth of the fire flowed around her to kiss their bare skin. The shiver that rippled through him had naught to do with the temperature.

It had everything to do with the longing in his heart, his soul, his flesh.

Perhaps it was wrong to want this forbidden one, yet want her he did. She reached toward him, the movement revealing one taut nipple. He licked his lips and bid the throbbing in his loins to be patient.

"Lovely," he whispered. "Grá."

Her breath caught as he reached forward to free her other nipple from the fabric. She was too beautiful for words, too perfect.

And she was his. How could he not take what she offered? She honored him.

He stepped closer, filling his hands with her luscious breasts, brushing his thumbs across their rigid tips. She gasped, bit her lower lip, but did not turn him away.

Instead, she slipped her slender arms about his waist and moaned as he dipped his head to flick his tongue against her nipple. She was so sweet, so soft, so warm.

He would die if she denied him now, though she had every right to do so. She kissed the side of his neck, freeing the last of the laces holding his tunic.

Guilt gnawed at him and he captured her wrists, staring into her glittering eyes. "Be very sure . . ."

"Jaysus." Riley shook himself from the daydream. He'd stopped his work for a sip of water, and the next thing he knew he was sitting in a field, imagining himself making love to a beautiful woman.

"*Shite*, Mulligan." He cut the engine and checked to make sure the brake was set, then jumped to the ground to pace. It was bad enough for a grown man to suffer through dreams of a carnal nature while sound asleep.

He gulped several deep breaths, noticing dark clouds beginning to gather. After a few moments, the throbbing ache between his legs eased and the sea-scented breeze dried the sweat coating his flesh.

Why had the dreams returned? And why now? Jaysus, but he was far too old to walk around with a willy hard enough to dig ditches.

He never saw the woman's features clearly in his

dreams—either awake or asleep—though he did see her eyes. Strange that even now he couldn't tell what color they were.

Aye, but he'd recognize her breasts anywhere.

"Enough of *that.*" The woman and her breasts didn't exist anywhere but in Riley's libidinous imagination. He took a long pull of cool water, then climbed back onto the tractor seat. He had work to do, and no time for daydreams of hot sex with beautiful women.

Or one, nameless, beautiful woman.

The sun slipped behind a cloud and he glanced at the sky again, but his gaze was drawn toward the sea. A cloud settled near the tower, growing darker and more threatening every minute. More clouds joined it until he could barely see the top.

A chill permeated the breeze that had been so warm earlier. He glanced toward the road, wondering if Maggie and her companions would get wet before they returned from Ballybronagh.

He'd rather enjoyed the sway of Bridget's hips as she'd walked along the road with his sister and Jacob. Had that triggered his daydream?

"What rot." He shook his head and sighed. The weather was turning soft and he still had hours' worth of chores ahead. "Get to work."

A gull called, drawing his gaze back to the tower. Uneasiness oozed through him, but didn't it always when he looked upon the woeful black stones of *Caisleán Dubh*? More of late, it seemed. But why?

"It's nothing but a bloody pile of rock," he muttered.

Then why couldn't he shake the feeling of being watched?

Ballybronagh looked like something from a travel guide. Bridget stood with Maggie and Jacob on a rise, gazing down at the busy village. Maggie pointed to various buildings, explaining their purpose. Ballybronagh had a school and a church, though they sometimes attended special services in nearby Kilmurry.

"Kill Murray?" Jacob repeated before Bridget could. "Why did somebody kill Murray?"

Maggie laughed, but Bridget thought her son's question made perfect sense, though she'd done enough research to remember that Kil was a common part of village names in Ireland. Even so, after a moment her sister-in-law seemed to realize she was the only one laughing.

"Kil means church in the Irish language," she explained. "Many villages are named after the local church."

Bridget gazed down at the village again, noticing the nearest building had a thatched roof and appeared very old. A wooden sign hanging out front dubbed it Gilhooley's Pub. Remembering Fiona's mention of that place earlier, she couldn't suppress the smile that tugged at her lips.

They continued into town, walking along the sidewalks, some of which were made of stones fitted together, rather than cement. Reedville had one cobblestone street still in existence, but this was even older.

"It's like something from a history book," she said. Even some of the older folks hurrying about looked like historical characters, though most people were dressed much like Maggie and Bridget.

An ancient woman leaning on a cane stopped in front of them. "Top o' the mornin' to you, Mary Margaret Mulligan," the woman said in a voice that sounded too strong to come from such a frail body.

"And to you, Mrs. Flaherty." Maggie placed a hand on Jacob's shoulder. "I'd like you to meet—"

"So this be Culley Mulligan's son." The old woman nodded, her faded blue eyes sweeping over Jacob. "You're the image of your da, lad. No one can deny you that."

Jacob fidgeted and mumbled his thanks. Bridget placed a supportive hand on her son's shoulder, barely able to keep from hugging him and telling him how proud she was of him right here and now. After all, he'd only recently learned about his daddy. Hearing folks other than his momma exclaim over how much he resembled Culley Mulligan was a brand-new experience for Jacob.

Then Mrs. Flaherty's gaze pinned her, and Bridget lost her ability to speak or even to think clearly. The woman had an uncanny way of seeing right through a person. Granny had been that way at times.

"And you're the one who stole Culley from Kathleen."

Confused, Bridget met Maggie's gaze. Her sister-in-law rolled her eyes and shook her head very slightly. "I . . . I'm Bridget Mulligan," she said, offering her hand.

The woman stared at her for several moments, then shook Bridget's hand. "You're a good, strong lass," Mrs. Flaherty said finally, turning toward the street. "A pity it is that you thought to divorce poor Culley." Muttering under her breath, the old woman crossed the narrow street.

Bridget stared openmouthed at the retreating figure. "I . . ." She opened and closed her mouth several times, unable to form words.

"Never you mind the likes of her," Maggie said, reaching over to give Bridget's shoulder a squeeze. "It's her generation. And the church."

"Your granny felt the same." Bridget thought back to the day Mr. Larabee had given her Fiona's letter. She had mentioned there that her mother-in-law had hidden the divorce papers. "I thought . . ."

"I understand what happened," Maggie said. "Mum explained it all to us. Now, you're not to worry yourself about it anymore, Bridget Mulligan. I won't hear of it, and neither will Mum."

No mention of Riley. Still, Bridget managed a nod and a fortifying breath. "Where's the market?" Later, she would ask about the mysterious Kathleen. Culley had certainly never mentioned having a girlfriend back in Ireland.

Mercy. Bridget already had a reputation here as a divorced woman who stole other women's men, and she hadn't done anything to earn it. At least . . . not deliberately. Yes, she definitely needed more information about Kathleen and her relationship with Culley.

The market was outside, where rows of fruits, nuts, and vegetables were displayed for shoppers. Bridget noticed a butcher shop next door. She hadn't seen a butcher shop since she was a little girl. After the Piggly Wiggly opened up in Reedville, the small grocery store and butcher shop had closed.

"Cherries aren't in season yet," she said as they walked up and down the aisles.

"I wonder if Mr. Clancy has any dried ones," Maggie said.

"And juice would help, too." Bridget followed Maggie into the small market. They read several labels and bought all the packages of dried cherries on the shelf, and four bottles of cherry juice.

Mr. Clancy was a robust man with a bald head and a red handlebar moustache. "Cherries, is it? I'm expectin' a shipment in a few weeks."

Maggie introduced Bridget and Jacob to Mr. Clancy, who greeted them without any snide comments about divorce or Americans or stealing other women's men. He winked at Bridget and said, "That Culley always did have a good eye."

Bridget blushed and managed to thank the man for his compliment. They walked back outside and saw the clouds gathering in the distance. Only now did Bridget notice that *Caisleán Dubh* was visible from the village, too. That danged castle was following her.

Silly. She glanced at Maggie who was staring at the sky, too.

"Welcome to Ireland." Her sister-in-law flashed Jacob and Bridget a smile. Her red hair turned flaming in the waning sunlight as the clouds gathered.

They had no umbrellas or raincoats, but neither did anyone else Bridget saw. "I guess we'll get wet."

"Let's duck into Gilhooley's for a bite." Maggie looked

at the sky again. "The weather might clear by the time
we're finished."

"A bar?" Bridget stiffened. "We can't take Jacob into
a . . . a honky-tonk."

"It's a pub." Maggie's brow creased in a frown. "I
don't know what pubs or honky-tonks are like in Tennessee, but it's really just a restaurant."

"It's not a bar?"

"Aye, they serve ale and whiskey, if that's what you
mean." Maggie turned toward Gilhooley's. "I promise it's
all right. Children go there with their families all the
time."

The interior of the pub was as interesting as the exte-
rior. Dark, gleaming wood was everywhere—the floor,
the bar, the doors, the ceiling beams. Scratches and worn
areas along the bar told of the pub's popularity over generations.

Bridget was relieved to see families inside having
lunch, just as Maggie had described. Booths lined the wall
of windows, and tables sat throughout the place, nearer
the bar. A fireplace with a huge stove occupied the longest
wall between the bar and the front door. Maggie led them
to a booth near a window.

A woman about Fiona's age approached and passed out
menus. She gave Jacob one with a cup of crayons. They
were obviously prepared for children. Bridget relaxed
even more when a family of four entered with children
even younger than Jacob. Several men came in as well
and occupied the tables and stools nearest the bar.

"You're still not interested in a job here, Maggie?" the
woman asked.

"No. Mum insists I go to university, like Da wanted."

"Well, I can't argue that. Fiona is a wise woman,"
Aileen said with a grudging nod. "Your da left the money
for college, and 'tis glad I am you'll be putting it to use."

"Thank you." Maggie cleared her throat and held her
hand toward Bridget and Jacob. "Aileen, this is Bridget
and her son Jacob. My nephew."

The look Aileen turned on Bridget made her breath hitch. Bridget had seen Mrs. Harbaugh's old tomcat look at General Lee with a kinder expression. "How do you do, Aileen?" Determinedly, Bridget thrust out her right hand.

Aileen chewed her lower lip thoughtfully, then shook Bridget's hand, though the look in her eyes was still wary. However, when she glanced down at Jacob, a look of surprise and downright delight replaced the suspicion she'd reserved for Bridget.

"By the saints," Aileen said, "he's Culley Mulligan all over again."

"Aye," Maggie said, reaching across the table to pat Jacob's hand. "Mum's tickled to have both Culley's son and widow with us now."

Bridget arched her brows questioningly at Maggie, who rolled her eyes toward Aileen. The message was clear that Maggie intended to tolerate no insults aimed at her sister-in-law or nephew. Bridget mouthed a "thank you" while Aileen went on and on about how much Jacob looked like his daddy.

"How old are you, Jacob?" the older woman asked.

"Six." Jacob looked up at the woman with a smile. "I'll go to first grade next year."

"You're gonna be a big strapping lad like your da and your uncle Riley." The woman sighed, smiling. "Lunch is on the house in honor of the newest Mulligan."

The rapid switch from resentment to open welcome startled Bridget. Confused, she waited until Aileen had taken their order and disappeared into the kitchen before she leaned across the table toward Maggie. "What . . . was that?"

Maggie laughed and took a sip of water. "The Irish are steeped in tradition. The old ways are valued and passed on from generation to generation." She lifted a shoulder and leaned her chin on her fist, her gaze holding Bridget's. "Being a Mulligan in Ballybronagh is tradition, so there you have it."

"And Jacob is a Mulligan by birth." Bridget gave a

nod. "The hills of eastern Tennessee are a lot like that, too. Kin's important, no matter who they are or what they've done. It's . . . unconditional, I reckon."

"Exactly." Maggie nodded and thanked Aileen when she brought their plates to the table.

"What's that?" Jacob asked, staring at a platter filled with something breaded and fried to a perfect golden brown.

"Fish 'n chips," Maggie explained as Aileen walked away, still mumbling about how much Jacob looked like his daddy.

"Looks like chicken," Jacob said, looking at Bridget. "Don't it?"

Bridget laughed quietly. "It's batter dipped like my catfish, Jacob."

His eyes widened. "I like that."

"I know."

Maggie showed Jacob how to dip his fish in the malt vinegar, smiling when his eyes lit up after his first bite.

Bridget pointed to the chips on his plate. "Those are like round french fries, Jacob."

"The lady said chips," he argued.

"They just call them chips here. Try one," Bridget said.

He took a bite and nodded, then turned his full attention to the food.

Maggie smiled. "You and Jacob are very close."

Bridget nodded. "Except for Granny, all we've had is each other since Grandpa died."

"I'm glad you've had that." Maggie took a bite of her sandwich.

Bridget tried the bowl of Irish stew she'd ordered and smiled. A bit of chopped celery would've livened up the broth some, but it was still tasty. She broke off a piece of the brown bread in the basket on the table and tasted it. "This is different," she said.

"Not to us." Maggie grinned. "Wasn't Riley's reaction to your breakfast just perfect?"

Bridget nodded. She couldn't deny her sense of satisfaction at watching the way Riley had so thoroughly enjoyed his breakfast. He'd asked for black pudding, though, and she couldn't imagine eating pudding for breakfast.

"Uncle Riley likes to eat," Jacob mumbled around a mouthful of fish.

"So does his nephew, I'd say." Maggie laughed. "A growing lad should."

If only the uncle would accept his nephew.

Maggie looked over Bridget's shoulder and her eyes widened. "Here comes trouble," she whispered fiercely, assuming a bland expression a split second later.

"Wha—"

"Maggie," a smooth voice said a moment before a heavy floral fragrance invaded their air space. The woman paused beside their table, her skirts perfect, her figure perfect.

Bridget's gaze traveled up past a red sweater with a broach on it, then rested on the long, slender column of the woman's perfectly white neck. Was there anything *im*-perfect about this woman?

Though the woman's words were for Maggie, her penetrating glare was for Bridget. "I don't believe you've introduced me to your new . . . friends," the woman said.

Maggie took the perfect woman's hand and gave it a noticeable squeeze. "This is Bridget and Jacob."

"Oh?" The woman's voice and smile were falsely sweet. "Hello, Bridget and Jacob. I don't believe I caught your surnames."

I'm drowning in molasses. If I was a diabetic, I'd be in a coma. Bridget bit the inside of her cheek to silence her churning thoughts. "Mulligan," she said, balling up the napkin in her lap with her left hand and offering her right hand to the newcomer.

"Mulli—*oh*." The woman's eyes snapped and she pulled her hand back from what Granny would've called a wet noodle handshake. "You're *her*."

"Her?" Bridget directed a questioning look at her sister-in-law.

"Bridget, this is K—"

"I'm Katie Rearden," the woman said, swinging her glare back in Bridget's direction. "The wronged woman."

Six

Rain streamed down Riley's face and neck in rivulets that collected in his collar with icy efficiency. Today's chores would have to wait. If he'd started as early as planned this morning, perhaps he could have accomplished more.

Instead, he'd dined like a king with a *cailleach*.

Bridget's arrival had thrown him off his schedule. Well, then, that made this all *her* fault. Didn't it? After all, he'd lost yesterday picking her up at the airport, and today's weather would prevent him from making up for it.

With a frustrated sigh, he stowed the tractor and put his tools in the barn, pausing as he heard a friendly whinny. He stopped to stroke *Oíche*. Night. The name suited him. The black horse nuzzled Riley's shoulder. "Aye, there's nothing I'd like better than a good run today, lad, but it's soft the weather's gone on us."

He gave *Oíche* an extra ration of oats, then made his way back to the house. Mum probably had something in need of repair. All Riley knew was that he needed *something* to keep him busy. The restlessness plaguing him of late had grown almost unbearable, and the intruder's arrival had made matters even worse.

He shouldn't allow her that much importance.

Wouldn't ignoring the woman be his best recourse? He ducked his head against the steady shower and wound his way around to the back door, trying not to remember the way Bridget had looked this morning in her nightgown, with her hair mussed, and her voice husky with sleep.

Aye, he'd like nothing better than to ignore Bridget-so-called-Mulligan, but he was a man, after all. She wasn't a woman easily ignored by anyone with a drop of testosterone in his veins. And from the way Riley constantly hardened at the sight of her, he must have more than his share.

"A curse, it is," he muttered, glancing up at the sky again and blinking against the slow but steady rain. "Another bloody damned curse."

He slipped through the back door and closed it firmly, then bent down to remove his boots.

"Mary Margaret, is that you, lass?" Mum called from the front room.

"No, it's Riley." He headed toward the stairs. "Just let me get some dry clothes, and I'll—"

"Never mind that," Mum said. "I need a word with you now."

"I'll be dripping all over the place." He paused a moment, waiting for her to change her mind about him fetching dry clothes. "Mum?"

"Bring yourself in here now, Riley Francis, or I'll be pushin' meself up the stairs after you."

With a sigh, Riley grabbed a clean rag and dried the worst of the drops from his head and neck, then went to the front room where Mum sat with her foot propped up and her dear face wearing a worried frown.

"What is it?" he asked, stooping beside her chair. "What's wrong?"

"Maggie took Bridget and Jacob with her to the village this morn'."

Aye, he knew that, but the reminder made Riley's belly lurch and his heart slam against his ribs. The thought of

Bridget parading herself around as Culley's widow was too much. "Maggie has gone too far."

Mum rolled her eyes. "I'll not be speakin' of your ridiculous mistrust of Bridget now." She drew a deep breath and exhaled very slowly. "'Tis worried, I am, about the weather turnin' soft and catchin' them in the wet."

Riley lifted a shoulder. "Mum, a bit of rain won't hurt them." Not as much as Bridget's lies could tarnish his brother's memory.

"The lad was wearin' cotton, Riley—not wool." She drew a deep breath, but the worry didn't leave her eyes. "Perhaps once they're used to our weather, but until then I don't want the lad takin' cold."

Naturally, Fiona Mulligan would worry about a child. The day she stopped worrying about children would be the day they lowered her into her grave. *Jaysus forbid.* "I'll bring the car 'round and fetch them myself."

"There's a good lad." Mum looked over her shoulder again at the droplets on the windowpane. "Be off with you. Hurry along now."

Riley grabbed a slicker near the back door and raked his fingers through his unruly mass of hair. He would fetch them all safely home all right, but he was considerably more curious about the villagers' reactions to the woman who claimed to be Culley's widow than he was about anyone getting a bit wet. Hadn't he and Culley been soaked through on a regular basis and still grown into men?

The thought of Bridget flaunting herself about Ballybronagh with Culley unable to deny her claims didn't set well with Riley at all. In fact, it made him furious. As he made his way around the house to the car, he kicked a clod of dirt, watching it disintegrate and blend with the mud.

Aye, that was precisely what he'd like to do with the intruder—make her vanish as quickly as she'd thrust herself into their lives. Culley's memory deserved better. All the Mulligans deserved better.

Mum had certainly taken to Bridget and her child. She'd never even questioned the woman's claim. Why? Fiona Mulligan was usually an uncanny judge of character. Why was this time different? Was Mum so eager to resurrect her dead son in any way possible, that her judgment was clouded? Aye, that had to be it. What else could it be? And was the same true of Maggie, then? No, more likely that Maggie simply wanted to annoy Riley.

"She's doing a bloody fine job of it, too," he muttered, swinging himself into the car and starting the engine. He'd rather drive the lorry, but there weren't enough seats in it. On the other hand, he could make Bridget ride in the open bed.

But even Riley wouldn't stoop to that. Besides—he drew a shaky breath—the rain would make her jumper cling to her breasts. The woman was already driving him insane with the constant craving without having her soaking wet before his hungry eyes.

Aye, he could picture her wet and shivering. The cold would make her nipples draw up and stiffen proudly. Tauntingly. Temptingly.

"Shite." He shook his head to rid himself of the image, but another took its place. His dream woman appeared in his mind's eye with her chemise clinging precariously to the tips of her taut nipples. "Bloody hell." Riley punched down on the pedal, making the car swerve as he rounded the curve near *Caisleán Dubh.*

He scanned the countryside as best he could in the rain and mist, but saw no sign of his sister or her companions. Chances were they'd holed up at a friend's house, or were shopping. Obviously they weren't walking home in the rain as Mum had feared.

And Bridget's jumper would be dry.

Riley snarled at no one in particular and a growl rumbled up from his chest. He had to put his mind around what needed doing, and not what a certain impudent part of his anatomy wanted to do to Bridget. No, what he needed to do was watch her until she made a serious mistake. Then he would prove her to be the liar he knew she was. Culley's memory would be cleared and all would be well again.

But even that couldn't bring Culley back.

Riley clenched his teeth, asking himself again why this mattered so much. "Because it's a bloody lie," he muttered, tightening his grip on the steering wheel as he swung the car into a parking spot on Ballybronagh's main street. All the shops and restaurants were within two blocks of where he'd parked. He would find Maggie and the others somewhere nearby.

He eased himself out of the car and stood there in the rain, looking up and down the sidewalk for any sign of his sister's red hair. A gust of wind made him shiver, and his breath created a cloud of vapor before his eyes.

The way this day was shaping up, he'd be the one to catch his death. But Mum, being Mum, was worried about Jacob. Regardless of Riley's feelings toward the lad's mother, he would honor Fiona Mulligan's wishes.

Culley would've done the same.

With that thought foremost in his mind, Riley tugged his collar closer and meandered in and out of the shops. He learned what time Maggie had left the market, and stood on the sidewalk beneath an awning to ponder the possibilities.

Where would *he* go to get out of the rain?

The answer came to him even as he made his way to the end of the block and his favorite establishment in Ballybronagh. *Aye, that's it.* And what healthy Irishman could disagree?

Riley pushed open the door of Gilhooley's and was greeted by the warmth and familiar scents of a good peat fire, hot Irish stew simmering in the kitchen, and the special tang of Guinness and Harp. He paused while his eyes adjusted to the dimness. His belly gave an audible growl and he had to chuckle. After all, he'd eaten enough breakfast for two men.

Kevin Gilhooley stood behind the bar, his apron already stained and his ever-present smile at the ready. "Afternoon to you, Riley."

"Afternoon." Riley leaned against the polished bar, his gaze sweeping the tables and booths. He really hoped Maggie hadn't brought Bridget here. Thanks to the weather and the fact that it was Saturday, the place was packed.

Besides the usual collection of old-timers and widowers who spent the bulk of their lives in front of Gilhooley's hearth, it appeared most of the village had dropped in for lunch. "Kevin, have you seen my ornery sister about?"

"Ornery, is it? Aye." The publican leaned across the bar, a mischievous smile on his too-lean face as he nodded toward the group before the hearth. "And haven't the lads been placin' bets on which one of 'em will be left standin'?"

Riley's blood turned to ice. "What are you blatherin' on about?"

Kevin inclined his head toward the opposite end of the restaurant. "Maggie and the others took the booth 'round the end there."

Riley pushed away to make his way toward his sister, then remembered everything Kevin had said. He turned to face Gilhooley again. "What do you mean 'left standing'?"

Kevin sighed and shook his head. "Hasn't the whole village heard about Culley's widow and son by now?"

Riley clenched his teeth, reminding himself that Kevin Gilhooley was an old and trusted friend. He wanted to blurt out that the woman was a liar and imposter—that Culley couldn't possibly have married a total stranger while betrothed to another. Besides, the marriage hadn't even taken place in a proper church. Culley never would have . . .

"I have to say it's been quiet enough, though, since herself went that way."

Riley blinked, focusing on Kevin's words. He'd lost

his own train of thought, not to mention Kevin's. "Quiet since who went that way? I've no time for riddles, man."

Kevin poured a shot of Jameson's and slid it toward Riley.

"Have you gone daft?" Riley asked his old friend. "You know I never drink so early in the day."

"I'm thinkin' you will today." Kevin leaned closer. "'Tis herself—Katie Rearden."

Riley downed the whiskey in one smooth gulp.

Granny had always said Bridget talked faster than a Baptist preacher after the devil when she was nervous. Well, she was nervous now, and the words just bubbled up from wherever words that didn't start in a person's brain were born.

"And the Larabees are taking care of General Lee while we're here, so—"

"What *are* you talking about?" Katie Rearden asked, blinking.

Bridget drew a shaky breath and met Maggie's twinkling gaze. A smile of approval stretched across her young face.

Well. Bridget smiled at the "wronged woman" again and said, "Home. The Larabees are the family I worked for back in Reedville, and Brother Martin is the preacher who performed Granny's funeral service, and—"

"Oh, stop your blatherin', already." Miss Rearden glanced upward. "I don't care to hear about all those people." She leaned on the edge of the table, pinning Bridget with an unsettling gaze. "I *do* care about you flaunting yourself all over the county as Culley Mulligan's widow."

Bridget felt her son's hand fumbling for hers. She found his and gave it a squeeze, holding it steadily while she faced this woman. *Sticks and stones may break my bones, but words can never hurt me.*

But they could hurt her son. And she wouldn't tolerate that from anybody.

She lifted her chin a notch, wishing she was standing

so she could look Katie Rearden in the eye. "I *am* Culley Mulligan's widow," she said simply. "I married him almost seven years ago in Reedville, Tennessee, and I have the marriage certificate and license to prove it."

"*If* it's true, you tricked him, you did." The woman tossed her golden hair over one shoulder and struck a challenging pose with one hand on her hip. "He never would have willingly married you while he was engaged to me."

"But he did," Maggie said as she slid from the booth and stood facing Katie. "I know it, Mum knows it, and that's the way of it, Katie Rearden. Accept it and move on."

Fury radiated from Katie, who blocked the end of the booth and any possible escape. Not that Bridget would have left Maggie here to face this crazy person alone even if she had a choice.

"What about Riley?" Katie's voice sweetened and she drew her words out in a slow drawl. "I didn't hear him named among those loyal to this . . . this doxie."

Bridget squeezed Jacob's hand again. "There will be no more of this now," she said. "Little pitchers have big ears, and none of this grown-up stuff is his doing. Understand?"

Katie glowered down at Bridget, then turned her accusing glare on Jacob.

That did it. The toe of Bridget's tennis shoe made contact with Katie's shin.

"Ow!" Katie reached down to rub her injury. "I'll ruin you," she warned, straightening. "Your so-called marriage to *my* betrothed was scandalous. How dare you shame us further by flaunting yourself a—"

"Culley's death was a tragedy to me—to us." Bridget glanced at her son, then pinned her gaze on Katie again. "You are perfectly welcome to try to 'ruin' me, as you wish. However, you'll not be taking your hurt feelings out on my son. On Culley's son."

"That's right." Maggie clenched her fists at her sides as

she stared at Katie with potent rage in her Mulligan blue eyes. "You have to go through me to get to them."

"And you're thinking that might be a problem, Maggie Mulligan?" Katie gave a nasty laugh and tossed her head again. "You'd be mistaken."

Bridget felt his presence before she saw him. Riley filed the space in the aisle between a table and chairs and the corner of their booth. The expression in his eyes was one of bewilderment and fury. He appeared betrayed yet confused.

"Uncle Riley," Jacob said, ducking under the table and hurrying to his uncle's side. "Make the bad woman stop bein' mean to my momma."

"He isn't going to make me stop." Katie Rearden's laughter sounded sick and vile. "*Are* you, Riley?"

Bridget felt as if all the wind had been knocked out of her as she turned her hopes and fears toward the man who'd rejected them every moment since their arrival. Let him continue to hate and resent her, but he had to accept Jacob. He just *had* to.

Now.

"My . . . my daddy would make the bad woman stop," Jacob said, tears streaming down his face.

Bridget's heart broke and she gave Katie a shove that sent her across the aisle and enabled Bridget to move to her son's side and gather him against her. But Jacob wiggled free and looked up at Riley, anger and heartbreaking trust flashing in his young eyes. "My daddy wouldn't let that bad woman be mean to my momma," Jacob repeated, blinking. "*Would* he?"

Riley drew a long, slow breath and Bridget watched his Adam's apple travel the length of his throat before he met her gaze. She pleaded with her eyes, praying he wouldn't break her son's heart again.

"No, lad. He wouldn't," Riley said, placing his hand on Jacob's shoulder. "Culley wouldn't have stood by and allowed anyone to speak to anyone that way."

Bridget lowered her gaze. Riley hadn't acknowledged

Jacob as his nephew, but he had come to his defense. It was a step in the right direction. A very good one. She wouldn't push it now, but she had hope.

Thank you, Lord.

"I think we've had enough excitement for our first full day in Ireland," she said, her voice amazingly steady. "Jacob must be exhausted."

"Aye, it's time we all headed home," Riley said, obviously avoiding Bridget's gaze. "Mum sent me in the car to fetch you. Come along, Jacob."

Bridget felt Katie's cold stare, but she refused to meet it. Instead, she focused on the undeniable birth of hero worship in her son's eyes as he gazed up at Riley Mulligan. Without hesitation, Jacob slipped his small hand into his uncle's and released hers, then walked toward the pub entrance with him.

She had to bite the inside of her cheek to halt the tears that threatened to burst free. Their new beginning was real. Riley *would* grow to love his nephew as an uncle should.

He would love Jacob because he'd loved Culley. Riley wasn't quite ready to admit anything openly, but the possibilities were there. The seeds had been sown.

Bridget turned to face Katie Rearden. "I'm sorry I kicked you, but I won't tolerate you or anybody else being cruel or unseemly before my boy." She drew a shaky breath and met Katie's hate-filled expression with every shred of compassion she could muster. "And I'm sorry you were hurt, but I'm *not* sorry I married Culley Mulligan."

Maggie linked her arm through Bridget's, all the while ignoring Katie's silent glare. "Come along, Bridget, let's go home. Mum will be worried."

Bridget stepped into the cool, damp air and saw Jacob buckled into the front passenger seat of Fiona's car. Tears pricked her eyes, but she blinked them away and gave a silent prayer of thanks.

They had a family. At least, Jacob did. Little by little,

his uncle would grow to accept and love him, then Jacob's future would be secure here. Even if they never completely accepted Jacob's momma, they would embrace her son.

Nothing else really mattered.

It rained the remainder of the day. Fiona called it an "auld soft day," but Bridget had difficulty thinking of it as anything but wet and cold. Maggie explained that Bridget would really learn to appreciate sunshine in Ireland.

"It's a perfect day for comfort food," Bridget announced as she and Maggie pored over the contents of the refrigerator and freezer. "Chicken and dumplings, I think."

"Oh, aye." Maggie's expression was uncertain. "Will you teach me to make it?"

"Of course, but I don't see a chicken in—"

Maggie placed her hand on Bridget's elbow. "This is a farm, Bridget. Remember?"

"A farm." Bridget thought for a moment, then smacked the heel of her hand against her forehead. "You have lots of chickens, but I don't know how to"—she swallowed hard—"*do* that."

"Mum usually does it, but I'll just ask Riley." Maggie grinned and sashayed into the front room, then returned a moment later. "He's bored to tears, so we should have one fresh chicken very shortly. We've an old cock Mum's been threatening to stew since he pecked her leg bloody last month."

Bridget's stomach lurched. "Will he . . . kill it?"

Maggie laughed. "Of course, silly, but we'll need to scald and pluck it."

"Scald and . . . and pluck it?" Bridget echoed, leaning against the refrigerator door for support. "I can buy chickens at the Piggly Wiggly, I can fry one, stew one, stuff one, filet one, bake one, and even barbecue one, so I reckon I can . . . pluck one." She drew a shaky breath and managed a lopsided grin.

"Some hillbilly you are." Maggie grinned and gave Bridget a hug. "From watching those videos on the piped telly at Gilhooley's, I—"

" 'Piped telly'?"

"Gilhooley's has a satellite dish."

"Like cable?"

"Aye." Maggie lifted a shoulder and her expression turned sheepish. "The country music videos and song lyrics made me think everybody with an accent like yours is from the country."

Bridget smiled. "There are cities and towns in Tennessee. Reedville is a lot bigger than your Ballybronagh."

"So you aren't a country lass." Maggie nodded. "A word I learned in school is 'stereotype.' I made a vow to the Virgin that I wouldn't be guilty of doing that to people, but I did it to you and Jacob. 'Tis sorry I am for it, too."

Bridget hugged Maggie again, then glanced at her son, who was occupied with the coloring books Mrs. Larabee had bought him for the trip. After their return to the farm, Riley had gone off to go over ledgers or something, leaving Jacob with the womenfolk again. The boy looked up at the archway between the kitchen and front room every few minutes, his expression filled with longing.

The weather will clear and Riley will accept Jacob.

That would be her mantra. Bridget drew a deep breath and willed it so.

"My people *were* country folk, but not since World War Two," she said, turning her attention back to Maggie. "My granny was born in the hills of eastern Tennessee, and that's where she learned to fix such fine comfort food. I reckon that means my cooking is country cooking."

"What should we do while we wait for the chicken?"

"We'll need onion, garlic, and celery for the broth." Bridget tapped her chin and considered the ingredients carefully. "Salt, pepper, parsley, basil, and the biggest pot you have."

Maggie gathered everything except the celery, which they didn't have. "What else?"

"I use sourdough for my dumplings, but I don't have a starter." She fumbled through the cupboard and found a packet of yeast. "Do you have a crock or jar that isn't needed for anything, and a piece of cheesecloth?"

A short time later, Bridget had the basic ingredients for sourdough starter resting in a small gray crock, with the cheesecloth covering it. "We need to keep this where it won't be disturbed."

"On the top shelf of the pantry, I think." Maggie moved a tin of what the Irish called biscuits and Bridget called cookies, then placed the crock on the top shelf. "No one should bother it there. What will happen to it?"

"The yeast and sugar will ferment and sour."

"Eeeeeeeeew." Maggie wrinkled her nose. "On purpose?"

Nodding, Bridget laughed. "Yes, on purpose, and in a few weeks you'll see why I've been missing it so."

"Can we still make dumplings without it?"

Maggie looked very young to Bridget just now, with her eyes wide and eager for knowledge, and her hair pulled up in a ponytail. "Yes, but they won't be as good without the sourdough. We'll need flour, salt, baking powder, and lard, but we won't start until the chicken's ready to bone."

"Bone?"

Bridget smiled to herself. "To take off the bone."

"Oh, aye, I've helped Mum do that."

I was beginning to wonder . . .

The back door opened a few minutes later and Riley entered, wiping his feet on the mat. Bridget averted her gaze from the limp bird in his hand. At least it wasn't headless, but she didn't want to know how he'd done the deed.

"Here's your chicken, Maggie," he said. "How burned will it be?"

Maggie smacked her brother's shoulder and took the chicken to the large utility sink near the back door and started working on it.

Bridget kept her distance, occupying her eyes with the sight of Riley Mulligan instead of the dead chicken that would become supper. His dark hair curled stubbornly around his face, softening his rugged features just a bit. He *needed* softening, for she'd never seen a harder-looking man in all her days.

Culley had been tall and strong like his brother, but also much younger. His hair had been neatly trimmed to graze his collar in back, and Bridget had fallen immediately and madly in love.

She blinked away the brief memories of Culley before they made the tears come again. She'd done more than her share of sniffling lately. Besides, Jacob was in the room.

She stole a glance at her son and found him staring at his uncle with that naked need shining in his young eyes. She caught her breath and held it, searching her mind for some way to urge her son and uncle together. If Riley spent more time with Jacob, he couldn't help but love the boy. Surely he would accept him as Culley's son—his own flesh and blood.

Something warm washed over her, much like it had during their walk to the village, and she jerked her gaze back to Riley, who stood staring at her as if trying to memorize every detail. The realization both chilled and thrilled her. What thoughts went through his mind while he stared at her? She was a woman, though not a very experienced one, but she still recognized lust when she saw it. There was no denying that Riley Mulligan found her attractive.

She patted her hair into place and smoothed her sweater as he continued to stare, and hated herself for doing it. *Pride goeth before a fall.* Dropping her hands to her sides again, she tried to ignore the heavy thud of her heart, the thickening of her blood, the longing warmth settling low in her belly.

Lust worked two ways sometimes. That certainty settled in her mind—and other places—and she licked her lips, allowing her gaze a leisurely journey down the length of the man and back to his handsome face. *Oh, yes.* He was one fine hunk of man. She couldn't deny that.

Maggie continued to chatter away as she did whatever needed doing to the poor, dead chicken. Bridget didn't really hear or begin to understand anything the girl said now. She was too lost in the self-discovery of feelings she'd thought long dead.

She licked her lips again, catching herself when she noticed the darkening of Riley's gaze as he followed her movement. Wave after wave of heat washed over her, consuming the distance between them and making her painfully aware of every breath, every beat of her heart, every throb of something *much* lower than her heart.

Enough of that. But it wasn't enough. She swallowed again and drew a shaky breath, shocked by her sudden and undeniable lust for this man.

Her husband's brother.

Seven

Riley spent what remained of the day in the barn sharpening tools that didn't really need it. His mood was ugly, as Mum would say, and he was of no mind to share it with anyone. Not even the woman who'd caused it.

The rain had stopped, but the air hung heavy with the threat of more. He stepped outside and watched the mist curl up from the base of *Caisleán Dubh* to twine about the tower like a snake. Aye, it seemed appropriate for a serpent to wrap itself around that particular tower, real or not.

Thanks to a serpent, Eve had tempted Adam. Bridget tempted Riley without any such assistance.

Riley clenched his fists at his sides, remembering the expression on Katie's face when she'd turned to him at Gilhooley's, expecting him to agree with her. Hadn't he asked her not to approach Bridget or the child? In time, Riley would have exposed the ruse and set things right again. Bridget would be packing her bags and returning to the States where she belonged.

Today's events had been a step in the wrong direction. He closed his eyes for a moment, recalling the pleading look in the lad's eyes when he'd asked him to intervene.

He'd called him "Uncle Riley" again—right there in Gilhooley's in front of almost half the village.

My . . . my daddy would make the bad woman stop, the lad had said, tears and snot streaming down his young face. And he'd looked to Riley to fill Culley's shoes.

Worse, he'd looked at Riley with Culley's eyes.

Jaysus. Could it be true? Was the lad Culley's son? The more Riley gazed upon the child, the harder it was to deny. Aye, it was possible that Culley had been seduced by Bridget, and anytime a man sowed his seed, the possibilities of it bearing fruit existed.

But that didn't mean Culley had turned his back on his fiancée, or that he had married a woman he barely knew. Culley had only been in the States ten days when he'd allegedly married Bridget. She couldn't possibly have had time to conceive his child *and* realize it within that time.

Riley didn't know much about the ways of a woman's body, but he knew that. If Culley had believed Bridget carried his child, he certainly would have married her, but that couldn't have been the case.

"So I'm right." Why didn't that knowledge ease his mind? Riley's breath puffed into the air in white clouds. He swallowed hard, his gut burning and churning from the confusion and anger roiling within him.

He didn't feel better, because he didn't want to lose Jacob. *Admit it, Mulligan.* But he couldn't. Not yet. Nor could he deny it.

Shite. He had to do right by Culley. If Jacob was truly his brother's son . . . *Jaysus.*

Riley glanced up at the darkening sky and drew a slow breath. "I wish you'd talk to me, brother. Tell me what it is you're wanting me to do. I need the *truth.*"

Only silence answered him. Riley shoved his fists into his pockets and scowled at the castle. The bloody thing should've been torn down decades ago, before Da ever—

"No, not now." Riley raked his fingers through his hair and closed the barn door, *and* the one protecting his memories. "Not ever."

Some things were best left buried. Forever.

Squaring his shoulders, he strode toward the house, his boots sinking in the turf and making a sucking sound with each step. He would keep the memories buried, and he would learn the truth about Bridget.

And Jacob?

Riley's heart skipped a beat and he paused just short of the back door. Squeezing his eyes shut, he remembered Jacob's expression again as he'd pleaded with him at Gilhooley's. And he remembered Bridget's when she'd asked him without words not to deny her son.

So he hadn't. Instead, he'd betrayed Katie—the woman his brother would have married—an old family friend.

There were blood tests these days that could prove or disprove a child's paternity.

He remembered those eyes again.

Culley's eyes.

Riley didn't want to believe it—couldn't believe it. Not yet. But he would do his best to treat the lad fairly and with the respect his brother's son deserved. For now.

As for Bridget . . . Riley's mouth went dry as he pictured her. The woman was a temptress of the worst kind. Aye, more and more, Riley understood how Culley could have been unable to resist the urge to bury himself in the woman.

An urge Riley understood too bloody well.

Another Mulligan curse?

Shaking himself, Riley stepped through the back door, determined to keep himself under control. He needed time and information. More than that, he needed to distance his thoughts from the entire notion of that bit of skirt.

Good intentions firmly in place, Riley removed his muddy boots and washed his hands at the utility sink near the back door. The aromas filling the kitchen set his mouth to watering and his belly to churning before he'd even rinsed off the soap.

He drew a deep, appreciative sniff and glanced at the

table, where various serving bowls sat steaming. Everyone looked up at him as he moved toward his empty chair.

"I was about to send Maggie after you," Mum said as he took a seat. "It's not like one of me lads to be late for supper."

Bridget laughed and Riley's face flooded with heat. Mum often treated him like a wee lad, but Riley always took it in stride. Until now. He didn't want to be presented in a vulnerable way before Bridget. He wasn't a lad. He was a man.

He glanced across the table at her. *Bad idea, Mulligan.* She'd put up her hair, revealing a long column of throat that he hadn't noticed earlier. A blue jumper he'd last seen on his sister stretched across Bridget's more substantial curves.

Aye, and despite her slimness, wasn't Bridget curvy in all the right places? The temperature in the room escalated—at least in his chair—and he tugged at his collar.

Her freshly scrubbed face glowed beneath the kitchen light, and he wondered if the warmth from the stove had put the bloom in her cheeks, or if she'd put makeup on them. No, he decided. This woman needed no paint, and he knew, somehow, that she wore none.

As Mum began grace, Riley bowed his head, but he found himself peering at Bridget through his lashes. With her eyes closed and her lips slightly parted, she was exquisite. Breathtaking.

His sinful gaze dipped lower, watching her pulse throb at the base of her throat, just above the edge of her jumper. Lower still, her breasts thrust forward just above the table, almost as if she'd arranged herself that way in order to achieve the best effect.

Oh, and it had worked.

The outline of her nipples showed through the lightweight knit, confirming that she wore no padding to entice a man. She had the natural equipment in place to achieve that without artifice.

Aye, a dangerous temptress.

Then he caught sight of Maggie crossing herself and he
followed suit, knowing he hadn't heard a word. Guilt sat
heavily on his conscience, more for his lustful thoughts
than for the missed prayer.

Disgraceful. That's you, Mulligan.

Men had needs, and it had been far too long since he'd
indulged himself. Once he remedied that situation, he
would be better able to deal with the likes of Bridget.

The huge bowl of chicken, gravy, and fluffy dumplings
came to him and he ladled a generous serving onto his
plate. Young Jacob was seated beside him again, and the
large bowl would be too unwieldy for his small hands, so
Riley served the lad as well.

Jacob beamed up at him, and Riley managed a grunt
but couldn't prevent his lips from curving a bit, too. The
lad had a way about him. There was nothing sly about
Jacob—Riley glanced across the table at Bridget—unlike
the lad's mother.

He cleared his throat and turned his attention to the
food, knowing that Maggie couldn't have prepared the delectable feast. No, Bridget had prepared the meal. The
thought of eating food prepared by her hands again an-
noyed him, but his hard work put food on their table in the
first place, so he speared a fork full of dumpling dripping
with gravy and popped it into his mouth.

An explosion of subtle flavors rewarded his effort, almost making him groan aloud. The dumplings were light
as a feather and perfectly seasoned.

"Oh, Bridget Colleen," Mum said between bites. "I've
never tasted better. Not even by me own hand. And you
didn't use spuds in them, you say?"

"Thank you. Assuming spuds are potatoes, no. But I
can next time if you want." Bridget's cheeks reddened and
she looked down. She was more reserved now. The incident in Ballybronagh must have been a warning. She was
obviously calculating her next move.

Riley would be ready for her. The next mistake she
made, he would expose her as a fraud and be done with it.

Jacob brushed against his sleeve, reminding Riley of his presence. He glanced down at the lad who wriggled in his chair as he shoveled food into his mouth.

A tightening in Riley's chest reminded him of his earlier thoughts concerning Jacob's possible paternity. By exposing Bridget as a fraud, he would hurt Jacob. He was but a lad who *believed* his mother—even her lies. As any good child should.

No, Riley had to proceed with caution. Bridget confused him, but in many ways her son confused him even more. The lad touched Riley in ways that had nothing to do with hormones, and everything to do with the past. And family.

Realization punched him in the gut. His breath caught. He swallowed hard. Aye. In a way, Jacob had brought Culley home.

At least, in Riley's heart. . . .

Restlessness clawed at Bridget as she paced her room, glancing in at Jacob every few minutes to assure herself he still slept soundly. She hadn't even bothered to change into her nightgown yet, because every time she stopped moving even for a moment, the memory of Riley coming to her rescue in town exploded in her mind. Along with the realization that she hadn't thanked the man. . . .

Granny had often said that guilt was life's best teacher. And—*dang it all*—the old woman had been right.

"Well, then I reckon I'll have to thank the man first thing in the morning." Resigned, she paused before the window and gazed out at the night. Silver moonlight beamed down on the earth and stars sparkled against the velvet sky. At least it had cleared and would rain no more tonight, but tomorrow could be another matter.

A huge yawn tugged at her mouth and she stretched. Now that she'd decided to thank Riley, she could get some sleep. She looked out the window again, mesmerized by the beauty of the dark landscape. It looked like something from a painting—too beautiful to be real.

Her gaze traveled across the meadow, knowing what she'd find. *Caisleán Dubh* marred the perfection of the night. Bridget's breath froze. She leaned closer to the glass, resting her forehead against its cool, smooth surface.

"That stupid castle can't hurt you," she whispered, her gaze riveted to the tower thrusting toward the night sky. Granny had always said the best way to get over a powerful fear was to face it head-on.

Bridget gulped.

Granny had been right about that, too. *Dang it.* Tomorrow, Bridget would march herself down to that castle and introduce herself. A smile curved her lips. All right, so introducing herself to a pile of rock was silly, but somehow it seemed right.

A woman with two big projects to face needed her sleep. Bridget pushed away from the glass just as her gaze fell on the figure standing in the meadow. He'd been there last night, and he was there again tonight. Standing. Staring.

Scaring the bejeezus out of her.

Her heart did a somersault and she shook herself. Instinct told her the man's identity, but that didn't prevent goose bumps from popping out all over her. She shivered and rubbed her upper arms, dispelling the sudden chill.

She drew a deep breath. Squared her shoulders. *You wanted to thank the man. Now's your chance.* He still stood there, but she realized now that his back was toward the house. Her gaze traveled beyond him to the castle, and a tremor slithered down her spine.

Gritting her teeth, Bridget rubbed her hands together and girded herself. Granny had always said Bridget had inherited more than her share of Frye stubbornness.

And now that Bridget had seen Riley Mulligan standing out there on a picture-perfect night, nothing would do but for her to hightail herself out there to do what she should've done today. He'd come to her son's rescue right there in Gilhooley's. He could have turned away and left them there with only humiliation to show for themselves. Instead, he had treated Jacob the way an uncle should treat his brother's son.

Courage spurred by gratitude prodded Bridget's feet to move toward the door. She peered in at Jacob first. The covers were tugged to his chin and his inky lashes rested against his fair skin. Nearly black hair curled across his forehead, making Bridget's heart ache for the man who had been hers for such a short while.

Yes, she would thank Riley. She would do it for Culley—she smiled down at Jacob—and for their son. And to silence that nagging guilt the Frye women were so doggoned good at.

She tiptoed down the back staircase, knowing Fiona and Maggie were already in bed. The back door opened silently, and soon Bridget was making her way across the moonlit meadow toward the man who still stood staring at *Caisleán Dubh*.

The night was cool. She should have grabbed her sweater, but if she went back for it now, she might never find the guts to do what needed doing. It wouldn't take long. She lengthened her stride, moving through the night with silent determination.

Moonlight poured over Riley from beyond him, casting his profile in sharp relief. Dark against silver. He didn't move as she drew closer. He continued to stare at the castle as if his life depended on it.

Bridget paused just shy of her goal and looked at the castle again. Her breath caught and her heart launched into a lively reel. Something called to her. Beckoned her. She wanted to follow the powerful urge to obey the invisible force pulling at her.

She took a step toward it. The sinister darkness of it pulsed against the silver moonlight and the sea beyond. She took another step, battling the urge to run toward the massive stones surrounding the structure, but the sane part of her held her back, allowing her only small steps toward a strangely coveted goal.

Why did she want to touch something that terrified her? She shook her head, then leaned her head to the side, listening. A soft soughing sound reached her ears. It reminded her of the mountains of Tennessee, when the wind came through the trees. But there were no trees here. It almost seemed as if—

"You hear it, too." Riley's deep voice came through the darkness.

He was close. So very close. Bridget dragged her gaze from the castle to study his profile. As if shaped from some precious metal, he stood there. He didn't flinch or even appear to breathe as she watched him.

"What . . . what is it?" she asked, turning her gaze back to the castle. "Is it the sea?"

"No, not the sea." Riley released a long sigh. "As a lad, I couldn't hear it, but Culley could."

Bridget jerked her head around to Riley again. He was looking at her now. "Culley heard it? It almost sounds like . . . whispering."

"Aye, that's what he said." Riley's face was shadowed, hiding his expression, but his voice sounded sad. Lonely. "Da never heard it. Neither have Mum or Maggie."

"That's downright strange." Bridget's heart pounded louder and louder, seeming to beat in rhythm to the whispering sound. "But you couldn't hear it when you were little?"

Riley shook his head. "I . . ." He cleared his throat. "The first time I heard it was the same night we learned about Culley's accident."

Air rushed out of Bridget's lungs and she swayed. "Oh." A sudden wave of dizziness gripped her and she reached for the nearest means of support—Riley Mulligan's muscular forearm.

"Are you all right?" he asked, his voice quiet. Emotionless. "Or would this be part of your evil game?"

Bridget struggled between anger and confusion. "I'm *not* playing a game, and I am *not* evil." She drew a steadying breath and released his arm, acutely aware of the break in contact. Some kind of silent energy hummed around Riley all the time. She'd been aware of it the first moment she'd seen him, but here in the silence of the night, that invisible force came alive. That knowledge cooled her temper even as it fueled the strange but exasperating attraction she felt for the man.

The odd whispering grew louder, as did the inexplicable need to touch Riley again. Her hand trembled as she reached for his arm and rested the tips of her fingers against his sleeve. But that wasn't enough. She pressed harder, feeling his muscles flinch.

An image of herself wrapped in his embrace exploded in her mind and she gasped, looking up to meet his gaze through the darkness. If only she could see his eyes. . . .

"You are a siren," he whispered, bringing the backs of his fingers to her cheek. "So beautiful. No wonder . . ."

She tried to speak, but no sound came from her lips. All she heard was the rich, deep rumble of Riley's voice, the soft whispering of *Caisleán Dubh*, and the steady song of her own blood as it whirred through her veins.

He gently stroked her cheek and took a step closer. Bridget's knees buckled and he reached out to steady her with his arm around her waist. The warmth of him stunned her, left her breathless and weak. What was happening to her?

His breath fanned her face, hot and enticing. She licked her lips, too aware of his arm around her waist and his face mere inches from hers even to breathe, let alone think.

Besides, a few moments ago, she'd imagined herself in his arms, and here she was. And she'd heard the same odd sound from *Caisleán Dubh* that Culley and Riley had heard. Why?

Thinking was dangerous sometimes. *Stop thinking.*

She drew a steady breath and released it very slowly, feeling the beat of his heart against her shoulder. After a moment, she ventured a peek at him through her lashes.

He'd turned his attention to the castle again, yet his grip about her waist tightened.

The strange whispers grew louder, drawing Bridget's gaze back to the tower. Voices from the past? Ghosts?

Hogwash.

But a sound that only Culley, Riley, and Bridget could hear? What significance was there in that? Was it merely a coincidence? It had to be. Even so, Granny had always sworn that everything happened for a reason.

Remember why you came out here, Bridget. She drew another deep breath, eased herself around to face him, and froze. In fact, her heart had surely skipped a beat. Or three.

Though her sexual experience was limited to her brief honeymoon, Bridget remembered enough to recognize the hard heat that pressed against her belly now. A very *impressive* hard heat.

"Oh." She wiggled, hoping to free herself, but his erection grew harder and hotter against her.

"Is this how you seduced Culley?" Riley's voice sliced through the night. "By rubbing yourself against him? Flaunting your wares?"

Rage licked through Bridget right alongside the robust longing that throbbed through her.

She hated him.

She wanted him.

She wanted to hit him.

She wanted to kiss him.

She just *wanted.*

He reached up to cup the weight of her breast in his hand, keeping his other arm about her waist like a leather harness. She couldn't escape. Heck, she could barely breathe.

"Or did you flaunt these in his face?" he asked, leaning closer, gently massaging her breast.

Her breasts felt heavy and swollen. As he brushed his thumb against her nipple, her knees gave out completely. He hauled her against him. Raw need ricocheted through her. Her insides were on fire, clenching and seeking fulfillment.

He traced circles around her nipple with his thumb. Her blood heated and flowed to the center of her, demanding satisfaction. Bridget's head swam with images of a man and a woman. They were faceless, just as Riley was now in the moonlight. Locked in a heated embrace, the imagined couple were joined in *every* possible way.

Liquid fire shot through Bridget and she pressed herself against Riley's erection, wishing there were no clothes between them. Wishing she could wrap her legs around his waist and swallow him deeply within her body. . . . It had been so long, and she wanted it. Wanted him.

There was nothing sweet about this hunger. She wanted sex and she wanted it now. She wanted it hard, fast, furious. Her body contracted and pulsed, weeping for fulfillment.

For Riley.

She shook herself, clamoring for the strength to end this. What in tarnation was she doing? She couldn't *do* this. It was wrong. *Remember Culley. Jacob . . .*

"No." She placed her hands squarely on Riley's chest and shoved as hard as she could. "I said no."

He released her so suddenly she almost fell, but she'd be damned before she'd reach out to him again. He moved as if to catch her, but she pointed her finger at him.

"Don't . . . touch . . . me." She could barely speak. Anger and an inconceivable craving pulsed through her, clouding her ability to think or move. Finally, she dragged in a shaky breath that sounded more like a sob, and straightened.

Facing him, she clenched her fists at her sides, kept her chin high. She had her pride, and she wouldn't let this man take that from her. Jacob would be proud of his momma, and Bridget would make certain she was worthy.

Trembling with rage, she said, "Don't touch me again

or I'll scream loud enough to bring Fiona and Maggie both out here to see what the ruckus is about."

He didn't speak, but his anger flowed through the night air to surround her.

"You hate me, and I don't know why." She held her hand up to make certain he didn't interrupt her now. "I came out here to thank you for today. Not to be insulted and . . . and ravished."

A choking sound came from Riley, but nothing intelligible. He fell silent again.

"I didn't 'seduce' Culley," she said, remembering the way her husband had swept her off her feet, how an unexplainable and sudden passion had driven them to the justice of the peace. There'd been nothing dirty about it. "I loved Culley Mulligan, and I married him because he asked me. I became pregnant, and bore his son. Jacob. That boy is the joy of my life and you aren't going to hurt him. Or me."

Still, the man didn't speak. Even the strange whispering sounds from *Caisleán Dubh* had ceased.

"I appreciate what you did for me and Jacob in town today," she said, calmer now. "But that doesn't give you the right to take liberties now."

"Liberties?"

"You know dang well what I mean." Bridget stiffened, suddenly so tired she could barely stand. "Now you go on thinking what you will of me, but don't be forgetting that Jacob is Culley's son."

"Maybe."

"No maybe to it." Bridget rubbed her arms against the sudden breeze that swept in from the ocean. "Now. That's settled, so I'll skedaddle on back to the house and we'll be done with it."

"You'd be lying to yourself, then." Riley turned back to the castle.

The whispering began again and Bridget shivered. She forced herself to walk away, to march to the house, open the back door, and quietly return to her room. Inside, she went immediately to the window.

Riley still stood there, but instead of staring at the castle, he now faced the house.

And her.

Eight

Riley always walked to mass on Sunday morning, but not alone. However, this Sunday Mum couldn't walk that far due to her gout—so much for the cherries—so Maggie would drive the car with Bridget and Jacob in the backseat. There wasn't room for all of them, which suited Riley just fine. He'd skipped breakfast to avoid Bridget, and riding in the car with her would have been the death of him.

That woman—that *cailleach*—had made him lose control last night. Riley tightened his hands into fists as he walked, growing angry with himself all over again. The feel of her against him, the weight of her breast in his hand, and the traitorous fire infiltrating his blood had all conspired against him.

"Shite." He reached up to massage the back of his neck. His head throbbed and his eyes burned like smoldering peat from lack of sleep. "You're a bloody mess, Mulligan."

To make matters worse, Bridget had heard the infernal castle whispering that had plagued him since Culley's passing. Wasn't that a puzzle?

He watched Mum's car pass with Maggie at the wheel.

Jacob waved and Riley managed to return the gesture, noting that Bridget faced straight ahead.

Well, fine. Didn't he need the peace of being alone? Aye, but not as much as he needed a woman. Sean Collins had asked him to play a session with him in Doolin next week. That was where Riley would find a woman to fulfill the lust threatening to seize his sanity. There were always anonymous, willing females hanging about the musicians in Doolin, unlike the farming villages where decency prevailed.

"And aren't you the indecent one now, Mulligan?" If that wasn't an understatement, he didn't know what one was.

He swallowed hard, rounding the bend that would take him inland toward Ballybronagh. Aye, but he wasn't headed toward the solitude he craved almost as much as sex just now. No, Riley Mulligan, the lustful and sinful— at least, he *wanted* *t*o sin—was headed for mass. To church. To confession?

No, he would confess *after* his trip to Doolin.

A smile tugged at one side of his mouth and the tension in the back of his neck eased at the thought. If it wasn't Sunday, he would go back for the lorry and head toward Doolin now. Ah, but there was no mercy for the lustful on Sunday. *More's the pity.*

He glanced toward the back of Mum's car and caught sight of Bridget through the rear window. Sunlight gilded her hair, displaying strands of red and even a bit of gold amid the rich brown mane. His breath caught and an odd tightening gripped him.

There was something about this woman that triggered a terrible madness within him. When she'd touched him last night, he'd gone off his nut.

After that, nothing would do but for him to touch her. And more. He'd been unable to prevent himself from pulling her against him and showing her just what she'd done to him. Aye, and wasn't that his shame to bear? Now the woman *knew* his weakness. Would she use it against him as she had against Culley?

Riley turned to cut across his own field, avoiding the castle, as he often did. Ah, poor Culley. Riley heaved a sigh, knowing now what his young and inexperienced brother had come up against so many years ago in Tennessee. Hadn't Bridget cast her siren's spell on Riley, too? Even *he* had been helpless to resist her charms.

If it had been Riley instead of Culley visiting the States seven years ago, would *he* have married Bridget in order to have her in his bed?

The question caught Riley by surprise. He chewed his lower lip, considering. Now that he'd experienced a taste of Bridget's power firsthand, how could he deny the possibility that Culley might very well have stooped to anything in order to have her? For that matter, hadn't Riley been near that point himself last night?

If Culley really had married the woman, then Bridget's legal claim to her late husband's share of the farm was genuine. Riley swallowed the lump in his throat and his empty stomach churned acid in lieu of the breakfast he should have eaten. Perhaps he'd been approaching this all wrong.

Perhaps? A snort of disgust broke free and he shook his head at his own foolishness. Hadn't Bridget won every round? She'd ingratiated herself into his family. She'd even been welcomed in the village. Only Riley and Katie had rejected Bridget and her son.

Culley's son.

Aye, the lad was a Mulligan. Resignation eased through Riley. That much, he could no longer deny. Maybe he couldn't deny the marriage, either, but he knew one thing to be true: When it came to Culley and Bridget, she had been the more powerful, the more seductive, the more experienced. And she had, no doubt, wielded that power ruthlessly.

Renewed rage threatened to whip through Riley, but he shoved it aside. Right now he needed reasoning—not anger. He was older, more experienced than Culley had been, and he must not fall victim to Bridget's wiles.

The memory of her soft curves melding against him last night flashed unbidden to his mind. He could smell her, feel her, hear her breathe. Oh, and when he'd cradled her breast in his hand, all thoughts but having her beneath him right there in the meadow had fled.

Her passionate response to his touch had shocked and inflamed him. Even now he throbbed and hardened expectantly.

"Bloody hell." How was he supposed to stroll into church with *that* on display? He paused half a block away. A little more time was all he needed. A cold swim would have been more effective, but this would have to do until he could get to Doolin.

His face warmed with embarrassment as he neared the church. By the time he reached the front steps, he would have himself under control again. After mass, he would determine how to handle the likes of Bridget Mulligan.

"So the traitor has arrived."

Riley froze at the sound of the familiar voice. Slowly, he turned to face Katie Rearden's wrath. "Aye," he said, unable to deny her charge.

She walked slowly toward him, her arms folded before her, the lines of her dress in perfect harmony with her stride. Crisp, freshly pressed, pristine. Culley had always said his Katie was the most perfect lass he'd ever known. How could he have betrayed her?

More shame finally brought Riley's lust under control—at least for now. Hadn't he betrayed Katie almost as much as Culley supposedly had, and all because of the same woman? *Jaysus.* As much as Riley wanted to deny it, he couldn't.

"'Tis sorry I am, Katie," he said, stopping in front of her. "I . . ."

"You what?" She stared up at him, waiting. "You're sorry for shaming me in Gilhooley's?" Her eyes narrowed and she drew a deep breath. "Or for embracing your brother's doxie and bastard?"

Katie's words slammed into Riley like a blow. He gnashed his teeth, struggling for a response. Finally, he cleared his throat and said, "None of this is the lad's doing."

"He's still a bast—"

"No." Riley held his hand up to silence her. "Don't, Katie. Don't lower yourself to blaming a child who wasn't even born then."

She stared at him in disbelief. "You believe her. The lies."

"I'm not sure what I believe right now." His voice sounded as confused as he felt, even to his own ears. "I know when I look upon the lad that he could be—probably is—my brother's son. I denied it for as long as I could, but you see it, too. Otherwise, you wouldn't have called him a bastard. . . ."

She looked quickly away, then pressed her lips into a thin line and nodded. "But . . ."

"The woman is dangerous," Riley said, trying not to remember *how* dangerous Bridget had been for him last night. "I'm convinced she tricked poor Culley into her bed."

Katie's lower lip trembled but without sacrificing a shred of her dignity. She would never have allowed that. She was always in control, or at least gave that impression. "Do you . . ." Katie bit her willful lower lip, then added, "Do you think he really married her?"

Riley lifted a shoulder, unwilling to share all his thoughts right now. Bridget was too powerful and his lust for her too great. Some of that might show in his voice or his words. The last person he wanted to learn of his lust for Bridget was Katie. Hadn't she been hurt enough without him adding to her pain?

"We'll learn the truth in time," he said, offering her his arm. "Come along now, or we'll be late for mass."

Katie flashed a quick, perfect smile. "Careful, Riley," she whispered. "People will think we're doing a line."

Riley missed a step and cleared his throat. Mum had been insisting for years that Katie had her cap set for Riley once she'd accepted Culley's death. *Stuff and nonsense.* "Let them think what they will," he said with more bravado than he felt. In truth, the last thing he wanted was for his family to believe he was courting anyone. He'd never hear the end of it.

Not that Katie wasn't attractive. She just wasn't his type—too cool, too sophisticated, he supposed. Besides, hadn't he known her all his life? She was more like a sister than anything.

Culley had been more interested in life beyond the farm after going to university, where he'd fallen in love with Katie. Riley, however, had always been content to work the land and tend the stock. It was as much a part of who and what he was as the Mulligan blood flowing through his veins.

And wasn't Mulligan blood the problem? He squeezed his eyes shut for a fleeting instant, remembering the last conversation he'd had with Culley. They'd been at the airport when Riley had asked his brother why he'd chosen Katie from among so many others. Culley's answer had shocked even Riley, who had believed he knew his brother better than anyone.

Because marrying Katie will stop the curse, Culley had said.

Riley blinked, glancing down at the woman on his arm. His brother had winked as he'd run to catch his plane without explaining that cryptic answer. After Culley's accident, Riley had put it out of his mind. But now . . .

Bridget and her son had changed everything.

Why had Culley believed that marrying Katie would stop the curse of *Caisleán Dubh?* And, more importantly, why had he married Bridget instead?

You've left me a mountain of questions, boyo.

If only Culley were here to speak for himself. Riley

sighed, vowing to find the answers he needed to set things right once and for all. It was the least he could do for Culley.

And his nephew.

Jaysus.

To complicate matters even further, Bridget had heard the ominous whisperings from *Caisleán Dubh.* Why? Was it because she'd borne a Mulligan child? *Aye, a Mulligan child.* But that didn't make sense, since Mum had never heard it. Only Culley, then Riley, and now Bridget. . . .

Yet Culley had believed that marrying Katie would stop the curse. Riley almost groaned aloud, but caught himself as he spied an elderly man waiting on the church steps, his face beaming when he spotted Katie.

"There you be, lass," he said. "I was beginnin' to worry."

"Granddad, you remember Riley Mulligan?"

"As I live and breathe, Mr. Rearden?"

"You still have bugs and rocks stashed in your pockets, lad?" Riley's former teacher grinned while embracing him and pounding him on the back.

"When did you come home?" Riley asked, remembering all the years as Mr. Rearden's pupil in the village school. "And isn't it grand to see you, sir?"

"Enough of that sir and mister business, lad," the older man said. "'Tis just Brady. Aren't you a man full grown yourself now?"

"Aye, but old habits are hard to break."

"That must mean you really do have bugs and rocks stuffed in your pockets."

"I do believe Granddad has kissed the Blarney stone this morn'," Katie said, rolling her eyes.

"Aye, and I intend to do that on a regular basis, lass." Brady's eyes sobered as he faced Riley again. "'Tis sorry I am about Culley. Such a waste."

Riley nodded, unable to form words just now. He remembered the countless hours he and Culley had spent walking between home and school. He drew a breath and released it very slowly, determined to change the subject. "What brings you home now?"

"'Tis time to fulfill a lifelong dream, and this be the only place to do it."

Riley waited for his old teacher to explain, but Brady turned toward the church entrance.

"He says he wants to write our local history," Katie said, shaking her head. "I can't imagine why anyone would want to read about our boring little village."

Riley chuckled, holding the door open for Katie and her granddad. As he turned to follow them inside, something dark against the horizon fell into his line of vision. A fist tightened around his heart.

Caisleán Dubh.

With cold clarity, he knew exactly what bit of local history Brady Rearden intended to tell.

Bridget couldn't breathe. After seeing Riley walk into the church with Katie Rearden, all she wanted was out of there. Heated memories of being in his arms last night warred within her against shame and jealousy.

Jealousy? She had no right or reason to feel jealous. Riley Mulligan could walk into church with anyone he pleased. In fact, the more time he spent away from *her*, the better. To make matters worse, she'd recognized the older gentleman who'd entered with Katie and Riley as the man she and Jacob had met on the airplane.

She was relieved the man passed by without spotting them, as she wasn't in the mood to be polite just now. However, she was even more relieved when she saw Katie sit on the other side of the aisle, leaving Riley to sit with his family. *Foolish, foolish Bridget.*

She barely heard the service, and didn't understand most of what she did hear. She'd never felt comfortable with the Southern Baptist church Granny had attended. Though she believed in God, Jesus, and the Scripture, she didn't know enough to feel comfortable with any religion.

She wanted that for Jacob. After all, she had decided to

convert to Catholicism for Culley after their argument on
a morning years ago, and since she'd never found her own
spiritual home, this choice seemed logical.

Her throat clogged and her eyes burned. Culley had
died without learning of her decision. She would make up
for that by raising her son in his daddy's faith.

The moment mass ended and they stepped out into the
sunshine, she knew what she had to do. She had fulfilled
one mission the previous night by thanking Riley. Her
face flooded with heat at the memory, but she quickly
banished the thought and drew a shaky breath. Riley had
remained inside to chat with friends—and Katie, no
doubt—but Bridget was relieved he wasn't close enough
to overhear her plans.

"I'd like to walk back, if you don't mind," she said
with a smile.

"Would you, now?" Fiona smiled her approval. "'Tis a
lovely morn'. If not for this gout, I'd join you, lass."

Maggie studied Bridget a few moments, seeming to understand that she needed some time to herself. "Jacob, I
could use some help gathering eggs."

Jacob's eyes grew round and a huge grin split his
young face. He turned to his momma. "Can I go help Aunt
Maggie?"

"I reckon." Bridget stroked her son's hair and gave her
sister-in-law a grateful smile. "I'll be along shortly. You
be careful, though."

"He'll be fine," Maggie said. "I promise."

"That he will." Fiona hobbled down the steps, leaning
heavily on her cane. "I do believe the cherries are startin'
to help some. At least I didn't have to go barefoot to
mass."

"And you would have, too." Maggie laughed as she
opened the car door.

"Do you think the Blessed Virgin would mind an old
woman's bare foot, lass?" Fiona asked as she lowered herself into the front passenger seat.

Smiling at their banter, Bridget waited until they were

in the car and driving away, then she started down the road toward *Caisleán Dubh*. She forced herself to look at the castle, and to remain focused on it as she drew nearer. Her heart thundered louder with each step she took, and a cold sweat coated her skin.

A gentle breeze from the sea washed over her damp skin, sending a shiver coursing through her. She felt much as she had that summer between her sophomore and junior years in high school, when she'd taken a job picking cotton. All day, she'd bend and pick and sort, then in the late afternoon, the breeze would swoop down from the mountains and dry the sweat from her skin.

A gull's cry pierced the air and she stumbled, barely catching herself before she fell. "It's just a bird, silly." She drew a deep breath, squared her shoulders, and continued her march toward *Caisleán Dubh*.

The closer she came, the more she had to crane her neck to see the tower. The main part of the castle was large and square, but the round tower soared into the sky. She shaded her eyes and paused, noting the presence of narrow windows near the top.

She turned her gaze to the ocean, imagining how far someone would be able to see from up there. Her mouth went dry and she pressed onward.

At the castle's base, she stopped to examine the lay of the land. On one side, the road separated the castle from the farm. "Fine, then let's go see what's on the other side of you."

She scrambled over huge boulders until she found a level area that she guessed had once been a path. Grass and wildflowers had nearly obliterated it, but at least it was smooth and it led around the castle toward the sea.

What would she find on the opposite side? Did the land drop away to the sea? Or would she find a drawbridge and something that at least resembled an entrance? From here, the old fortress didn't appear to have a single door, and the windows were high and covered with old, rotting boards. However, the castle itself looked solid and sound.

An odd sensation tingled through her. She wanted—no, needed—to touch the castle. The urge to go inside gnawed at her, and the closer she came to what she believed was the front, the louder her heart thundered. Her fingertips tingled as she paused and reached toward the sturdy stones, but she stopped short of actually making contact.

Fear coiled through her, but the longing to see and feel the castle refused to die. Still, she would wait. The knowledge that she *would* touch this castle settled in her heart with a certainty that made her stop. She pressed the heel of her hand against her breastbone, drawing strength from the solid beat of her heart.

Did she believe in fate? Why couldn't she shake the notion that she belonged here? Was it Culley's memory? No, though that would have been a simpler explanation. This was more. Much more.

Excitement and fear joined forces within her, prodding her into motion again. She rounded the corner nearest the sea and lifted her face to the steady breeze flowing in off the water. Whitecaps glistened in the Sunday sunshine, and gulls darted and sailed overhead. Even from this vantage point, she could see forever. The men who had built *Caisleán Dubh* must have needed to see far. She looked upward again, but standing this close, she couldn't begin to see the top of the tower.

Squaring her shoulders, she drew a deep breath, knowing that once she turned the corner, she could never go back. Something called to her here—something powerful.

She closed her eyes and prayed, "Well, Lord, I reckon death is a powerful thing, too, but I don't have any urge to meet mine just yet. Amen."

She kept her eyes closed as she stepped around the corner to face both her greatest fear and her greatest desire. Well, last night in Riley's arms, she'd desired something a whole lot more earthly than whatever drew her to this castle.

She just stood there, her mouth turning dry. She tried to swallow the lump in her throat, but failed. "Just do it,

Bridget, like they say on those sneaker commercials." She drew a deep breath and blew it out, opening her eyes at the same moment.

Caisleán Dubh stood before her in all its glory. "Wow." Curiosity and excitement overruled the niggling fear in the back of her mind as she circled along the grassy area for a better view. A small section of stones near the massive closed doors had crumbled away, but she saw no other visible damage beyond blatant neglect and simple age.

"You are really something," she whispered, shaking her head. An invisible band tightened around her chest and she walked slowly toward the crumbled stones next to the doors.

The gap between the wood and the stones was wide enough for someone to slip through. She licked her parched lips as she drew nearer, reaching toward the castle wall with her trembling hand.

The whispering she'd heard last night beckoned to her again now. Her breath came in short bursts, and only one thought filled her mind: *Go inside. Go inside. Go inside.*

She stumbled over a rock near the entrance, pitching forward toward the jagged stones that formed a border along the overgrown pathway. A shriek erupted from her just as a pair of strong arms gripped her about the waist and hauled her to safety.

All the air rushed out of her lungs as those same arms snapped her firmly against a solid wall of chest, then wrapped themselves around her waist from behind. "What the devil do you think you're doing?" Riley asked, his breath scorching the side of her neck.

Bridget tried to pull away, suddenly desperate to break free and run headlong into the castle. She'd been so close. "Why did you stop me?" she asked, squirming and trying to jab him in the ribs with both elbows.

"Are you after getting yourself killed?" His voice sounded calmer now, though his breathing grew even more ragged. Hotter. "Are you so eager to leave your son an orphan then?"

"Jacob." A wave of weakness descended upon her like a cloak made of lead. "What am I doing here?" Then she remembered and closed her eyes. "I know. I remember."

"If I let you go, will you promise not to do anything foolish?"

"I promise I'll *try* not to." Bridget smiled to herself as he made a snorting sound, then gradually released his hold. She turned to face him, so close the warmth of him seeped through her clothing and into her bones. "Thank you for rescuing me again."

His eyes were hooded, his lips set in a stern line of disapproval. "What is your game?" he asked, gripping her upper arms in his strong hands. "One minute you're trying to seduce me, then the next you're trying to get yourself killed."

"Sed—" She sputtered for several seconds, his image blurred through the veil of rage that exploded from within her. *"Seduce?"* She tried to pull free, but he held her fast. "Fine, be a big old bully. Your momma will ask me about the bruises you're leaving on my arms."

His grip eased immediately and his expression softened. "I'm sorry." He sighed and shook his head. "I've never harmed a woman, and I don't intend to start now." He gave her a look that was more curious than anything. "Why do you go out of your way to irritate me?"

"I'd wager you were born irritated." Bridget put one fist on her hip, concentrating on this flesh-and-blood man before her rather than on the persistent and perplexing lure of the castle behind.

A powerful sadness filled Riley's eyes and Bridget's heart. "What is it?" She took a step toward him.

He released a shaky breath and gazed out toward the ocean, and at something else she suspected only he could see. "It's nothing to concern you, and I'm sorry for being so rough."

Absently, she rubbed her upper arms. "You didn't hurt

me. I'm tough peasant stock." She grinned when he half-smiled in her direction. "My grandpa told long tales about how his family fled Ireland during the Potato Famine, so I reckon that makes me *Irish* peasant stock."

"Bridget is an Irish name. A saint's name, be it fitting or not."

"I'm not a saint," she said quietly, "but I'm not bad, either. Maybe someday you'll open the eyes God gave you and realize that."

He folded his arms in front of him and a muscle in his jaw clenched. His eyes appeared icy as they swept over her. "Irish peasant stock, I believe. I'm not so sure of the other."

"You'll believe what you want, I reckon." Riley Mulligan's opinion shouldn't matter to her, but it did.

"Aye, that I will." He sighed and dropped his hands to his sides. "What are you doing here, snooping around *Caisleán Dubh*?"

"I wouldn't call it snooping." She clenched her jaw, wishing she could ask him about the castle. Why did it call to her so? Now wasn't the time. She would try again, though. *Caisleán Dubh* wouldn't have it any other way.

And that assurance both terrified and tantalized her.

"No one enters *Caisleán Dubh*." His voice echoed off the castle wall.

"You Mulligans weren't peasants," Bridget said, determined to steer their conversation in another direction.

"Aren't you the most exasperating . . ." He shook his head. "No. The Mulligans became simple farmers by choice," he said, half-facing her now.

He seemed almost friendly now as Bridget allowed her gaze to travel the length of him and back. Wind ruffled his overly long hair and made her heart do a little somersault right there in her chest. What would old Doc Boliver back in Reedville have called that? A ventricular something-or-other, no doubt.

She called it downright disturbing.

Her breath caught as Riley turned more fully toward

her. The man could have stepped from the pages of one of the historical romances Mrs. Larabee devoured, and had passed on to Bridget. He was rugged, square-jawed, with long dark curls any woman would have loved to run her fingers through.

The urge to do so overtook her and she raised her hand to trail her fingertips through the longest strands near his massive shoulder. A flame flared in his bright blue eyes, so hot it threatened to incinerate them both.

A tremor coursed through her, compounding her need and her confusion. The castle's infernal whispering commenced again and she took a step toward him. What was it about this man that made her want to do things she hadn't wanted to do with anyone since before her husband's death?

"I wish I could understand what it's saying," he said, not pulling away as she stroked his hair. "And to whom."

"So do I." She didn't have to ask him for an explanation, for the same thought plagued her. *Caisleán Dubh* was speaking to them, and only to them. It had also spoken to Culley. The brothers belonged to the castle and the land, but Bridget didn't. Why her?

"And why do *you* hear it?" he asked, echoing her own thoughts.

There was no harshness in his voice as he stood facing her while she shamelessly trailed her fingers through his gleaming black hair.

"I don't know." Her voice sounded huskier than usual—downright sultry. Her cheeks warmed and she struggled against the need to bury both her hands in his hair and pull his lips down to meet hers. Yes, a kiss. She wanted—no, needed—to kiss this man more than she needed to draw her next breath.

It was nonsense.

It was destiny.

Listen to yourself. The voice of reason tried to argue, but the castle's whispering and the bewildering flame that burned within her defeated logic and common sense.

Still, she didn't move any closer, though she wanted to more than anything. Instead, she waited and listened as the rhythm of her pulse melded with the cadence of the castle's whispers.

"We'd best get back before Mum starts worrying herself," he said thickly, though the spark in his eyes said he wanted to do something far different.

"You want to kiss me," she said, then bit her lower lip as she realized what she'd said.

The blaze in his eyes flared and he nodded once. "But I won't."

"No, of course not."

They were both pitiful liars.

Nine

Riley had skipped breakfast, barely tasted lunch, but he absolutely gorged himself at supper. The roast Bridget had prepared practically melted in a man's mouth. Cabbage, onions, and spuds swam temptingly in the rich, brown gravy surrounding the meat—a bit of heaven in every morsel.

Filled to near bursting, he leaned back in his chair and knew he had to pay his compliments to the cook. Everyone had watched him savor each bite, and to ignore the person who had prepared the feast would be inexcusable.

Bridget confused him. One moment she seemed so genuine he almost forgot that she'd lured his gullible young brother into her bed. Furthermore, he mustn't forget that if Culley hadn't been with Bridget in Tennessee, he might still be alive. Wondering wouldn't bring Culley back, but Riley had best not forget that again.

He'd come far too close to kissing her this afternoon. Swallowing the lump in his throat, he vowed to work harder on his self-control. Unfortunately, his anatomy had other ideas. Bloody inconvenient.

All the food Riley had consumed set well in his stomach, and he sighed. Without looking at Bridget, he made the sacrifice and said, "Fine meal."

Maggie gasped.

Mum said, "Praise be."

Bridget remained silent. He ventured a look at her and found her cheeks flushed and her gaze directed toward her lap. She was easier to tolerate when she chattered nonsense like the infernal bird that perched outside his bedroom window every bloody morning. This silent Bridget was more disconcerting.

More dangerous.

"I hope Maggie learns to cook as well," he continued, forcing himself to play the role. Why were they all so shocked by common courtesy? He wasn't *that* much of a boor. Was he? Aye, well, toward Bridget he had been, but nothing had changed.

"Granny taught Momma to be the best cook in the whole world," Jacob said, wriggling with obvious pride.

"Aye, lad, I believe she may be just that," Mum said.

Riley added, "If she can teach our Maggie to cook anything edible, won't I be dancing a jig in the center of Ballybronagh?"

"Well, now, isn't that something I'd like to see?" Maggie asked. "Riley Mulligan dancing. Maybe he'll even smile. Imagine that."

"Never happen," Mum teased.

Riley's face grew hot as the exchange of good-natured barbs continued. *Jaysus.* He wasn't an ogre. He knew how to smile. How was it that his family thought so little of him?

"Ah, boyo, 'tis funnin' with you, we are." Mum reached behind Jacob and gave Riley's shoulder a squeeze.

Shite. He wasn't a lad in need of comfort. He pushed away from the table and rose. "I'm going to the stable, where a man might get a bit of respect."

"Can I come?"

Riley froze at hearing the lad's softly asked question.

His breath stuttered free and he inclined his head without looking at anyone else. "Aye." He shot a quick glance at Bridget. "If it's agreeable to your mum."

Riley Mulligan was going soft.

The gratitude shining in Bridget's eyes nearly unhinged him. He couldn't draw a decent breath for several seconds.

"Be careful," Bridget said, her gaze still fixed on him.

Something tightened around Riley's chest as Jacob jumped up and hurried to the door. The lad's enthusiasm reminded him so much of Culley, he was taken back more than twenty years to this very same kitchen.

Jaysus, this child is my brother's son.

Shame for the way he'd treated Jacob at first pricked at Riley as he tore his gaze from Bridget's and made his way to the door. He stared at the peg holding his heavy, old fisherman's jumper. Beside it, Jacob's much smaller sweatshirt hung as if it belonged there. And it did belong there.

Just as Jacob belonged here at his side.

Memories flashed unbidden to Riley's mind. He and Culley racing across the field toward the sea. He and Culley in the meadow, staring up at the clouds. He and Culley duking it out over something or another. A smile curved Riley's lips.

"Uncle Riley can too smile," Jacob announced. "See?"

Riley's smile faded as he stared at Jacob's pointing finger. He glanced across the room and met his mum's knowing gaze. The old woman saw Riley's heart, but knowing that didn't gnaw at him at all. She was his mum.

A cap hung on the end peg that hadn't been worn in more than seven years. Riley reached for it, his heart thundering against his ribs as he closed his fingers about the brim and removed the dusty wool beret. For a few moments, all he could do was stare at it. And remember . . .

Tenderly, he brushed dust from the cap and pulled the leather tab inside the brim to tighten the band as much as possible. He cleared his throat and faced Jacob, focusing only on the lad.

"This is for you," he said, holding the cap out to Jacob.

A muffled sob came from Mum and Riley blinked away the stinging sensation behind his eyes. He didn't dare look at his family right now.

"For . . . me?" Jacob took the cap and turned it around in his fingers to examine it. A huge grin split the lad's face, displaying a missing tooth right in front. "Really and truly mine?"

"Really and truly yours. On the Blessed Virgin." Riley swallowed the lump in his throat and lifted the cap from Jacob's hands, placing it on the lad's head at a jaunty angle. Just the way . . .

He cleared his throat again and heard a sniffle from behind him, but he didn't look. He couldn't.

"There now," he said, girding his resolve and squaring his shoulders. "Aren't you dapper wearing your own da's cap?"

"Jaysus, Mary, and Joseph," Mum said quietly from behind them.

"My . . . daddy's?" Jacob's lower lip trembled a bit and his green eyes were like giant shamrocks. "Really?"

"Aye." Riley released a long, slow breath and placed his hand on Jacob's shoulder. "Now, let's go out and introduce you to *Oíche*, right proper like."

"Who's that?"

"My horse. *Oíche* means night."

"A real horse?"

"Well, now, what would I be doing with a fake one, lad?"

"A *real* horse!"

"A real horse." Another smile tugged at Riley's mouth and at his heart as he reached for the doorknob. He looked back over his shoulder once and found all three women staring at him.

Tears streamed down Mum's face, but he knew they

were tears of joy, so he didn't worry. Maggie smiled with approval shining in her eyes.

Bridget held her chin high and her lips pressed together tightly. She met his gaze with a bewildering expression. Was it still a mother's gratitude he saw shining in her eyes now?

Or fear and suspicion?

Bridget chose her words with great care. Using the stationery Mrs. Larabee had given her, she asked Mr. Larabee the burning question that had plagued her since the moment she'd realized that Riley had accepted Jacob as Culley's son.

Can the Mulligans take my son?

She looked down at the light green paper, her eyes blurring and her hands trembling. For some reason, the moment Riley had referred to Jacob as Culley's son, Bridget's sense of security had shattered.

But isn't that what you wanted?

She leaned back in the chair at the small writing table in her room. The sun hadn't yet set and Jacob was still at the stable with his uncle.

Riley had made no secret of his hatred for Bridget. Now that he'd accepted Culley's son, would he try to push Bridget out of Jacob's life?

Would—*could*—he steal her child?

Her fingers fluttered and she dropped the pen. It rolled across her desk and landed in her lap. She made no effort to retrieve it, but continued to stare at the words she'd written.

She had to know her rights. This was a strange land and though the Mulligans were Culley's kin, they were still strangers to her. She trusted Fiona and Maggie. They wouldn't try to take Jacob.

But what about Riley?

If he truly believed Bridget had tricked Culley into her bed, would he consider her unfit to raise Jacob? Did he have that right? That power? What rights did uncles have in Ireland? With her husband dead, would Bridget have any defense if Riley chose to seek custody of his nephew?

"Don't listen to yourself." She drew a shaky breath and collected her pen. Common sense demanded this wasn't possible. Jacob was her son—her life. No one could take him from her.

However, a sinking sensation gripped her each time the thought crossed her mind. She *had* to ask Mr. Larabee. He was her friend and her lawyer. He would give her an honest answer. It might take weeks, though. For now, she would watch and listen.

And worry.

Forcing her hand to remain steady, she completed the letter and sealed the envelope. She would ask Maggie or Fiona where to mail it in the morning.

She propped the envelope against a paperweight that boasted a shamrock encased in clear glass. Maybe it would bring her luck.

When she'd first learned about the Mulligans and planned her trip to Ireland, she'd considered this the luckiest thing to have ever happened to her. Short of Jacob. Now . . . she wasn't so sure. She couldn't deny how fond she'd grown of Fiona and Maggie in just a few days. But Riley . . .

Could she trust him with the most precious part of her life?

If only she had some money of her own. That would give her independence, and a smidgen of power. Then if Riley did try anything underhanded, she wouldn't be helpless.

She couldn't very well take a job in the village and leave Jacob here all day. What could she do to make money? *Cook, of course.* But where? Did anyone in Ballybronagh need a cook or housekeeper? The Larabees would give her a reference. She had no doubts there.

She went back downstairs and heard the television in the parlor. Fiona and Maggie were both seated in front of the hearth, chuckling at a program. Feeling restless, Brid-

get slipped into the kitchen and stared out the window beside the back door. There was a good hour of daylight left.

Across the meadow, she watched as a dark shape
moved away from the house. Her heart swelled. Jacob was
riding that gigantic horse.

She saw Riley holding the reins, leading the horse, and
her breath eased from her lungs. Now that Riley had accepted Jacob as his brother's son, she knew that he would
never allow any harm to come to the child. If only she
could be as certain of Riley's intentions toward *her.*

Remembering their earlier encounter at the castle, she
looked at the dark image against the twilight. She'd tried
to confront that stupid castle, but Riley had stopped her.
She would never stop fearing it unless she faced it and
gave it what for.

Now was the perfect time. Riley was occupied, as were
Fiona and Maggie. Her heart pounding in her ears, Brid-
get pulled her sweater close and slipped out the back door.
As she walked across the meadow, her gaze was riveted to
Caisleán Dubh. This was her hour of reckoning with that
pile of rocks, and no one was going to stop her this time.

Face what scares you, and give it heck, Granny had
said.

"All right, Granny," Bridget whispered as she marched
around the castle's foundation for the second time today.
"I'm doing it. Be proud of me."

And, somehow, Bridget knew the old woman was smiling down on her from heaven, probably between rounds
of Bingo. A smile of remembrance tugged at her lips and
she knew she was doing the right thing.

She kept her pace steady and tried not to look directly
at the castle until she'd reached the front of it again. Then
she put a fist on each hip and swung around to face the
thing.

As always, the sight of *Caisleán Dubh* gave her a jolt.
She'd never get used to the size of it, but that wasn't what
terrified her. It was something invisible. And powerful.

"Now that's just nonsense." She shook her head and

drew a deep breath, then released it in a loud whoosh. "Ready or not, *Caisleán Dubh*, here I am. Bridget Colleen Frye Mulligan, in the flesh."

Icy wind circled around her and she blinked, but continued to stare at the closed doors. "I'm not afraid of you," she said, noting a slight quaver to her voice. "Well, dang it all, you're nothing but a pile of really old rocks."

The whispering surrounded her, louder than before. More insistent. "What is that?" she whispered back. "Who are you? *What* are you?"

A shudder rippled through her. Which would be worse? A who or a what? Granny had always said not to ask questions you didn't really want answered. "Forget that," she said, trying to sound flippant and failing.

She sounded downright scared. Petrified. And of *what*? She was a Mulligan, albeit by marriage, and she had a perfect right to be here.

"Are you trying to scare me away?" She lifted her chin, listening to the whispers. "Because I'm not going anywhere." She took another step toward the castle, keeping her breathing steady and her concentration on only one goal.

Touching *Caisleán Dubh*.

The whispering grew louder, and it sounded like many voices murmuring in different languages—nothing identifiable. All she knew was that the whispers, the ghosts, the castle—whatever—was trying to communicate something important.

To her.

"Why me?" She took a half-a-dozen more steps until she stood within arm's length of the space beside the entrance. "I understand Riley and Culley, but why me?"

She inched a bit closer, holding both hands chest high, palms open. The cold of the stone closed the distance between her and the castle. The whispering swirled around and through her.

Beyond the point of no return, Bridget drew a great breath and leaned against the castle wall. Her palms touched it first, and the roughness of the cold stone felt somehow comforting—as if she'd achieved a long-coveted goal. Well, in a way, she had.

The stone seemed to warm beneath her hands and she moved closer, pressing her entire body against it. An ache commenced deep in her chest. She felt the pull of the castle, a calling of sorts. She belonged here. She was welcome. Wanted.

The whispering stopped and only she and *Caisleán Dubh* remained.

"It feels like . . . home." Her breath came on a sob and she bit her lower lip as her hands rubbed against the stones. She'd never experienced anything like this, but she knew in her heart that this was right.

She wanted desperately to go inside, but even in her state of discovery, common sense reminded her that it might not be safe to enter the centuries-old castle. But it could be made safe. The structure seemed sound from the outside. Was it possible to enter and even to live in the castle again?

What about the curse?

She forced open her eyes to the deepening twilight, anchoring herself in reality. Deeply, she breathed in the salty scent of the ocean below the cliff. "I don't believe in curses." Besides, the castle felt good to her—not evil. She was welcome here. It wouldn't harm her. It wanted her here. "Crazy."

But undeniable.

With great effort, she pulled herself away, staggering as she moved back far enough to gaze up at the tower again. The beauty of the waning sunlight shimmering against the stones brought tears to her eyes. Before, she'd only thought of it as a terrifying structure. But now . . .

She couldn't define how she felt, but she knew she had to do something with *Caisleán Dubh*. Maybe she could open some kind of business in it. But what? Something. She would talk to the Mulligans about restoring and using it.

Excitement made her walk in circles before the doors. She envisioned a parking lot on the level area over there. Near the entrance she would plant flowers and hang baskets of more flowers overhead. She would make it a welcoming place. A friendly place.

"Food." She froze as butterflies fluttered through her veins. "A restaurant. A bed-and-breakfast?" Hadn't she read something about castles that had been converted to bed-and-breakfasts?

"Oh, Lord, that's it." She held her breath and squeezed her eyes shut, envisioning the place. "Mulligan Stew." After all, her relationship with the Mulligans had been quite a stew. A smile spread across her face as she opened her eyes again to look at the castle. Her castle. No, not quite, but part Jacob's. Hadn't Mr. Larabee said as much?

She would work hard and make the castle into something her son would be proud of . . . and he would be proud of her, too. His momma. Tears stung her eyes and she blinked them away.

One thing at a time. She needed to broach the subject with Fiona and Riley—that wouldn't be easy— then get someone out here to inspect the place. A restaurant first, then maybe a bed-and-breakfast later. Assuming the Mulligans agreed to her proposal. . . .

"Mulligan Stew." She hugged herself as a cool breeze wafted in from the sea and lifted her hair off the back of her neck. "Won't folks be surprised to find Tennessee cooking right here in County Clare?" The idea felt so right.

What could go wrong?

Riley lifted Jacob from *Oíche*'s back and set the lad on the ground. "Well, now you've had your first horseback ride."

"Let's do it again." Jacob's cheeks glowed and his smile was huge in the waning twilight.

"Too dark, but now that you and *Oíche* have made friends, we'll be sure to do it again." Riley saw disappointment spread across his nephew's face. "Come full summer, the daylight will be much longer, lad."

Jacob's grin returned. "Then we can ride longer?"

"Aye, sometimes." Riley showed Jacob how to rub *Oíche*'s sleek black coat with a rough cloth, then he turned the horse into his stall with an extra ration. *"Buíochas, Oíche."*

"What's that mean?" Jacob asked.

"It means thank you, Night."

"Oh." Jacob reached into the stall and stroked the horse's muzzle. "He likes me."

"Aye." Worry oozed through Riley. "But he's still a horse, and you must promise never to ride him without me—at least, until you're older."

"Oh." Jacob's face fell.

"Ah, so you were thinking of it." Riley drew a deep breath, trying to get his mind around these new, protective feelings he had for Culley's son. "Your da was my brother, Jacob. Wouldn't he want me to look after his son?"

"Momma looks after me." The lad's eyes were filled with innocence. "She's the best momma in the whole world."

Riley bit the inside of his cheek, vowing never to share his opinion of Bridget with her son. That would be wrong. Besides, he still hadn't completely defined *his* opinion of her. A more perplexing creature had never walked this earth.

"Jacob, would there be anything wrong with having an uncle look after you, too?" He kept his tone and expression light, though his heart and mind were at odds. "If your da were still alive, he'd be looking out for you, so I'm the logical person to fill in for him."

Jacob chewed his lower lip and squinted his eyes. "Yep, I reckon."

"Well, then." Riley draped an arm across his nephew's shoulders. "It's all settled then, and you won't be visiting *Oíche* alone."

"All right," Jacob said on a sigh that was bigger than him.

"We'd best get back to the house before the women

come looking for us." Jacob walked beside Jacob, still pondering the enormity of his responsibility to the lad.

His brother's son. Culley's flesh and blood.

He had to do right by the lad. His step faltered as another thought gnawed away at him. By accepting Jacob, would he have to accept Bridget as well? Couldn't he have his nephew any other way? Then again, if Bridget hadn't lured Culley to her bed, there would be no Jacob. In a way, Culley lived on through his son. The thought comforted Riley even as all the implications of it tormented him.

He would have to find a way to do his duty without letting down his guard where Bridget was concerned. Sullying the lad's opinion of his mum was too drastic. Didn't Riley know how important his own mum was to him? No, he couldn't do that to Jacob, but he couldn't allow Bridget to reap any undeserved rewards, either.

He wiped his boots at the door and Jacob imitated his action. A smile curved his lips. It was heartwarming and disconcerting at the same time, as Riley had never been anyone's role model before. He hung up his jumper and cap. Jacob hung up his sweatshirt and cap. Riley washed his hands, and Jacob did as well.

"Well, then, shall we see if there are any milk and biscuits for a bedtime snack?"

"Cookies," Jacob said with a grin.

"Cookies, is it?" Chuckling, Riley pulled down the tin of biscuits and poured two glasses of milk. He and Jacob sat across from each other, eating in companionable silence. Men didn't need to chatter constantly as women did. This felt right.

Riley's throat clogged with a flood of emotions as he saw his brother's face in the lad's. Aye, this was right.

The door between the kitchen and parlor swung open and Bridget said, "There you are."

"I told you he'd be fine," Maggie said, following her into the room.

"Aye." Riley winked at Jacob. "Our peace and quiet is over now, lad."

Jacob grinned. "Yep."

"Finish your milk and cookies, then it's bedtime for you, young man." Bridget stood behind her son and rested her hand on his shoulder. Her gaze met and held Riley's. "Thank you for returning my son to me safely."

Was it Riley's imagination, or had the woman emphasized "my son"? Curious, he simply nodded and drained his glass of milk. "I've a bit of reading to do, Jacob. I'll see you at breakfast."

As he rose, Riley felt Bridget's gaze on him. He couldn't read the woman. One minute she seemed grateful, the next minute her eyes were filled with suspicion or accusation. "Good night," he said, determined to put some distance between them.

"'Night, Uncle Riley." Jacob rose and ran around the table, throwing himself against Riley as he embraced his legs.

Stunned by the lad's display of emotion, Riley hesitated a moment, then reached down and pulled Jacob closer, patting him on the back as he remembered his own da doing to him. "Sleep well, lad."

When he met Bridget's gaze again, he shook his head. Aye, suspicion was what he read in her green eyes. But why? Perhaps she feared he had learned her secret. If only that were true. In truth, she confused him more with each passing day.

"I'll be back in a few minutes," she said, then went up the stairs with her son.

"Bridget wants to talk to us all," Maggie explained. She reached out and touched Riley's forearm. "It's glad I am to see you and Jacob together."

"Aye." Riley cleared his throat. "What would she be wanting to talk to us about?" Maybe she was going back to the States. Wasn't that what Riley had wanted? Aye, but the last thing he wanted now was to lose Jacob. He wanted time to know his brother's son.

"She said she has to tell us all together." Maggie grabbed a biscuit from the tin and took a bite.

"And you've no idea what it's about? I've work to do."

"You can spare your sister-in-law a few minutes." Maggie lifted her chin in a challenging pose.

"Just because I've accepted the lad as a Mulligan doesn't mean—"

"Thanks for waiting," Bridget said as she emerged from the stairway. "Jacob fell asleep practically before his head hit the pillow."

"Fresh air and exercise will do that to a lad." Riley suppressed a yawn. And to a man.

"I need to talk to y'all together," Bridget continued, leading them into the parlor, where Mum sat in her rocker with her foot propped. She took a sip of cherry juice, and set her glass aside.

"Did the lad enjoy his ride?" Mum asked, her eyes warm and her smile sweet.

"Aye, that he did." Riley bent to kiss his mum's soft cheek, and asked, "How's your foot feeling?"

"Much better, thank you." She wiggled her toes, wincing only slightly. "By tomorrow I'm hopin' to be up and about as usual."

"I hope you're right." Riley pulled the chair from under his da's old writing desk and straddled it, facing the women. The feeling that Bridget was up to something wouldn't leave him be.

"I'm not sure where to start." Bridget paced nervously, wringing her hands in front of her.

Ah, was the woman about to confess her sins? Riley narrowed his eyes, waiting for her to reveal herself.

They all sat quietly. Waiting.

"I . . . went down to visit the castle earlier."

"Aye, and almost fell, as I recall," Riley said, trying not to remember how close he'd come to kissing her then.

"Not that time." Bridget's cheeks turned fiery red and she looked away from him. "I . . . I went again this eve—"

"You did *what*?" Riley shot out of his chair, clenching his fists at his sides.

"Jaysus, Mary, and Joseph." Mum pressed her hands to her chest and looked upward. "Tell me you didn't go inside, lass."

"N . . . no." Bridget looked anxiously at Mum and Maggie, but still avoided Riley's gaze. "But I wanted to."

"Bridget, it's not safe," Maggie said, slumping back in her chair. "The curse."

Bridget lifted her chin and squared her shoulders. "I don't believe in curses."

"We do." Riley kept his voice calm, though he felt more like roaring. "I told you and Jacob that *Caisleán Dubh* is forbidden."

She met his gaze now, her eyes glittering like emerald shards. "You told us a lot of things."

Was she about to remind him how boorish he'd been to Jacob at first? Didn't he regret that enough without her throwing it back at him?

"*Caisleán Dubh* is dangerous," Mum said, her voice quivering slightly. "So much misery . . ."

"Aye, Bridget, you haven't heard the half of it," Maggie said. "Deaths, tragedies—one after another."

"Until the Mulligans moved from the castle and into this cottage."

"I understand," Bridget said, "but I don't think we should let the curse keep us from using the castle."

"Using?" Riley shook his head. "You're talking nonsense."

"What would you use that dusty old castle for, lass?" Mum asked in her calm, patient way.

Bridget hesitated, her gaze darting to each of them, then back. "Fiona, I need to work. To make money."

"You're family," Mum argued.

Riley's gut went topsy-turvy and he retrieved the roll of antacids from his pocket, popping two into his mouth. Bridget would fall from grace with his mum now, if she kept talking this nonsense.

"I still need to make money," Bridget continued. "What I do best is cook."

"What does cooking have to do with *Caisleán Dubh*?" Maggie asked, lifting a shoulder. "I'm lost."

"And you wouldn't be alone there, Maggie," Riley muttered, rolling his eyes.

"Like I said . . ." Bridget sighed and cleared her throat. "I went down there and introduced myself to the castle. Granny always told me to face what scared me and give it heck. So I did."

Riley shook his head, barely resisting the urge to laugh at the woman's insanity. "You're off your nut."

"Riley, there's no call for meanness." Mum smiled at Bridget. "Go on, lass. We're listenin'."

Again, he'd been made the villain when Bridget was their enemy. Not him. Riley gritted his teeth and vowed himself to silence. Let the woman spout nonsense. She would soon regret her words, and perhaps she'd simplify things for him all the way around.

The thought had merit.

"Would y'all mind if we had somebody out to take a look inside the castle?" she asked, wringing her hands and pacing. "I mean, to see if it can be fixed up."

"'Fixed up'?" Mum echoed.

"Restored," Bridget corrected. "I thought we could start with a small section—something big enough for a kitchen and a dining room."

Riley had to bite his tongue to keep himself quiet. Jaysus, but she was mad.

"Why would you want a kitchen in that old castle, Bridget?" Mum asked. "Isn't the kitchen here big enough?"

"For a restaurant." Bridget's eyes glowed with excitement and she perched on the footstool beside Mum's injured foot and reached for the older woman's hands with both her own. "We could put a parking lot right in front, and plant flowers everywhere. Folks would come just to see the mysterious *Caisleán Dubh*, but also to eat genuine down-home cuisine. Comfort food. Mine."

Now Riley did laugh. The chuckle was so determined to escape, no amount of self-chastisement could contain it.

"You don't like my cooking?" Bridget rose, hands on hips, cheeks flushed. She met his gaze now. "Did you eat three helpings at supper because you *didn't* like my pot roast?"

Riley's face heated and that pot roast turned on him. His gut churned. "You're a good cook, Bridget," he said in a low voice. "But the whole idea is ludicrous. The castle is dangerous. The curse . . ."

"So you're content to let that stupid old curse win?" She turned her attention back to Fiona. "We need to face that curse and give it heck like my granny said."

"Your granny was a wise woman." Mum pursed her lips, and finally sighed. "But Riley's right. This is dangerous."

Well, finally. Riley folded his arms and pinned Bridget with his gaze. She didn't appear defeated, though. In fact, she seemed more determined than ever.

This was what she'd been after all along. She wanted *Caisleán Dubh*. Of course.

"Fiona, can't we please try?" Her lower lip trembled. "I want to earn my own way, and my boy's."

"Jacob is family," Riley said. "He'll always have a place in his da's house."

"Yes, but you've pointed out more than once that *I'm* not." Bridget rose and faced him again. "I want the chance to earn my own way, and I think I can do that with *Caisleán Dubh*, if you'll give me a chance."

"No."

"First," Mum said quickly, "Bridget *is* family. She was our dear Culley's wife, and you'll show her the respect she's due." She paused to draw a breath, her face flushed and her eyes sparking with a good temper. "The lass has a right to speak her piece."

Riley fell silent for a few minutes, struggling between

a sense a betrayal and trying to understand his mum's position. "I believe she already spoke her piece."

"You two are at it again." Maggie came to stand between Bridget and Riley. "Arguing like children."

"Are you saying I'm not right?" Riley asked, never shifting his gaze from Bridget's eyes. "And that she is?"

"No, I'm not saying anything of the kind, but—"

"Then there's nothing more to be said on the matter." Riley rarely used his position in the family, but this seemed like the ideal moment to wield any power he could. He pinned Bridget with the fiercest gaze he could summon. "I forbid it. *Caisleán Dubh* was closed for a reason, and I respect the wishes of my ancestors."

With that, he spun around and marched into the kitchen just in time to see Jacob scurrying up the back staircase. *"Shite."* He started to follow the lad, but Bridget gripped his arm, digging her nails into his flesh.

"I'll see to my son." She pushed past him, pausing with one foot on the bottom step. "You've done enough." Then she disappeared up the stairs.

Riley shoved his fingers through his hair, hoping he hadn't destroyed the relationship he'd just begun with his nephew. The lad loved his mother, and—right or wrong— he wouldn't be likely to forgive anyone who upset her. Riley didn't want to lose what he'd gained today with Jacob. Nor that link to Culley.

Another traitorous voice deep inside him wondered if Bridget would ever look at him again with desire in her eyes.

Ten

Bridget fought the tears until she reached the safety of her room. She leaned against the closed door, gulping a lungful of air and trying to hold the tears at bay, but the liquid Benedict Arnolds betrayed her. Hot and fierce, they ran down her cheeks and neck. She had to bite her tongue to suppress a sob.

"Momma?"

Gasping, she swiped the damp trails off her cheeks with the backs of her hands. She reached down to brush her son's hair away from his face. "Jacob, you should be asleep."

"I heard Uncle Riley yelling." Her son looked up at her with trust shining in his eyes. "Is he mad at you?"

Bridget had vowed never to lie to her son, and this was one of those times when she wished she could withdraw that promise. But she couldn't. Promises were important, and if she expected her son to grow up to be a man of honor, she'd best show him what honor was.

"Y-yes." She sniffled and tried to smile, but knew she failed miserably. "I'm afraid he's very mad at me."

"Why?" Jacob tugged on her sleeve. "Why, Momma?"

She drew a shaky breath and led her son to her bed,

where they sat facing each other. Jacob crossed his legs beneath him, waiting with amazing patience.

"You were listening," she said quietly, watching her son for any reaction. He lowered his gaze and nodded. "Then you know why your uncle is mad at me."

"I . . . I'm sorry for spyin'." Genuine regret filled his young eyes as he met her gaze again.

"I know you are." She scooted closer to him and put one arm around his shoulders. "But you did, so I reckon you know why he's mad at me."

"I heard what you asked him." Jacob pulled back to stare at her unblinkingly. "He got mad, but I don't know why."

"Well, Jacob, you remember the first day we were here, don't you?"

He nodded, but didn't speak, leaving Bridget no choice but to continue with her pitiful explanation.

"Then you know your uncle doesn't believe the castle is safe."

"'Cuz of that dumb old curse?"

Bridget squeezed her eyes shut for a moment, searching for strength. "The folks here believe there's a curse, but I think the castle being so old is another reason."

Jacob appeared thoughtful, and said, "But old buildings can be fixed."

"Some can." Her son made so much sense. Of course, he must have heard her say almost the same words. "Your uncle and *mamó* don't think the castle can be fixed." *Or* should *be fixed.*

"Well I think we oughta try." Jacob set his jaw in that stubborn Frye way.

"I know. So do I." She cupped her son's cheek and kissed him on the forehead. "I'm not going to give up yet, but they have the final say. Okay?"

She saw his young mind churning ideas around, but she had to let this subject drop. She didn't want to cause any friction between Jacob and the Mulligans. Lord knew she'd caused enough of that between *herself* and Culley's kin.

"Okay, Jacob?" she repeated.

"I reckon." He didn't look at her as he spoke.

"Do you remember how angry I was at you that time you followed General Lee onto the highway?"

"Y-yes." Jacob sniffled and his lower lip trembled. "I coulda got squashed like . . . like Granny."

She gave him a quick, fierce hug. "But you didn't, darlin'." She pulled back and stroked his cheek. "Maybe Uncle Riley got mad at me, because he doesn't want anybody getting hurt in the castle."

I'm not really lying, Lord.

"I reckon." Jacob sniffled and scrubbed his eyes.

"Now, stop worrying about me and get some sleep." She eked out a smile of sorts. "It's late."

"All right." Jacob stood and padded barefoot to his narrow bed beneath the eaves.

Bridget followed him, pulled the quilt around his shoulders, and kissed him good night. "Sweet dreams, darlin'."

"'Night."

She turned off the small lamp beside his bed and returned to her room. Sleep wouldn't come easily tonight. She rubbed her arms and turned off her bedside lamp.

Slowly, she walked to the window and stared out at the night. No rain or clouds marred her view now. *Caisleán Dubh* stood majestically by the sea, its tower lording over the Mulligan farm, the village, and everything within sight.

That strange tugging called to her again. Something about that castle spoke to her, and she knew it was far more than merely the whispers. What called to her was something unheard and unseen. It came from inside her.

Bathed in moonlight, *Caisleán Dubh* was the most beautiful place she'd ever seen. "Mulligan Stew," she murmured.

She had to find a way to make her dream come true.

She wanted this more than anything. The idea had only come to her a few hours earlier, but she felt as if she'd lived with it and worked toward it all her life.

Maybe longer.

That thought sounded so foolish, she shoved it aside, though something continued to niggle at her brain. It almost seemed as if she should remember something that she'd forgotten. Something important.

She gazed down at the meadow between the cottage and the castle. He was there, as she'd known he would be. Riley Mulligan stood staring up at the house as if willing her to defy him.

Bridget struggled against the urge to show grouchy old Riley her middle finger, as Granny had been known to do back in Reedville when properly provoked. No, Jacob's momma wouldn't resort to that, though she would sure as heck think about it. A lot.

A smile tugged at her lips. "So there," she whispered.

Enough of that nonsense. She needed sleep, because one way or another, she would find a way to get inside that castle. She had to do it, even if in secret.

Maybe once she saw the inside of *Caisleán Dubh* for herself, she would realize that it was a lost cause. Maybe then she could accept defeat. Maybe.

But she doubted it.

She changed into her nightgown, washed her face, and brushed her teeth, but still didn't feel sleepy. "Enough of this," she whispered. She needed to rest so her brain would work right in the morning. After all, she had a mission.

She lowered herself onto the feather mattress, deciding this was the most comfortable bed in the world. Surely she would be able to sleep. She stared at the ceiling for some time, then rolled onto her side and pulled her legs in close.

Gradually, her body warmed and relaxed, allowing dreams to carry her away. . . .

• • •

He was back—her dream lover. Who was he? She knew now that the language he spoke was Irish, but that didn't help her understand a word.

Standing across the room from her, he crooked a finger. Well, she understood that. He was bathed in shadow, making his face completely indistinguishable. The only light in the room came from the fire burning in the hearth, and it created a golden glow that flowed around the man from behind. Faceless, he stood there. Waiting.

She didn't need to be told that he waited for her. Somehow, she just knew. Maybe because of the other dream. This was the same man—of that she was certain, face or no face. As she walked slowly toward him, she savored the fact that his massive chest was bare. Muscles rippled across his chest and arms. He placed a fist on each hip, and continued to speak to her in his deep, rumbling voice. If only she could understand his words. Maybe then she would know who he was and why she kept dreaming of him. Heck, seeing his face might help, too.

However, his body was a fine sight. Was he naked again? Curiosity overcame her and she glanced down the length of him. Through the shadows, she saw his erection clearly. It thrust outward from his body like the tower of Caisleán Dubh. . . .

"Oh, my." She tilted her head to one side to examine him more carefully. After all, this was a dream. She didn't have to be shy or even decent. Did she? Wasn't that why people had these kinds of dreams? So their secret fantasies and thoughts could find a release?

She fanned herself with her hand, noticing a cold draft. Glancing down, she stifled a small gasp. She was almost naked herself, with a thin excuse for an undergarment barely covering her breasts, and no panties at all. Scandalous.

She giggled at herself and decided to enjoy her dream. She swung her hips a bit more than necessary and felt the straps of her chemise, of all things, slip lower. The soft fabric brushed along her nipples, catching near the peaks, which were tight with longing.

She wanted him to touch her again. To kiss her. Oh, she wanted him to do a lot more than that. Why not admit it? It was her dream.

By the time she stood before him, a heated flush had crept over her entire body. Her blood sang through her veins, pulsing wickedly right between her thighs. Between the heaviness of her breasts and the gnawing hunger in her most private place, she knew exactly what she wanted.

Her gaze dropped to his erection again and she licked her lips. Exactly.

He reached out with one finger beneath her chin, urging her to meet his gaze. The infernal shadows still hid his features from view, but she looked in the direction of his eyes anyway.

Easing the tip of his finger down her throat, he whispered, "Bronagh."

Did he mean the village?

He looped his fingers through the straps of her chemise. A shiver coursed through her, but not from the room's temperature. He filled his large hands with her breasts and brushed his thumbs across her nipples. Her knees threatened to give, but desire kept her upright.

She wanted this. Needed this. A release, even if only in her dreams. . . . My wildest dreams, she thought, and prayed that would prove true.

"Bronagh," he repeated, then dipped his head to draw her nipple through the thin fabric.

"Mercy." She gasped and wrapped her arms around his muscular neck for support. Rivers of warmth eddied through her, zeroing in on the part of her that wanted him most.

His tongue stroked her through the fabric, and he nipped her with his teeth. He drew her deeply into his mouth, sending rivulets of need spiraling through her.

She buried her fingers in his long hair, holding him against her breast, and praying her dream wouldn't end

*too soon this time. She wanted to finish this—not that she
was in any hurry to have it end.*

*A low, primal growl rumbled from him and vibrated
against her tender flesh. He straightened and the cool air
circled her damp nipples, compounding her sense of loss
at his abandonment.*

"Bronagh?" he asked.

*"What do you mean?" This was how she'd lost him
last time—by not understanding his questions. "Please,
don't go. Don't leave me again."*

*Since she couldn't make him understand her words, she
decided to show him. With trembling fingers, she grasped
his red-hot erection. He pulsed with power. Life. Promise.*

*A small sob erupted from her and he growled again as
he covered her mouth in a smoldering kiss. He thrust his
tongue into her mouth, imitating the movements of her
hand on his body.*

*Oh, but she wanted more. She stroked the petal-soft
skin covering his engorged penis, knowing that nothing
less than having him inside her would satisfy the fierce
hunger he'd awakened. Her movements became more
frantic as he kissed his way along her jaw and down her
throat, leaning her back against his strong arm.*

*Her breasts spilled from the confines of the chemise,
baring her flesh to his insatiable lips. "Yes," she whispered as he devoured her. He moaned against her as she
slid her hand down his full length then back to his moist
tip.*

*With his lips brushing her nipple as he spoke, he said,
"Grá." His voice was hoarse and thick.*

*"What?" She continued to caress him until he grabbed
her wrist with a grip of steel. "Oh." He'd wanted her to
stop. They really could communicate.*

*"Aye." He swept her into his arms and carried her
deeper into the room's shadows, then placed her on what
felt like a silk sheet. The bed dipped when he joined her
there, hovering over her.*

He was so large, he blocked most of the light from the

*fire, but she didn't care—not as long as he finished the job
this time.*

*All right, in a dream she was allowed to be tacky. Make
that trashy. She rolled onto her side and found his erection
with her hand again, pulling him toward her.*

*He chuckled low in his throat and pressed her onto her
back, pinning her hands over her head. He leisurely
feasted on her breasts while she writhed beneath him.
She'd never wanted like this before. Her body clenched
the emptiness, aching for him to fill her. She wanted him
to claim her, to bury himself inside her, and even to ravish
her.*

Oh, yes. "Ravish me," *she whispered.*

*He chuckled almost as if he'd understood, though she
suspected that was impossible. He released her hands and
kissed his way down her belly, tickling her navel with his
tongue.*

*"Mercy." She stroked his hair, afraid he would stop.
Afraid he wouldn't. He was doing things to her she'd
never experienced before, but right now she wanted nothing but this. She wanted him to give her everything he had
to give.*

"Now?" she pleaded.

*He cupped her bottom in his large hands and angled
her pelvis toward him. Then, amazingly, he covered that
most sensitive part of her with his molten lips. . . .*

"No!" Bridget whispered, bolting upright in the bed.
She slapped at the mattress and noticed the blankets
bunched between her legs as if she'd been—

"Oh." Her face flooded with the heat of embarrassment
and she darted a glance toward the archway that led to
Jacob's alcove. At least her son wasn't standing there
watching his momma have a wet dream.

Embarrassment might make her behave while awake,
but frustration was still her ruling emotion. She ached and
throbbed with the hunger her dream lover had created.

What kind of torture was this? Her body quaked with

an overpowering weakness as she swung her legs over the side of the bed and straightened her bedding.

"Positively indecent," she muttered. "Shameful." She drew several huge gulps of air and pushed to her feet. On wobbly legs, she staggered into the bathroom and closed the door before flipping on the light.

She stared at her mussed image in the mirror. Her hair was a wild, knotted mane. Her lips looked swollen, almost as if . . . they'd been kissed. Her breasts still ached for the feel of her dream lover's lips.

Instinctively, she brought her hand to her breast and gasped.

The worn flannel covering her nipple was damp.

The mysterious woman haunted Riley's dreams again. He hadn't experienced a good night's rest in nearly a week.

Rising slowly, he stretched the kinks out of his muscles. He splashed his face with cold water and felt almost awake, so he dressed for a day's work. Hard physical labor might make him tired enough to sleep without dreaming tonight. He stifled a yawn and pulled on his socks.

Tea, strong and hot, was what he needed. He made his way into the hall, pausing at the narrow door that led to the attic. To Bridget. No, to Jacob, he amended with a scowl.

He ducked under the low beam and went downstairs to put the kettle on, but Mum was already up and bustling about the kitchen. She wore shoes and walked without a limp.

"Mum?" He kissed her cheek. "Is the gout gone, then?"

"Aye, pretty much." She patted his cheek and poured tea into his cup. "Nice and strong, the way you like it."

"Thanks." He took the cup and seated himself at the table. "Don't overdo, though, with this being your first day of feeling better."

"I promise." She flashed him a smile that took twenty

years off her face. "I'm so happy to be back on me feet I could sing."

"You wouldn't."

Laughing, she flung the tea towel at him. "I just might if you keep blatherin' on about me miserable voice."

"Fortunately, I got my musical genes from Da."

"Aye, so you did." Mum's expression grew thoughtful. "Tell me, Riley," she said, stirring something at the stove. "What do you think your da would have to say about Bridget's idea?"

Riley released a long, slow breath and took a sip of tea to brace himself. He should've known the subject of *Caisleán Dubh* wouldn't die peacefully. "I don't know," he finally said, shaking his head.

"I was rememberin' . . ." Mum bit her lower lip and, lifted one shoulder. "'Tis like it was only yesterday."

"Aye." Riley didn't want to remember. Mum seemed to take comfort in remembering, but he wanted to bury the memories so deep they'd never return. "It never goes away."

"Does a body *and* a heart good to remember, lad," she said seeming to understand exactly what he was thinking. She often did.

"I'd rather not." He drank his tea in silence for several blessed minutes while Mum prepared their breakfast. "Did everyone else sleep late?" he finally asked.

"Riley Mulligan was the layabout this morn'." She smiled again. "I heard you tossin' and turnin' half the night, so I figured you hadn't slept well when you didn't come down earlier. Bridget and Jacob haven't come down either, though."

He didn't want to hear about Bridget. The less he heard about her, the better. "Maggie gone to school, then?"

"Aye. A few minutes ago." Mum sighed. "I believe Jacob will be old enough to go next year. Bridget said he went to kindergarten in Tennessee."

"If he's still here." Riley regretted the words the moment they left his lips.

Mum turned down the fire beneath the pot and walked over to the table, her blue eyes snapping. She shook her index finger at him. "Riley Francis Mulligan, if you were a normal-sized man instead of the giant you are, I'd turn you over me knee and—"

"Good morning," Bridget said as she entered the kitchen.

Riley didn't look at her. Instead, he returned his attention to his tea. Tea was safe. Women—including mothers—were not.

"Have you seen Jacob this morning?"

Riley had to look at Bridget now, and was both relieved and disappointed to find her properly dressed. "He wasn't in his bed this morning?" he asked, worry slithering through him.

She shook her head, concern puckering her brow. "I . . . I didn't sleep well, so I didn't wake as early as usual."

"You weren't the only one," Mum said. "Riley, have a look 'round the house for young Jacob, and if the lad doesn't turn up, we'll look outside. 'Tis a sunny morn'. Chances are he went out to frolic with the fairies."

Riley was out of his chair before Mum completed her whimsical statement. He took the steps two at a time, bumping his head on that wretched low beam. His ancestors must have been pint sized.

Rubbing his skull, he searched all the rooms, including the attic. No sign of Jacob. Icy fingers of fear spiked through him. The horse. *Oíche* He almost hit his head again dodging down the stairs.

"Where are you—"

"The stable," Riley called, foregoing his boots. He raced along the well-worn path, unmindful of the small rocks that bruised his stockinged feet.

The lad had promised not to go near *Oíche* alone. He'd promised. But Jacob was just a lad. Riley should have known. He should've been wiser, a better uncle. A better protector of his brother's son.

"Jaysus, let him be safe." He flung open the stable door, startling *Oíche*. There was no sign of Jacob anywhere. Just to be sure, Riley entered the stall and moved straw around, terrified he might find the lad beneath it. Trampled.

"Nothing." He leaned against a post, recovering his breath. Where could the lad be?

"Did you find him?" Bridget burst into the stable without stopping.

Riley grabbed *Oíche*'s bridle. "Easy, lad." He pinned Bridget with a glare. "You scared my horse."

"I'm more concerned about my son than your stupid—"

"As am I." Riley released *Oíche* and left the stall. "Do you have any idea where—"

"Oh, my God." Bridget's face blanched and she swayed, grabbing a post for support. A moment later, she swung around and bolted out of the stable as if the devil were on her tail.

"Shite." Where the devil was she going now? Riley pulled on a pair of old Wellies he kept for mucking out the stall. "Bridget, wait."

But she was far ahead of him by the time he started after her. Where was she going? And where was—

"Jaysus." *Caisleán Dubh.* The lad had overheard them last night. "Not him, too. Not him, too."

Riley ran as if his life depended on it, and maybe it did. He passed Bridget and kept running. *Please let me be in time. Please . . .* Memories bombarded him, echoing the panic-driven thud of his heart. The vault at the back of his mind that he'd guarded so carefully edged open a bit more.

Not now. He needed to save Jacob. *Please, Mother Mary. Please.*

Someone else was running toward him from the direction of the road. Maggie. Her twisted features spoke of panic. "Jacob," she said, gasping for air. *"Caisleán Dubh."*

Riley left her there and kept running. As he rounded the

front corner of the castle, his floppy Wellies tripped him and he landed on his face in sand and grass. A moment later, he was back on his feet. He hazarded a glance back to find Bridget and Maggie racing toward him.

Sweat trickled into his eyes, blinding him. He mopped it away and bridged the distance between him and the opening beside the massive doors. *I should've torn it down. I should have. Why didn't I after Da . . . ?*

His throat swelled, almost closed, but he cleared it and shouted though the crevice. "Jacob?" Then louder and louder.

Only his echo answered.

Eleven

Panic gripped Riley as memories bombarded him. For a few terrifying moments, he again became the lad in search of his missing da. Cold sweat seeped from his pores, and his throat squeezed shut. How could he ever forget that day?

That horror.

"No." He drew a shaky breath and anchored himself in the present. Jacob was here and now. Da was long dead and nothing would change that. "Jacob, can you hear me? It's your uncle Riley come to fetch you home."

Silence.

"Come along now like a good lad."

Please, Jacob. Please.

Riley heard a sneeze from the bowels of the black castle and angled himself into the opening. "I know you're in there, lad, and if I can hear you sneeze, you can hear me shouting like a bloody fishwife."

Riley edged sideways through the opening, jagged edges of broken stones scraping his flesh through his clothing. Of course, the last time he'd entered *Caisleán Dubh*, he'd been much smaller. Remembered images invaded again—the darkness, the fear, the tragedy.

Don't think about that. Don't. "I'm not leaving here without you, Jacob." Riley didn't want to go any farther. His feet were rooted in place, though his memory kept walking deeper into the castle. *Jaysus.*

Again, he forced the vault door shut and mentally turned a key. *Not now. Jacob is now. Jacob is now. Jacob is now. . . .*

Culley's son.

"I'm coming in after you," he said more firmly, listening for any sound. The only light in the main chamber came from broken windows high overhead. All the lower ones had been boarded over more than a century ago.

Memory told Riley that the stairway curving toward the tower was to his right and he prayed Jacob hadn't gone up there. The ground floor might be sound, but the tower was another matter. Besides, that was where the curse had commenced. To his left, another stone stairway led to the bowels of the castle.

"Jacob, don't hide from me, lad," he said, forcing his tone to remain steady, without a trace of anger. "If you show yourself now, maybe your mum won't punish you." *And maybe I won't.*

Another sneeze came from the direction of the massive stone steps. Riley remained frozen, inhaling dusty air and trying to ignore the flapping of wings far overhead. He had not time for bats.

Or memories.

He clenched his jaw so tightly, it was a miracle his teeth didn't shatter. Gradually, his eyes accustomed themselves to the darkness and he made out several shapes. He'd never been any farther into the castle than this main chamber, but that had been more than enough to last him a lifetime.

"Jacob, lad . . . ?" He walked slowly toward the stairs, discerning their shape through the darkness. "It's time to go. The women are worried."

Riley heard a sniffle and wondered if the lad was crying. Well, he'd been older than Jacob that day long ago, and he'd wept, too. Of course, he'd had more reason.

His gut twisted and his heart pressed against it. "You're keeping me from my work," he said, forcing his tone to sound light. "I thought you were going to help me drive the tractor today."

"You . . ." Jacob's young voice echoed off the stone walls. "You're mad at my momma."

Riley squeezed his eyes shut and searched for words. "Aye, but that's no reason to—"

"There isn't any stupid curse," Jacob said, his voice stronger now. "We're inside and nothin' bad has happened to either one of us."

Yet. Riley clenched his fists. "And I'm glad of it, but it's still not safe, lad."

"Don't be mad at my momma."

"Jacob, I—"

"Jacob," Bridget's voice came from directly behind Riley and he spun around to see her silhouetted against the light filtering in around the massive wooden doors.

"Don't come any farther," he warned. "It isn't safe."

"Is, too," Jacob argued.

The little muzzy was pushing too far. Riley clenched his fists and buried his temper beneath a mountain of worry. "We don't *know* if it's safe or not, Jacob."

"I don't care," Bridget said, her voice quivering. "All I care about is my son."

"Will Uncle Riley let you use the castle?"

Blackmail! And from a child, no less. Riley chewed his lower lip, wondering what the lad would do if he gave the wrong answer. Would he vanish deeper into this hideous place? Would he fall to his death?

Would the curse take yet another Mulligan?

Riley's breath froze in his throat and he struggled to fill his lungs for several seconds. "I can't . . . promise," he said finally, expecting to fall dead at any moment.

"Jacob, come out now," Bridget said, her shuffling

steps coming closer to Riley as she spoke. "I want you to forget about what you heard last night."

"No."

Riley could just see the lad's flashing green eyes, his chin thrust out defiantly, his little arms folded over his narrow chest. "Aren't you the stubbornest lad?" He exhaled in a loud whoosh, pondering his options. Any reputable inspector would find *Caisleán Dubh* unworthy of renovation. Wouldn't he?

"I'm a Frye," Jacob said. "We're stubborn. Granny always said so."

"And Mulligans aren't?" Maggie said from outside the opening.

At least one of them had the sense to stay outside. "Well, then, that means Jacob is doubly stubborn," Riley said, forming a plan as he spoke. He couldn't trust a six-year-old's judgment enough to be certain the lad wouldn't run deeper into the castle and into harm's way if Riley refused to succumb to the blackmail.

"All right, Jacob," he said, the darkness closing in around him. "If you'll come out now, we'll have someone inspect the castle, but only if you agree to abide by his findings."

Bridget gripped Riley's arm and he felt her tremble against him. Her breathing sounded ragged, and he suspected she felt much like he had the day he'd followed someone he loved into this hellhole.

Today would have a different conclusion. Already, Riley sensed the difference. Later, he would ponder the why of it. "Are you ready now, lad?" he asked, keeping his voice calm.

"What's that 'abide by' thing mean?"

Riley couldn't suppress the smile that tugged at the corners of his mouth. "It means that you"—he looked at Bridget's shape standing at his side—"and your mum accept the inspector's word as final."

"Okay. You promise to really do it?" the small voice

asked from the darkness. "Cross your heart and hope to die?"

Riley bit his lower lip. "Now why would I be hoping such a thing?" He forced levity into his voice, though the mere mention of death in this place made him want to run screaming. "Of course, I promise."

Jacob's footsteps approached them, then he took shape a few feet away. "All right."

Bridget released her death grip on Riley and gathered her son into her arms. She wept and laughed intermittently, smothering the lad with kisses. A moment later, she pulled back to scold the child.

"Jacob Samuel Mulligan, you scared ten years off my life. Don't you ever run off like that again." She drew a ragged breath and started sobbing again.

Weren't women the most confounding creatures?

"If you don't mind, I'd like to get out of here before *Caisleán Dubh* comes down around our ears." He wasn't teasing. This was the place of his most hideous nightmares. "And we'll find you an inspector."

The stepped into the sunlight to find Maggie and Mum huddled together. He recognized fear in their eyes, and he knew his own mirrored theirs.

Maggie might not remember the day that had changed all their lives forever, but Riley would never forget it. His gaze went to his mum. Tears spilled from her eyes.

They were part relief, and part mourning for the man they'd both lost to the curse of *Caisleán Dubh* so long ago.

Riley went to her while Maggie and Bridget fussed over the wee blackmailer. Riley purposely turned Mum away from the castle to face the sea, placing his arm across her shoulders. They stood there for what seemed like forever, remembering and trying to forget at the same time.

Finally, Maggie appeared in front of them. "Thank you, Riley." She stood on tiptoes and kissed his cheek. "You're a hero. Why, even St. Patrick would be proud."

"Women." He shook his head. "I'm a bloody extortion victim—not a hero and not a bit proud." Riley swallowed the lump in his throat and felt Mum shiver against his side. "I did what needed doing, and we'll all have to live with the consequences."

"What did you do?" Mum pulled away and looked into his eyes.

"I let a six-year-old blackmail me," he said on a sigh. "And I'll rue the day, for certain. Jacob definitely has his da's gift for tossing words about."

He glanced over his shoulder at Bridget and Jacob, who were walking around discussing the castle as they pointed to various parts of it. A shudder rippled through him and his knees wobbled, though he managed to hide it.

They were all alive. *Why?* They'd entered that wretched tomblike place and all walked out alive. It didn't make a bit of sense.

An image of his childhood self dragging his da from inside *Caisleán Dubh* exploded in his mind. Nausea welled within him and for several moments all he could do was concentrate on breathing. Mum patted his arm.

They were having the same thought. Why hadn't it taken *his* life? Riley looked over his shoulder again at his nephew. Or Jacob's? They were both Mulligans by blood.

What was different? Why had they been spared?

"Maybe the curse expired," Maggie said as if reading their minds.

"Expired, is it?" Mum asked, making a tsking sound with her tongue. "*Expired*, lass?"

Riley tilted his head back to look up at the tower. Still staring, he drew a deep breath and said, "No, Maggie. Evil doesn't expire."

"Well, you're all out now," she said. "Safely. Nothing happened."

"Aye," he said, turning his gaze upon the sinister black stones of *Caisleán Dubh* again. "For now."

• • •

Still shaken from this morning's adventure, Bridget decided to bake bread. Not Irish soda bread, but *real* bread. She would have preferred sourdough, but the starter wasn't quite ready. A few more days, maybe a week, and it would be fermented enough to have a good bubble to it.

Maggie went on to school tardy, and Fiona bustled around the cottage, catching up on her chores. She was so happy to be up and about again, she seemed to have put the castle incident out of her mind.

Somehow, Bridget doubted that. Fiona was an amazing woman who'd learned to live with whatever life threw at her. In many ways, she reminded Bridget of Granny.

Bridget had reluctantly allowed Jacob to accompany Riley on his chores today, but only after she'd reminded her son that if he ever disappeared like that again, she would break her own rule against spanking. She'd never raised her hand to him, but maybe Granny had been right about even good children needing an occasional swat on the rump.

Thank you, Lord, for keeping him safe. She chewed her lower lip and shook her head. She should've been sterner with Jacob, but her relief that he'd been found unharmed had left her weak. Later, she would talk with him again and make absolutely certain he realized how serious his actions were.

At least working on the farm with Riley wasn't like being taken out for ice cream. It wasn't a *reward.* Exactly. Besides, if they were staying in Ireland permanently, her son would need to work the farm alongside his uncle. The fresh air and sunshine would do the boy good, and Riley would keep him safe.

Still, she kept glancing out the window to watch her son sitting in front of Riley on the tractor seat. At least Jacob hadn't run off to *Caisleán Dubh* again.

Her heart skipped a beat as she recalled the fear all over again. A metallic taste filled her mouth and she realized she'd bitten the side of her tongue. Foolishness. Jacob was fine. They all were.

Curse or no curse.

She'd vowed to enter the castle, but not this way. There had been no powerful feelings of a personal connection today. Only fear and desperation. She hadn't even heard the whispering.

And the roof hadn't caved in on their heads or anything. Maybe the castle really was safe. Maybe it *could* be restored.

Maybe Mulligan Stew would really happen.

She almost smiled, but caught herself in time. *Don't count those chickens before they're hatched.*

She *would* go back to the castle, though. Alone. And she would take a doggoned flashlight this time.

Smiling to herself, she checked the dough again to see if it was ready. Both loaves had at least doubled in size. She placed them in the oven just as someone knocked on the front door.

"Well, if it isn't Brady Rearden himself come home where he belongs," Fiona said as she opened the door and admitted their visitor.

Rearden? Bridget peeked into the parlor to confirm the man's identity. Was he related to Katie? Would he remember Bridget and Jacob? Had Brady heard terrible things about her from Katie?

The elderly man stepped into the cottage and doffed his hat, before sweeping Fiona into his arms for a hug and a big sloppy kiss. "And isn't Fiona Mulligan still the prettiest lass in three counties?"

"Oh, go on with you, Brady. And don't you be forgettin' that you're old enough to be me own da." Fiona blushed and giggled like a young girl. "You always were full of the blarney."

"Aye, and I never intend to stop, no matter how old."

He caught sight of Bridget in the doorway and smiled again. "Ah, the lass from the plane has found her Mulligans."

"Yes, thank you. It's a pleasure to see you again, sir." Bridget smiled and wiped her floured hands on her apron.

"Sir? What is it with all the young folks callin' me sir, Fiona?"

Laughing, she shook her head.

"Good manners, you suppose?"

"Well, 'tis better than bad ones."

"Jacob mentioned meetin' you on the plane after he saw you at mass." Fiona turned toward the kitchen. "Kettle's on. I'll just wet the leaves and we'll have us a nice chat with Bridget here."

Bridget puttered around the kitchen while Brady and Fiona shared stories about Culley and Riley's childhood antics. A band tightened around her heart each time she heard her late husband's name.

He shouldn't have died. Yet, somehow, she felt his presence here with his family. She wasn't pining away for him or anything like that. The loss of a young life was such a waste. That was what touched her most now—not the loss of her husband or the love of her life.

Culley would have been so proud of Jacob. Smiling, she opened the oven door and removed two perfect, golden brown loaves of bread and set them on a rack to cool.

"If that isn't a scent from the angels, I don't know what is," Brady said, sniffing the air appreciatively.

"Our Bridget cooks like an angel," Fiona said, beaming with pride. "The lass hasn't prepared anything but food fit for saints since she got here."

Bridget blushed and thanked her mother-in-law. Cooking was the only thing she really knew she did well. "I'll get plates," she said, managing to loosen the bread from the sides of the pan enough that it came out cleanly. She placed it on a board with a small dish of butter, and took it all to the table with the long-bladed bread knife and three butter knives.

Even *she* couldn't resist freshly baked bread. With a glass of soda, she sat at the table and munched the yeasty bread while listening to Brady's stories.

"So what brings you home?" Fiona asked between bites of warm bread. "Really?"

"Me life's dream." Brady shook his head and his brow furrowed. "I'm sure you remember how much research I did over the years on local history."

"Aye." Fiona nodded and sipped her tea. "Didn't you come 'round here askin' questions often enough?"

Brady blushed to his ears. "Well, why do you think I'm here now?"

Fiona laughed and Brady's eyes twinkled. Bridget couldn't prevent herself from smiling at the pair. They'd obviously been friends for many years.

"When I went to the States, I left all me notes here with me son Colin. They were in his Katie's closet, safe as can be." He sighed, shaking his head.

Bridget's appetite fled and she washed a lump of bread down with tepid soda. She didn't make a sound, because she didn't want to miss anything Brady said now. He was an historian who knew about the castle. . . .

And the curse? Could he help her understand why the Mulligans insisted there was a curse? After this morning, she was more convinced than ever that *Caisleán Dubh* was just a very old, very lonely castle. It needed her.

She needed it. Warmth oozed through her and she glanced out the window at the tower. Why had she been so frightened of it at first? *Well, no more of that nonsense.*

"One whole box of me notes is missing, and it's the one that deals with *Caisleán Dubh*," Brady said. "And isn't the curse the most interestin' part of Clare's history?"

Bridget leaned on her elbows, resting her chin in her hands.

"Interestin' is one way of puttin' it, I suppose." Fiona sipped her tea. "Too much pain and misery."

"Aye." Brady reached over and patted Fiona's hand. "We all remember what happened to your Patrick."

Fiona nodded but said nothing.

"Patrick was Culley's da?" Bridget asked.

"Aye. He was me husband, lass. All me children's da."

Fiona stared through the window. "'Tis best not to speak of what happened. It will only upset Riley." She blinked rapidly as if to clear her vision. "And me."

Bridget's pulse thudded louder with every breath she took. Patrick Mulligan's death was important, and it was something she needed to know. If Fiona wouldn't speak of it—and she knew Riley wouldn't—then how was Bridget to learn the truth?

From Maggie. Yes, that was it. She would ask Maggie.

"'Tis bewildered, I am, to have only that one box of notes missin'." Brady sighed, obviously determined to change the subject away from anything that upset Fiona. "I'll have to reconstruct the lot of it."

"You know where to find what you need."

"Aye, that I do, but . . ." Brady patted Fiona's hand again. "I wanted your blessing, lass."

"Keep callin' me lass, you old charmer, and you can have anythin' you want."

Brady blushed to his ears and Bridget decided she still liked this man, even if he was related to Katie.

"I left for the States when Katie and Culley were first court—" Brady stopped abruptly and looked at Bridget. "'Tis sorry I am to mention the subject, dear Bridget. Forgive me."

"I've already heard that Culley was engaged to Katie," Bridget said carefully, studying Brady's expression as she spoke. "Is she your kin?"

"Aye, me granddaughter."

Bridget held his gaze, deciding to go ahead and ask the question burning in her heart. "Why don't *you* hate me?"

Brady didn't seem a bit taken aback by her blunt question, but Fiona's eyes grew wide.

"Riley and Katie both hate me," Bridget continued, keeping her voice calm and her gaze on Brady.

"Well, now, I can't be speakin' to someone else's feelin's, but I've no cause to hate you or anyone, lass." Brady drew a deep breath and held her gaze. "I was already livin' in the States with me daughter's family when

Katie and Culley became engaged." He lifted one shoulder and a sheepish grin brightened his wrinkled face. "I never believed them well matched anyway."

"Well, then I guess it won't shock you to learn I felt the same," Fiona said with an emphatic nod. "A more mismatched pair never lived."

Bridget managed a weak smile and said, "Thank you for that. I didn't realize I've actually felt a little guilty about Katie until now."

Brady shot her another of his crooked grins and said, "And how could it have been wrong for you to marry a charmer like Culley Mulligan if you loved him?"

"Especially since you couldn't have known about Katie," Fiona added.

Bridget realized now why Fiona had accepted her so easily. "I wonder why Riley . . ." She bit her lower lip. "Never mind. It doesn't matter now."

"'Tis in the past," the old teacher said. "We live in the present, except for old fools like me who'd rather be diggin' up history than livin' in the here and now."

"You were a good teacher," Fiona said. "And not just about history."

"'Tis a flatterer you are, Fiona Mulligan." The twinkle in his eyes gave him away as he said, "If I didn't know better, I'd say you're after a husband."

Fiona blushed and stuttered, then said, "You old fool."

"I'm old, but not a fool." Brady squeezed her hand, his expression solemn. "I'll be askin' Father O'Malley for the parish records again then. With your blessing?"

"You have it," Fiona said. "But don't be botherin' Riley about it, please."

"I promise." He rose. "I'd best be about my business then. Thank you for the tea."

"You're always welcome." Fiona stood, turning toward the door to see him out, then she snapped her fingers. "Brady, would you know of someone who could inspect *Caisleán Dubh* for us?"

"Inspect it, you say?" Brady scratched his bald head,

his eyes growing wide. "Well, now, 'tis an interestin' question, that."

"Bridget here wants to see if it's sound enough to restore."

"At least part of it," Bridget added, standing near them now, her heart pounding as she waited anxiously for Brady's answer.

"Aye, just call the Irish Trust in Dublin," he said. "They have engineers and architects on staff who'll come out and look it over for you."

"Thank you, old friend."

Fiona wrote down the number Brady gave her. As soon as he'd left, she went to the phone and dialed while Bridget stood by, still holding her breath. They really were going to inspect the castle.

And so was she.

Tonight.

Twelve

Riley took another bite of what Bridget called "chicken-fried steak" and almost moaned aloud. As much as he hated to admit it—again—the woman's cooking could bring entire armies to their knees.

He'd planned to walk into Ballybronagh to eat at Gilhooley's, just to avoid this. And her. Aye, and hadn't that been a good plan, too? He took another bite. Then another. Aye, it *had* been an excellent plan.

Mulligan, you're weak. He'd been felled by a piece of beef and gravy rich enough to make a grown man weep with joy. Mum had made his favorite fried cabbage with rashers crumbled in it, and he really hoped there were no afters. If he ate like this every day, he'd be too heavy to ride *Oíche*.

"Maggie made the dessert," Bridget said, smiling.

"Oh?" *I'm saved.* Riley could easily resist sampling something his sister had prepared. "I don't think I'll have room for afters."

"Aye, you will." Mum's eyes twinkled mischievously, and she turned her attention back to Bridget. "Bridget, tell me again how you make this meat with your sourdough? I can't believe it could taste any better."

"The sourdough helps make the outside even crispier," Bridget explained. "I dip the meat in the sourdough starter, then dredge it in flour and spices like I did this time."

"Then you cook it the same way?"

"Yes. I'm glad y'all like it." She smiled and her entire face glowed.

Riley's throat threatened to close around a half-swallowed piece of meat. The woman's smile did things to him—different things than looking lower would do. Heat rose to his neck and he took a sip of cool water before his entire face turned crimson.

Something swelled within his chest as he watched her chat with Mum about cooking. She obviously loved to cook, so it wasn't hard to understand why she'd thought of opening a restaurant.

A restaurant in *Caisleán Dubh*. Had he ever heard a more ludicrous notion?

At least Jacob hadn't blathered on about the wretched castle all day. In fact, the lad had behaved himself in every way after his little disappearing act. Riley cast a sidelong glance at his nephew—master con artist—who shoveled mashed spuds and gravy into his mouth faster than old Seamus Doone could down a pint after Lent.

"Riley, are you listening?" Maggie asked, spearing his attention.

"Aye. What?"

All three women snickered. Would this be another of those "Funning Riley" evenings? He drew a deep breath and vowed that he would not let them bother him this time.

"No," he said, smiling at his sister. "What did you say?"

"I asked if you're ready for the afters."

The expression on Maggie's face reminded Riley of the time she'd begged him to teach her how to ride his bike. Of course, it had been much too tall for her, but she'd finally managed to ride it to the road and back. Had he ever seen her look as proud as she had that day, with her missing tooth and her hair curling wildly around her freckled face?

Aye, he was really going soft. *Eejit. Sap.*

"You promise not to kill me?" he teased, though there had been a time or two when he'd feared just that from his sister's disastrous cooking.

She wrinkled her nose at him. "I just might, boyo." She pushed away from the table with Mum right behind, leaving Riley at the table alone with Bridget and Jacob.

"I saw Brady Rearden out on the road," he said, watching Bridget's expression.

She looked up at him suddenly, her gaze darting to Mum's empty chair, then back to Riley. "He came by to see Fiona," she said.

"Aye, old Brady is a charmer." Riley managed a smile, though suspicions continued to press to the front of his mind. "Did he tell you he's Katie's granddad?"

"Y-yes. Yes." She leaned back in her chair and took a deep breath, filling out far too well the same green jumper she'd worn the day she'd first arrived.

Riley drank more water, keeping his gaze on her breasts. And weren't they fine breasts, too? Lightning struck right between his legs. Served him right for staring, but they were right there. Tempting him.

Jaysus. He sucked in a sharp breath and shifted into a more comfortable position. Self-consciously, he cleared his throat and reminded himself about Brady.

"Is Brady the man from the airplane?" Jacob asked between bites.

"Yes, he is." Bridget smiled again, but this time it wasn't for Riley.

"Did he remember us?" Jacob finally set his fork aside.

"He sure did." Bridget relaxed visibly as she spoke to her son.

"I didn't realize you knew Brady." Riley tried to keep his gaze above where Bridget's pulse beat at the base of her throat. All points below that were unsafe for a man in his current state of sexual deprivation.

"He sat beside us on the airplane," Jacob explained. "He told us about the curse and the Cliffs of . . . of . . ."

"Moher," Bridget finished. "The Cliffs of Moher."

"Yeah, them."

"You're saying you already knew about the curse before you arrived?" Riley wasn't sure yet what this information meant, but he intended to give it considerable thought. "You can't see the cliffs at all from *Caisleán Dubh*," he pointed out, wondering why he'd connected the two thoughts.

Because a castle with a view of the cliffs is valuable. Well, Bridget would be disappointed, if that was her—

"Here we are." Mum and Maggie carried plates with something gooey and chocolatey on each one.

"What is it?" he asked, narrowing his gaze. Maggie swept away his empty dinner plate and placed the concoction before him. The rich aroma of chocolate wafted to his nostrils and he inhaled appreciatively. "Smells edible."

Maggie punched him in the arm. "It's more than edible, you oaf," she said. "Bridget says it's decadent."

"Decadent, is it?" Riley grinned and lifted one shoulder. "Well, I'll be the judge of that, but what is it?"

"Mississippi mud pie," Jacob answered.

"Mud pie?" Riley chuckled at the lad and elbowed him. "And did you go out in the yard and collect the mud for the pie yourself, lad?"

"Nope. Chocolate mud." Jacob scooped a huge bite of the mud in question, along with nuts and other tasty-looking morsels, into his mouth.

"'Tis tasty, then?" he asked, and the lad nodded and kept shoveling.

"You're using poor Jacob as a tester?" Maggie asked, placing a hand on each hip as she hovered over him. Waiting. "Well?"

"Well, what?" Riley looked from her to his plate, then around the table at the others.

Mum took her seat and started eating, too. She rolled her eyes and glanced heavenward. "Isn't this fit for the Virgin Herself? 'Tis divine, Maggie."

Maggie giggled and clapped her hands together. "See?" She turned her glower on Riley again. "Eat."

Riley squeezed his eyes closed, prayed, and crossed himself.

Maggie punched him again.

"Ow." He rubbed his arm and reached for his fork. "All right, then. I'll taste this Mississippi mud pie of yours, but if it's really mud, you'll be wearing it."

She folded her arms in front of her and waited.

He brought the fork to his mouth and hesitated, remembering the last dessert Maggie had made. A shudder rippled through him and she punched him again, sending the bite balanced on his fork back to his plate with a plop.

"How do you expect a body to taste it if you keep knocking it away?" He pointed at her chair. "Over there or I'll not take a single bite."

"Your loss," Bridget said, licking her fork.

The sight of Bridget's tongue stroking the silver tines sent another lightning bolt through Riley. He gulped and forced himself to look at his food and not at her. He heard Maggie walk around the table and pull out her chair beside Bridget.

Slowly, he put the fork between his lips and deposited gooey, creamy chocolate and nuts upon his tongue. He chewed once and stopped, narrowing his eyes and pinning Maggie. "You didn't make this," he accused.

Maggie sputtered in outrage and pushed her chair back, leaping to her feet. Bridget grabbed her arm and pulled her back into her chair.

"Granny always said that if somebody says something unkind *and* untrue, that knowing the truth is every bit as good as winning."

"Was that supposed to make sense?" Riley asked, yelping when the toe of a shoe made abrupt contact with his shin. "Mary Margaret, I told you—"

"It wasn't Maggie."

"Who . . . ?"

She just kept smiling while Maggie and Mum snickered. Bridget's smile was way too confident. Why? Where had the nervous hillbilly gone? She folded her arms beneath her breasts, leveling them at a nice angle for his perusal. He took another huge bite of pie and swallowed it without taking his gaze away from the woman who had turned his life arseways.

She tempts a man.

"Do you like mud, Uncle Riley?" Jacob asked, swinging his feet back and forth beneath the table.

"Aye, 'tis the best mud I've ever tasted." He darted a look from Maggie to Bridget, then back. "No matter who made it."

"I did, you bloody—"

"Ah, Maggie," Mum said, shaking her infamous index finger. "You know better than to swear at me table."

And wasn't it a good thing Mum couldn't read her son's mind? The thoughts Riley had had about Bridget right here in Mum's kitchen were scandalous. Aye, he wanted to do every scandalous thing he could think of to Bridget's body, and he could think of plenty.

Correction: *had* thought of them.

Awake, all he could do was think of her in anger or lust—either way, with passion. Asleep, he was plagued with dreams of a faceless woman who'd haunted him for years.

You're a pitiful excuse for a man, Mulligan.

He finished his "mud" and pushed away from the table. "Well, now. From what you've told me, I'm to thank three cooks this time?"

"Aye," two women said, while Bridget said, "Yes."

"Thank you. Thank you. Thank you." He looked at Maggie but not Bridget, and planted a kiss on Mum's cheek. "A fine meal. Even the afters."

He left the kitchen before Maggie could do him any further bodily harm, and went into the parlor. If he was going to play in Doolin on Saturday, he'd best be practicing his music. He pulled the fiddle case from the shelf where the instrument had been stored since long before Riley's birth.

He opened it and the sight of the old fiddle made him smile. His fingers itched to play, so he rosined the bow and tuned the strings, then played a bit to limber his fingers.

Jacob sat on the ottoman nearby, staring at Riley with open curiosity.

"My da taught me to play on this very fiddle," Riley explained, remembering.

"My grandpa?"

"Aye, lad." Riley cleared his throat. "Culley—your da—always played sweeter than me with his long, skinny fingers." He held his own work-roughened paw out to show Jacob. "I have farmer's hands, but I can still play a bit."

"Ah, don't let Uncle Riley be joshin' you, Jacob," Mum said as she sat in her rocker and picked up her knitting basket. "He's the finest fiddler in Clare."

"Really?" Jacob's eyes grew round.

"*If* that's true," Riley said quietly. "'tis only because your da isn't here."

Jacob nodded, seeming satisfied with that explanation. He held his hands out toward Riley, palms down. "Do I have long, skinny fingers?"

Riley made a great show of turning the lad's small hands for a thorough examination. "Aye, you do. I'll wager you'll be a fine fiddle player."

"Really?"

"Aye."

Bridget and Maggie clattered pans and dishes as they cleaned the kitchen. Somehow, it felt right after a fine meal to sit here with Mum, Culley's son, and knowing his sister and—

And if that isn't dangerous thinking. . . .

He mentally shook himself and turned his attention back to making music.

"Play a song," Jacob said. "Please?"

"I think I can manage that." Riley played "She Moves Through the Fair," because it was one of Mum's favorites. Her foot tapped, her knitting needles quieted, and her chair rocked to the music.

"Wow, you're good," Jacob said when Riley lowered the instrument. "Will you teach me?"

Riley's throat clogged and his vision blurred. He blinked away the sensation and cleared his throat. "I'd be proud to teach you, Jacob."

Mum made a sniffling sound and Riley looked across the room to find Maggie and Bridget seated near her. He hadn't even seen them enter the room while he played.

He met Bridget's gaze and his breath froze at the softness in her expression. "With your permission, Bridget?" he amended.

"Please, Momma?" Jacob asked, stroking the side of the fiddle Riley held.

"Yes," she said, still staring at Riley with an unfathomable and disturbing look in her eyes. "I'd like that. Very much."

"Well, then." Riley showed Jacob how to hold the bow, then he positioned the fiddle the way his own da had shown him so long ago. "Go ahead, Jacob. Make music like your da did."

An unholy screech and scratch filled the house, but the grin on Jacob's face made it bearable. The vault door on Riley's memories eased open a wee bit farther.

But this time he couldn't quite close it.

Bridget waited until the house was quiet and Jacob was sound asleep. From her dark bedroom, she looked out at the moonless night and found no sign of Riley. Jacob must have worn his uncle out today.

Between the stunt Jacob had pulled this morning and the long evening of music and laughter, they were all tired. Bridget yawned and shook her head. She *would* see the castle again, and she would do it tonight.

She looked at the tower's dark shape, barely visible across the meadow. *Caisleán Dubh* called to her. Beckoned, really.

It all sounded downright crazy, but she couldn't explain it. She *wasn't* crazy, but there was something about her that was connected to this castle. That certainty had continued to grow within her until she'd had no choice but to accept it.

Granny would have called her "tetched." Well, she was "tetched," but not in the head. She pressed the heel of her hand to her breastbone. In her heart. Her soul.

Maybe I really am crazy.

She shook her head and smiled. A logical woman would wait for the inspector, but she was feeling anything but logical. She bit her lower lip and tried to convince herself to wait, but in the end she pulled on her cardigan and grabbed the flashlight she'd found in the shed.

Quietly, she tiptoed down the front staircase—farther from Riley's room—and back through the kitchen to the door. She remembered that the front door had a squeak that might ruin everything.

If Riley knew what she was doing, he would raise all kinds of old Billy Hell. Whatever that meant. Granny had said it all the time, but Bridget really had no idea who or what Billy Hell was. Maybe it had something to do with that Billy Beer Grandpa had hated so much.

Billy Hell or not, Bridget had a mission.

Once outside, she switched on the flashlight and started across the meadow. She followed the path that had been worn between the house and the stables, knowing that another path continued on ·toward the road and *Caisleán Dubh* from there.

She looked up at the tower thrusting toward the night sky, and smiled. The whispering started again, surrounding her, filling her, calling her.

The castle wanted her. Maybe it even needed her. All

Bridget knew was that *she* needed it. She lengthened her stride and crossed the road, smiling as she remembered the first time she'd walked this close to *Caisleán Dubh*.

She'd been frightened enough to dang near wet her pants.

How quickly things changed. She drew a deep breath, rounded the corner nearest the entrance, and paused. The whispering sounded almost like singing now. She moved toward the opening and pressed her cheek against the rough doors.

"Home," she whispered. At least, it *felt* like home. She'd never been to Ireland or *Caisleán Dubh* before, but she belonged here. Right here. Right now.

After a moment, she drew a deep breath and steadied herself, aiming her flashlight at the same opening she'd passed through this morning in search of Jacob. Mostly, she saw dust. Something scurried across the floor and she followed it with the flashlight. A mouse?

Bridget was *not* afraid of mice. Snakes were another matter, but they ate mice. However, hadn't St. Patrick driven the snakes out of Ireland?

"Stop it, Bridget." She rolled her eyes at her own silliness and slipped through the opening, clearing the jagged stones with ease. The flashlight beam was broad enough to create a good sweep of the room. When she found the staircase curving toward the tower, her breath caught.

It looked . . . familiar? She squeezed her eyes closed, trying to figure out how the staircase *could* look familiar. Had she seen something in a book or magazine? Nothing made sense or connected. Finally, she shrugged and opened her eyes to continue her exploration.

Huge paintings hung along the walls. They were covered with dust and cobwebs, but those could be cleaned. Perhaps the canvas had remained undamaged beneath the grime. Would she find portraits of Mulligans who'd lived centuries ago? The thought made her pulse quicken as she walked to the side of the chamber opposite the staircase.

The temptation to climb those stairs was too great, but

she didn't want to risk injury. If she disappeared, Riley would find her inside the castle, and, well, there'd be old Billy Hell again.

She shined the light up at a painting over the hearth. It was massive, easily as tall as a grown man. Dust, damp salty air, and age had nearly obliterated the image, though she could tell it was a painting of a person standing. The frame was heavy gold with an intricate design.

She reached for the bottom of the frame and the whispering grew more frantic, as if urging her to touch it. "Now I'm really being silly." Besides, she couldn't quite reach it without a stepladder.

Archways led to other rooms—some with heavy, planked doors and some without. The floor beneath her feet was made from some kind of stone, too. Perhaps after all the layers of filth were removed, she would learn it was marble. The thought of a clean marble floor with massive tables covered with Irish lace tablecloths exploded in her mind. She would hire a musician to play the harp, or maybe even Riley would play some quiet music one night.

The thought of Riley destroyed the image. He would never do anything to support her dream, though he had agreed to the inspection.

Under duress.

Bridget grinned, remembering her son's outrageous blackmail attempt. Well, it had been more than an attempt. Perhaps there was more Frye in that boy than she'd realized.

Her thoughts returned to Riley—the way he'd shown Jacob to hold the fiddle, and how patiently he'd tolerated the ungodly screeching her son had produced. To make matters worse, the man was unbelievably handsome, and Bridget suspected he didn't even realize it. That made him all the more appealing to her.

And dangerous.

She would never forget the way he'd touched her that night in the meadow. And how desperately she'd wanted him to kiss her.

And more.

"Enough of that." She drew a deep breath and sneezed.

Focusing again on her mission, she circled the perimeter of the room, not venturing into any others now. It wouldn't kill her to wait for the inspector before seeing the rest of the castle.

She'd just needed to confirm her belief that *Caisleán Dubh* could be restored. So far, she'd seen nothing to make her believe otherwise.

Again, her gaze and the flashlight drifted toward the massive, curving staircase. The banister was intricately carved. Perspiration coated her flesh and her mouth went dry as she approached it. Touched it.

Her breath froze in her throat and her entire body went rigid. "Oh, my God." Memories of her most recent dream flashed through her brain like a slide show.

The man—her dream lover—had touched her. She rested her hand over her breast. He'd kissed her. She brought trembling fingers to her mouth. He'd suckled her until she'd nearly wept from the pleasure of his warm mouth tugging at her aching breasts.

Fire pulsed through her. The images grew more detailed, and she felt him touching her. Weak with desire, she fell to her knees at the base of the steps, clutching her flashlight in one hand and the banister in the other.

Her private parts contracted against her sharp need. She tugged at her sweater, suddenly wanting to be free of it and all her clothing. Then he could touch all of her again.

She wrenched her cardigan off and flung it to the dusty floor. Too many barriers still separated her from him. He was here. She felt him waiting for her.

Wanting her.

She pulled the clip from her hair. His fingers combed through the tresses until they tumbled about her shoulders. Her pullover sweater slipped over her head at his urging, though she wasn't sure whether she or he had done it.

She couldn't think.

All she could do was want.

And need.

He pulled her to her feet and leaned her back over the banister, tasting her bra-covered nipple with hungry lips, his sharp teeth nipping her through the fabric. She wanted more. So much more.

He cupped her breast in one hand, holding her with one strong arm behind her waist. Her breast swelled into his mouth, urging him to drink from her, to take her to a place she'd never been before.

Strong hands gripped her waist and hauled her against a rock-hard body. Something was different, though hunger still pulsed within her. The flashlight was at her feet, shining up at the man who held her so roughly.

His eyes gleamed with colorless intensity. The planes and angles of his features were hard, as if chiseled from the same substance as the banister.

"What the devil are you doing here?" he asked.

That voice. This man spoke English. Familiar. Bridget tried to force her mind and her desire into synch, but all she could think about was being touched. Kissed. Wanted.

"The whispering," he said so softly that she barely heard him.

"I hear it," she said, pressing her lips against his, and groaning as his hard, heated length throbbed in response.

With a growl, he threw her over his shoulder and carried her back outside.

Thirteen

Riley was mad. Angry.

Horny.

Since the second he'd lain eyes on Bridget, all he'd been able to think or dream about was having a bit of a ride. More than a bit.

Admit it, Mulligan—you're like a bull in autumn after the nearest heifer.

He'd gone for an innocent walk and seen a light shining through the shuttered windows. Afraid Jacob had snuck out of the house for an adventure, Riley had raced into *Caisleán Dubh* for the second time on this *fecked*-up day.

To find Bridget—not the lad—writhing in what appeared to be the throes of, well, ecstasy.

Shite.

After the sizzling dreams Riley had been having of late—not to mention lusting after Bridget while awake—finding her thus had unhinged him.

A shudder of longing rippled through him as he lowered her to the ground before him, her delectable body sliding along the length of his until she landed on her feet and swayed toward him. The castle's infernal whispering circled him—them—driving him to keep her snug against him. Their hearts thudded in unison, echoing in regions below their waists, and their breath came in short, ragged gasps.

"Kiss me," she invited, her breath warm against his cheek.

Jaysus, how he wanted her. He inched closer to her mouth—her soft, full, tempting mouth. He'd resisted the powerful urge to kiss her for days, but once he'd entered the castle, any semblance of control had burst. Vanished. Dissipated. He'd merely touched her about the waist at first, but her response had left him defenseless to her charms.

Aye, and weren't her charms desirable?

Poor Culley had surely lost before the battle had even begun. And Riley was no better, no stronger.

He swallowed hard as Bridget rubbed herself against him, driving him mad with the hunger that had become as much a part of him as the air he breathed since the moment he'd first lain eyes on the *cailleach.*

Cailleach? Aye, she was a witch, a goddess, a temptress—all rolled into a package he craved more than air and water and decency.

He cupped her chin in his hand, none too gently, tilting her head back to bring her lips to just the right angle. When he'd found her writhing and moaning—and alone—he'd gone mad with need. He wanted nothing more than to satisfy her longing. And his.

In fact, he couldn't imagine *not* doing just that. Now. Here on the earth itself at the castle's base, with the whispering whirring mercilessly about them. Aye, he would kiss this woman at last, and he would do a bloody fine job of it.

With a single powerful tug, he brought her even more fully against him, her softness melding deliciously with his hardness. Oh, aye, and had he ever been as hard as he was now? Heat spiraled through him, culminating right between his thighs. He groaned in agony and anticipation.

She rotated her pelvis against him again. He growled as he lowered her to the ground and fell atop her, hovering over her for several moments of pure torture. Their breaths mingled; their hearts thudded in unison. Time stopped.

Then he kissed her. Oh, but he shouldn't have. The moment his lips met hers, he was lost. She was not only the most tempting woman he'd ever met, she was the sweetest tasting. He claimed her mouth, parted her lips, staked his claim of her with each thrust of his tongue.

And his tongue wasn't the only part of him with a mind toward thrusting.

Blood sizzled along his veins, converging between his thighs. He couldn't think. He couldn't reason. He could barely breathe.

All he could do was want and need. He had a bad case of what Gilhooley called Irish craving. After all, it was common knowledge that Irishmen made the best lovers.

And Riley desperately wanted the chance to prove that to Bridget. For a fleeting moment, he remembered that he wasn't her first Irish lover; but raging passion defeated logic.

Her mouth was warm. Moist. Sweet. He explored the smoothness of her teeth, the silkiness of her tongue, the warmth of her palate. He needed her like he needed his next meal. Nothing in his life had prepared him for this.

For her.

For Bridget.

The castle's whispering spun around him like a devil wind, driving him closer to the brink. He couldn't hold himself back. He would take her here in the sand like a rutting beast, and he would *like* it.

Nay, he would savor it.

Mad with the lust thrumming through him, Riley filled his hands with her breasts. He'd never admired a woman's breasts more than Bridget's. He wanted to taste them. He wanted them naked and pressed against his chest while he rode her hard and deep and long.

Gasping, he broke their kiss, licking his way along the side of her throat, resting for an instant at the base. He pressed her breasts together, just now noticing that she wore only a bra and her jeans. He had no idea where her jumper had gone and he didn't care.

All he knew was he had to get rid of all the physical barriers separating them. He wanted her flesh against his. He wanted to feel her smoothness against his roughness. He wanted it all.

And he wanted it now.

He reached behind her and released the tricky clasp on her bra. She wriggled free of the wretched thing and he froze above her just as the moon rose above the tower of *Caisleán Dubh*. Bathed in silver, her breasts rose and fell with her rapid breathing, her nipples dark and erect against the plump, silvery firmness.

He made a sound that dangerously resembled a whimper as he lowered his face between her luscious breasts and inhaled her essence. Then he kissed his way up the inner slope and circled the sweet nub with his tongue. He trembled over her, wanting this so much it frightened him.

Riley Mulligan had feared only one thing in his life. Before Bridget.

The curse.

Feck the curse. All he wanted was this woman, this temptress. *Sex!* He drew her deeply into his mouth, moaning with pleasure as he tasted her sweetness. He'd never desired a woman more. Never wanted to act on that desire less.

He *burned* for her. Burned with a need so fierce he couldn't fight it. His blood bubbled through his veins, driving him to find the release that he knew only Bridget could provide. No other woman would ever sate this mad hunger.

Not in Doolin. Not anywhere.

Not ever.

"Sweet," he murmured against her, brushing his thumb against her other nipple.

She wrapped her legs around his waist and pulled him against her. He rocked against the cradle of her womanhood, wanting so much more. Just thinking about burying himself within her heated folds was enough to make him shudder and throb against her. She squirmed and writhed and whimpered, pleading with him to take her, to fill her.

That did it.

He reached between them and released the snap and zipper of her jeans, shoving them down her slim hips. She squirmed and attempted to assist him, making supremely sexual sounds of encouragement.

He was a dead man.

For a fleeting moment, he thought of Culley. And empathized. His brother had fallen victim to this woman at a much younger age than Riley.

And Riley couldn't resist her either . . . didn't want to. . . .

One leg of her jeans lay impotently beneath her, while the other was still in place. He slid his hand inside her plain cotton drawers and found her mound beneath the tight curls. Lower still, he found her hot and moist as he discovered the center of her desire and stroked until her hips left the ground to meet him.

"Take me," she said, her voice barely more than a strangled whisper. "I want you. I want you." She rocked her pelvis as a woman did with a man buried to the hilt within her. "I want you inside me."

Oh, Jaysus.

She couldn't have known he would find her moaning and writhing, alone and undressed, in the castle. She couldn't have known he would *need* to finish what her imagination had begun. Could she?

Did he care?

No. Right now, all he cared about was surround himself with her heat, her softness, her womanhood. He would die if he couldn't.

He dipped one finger inside her, felt her muscles contract around him. Sucking in a breath, he held it until he brought the urge to explode right here and now under control. Barely. She contracted, drawing his finger deeper inside her. He slid two more in to join the first, mimicking the very action he ached to do with another, much larger, much *needier*, part of his body.

He was going to explode if he couldn't do it now. She'd driven him mad with this constant craving since the day she'd arrived. He'd go off his nut and lose what remained of his mind if he couldn't join with her *now*. As he so desperately wanted. Needed. *Must*.

He had to have her.

Possess her.

Love her.

Love? He tore himself away, pulled his trembling hand from inside her drawers, and stared down at her passion-stricken features. The moonlight gave her a surreal appearance, making her even more beautiful.

"*Shite*," he said, his voice harsh in the night. "*Cailleach*. Witch." She'd cast a bloody spell on him.

The only other sounds were the waves crashing against the rocks below, and the infernal whispering of *Caisleán Dubh*. The castle seemed determined to drive him toward the biggest mistake of his life.

Toward his brother's wife.

But when he gazed upon her bathed in moonlight, he didn't see Culley's wife or Jacob's mum. He saw Bridget—the woman who'd turned his life arseways and topsy-turvy.

And he wanted her. Only her.

The fire pulsing through Bridget almost hurt. No, it *did* hurt. She needed Riley to fill her so full she would never want again. He stretched her with his fingers, but that wasn't enough. She wanted more.

She wanted *him*.

Without warning, he bit off a curse and called her a witch again. She wasn't a witch. She was a woman who needed him more than her dignity. He withdrew his fingers and hovered over her. Torturing her.

"Bronagh," he whispered.

"What?" Her flesh turned icy as the ocean breeze swept over her nakedness. "What did you say?"

He shuddered and stood, facing the sea. "Get dressed." He shoved his hands in his pockets and didn't look at her again. "Just . . . get dressed."

The fire subsided and Bridget shivered. He'd used the word from her dream. Or was it a name? Trembling, she realized just how naked she was and shame washed over her. What if someone had seen them like this?

"Oh, God," she muttered, squirming until her panties and jeans were righted. Her bra lay a few feet away, bathed in moonlight. She shook sand from it and put it on. "Where's my sweater?"

He looked down at her without turning away from the sea. "Don't your remember?" His tone was mocking. "It must be inside."

Confused, she looked toward *Caisleán Dubh*, where her flashlight still glowed from the base of the stone steps, aimed toward the high ceiling. Remembering what had happened when she'd touched the banister, she made a choking noise.

"What . . . what did you do to me?" she asked, her voice quavering.

He spun around and grabbed her hand, hauling her to her feet. Dizzy, she slammed into him, but quickly recovered her balance and maintained her distance—if not her dignity. Touching him was dangerous. "What did you do to me?" she repeated, aiming her thumb over her shoulder. "In there?"

He stared at her with moonlight bathing his features. "Are you bloody daft?"

"No, I'm confused." She shoved her hair back from her face. "I'm standing here without my clothes and I don't know what . . . happened to them." Her voice fell to a whisper as she spoke. She turned toward the castle. Her sweater was inside. She remembered now.

And he'd called her "Bronagh."

Oh, God. Was Riley her dream lover?

"Have mercy!" She clutched at her throat as the enormity of it all pressed down on her. "It was you. All along, it was you. You said . . . you said 'Bronagh.' Just like him. . . ."

He looked at her as if she'd lost her mind, and at this moment she wasn't sure she hadn't. "Just like who?"

"My dre—" She looked away. The last thing she wanted this man to know was that she'd been having erotic dreams starring him. *Is it true?* "Why did you say—call me—Bronagh? Is it a name? What does it mean?"

"You're very good at trickery," he said, his voice low but fierce. "Poor Culley."

Rage sliced through Bridget. With a roar of anguish, she slapped Riley Mulligan's smug face, the loud crack echoing off the castle walls and out to sea.

His head snapped to one side, but he quickly returned his gaze to her, unharmed. His ragged breathing and the wash of the tide against the rocks below were the only sounds. Even the whispers of *Caisleán Dubh* had fallen silent.

"I . . ." She bit her lower lip and crossed her arms over her chest, remembering that only her bra covered her above the waist. "I'm sorry I hit you," she said. "I've told you before that the only thing I ever did to Culley was love him. I can't force you to believe me."

"You would be right about that." Rubbing his cheek, he turned toward the sea again. "You and your son have made me break a lifelong vow today. Twice."

"There is no curse." She brushed sand from her arms and off her back as far as she could reach. "We've been in there two times now and nothing's happened." Determined to find her clothes and cover herself, she spun around and marched toward her flashlight.

What in tarnation had happened to her? How could she

have stripped off her clothes inside and ended up rolling in the sand out here with Riley? And why had he called her Bronagh? The more Bridget thought about it, the more convinced she was that it was a name. A woman's name.

The woman from her dreams? But that had been Bridget. Hadn't it? Otherwise, she wouldn't have felt it all so . . . so . . .

"Don't go in there," Riley said just as she reached the opening. "I forbid it."

Up yours. Granny would have been more proud of Bridget if she'd said it out loud, but thinking it would do for her now. She was too shaken, too confused, too aware of all the ways and places Riley Mulligan had touched her to be logical or brave.

Already inside the castle, she found her sweater and shook the dust from it as best she could, then pulled it over her head. Her cardigan was in worse shape, so she shook it and draped it over her arm instead of wearing it. Besides, she wasn't a bit cold now.

Not after . . . She stood a few feet away from the banister where her flashlight lay near the bottom step pointing toward the ceiling. The fluttering of wings overhead made Bridget shudder, but she reminded herself that bats would eat mice since there were no snakes.

Definitely "tetched."

She almost managed a breath, but she had to reach too near the banister to retrieve her flashlight to manage that. The urge to grab that banister again clawed through her and the whispering commenced again. "Stop it," she whispered. "Just stop. Not now."

Amazingly, it did.

All of it was too bizarre. She clutched the flashlight in a death grip and headed back toward the opening, where Riley's big body blocked all the light from outside.

She stopped near the opening and shined the flashlight right in his eyes. "Move." She was too tired and confused to be polite now.

He didn't budge, and his smirk really grated on her.

"Won't y'all please move? Pretty please?" she asked with false sweetness. *"Now?"*

He leaned against the edge of the exposed door frame as if he had no intention of ever moving from that spot. "I told you not to go in there again."

"My clothes were in there, as you well know."

"How would I know that, since I wasn't there when you removed them?"

"I didn't—" She stopped, holding her breath. "I'm not sure how that happened." And that was the truth. *Dang it.* "But I'm dressed now and I just want to go to sleep. Move." Why couldn't they just use a door like normal people?

He shifted to one side, remaining close enough that she had to brush against him as she exited the castle. Awareness spiked through her again, and she sucked in a breath. Her nipples perked up expectantly as she eased her way past his broad chest. *Traitors.* No matter how much her body wanted Riley Mulligan, *she* was determined to maintain her dignity.

What was left of it.

He placed his hand on her shoulder and the jolt that shot through her was almost as powerful as the one that had seized her when she'd touched that danged banister. His left shoulder was against the door frame, and her backside pressed against the castle wall. She wasn't pinned by him, but by the complete force of her own desire.

"What are you doing to me?" she whispered, staring up at his face through the shadows.

"Bronagh." His voice sounded strange and his grip on her shoulder tightened as he pulled her toward him. "Bronagh," he repeated.

Bridget wanted nothing more than to lean into him, to seek his lips, his touch, his possession again and again. She forced herself to remember her son and their precarious situation. If she slept with Riley, she'd lose her self-respect. And if Fiona ever learned of it, she would surely lose her place in the family.

And, worst of all, Riley would believe himself right about her and Culley.

That thought gave her the strength to force herself through the opening and past him. The moment she emerged from the castle, she felt some control return. With the flashlight still clutched in her fist, she bent over at the waist and gulped the cool night air, bracing the heels of both hands against her knees.

Strengthened, she straightened and turned to face Riley. Still leaning against the castle, he seemed to be in some kind of trance. He kept staring straight ahead and his breathing sounded labored.

"Riley?" Cautiously, she walked toward him.

"Bronagh," he whispered.

"No, I'm not Bronagh." *Whoever she is.* Or was.

He blinked and she aimed her flashlight in his face again. His scowl returned and he shoved himself away from the castle. "What the devil just happened?"

"I asked you the same thing earlier," she reminded him. "I wish I knew. I don't believe there's a curse, but there is some kind of . . . power here."

He nodded. "Would you mind not shining that bloody light in my eyes?"

The real Riley Mulligan had returned.

Grinning, she lowered the flashlight. With the half-moon rising higher, she didn't need it now and turned it off. Later, she would try to determine just what had happened here tonight.

The castle's whispering encircled her again and she squeezed her eyes closed. She'd proven three things to herself this evening.

First of all, *Caisleán Dubh* was safe—at least part of it was—and it could be restored. She didn't need an inspector to confirm it. She just *knew.*

Second, the castle possessed some kind of power or magic. She'd never given supernatural things much thought before, but whatever force had seized control of her when she'd gripped that banister wasn't something to ignore.

And that power had taken control of Riley, too. Why had he called her Bronagh? *Why?* Was he *really* her dream lover, or had he just been here at the right—or wrong—time? A tremor raced through her and she hoped the dreams would end now. Maybe now that she'd faced *Caisleán Dubh* and her ridiculous fear, they would.

She watched Riley's profile as he gazed out to sea, as lost in thought as she. Was he asking himself the same questions? Did he realize he'd called her that name? And what did it all mean?

With a sigh, she swallowed hard and admitted her third discovery. There was nothing magical about this one. Nothing supernatural. But it was every bit as dangerous and uncontrollable.

She *wanted* Riley Mulligan. The mortal man. Not any dream lover. The flesh-and-blood, dangerously handsome, gentle and patient man. Though he'd shown her his ugly side, she'd seen his goodness in the way he treated his momma and sister. And especially Jacob.

He was confusing—angry one minute and brooding the next. Then without any warning at all, he'd wax as charming as that used car salesman who'd lived in the trailer next door to Granny's.

Bridget had to resist her attraction to the flesh-and-blood Riley, though she had no control over what happened in her dreams. Maybe someday, if the dreams didn't end now, she'd find satisfaction in her sleep.

A hot flush crept over her and her heart did a flip.

One thing at a time. First, she needed the inspection and the restaurant. Once she had an income, she might consider separate living quarters for her and Jacob, though she dearly loved being near Fiona and Maggie. Still, it might be for the best to put some distance between herself and Riley. Meanwhile, she had to keep her crazy libido under control.

And remember never to touch that banister again. . . .

"Well, I'm heading back now," she said. "Do you want the flashlight?"

He pinned her with his gaze. "Why did you have to come here and cause so much trouble?"

She lifted her chin a notch. "I haven't done anything to cause trouble."

He made a snorting sound and shook his head. "What do you call what happened—or almost happened—here this evening?"

"Magic." Bridget looked back over her shoulder. "There's magic here."

"There's a curse here."

She stomped her foot and thought every dirty word she'd ever heard Granny utter. "I reckon we'll see what the inspector has to say."

Riley sighed and lifted one shoulder. "I agreed to an inspection. Nothing more."

Realization slammed into Bridget. Speechless, she stared at Riley for several moments. He'd never had any intention of letting them renovate and open a restaurant. He'd only agreed to the inspection because of Jacob.

Instead of calling him all the names that exploded in her mind, or telling him just what she thought about his obstinance and that stupid old curse, she squared her shoulders, lifted her chin a notch, and did what Granny would have done.

She showed him her middle finger and walked away.

Fourteen

Riley worked like the devil himself was on his tail. He plowed, mowed, raked, fed the cattle, birthed a calf, and sheared a few sheep. He was ready to drop. However, it was considerate of the calf to give him something to do. Busy hands . . .

Jacob had helped him for part of the morning, but had opted to help his *mamó* the rest of the day. Mum was putting in the later additions to her kitchen garden and insisted she needed Jacob's help.

However, Riley suspected his mum had sensed his surly mood and intervened to give her son a bit of privacy, or to spare the lad from his uncle's temper.

Wise woman, Mum.

He straightened from the angry sheep and released the wild, woolly thing into the pasture. He was filthy. Dirt and wool had stuck to the sweat he'd worked up while mowing and raking.

"Go on with you now, you little she-devil," he said, nudging the ewe away when she just stood there staring at him after her haircut. After the way she'd fought him, he'd expected her to run fast. "Silly sheep. Female, of course." He sorted the contaminated clumps of wool and bagged the good for Mum.

He paused to take a long drink of water. Nothing—not even an unholy amount of hard labor—could make him forget last night. He stood staring toward *Caisleán Dubh*. Remembering.

His throat contracted and he shoved his hair away from his face. He couldn't decide which part was worse—the memory of almost succumbing to Bridget's charms, or the crazed way the bloody castle had made him feel and act.

"Aye, crazed." He released a long sigh and took another sip. The problem was, he couldn't deny the painful truth.

Even without the bloody curse, he would still want Bridget.

Eejit. Aye, but truth was Riley's way. He couldn't fib to himself. Pity, that. Wouldn't lying to himself ease his tortured brain, if nothing else? He glanced down at the fly of his jeans. Not even a well-turned fib would control *that*.

Had he ever wanted a woman more? He drew a deep breath of salt-tinged air. No. Never.

"Jaysus. I *still* want her," he whispered.

I always will.

He squeezed his eyes closed and swayed, remembering the way she'd felt in his arms. Tasted. Looked. And his foolish body responded to the memories with more enthusiasm than Riley could stand. He grabbed the rake leaning nearby and flung it halfway across the pasture. There was nothing in harm's way. At least he was still sane enough to know *that*. Unfortunately, it didn't help. Nothing would. Not now. Not ever.

"Shite."

"Who are you trying to kill?" a female voice asked him from the rock wall several feet away.

Riley looked over quickly, both relieved and disappointed to find Katie sitting on the wall instead of Bridget. "When did you take up spying on workingmen?"

Hoping her gaze didn't wander below his belt, he

walked toward her, acutely conscious of his appearance and, undoubtedly, his odor. A man didn't sweat this much without working up a good stink. Aye, but wouldn't he rather she smelled him than noticed his blatant erection?

Working himself practically to death was supposed to eliminate those urges. Any other time, about any other woman, it might have. This time, there was only one cure. . . .

"My, but aren't we in a sour mood?" Katie shook her head and slid off the stone wall. "I suppose living under the same roof with . . . with *her* would make me surly, too."

Riley had to chuckle at that. "And I wonder which one of you would be left among the living if that were true."

Katie narrowed her gaze. "Don't wonder."

The woman is vindictive. He'd never noticed that about Katie before. Of course, she'd been engaged to Culley— not Riley. He'd never really paid her much attention before Bridget's arrival. For that matter, Katie had spoken to him more in the last few weeks than in the last ten years.

"What brings you out here so late in the day?" he asked, deciding it best to change the subject.

"Granddad." She sighed and pursed her perfectly painted lips. "He's annoying."

"Brady?" Riley frowned. "I'm surprised. I always thought you were close."

"Aye, when I was a wee lass." She gave an exaggerated sigh. "Now he keeps nagging me about some old papers he left stored in my closet before he went to the States."

"Papers?" Riley's stomach growled and he took a deep breath in hopes of silencing it. He'd worked like the devil and smelled worse. On top of that, he was half-starved. However, he forced himself to make polite conversation with the woman who *should* have been his sister-in-law. "What papers?"

"Research papers. What else?" She rolled her eyes. "He's so determined to write his silly book that he came out here to get Fiona's blessing."

Riley frowned and rubbed his chin. "I don't follow. What does Mum have to do with—"

"The curse, Riley," she said dramatically. "Remember?"

"Ah, that."

"Aye, that."

"And he wanted Mum's blessing for what purpose?" Riley still didn't understand the connection. "He can do research without asking her permission."

"Aye, but he said it would be disrespectful to go through the parish records without her blessing."

"Mulligan records?"

"Aye."

Riley lifted a shoulder. "Brady has always been fascinated with the history of *Caisleán Dubh.* There's no law against doing research." He tilted his head slightly and narrowed his gaze. "Why does that bother you?"

"Well . . ." Her face flushed and she looked downward for several seconds, as if contemplating her next words. "Did Culley ever tell you why we had to get married?"

"*Had* to?" Didn't the woman realize what that meant? "I'm thinking that's not exactly what you—"

"Oh, no. Not . . . not *that.*"

Riley had always considered Katie somewhat cold. Unlike Bridget, who had passion and sexuality to spare. *Don't think about that.* He seriously doubted that Katie and Culley had ever been intimate, despite their engagement.

"About the curse, Riley."

"What?" He mentally shook himself, trying to figure out where and when he'd lost the thread of their conversation. "You lost me, lass. What do you and my brother have to do with the curse?"

She leaned closer, a conspiratorial look in her eyes. "We were soul mates."

A burst of laugher forced Riley to choke and feign a fit of coughing to disguise it. "Well, now, I didn't realize . . .

that," he said, hoping he appeared more sincere than he felt.

So much for never lying, Mulligan. Well, he hadn't *exactly* lied—simply didn't offer his complete thoughts on the subject at hand. He cleared his throat.

"Aye, 'tis true." An odd twinkle appeared in her eyes. "I found the proof in Granddad's notes."

Suspicion slithered through Riley. "Would that be in his *missing* notes?"

Katie's face reddened and she took a step back, her eyes widening. "I didn't *steal* them, though I probably did misplace them." She lifted one shoulder and gave him a sad smile. "I was heartbroken after Culley . . ."

You big oaf. Guilt, guilt, and more bloody guilt tormented him. "There, now. Culley wouldn't—Ooof."

She threw herself into his arms, tears mingling with his sweat to thoroughly soak his sleeve. He had no choice but to put his arms loosely around her shoulders and pat her back. What else could a man do when a woman threw herself against him in a crying jag?

After several minutes of Katie's weeping and carrying on, Riley pushed her away and gripped her shoulders. "We'll have enough of that, now," he said firmly, but without cruelty. "Culley's been gone over seven years. The time for tears is long past. Besides, I'm filthy."

She sniffled and made a great show of bringing herself under control. "Aye, he wouldn't want me to cry."

"So don't." *Please.*

"I'll be strong."

"Good."

"As I was saying, the papers told about the reason for the curse."

Riley's heart thudded against his chest. "And haven't the Mulligans all cut our teeth on that tragic tale?"

"I'm sure, but the priest at the time claimed that a *cailleach* cast a spell on *Caisleán Dubh* after the tragedy."

"The tragedy happened on Aidan Mulligan's wedding day." Riley knew the story by heart, as his da had told it to them dozens of times. "Aidan fell in love with a local lass—a peasant girl—but he was promised to another."

"You *do* know the story." Katie appeared smug now. "The *cailleach* was the peasant girl's aunt or something."

"I've not heard anything about a *cailleach*."

"That's the important part that most don't know," she said quietly. "Granddad's notes said the curse will end when Aidan weds his true love."

"That's rubbish and nonsense." Despite the voice of reason, Riley's throat constricted and his heart thudded louder. "Aidan Mulligan and his peasant girl died centuries ago."

"Aye. That's how I knew Culley and I were soul mates."

Katie pouted again.

"I'll not stand still for one more tear, Katie Rearden," Riley warned. "I'm tired, filthy, and hungry, and you're spouting folly."

She gripped his arm and leaned closer. "Not nonsense, Riley," she said, her tone intense. "'Tis true that the theory Granddad wrote about in his notes sounds like a fairy tale. A romantic fairy tale at that. But ask yourself what could happen if Aidan's spirit has lived on in his descendants?"

The Irish placed great importance on the power of blood—the traits handed down from generation to generation. Riley shook his head. "I'm not sure such a thing is possible."

"*I'm* sure." Katie straightened. "And so was Culley."

The memory of the last time Riley had seen his brother surged to the front of his mind. *Jaysus.* Was that what Culley had meant when he'd said that marrying Katie would end the bloody curse? Was there something in Brady's notes that said as much? Riley's empty stomach churned acid like liquid fire.

More importantly . . . was it true?

"My people have been in County Clare for centuries, just like yours," she continued. "However, the Reardens were peasants, and the church records aren't as detailed for us as they are for the Mulligans."

"I still don't understand." Riley swallowed hard, trying not to dwell on his brother's words that long ago day. "What do you mean? The crux of this, Katie, if you will."

"As near as we could tell from the notes—"

"You mean Culley saw them, too?"

"No." She blushed again and shook her head. "No, but I told him what I'd found."

But did you tell him the truth? For some reason, Riley sensed that Katie was lying—at least, in part. And wasn't it his job to determine which part?

"How does what you found lead you to believe in this ridiculous notion of soul mates?" He folded his arms and kept his expression as stoic as possible.

"The lass Aidan loved." Her eyes glittered with excitement, as if she were imparting some great secret. "I *think* my *mamó* from mum's side was descended from the same family. *Mamó* has been dead since I was a wee lass, so finding her family records has been hard without help."

Stunned, Riley took a step back, never shifting his gaze from Katie's face. He didn't trust her, yet he couldn't deny that his brother *had* seemed certain that marrying this woman would make things right again. "You're saying Brady's notes named the lass Aidan loved?"

"Aye." Katie's expression was smug. "I'll not tell you, though, until I'm sure."

"How can you be sure?" he asked. "*When* will you be sure?"

"As soon as the letter arrives from *Mamó*'s parish, confirming her birth name." She sighed. "I didn't pursue the information after . . . after Culley. But now . . ."

Riley gnashed his teeth, wondering if Brady would have the answers he needed.

"Culley heard sounds from the castle," she continued, looking toward the tower in the distance.

Riley swallowed hard and gave a curt nod. "Do you?" Why had he asked such a question?

Because Bridget hears it.

Riley's heart swelled upward, pressing against his throat, and he clenched his jaw until it ached. He watched Katie for any reaction, but she seemed unaffected by his question. "Do you?" he repeated.

"Well, no," she said. "Of course not. After all, I'm not a Mulligan."

Neither is Bridget by blood. . . .

"No, you aren't a Mulligan." Riley kept his tone bland, as he wanted to end this conversation as soon as possible. "I still don't understand what this has to do with the curse or anything else," he said. It wasn't a fib. How could anyone actually *understand* this soul mate business?"

"Culley and I believed that once we married, the curse would end."

"I see." But he didn't. Katie didn't hear the castle's whispers.

Bridget did.

"Do . . . do you hear the castle?" Katie asked, her expression somewhat sly.

Every thread of Riley's common sense screamed that he should make a second exception about lying. Instead, he drew a deep breath and said, "Aye."

Katie's eyes widened. "You *do*?"

"Why are you so surprised?"

"Culley told me—" She bit her lower lip.

"He told you that I couldn't hear the castle," Riley finished, still wary.

"Aye."

"That was true. I couldn't hear it as a lad." Riley didn't tell her that he'd started hearing the castle right after Culley's death. Maybe he couldn't fib to the woman, but he wasn't a total *gobshite*. Some things were none of her bloody business.

"I see." She eyed him in a way that made Riley feel like a leg of lamb in the butcher's display case. "Why don't you wash up and come over for supper this evening?"

Riley shook his head, trying to follow her sudden change of subject. "What?"

"Food, Riley?" She laughed and leaned into him, gazing into his eyes.

Warning bells rang in his brain, and he stiffened. "Not this evening, but I thank you for the invitation."

She pursed her lips in a pretty pout that made Riley even more suspicious. "Well, another time, then," she said.

"Maybe." He took another step back for good measure. "It's a busy time of year for a farmer."

She ran her tongue over her bottom lip and said, "Even busy men have to *play* sometimes."

Shite. Realization stumbled through his mind. The woman had never been interested in the older Mulligan brother, but suddenly she had the look of a female cat in heat. He didn't have to wonder why. If she believed this soul mate story, then how could she transfer her feelings for Culley so easily?

She'd wanted to marry Culley because, though younger, he was the "chosen" son—the one who heard the whispering. Now she had her mind set on the remaining son. Why? The Mulligans weren't wealthy, though the farm was one of the largest and most prosperous in Clare.

He shouldn't have told her he could hear the wretched castle. *But* she *doesn't hear it, Mulligan.*

"I have to go," he said. "Mum's expecting me."

"I'll ring you up," she said, turning toward Ballybronagh with a spring in her step he hadn't noticed before. "We'll get together another time. Soon." She waggled her fingers at him.

The moment she turned her head, Riley made sure his back was to her in case she waved again. The woman had made her intentions clear, and he was having no part of it.

After stowing his tools, he tended *Oíche* and headed toward the cottage. The sun had sunk low beyond *Caisleán Dubh*, and the tower cast a long shadow across the meadow. A rainbow arced over the cottage, giving it a fairy-tale appearance.

Aye, a fairy tale.

He hadn't given voice to the thoughts raging through his mind since piecing together the bits of Katie's theory he'd heard. Before he entered Mum's kitchen and faced them all, he'd best get it sorted out in his mind as best he could.

He believed in the curse—always had. Aye, and hadn't he always had good cause for believing? Though he'd never heard of a *cailleach* having anything to do with it, didn't it make sense for a curse to have a cause?

Still, the notion that the souls of Aidan and his lover could return, seeking the union fate had denied them . . .

Could it be true? And if it were, then . . . then . . .

He stopped several feet from the back door and turned toward the castle. Drawing in a deep breath, he welcomed the expected whispering that surrounded him.

Culley had heard it, but he'd died. Now Riley heard it. Aidan Mulligan had been a younger son, as had Culley. It seemed odd for an older sibling to "inherit" something from a younger, but Riley found himself certain that this was precisely what had happened to him.

He lifted his face toward the sun and the top of the tower, trying to deny the obvious. Culley had heard the whispers. Truth. Now Riley did. Also true. Katie did not and never would.

But Bridget *did.* Another truth.

She claimed to have loved Culley, and the saints knew how Riley burned for her. The memory of last night made him shudder with the same powerful craving and his pulse quickened. He would go to his grave wanting her, as Culley had.

Was it true? *If* Katie's crazy theory about soul mates proved true . . .

"Jaysus, Mulligan. Listen to yourself." Aye, he would listen, because he had to, no matter how mad it all sounded, or how desperately he wanted to deny it.

Riley had some serious research of his own to conduct. He would pay Brady a visit and they could discuss his missing notes. And *why* were they missing? Another mystery.

If Katie was right about this soul-mate nonsense . . . *Shite.* Riley forced himself to speak the rest of his dreaded thought aloud, since his mind continued to fight it.

"Bridget . . ."

Bridget needed answers. She'd lain awake for three nights, afraid to go to sleep. If the erotic dreams returned, would she finally learn her lover's true identity? She knew in her heart, and absolute confirmation it would do her no good. Then again, neither had denial.

Riley had driven his momma to the doctor in Kilmurray for a checkup, and Jacob went along for the ride. Alone with Maggie after school, Bridget did what she should have done days ago.

In the kitchen garden, which was bathed in sunshine after three days of rain, she straightened and asked, "Maggie?"

The girl straightened and met Bridget's gaze. "What is it, Bridget? Is something wrong?"

"No, I just need to talk." Bridget glanced down at the basket of greens slung over her forearm. "I think we have more than enough for supper. Let's go inside for a cold drink and a chat."

"All right." Maggie gathered the scallions she'd pulled and followed Bridget inside. "You're not planning to leave us, are you?"

"No," Bridget said slowly. "Not yet, anyway."

"Mum and I both want you and Jacob to think of this as home." Maggie set her onions in the sink and washed her hands.

Bridget followed her sister-in-law's example. They retrieved two glasses and two cans of soda pop, then sat at the table.

"Jacob and I like it here," Bridget said after a few bubbly sips of pop. "I want to talk about Riley."

"Oh." Maggie shook her head and sighed. "He can be such an old grumble puss sometimes."

"Yes." Bridget certainly couldn't deny that. "Why is that, Maggie? How can a boy who grew up with the same momma as you and Culley be so . . . different?"

Maggie's expression grew solemn and she fell silent for a few minutes. Finally, she cleared her throat and said, "It was a long time ago."

So something had happened to change Riley. Bridget had sensed it. "Tell me, please. I . . . I need to know." She sighed and worried her lower lip with her teeth. "I think it might help me understand him better."

Maggie nodded. "He'll be furious with me for the telling, but I think you're right." She took a sip of pop, then set it aside and clasped her hands before her on the table.

"Riley was but a lad, and I was still in nappies when it happened, so I don't remember firsthand." Her expression grew distant, her tone very serious. "Mum told me what happened that terrible day. Why Riley changed from a happy lad to a sad old man so suddenly."

"That describes him." Bridget concentrated on Maggie, wanting—no, needing—to understand Riley. She couldn't really explain the need, any more than she could explain why touching the banister in *Caisleán Dubh* had sent her into sexual hyperdrive. The memory made her cheeks burn.

"Did you take too much sun, Bridget?" Maggie started to push away from the table. "Mum has some salve—"

"No." Bridget gripped her sister-in-law's arm. "Please, just tell me the rest."

"All right." Maggie settled herself in the chair again. "The potato crop was poor that year, and some kind of disease took half the sheep. We were poorer than we'd ever been, and Da was worried.

"He told Mum he was going fishing one day, but in-

stead he went to *Caisleán Dubh*. Mum thinks he was looking for antiques to sell, as he'd mentioned before that
there were things inside worth a fortune."

"That makes sense." Bridget nodded encouragement,
remembering the huge framed portraits and such.

"Aye, but there was the curse." She held her hand up to
silence any protest Bridget might have made. "I know you
don't believe in it, Bridget, but we do. In fact, the curse
took Da's life."

"Oh, God." Bridget rubbed her temples and forced herself to concentrate on Maggie's tragic tale. "How awful."

"Aye." She fell silent again. "I would've liked to know
me da, but it wasn't meant to be."

Bridget reached across the table and took her sister-in-
law's hand. "I'm sorry for that. I lost my parents when I
was young, too."

"But I had Mum, Culley, and Riley, and you had your
granny and grandpa."

"Yes." Bridget smiled in remembrance. "What happened that day—to your daddy? And to Riley?"

Maggie cleared her throat. "A terrible thing. Riley saw
Da go into the castle, and being raised a Mulligan, hadn't
he heard of the dreaded curse from the womb?" Maggie
shoved a wiry red curl behind her ear.

"Riley followed Da inside." Maggie's lower lip trembled. "*So* young."

Bridget's stomach heaved and she drew a deep breath
to quell the rising nausea. Another sip of soda pop steadied her. "I'm listening."

"Poor little lad." Maggie sniffled and blinked rapidly,
her eyes glistening with unshed tears. "He . . . he found
Da in the center of the main chamber. Dead."

Bridget squeezed her eyes shut for several seconds and
drew a shaky breath. "What happened then?"

"Riley pulled our big, strong da's body out of the castle, which had been empty for a hundred years by then."

A chill swept through Bridget. No wonder Riley believed the curse was real. "How did your daddy die, Maggie?"

She shook her head, a mournful expression in her blue eyes. "No one knows. The doctor said he was fit as could be, and there was no reason for such a healthy man to just drop dead. The curse was the only explanation."

Bridget had heard stories of allegedly healthy individuals dying suddenly from heart attacks or strokes. "So Riley pulled his da out of the castle alone?"

"Aye, all by himself."

"Then what happened?"

"From what Mum has said, Riley took it upon himself to become the man of the family. He vowed to run the farm for Da." She sniffled and dabbed her eyes. "The next crop was a bountiful one. With Riley working like two grown men, and the help of good friends and neighbors, all was well by the next harvest."

"But Riley will never forget," Bridget whispered, understanding why he hated the castle so desperately. "I still don't believe there's anything evil about *Caisleán Dubh,* Maggie. But . . ."

Bridget looked out the window at the tower, dominating the horizon. "There is something powerful there."

"You felt it?"

"Yes." Her cheeks warmed again. "The castle seems to . . ." Dare she tell Maggie that the castle spoke to her? It sounded so crazy. Mad.

"What is it, Bridget?" Maggie scooted closer. "Something is wrong. I can tell."

"Do you ever hear any . . . sounds from the castle, Maggie?" she asked.

"No, but Culley said it whispered to him every time he went near it."

And sometimes from clear across the dang meadow.

"I wonder why," Bridget said, deciding to keep her secrets to herself for now. "Was it calling to him for some reason?"

And me?

"Aye, he said it did." Maggie appeared thoughtful. "He never talked about it much, except to say it wasn't scary." A visible shudder rippled through Maggie. "Well, it terrifies me enough sometimes to wet me knickers."

But not me.

Bridget gave Maggie's hand another squeeze. "Thank you for telling me. I think I'll be able to understand Riley a mite better now."

"I'm glad of it," Maggie said on a sigh. "It's time you two stopped bickering like a couple of roosters."

Bridget almost smiled, for she knew beyond any doubt that Riley didn't think of her as a rooster. A hen, perhaps. Well, the thought was still unflattering.

"I have one more question, if you don't mind." Bridget waited for Maggie to meet her gaze. "What does *bronagh* mean?" She'd deliberately asked the question as if she believed the word was *not* a name, though nothing could be further from the truth.

"Oh, like the village?"

"Well, yes. I guess the village was named Ballybronagh for a reason." Bridget held her breath, waiting.

"Bronagh means sorrowful," Maggie explained. "No one knows for certain, but the locals believe the village was named by Aidan Mulligan after the tragedy, since his life was filled with sorrow."

"Tragedy? And who was Aidan Mulligan?"

"Aidan lived long ago when *Caisleán Dubh* was brand new. His da built it. 'Twas Aidan's tragedy that brought the curse." Maggie patted Bridget's hand. "Mum is probably the one to tell the whole story when you're ready."

"So . . . Bronagh isn't a woman's name?"

"Oh, aye, it can be, but who would want to be named 'Sorrowful'?"

Who, indeed? Bridget still believed that Riley and her dream lover had used the word as a name. She shook herself and vowed to find the perfect moment to ask Fiona to tell her the whole story.

Rising, she placed her hands on her hips and said,

"Let's cook something guaranteed to make even the grouchiest man smile."

Maggie put her arms around Bridget and laughed. "I'm so glad you and Jacob came home to us, Bridget."

Bridget's throat tightened and a scalding hot tear crept from the corner of one eye as she focused on the view through the window. "Home," she whispered.

To *Caisleán Dubh.*

Fifteen

On Saturday morning, Sean Collins rang up Riley to cancel their session in Doolin. A week before, Riley had looked forward to the opportunity to find some casual female companionship for an evening. As he hung up the phone in the kitchen, he realized that now he was relieved that the opportunity wouldn't present itself.

Oh, he still had the hunger, but what he wanted wouldn't be at all casual, because he craved his brother's widow. Of course, a week ago he hadn't known about Katie's bloody notion about soul mates.

Maggie burst through the back door with the mail she'd gone to Ballybronagh to fetch. "Where's Mum?" she asked, out of breath.

"Fetching spuds." Riley narrowed his gaze as his sister went through the door to the cellar, calling for her. A few moments later, they returned together.

"Where's Bridget?" Mum asked as she tore open an envelope. "She'll be wantin' to hear this."

"I'll get her." Maggie bounded up the back staircase.

Pity she was too short to knock her noggin on that low beam. Ah, but he didn't mean that, though it did seem unfair that he should be the only Mulligan tall enough to . . .

Jacob skipped into the room. The lad was tall. Not that Riley would wish the child harm . . . but maybe there would be some justice, all the same. Family traditions and all . . .

Riley smiled as he caught Jacob in a headlock while tickling him mercilessly. He'd grown fond of the lad in a short time, and he wanted him to stay and grow up here on the farm. Long enough to bump his head. Long enough to have his sons bump theirs. It was right to have them here.

Both of them?

Riley stopped tickling, but didn't release the lad. Jacob seized the opportunity to jab his uncle in the ribs. "Ow!"

"Stop this nonsense and pay attention now," Mum said as Bridget hurried into the room behind Maggie. She held the letter up in front of them. "'Tis from the Irish Trust."

Riley reached for the envelope, but Mum gently slapped his hand away. "'Tis addressed to me, boyo."

Clenching his teeth, Riley folded his arms and waited while Mum opened the envelope.

"Well, I'll be," she said, looking around the room. "The inspector says he'll have a team out here on Wednesday."

So soon. Riley released the breath he'd been holding and dared a glance at Bridget. She looked nervous but happy. Maybe "hopeful" was the proper description.

And beautiful.

Her unpainted face glowed with health as she hugged her son, who looked up at her adoringly. Nagging doubts had plagued Riley for days, and now they grew tenfold.

Was Bridget really the deceitful seductress he'd accused her of being? His entire sense of logic and justice tilted and he felt off-balance.

The time for the research he'd promised was now. He could wait no longer. Before the inspectors arrived, he would have the information he needed.

He couldn't drag his gaze from Bridget for several moments. The way her silky hair waved about her shoulders made him ache to run his fingers through it. Her lips were moist and inviting. Her breasts filled out her jumper in a way that made his blood heat and thicken with need. Bridget bent down to feel the toes of Jacob's shoes, her jeans pulling tight against her nice bum.

Lust whipped through him like bees buzzing around a hive. He arched an eyebrow as he stared at her appreciatively. Aye, bees were drawn to sweets. . . .

Remembering that he wasn't alone, Riley forced himself to look away as Maggie joined Bridget in examining and discussing the fit of Jacob's shoes. At least his sister hadn't noticed Riley practically making love to Bridget with his eyes. He'd never have heard the end of that bit of funning.

"Well, I'll be," Mum whispered under her breath.

Riley met her knowing gaze and his stomach gave a lurch. *Jaysus.* Having Maggie see his secret would have been better than Mum. He sighed and she arched her eyebrows at him.

One thing about Mum, though—she would keep his secret.

The question was, could *he*? Obviously not, since he'd just allowed his mum to see his naked desire for Bridget.

"I'm going into Ballybronagh," he announced, needing some air and definitely some privacy. Avoiding Mum's gaze, he grabbed his cap and waved to them all as he slipped out the door.

Jacob's voice sounded as the door closed behind him. Riley walked at a brisk pace, riddled with guilt about his nephew. The lad would have loved to go into the village with him, but not today. Riley had to speak with Brady alone.

The bloody inspector would be here on Wednesday. Riley strolled past *Caisleán Dubh.* The whispering and sighing of the thing swept over him, but he refused to offer the castle so much as a glance this day.

Caisleán Dubh had caused enough trouble, and would cause more before this nightmare ended. If it ever did.

The Reardens lived in a small stone cottage on the edge

of town. Riley looked around the tidy yard and spied old Brady sitting in the shade, poring over a lapful of books. The gate squeaked as Riley pushed it open, alerting Brady of his presence.

"Top o' the mornin' to you, Riley Mulligan," his old teacher said. "Pull yourself up a chair and have a visit with an old man."

Riley looked around anxiously, relieved to notice that Katie's car wasn't here. "Are you alone today?" he asked, hoping he didn't sound as eager as he felt.

"Aye, they all ran off to some festival in Galway."

Thank the Blessed Virgin. Riley mentally crossed himself and relaxed. "And what are you so busy with this fine day?" he asked, determined to lead into his topic as casually as possible.

"Sit, sit." Brady patted the book in his lap. "These are church records that Father O'Malley let me bring home. He trusts me, the old fool."

Brady grinned as Riley pulled his chair closer and peered down at the faded scrawl on yellowed parchment. "How can you even *see* it, let alone understand it?"

"'Tis hard, lad." Brady leaned back and adjusted his glasses on his nose. "Sometimes I have to use a magnifyin' lens."

Riley nodded. "What is the subject you're studying so hard?" His heart fluttered, then raced forward.

"*Caisleán Dubh.*" Brady's eyes twinkled behind his spectacles. "Didn't Fiona tell you me plans?"

No, but Katie did. "About your book? You mentioned that at mass."

"Aye, so I did." Brady pointed to a passage near the top of the page. "Here's a bit I missed the first time. 'Tis fascinatin'."

Aye, fascinating. Riley swallowed hard. "What did you find?"

"All these centuries, the villagers have assumed that Ballybronagh was named for the sorrow Aidan felt after his beloved's tragic death."

"Aye." Riley studied his old teacher's expression very carefully. "Wasn't it?"

"See, this is the fascinatin' part." Brady nodded, a grand look of satisfaction on his face. "Even the Mulligans didn't realize how the village was named."

How long would it take to get Riley the information he needed? Of course, if Riley *knew* what he needed, it would be much simpler. "How was it named?" *One wee step at a time.*

"'Twas her name, lad."

Riley shook his head. "Whose name?"

"Aidan's love. The peasant girl who threw herself to her death from the tower of *Caisleán Dubh.*"

Riley suppressed a shudder at hearing the tragedy spoken so plainly. "What was her name?" No wonder Katie was so hard to follow in a conversation. She'd inherited the trait from her granddad.

"Bronagh, Riley. Bronagh." He pointed to the faint, spidery crawl. "'Tis right there, where it names the poor lass."

Riley leaned closer. "Bronagh," he whispered, remembering the night at the castle with Bridget. She'd accused him of calling her Bronagh. "Jaysus."

Cold sweat coated his skin and his pulse skittered like a spider's web along his veins. "What was her surname?" He held his breath.

"Look here, lad. Me old eyes can't read that part." Brady tilted the old book toward Riley. "Can you see it? What was Bronagh's surname?"

Riley looked at the word from every angle, and even borrowed Brady's magnifying glass, but he still couldn't read it. Wasn't learning her first name proof enough?

Proof of what, Mulligan?

If only he knew. "I'm sorry, but in this case, my eyes aren't any better than yours, Brady," he said.

"A pity, but thanks for tryin', lad." Brady pointed to another book sitting on the table beside him. "In his diary, the priest who was here in Aidan's time writes about Bronagh's aunt—a *cailleach*, by all accounts."

Riley blocked the memory of Katie's words from clouding his judgment. He only wanted to hear this from Brady. He trusted Brady. For some reason, every shred of common sense he possessed told him not to trust Katie. Not anymore. Maybe he never could.

Maybe Culley shouldn't have. . . .

Don't be going there now, Mulligan. Culley was dead and the past was history now. Yet . . . the very history Brady was researching might very well affect the future.

"A witch, you say?" Riley tried to sound flippant. "Da never spoke of her."

"Aye, that's because much of this information comes from Bronagh's clan—not the Mulligans." A satisfied gleam danced in Brady's eyes. "The other side of the story, if you will. The untold one."

"But you will tell it."

"Aye, though it may take a miracle to read some of this. Time has been unkind."

"Aye." Riley craned his neck to look at the spine of the diary, which had obviously been damaged by moisture and was illegible. "And nowhere else in all those notes does it mention Bronagh's surname?"

"I've not finished reading them all just yet," Brady said. "But I can see that you recognize how important this could be."

"Aye, well . . ." Riley couldn't deny the hum the excitement whirring through him, almost as insistent as the whisperings of *Caisleán Dubh*. Almost. "Have you figured out what role the *cailleach* played in all this?"

"The priest believed she placed an evil spell on *Caisleán Dubh* to avenge her niece's tragic death."

Riley fell silent for a moment, remembering how his da had described the events. "Aye, the lass was treated unfairly."

Brady nodded. "She loved Aidan, and he loved her." He pointed to another book. "The priest speaks of Aidan's mourning here. 'Tis quite a sad life he led after that, though he did rear strong sons. Alas, not with the woman he loved."

"Da said the lass came to the castle the day of Aidan's wedding, but was forbidden entrance. She even told Aidan's da that she was with child."

"Aye. That's all in here, lad." Brady's head bobbed again. "Just as your da told it."

"Except for the *cailleach*, and the lass's name."

"Aye." Brady frowned. "When I did this research before, years ago, I had notes about the priest's interview with the *cailleach*. Some of it was ugly, lad, as the old woman was grieving and angry."

"That's understandable," Riley said, pointing at the priest's diary. "Does he reveal the nature of her so-called spell in there?"

"No, and 'tis angry I am that me earlier notes were lost." He heaved a weary sigh and scratched his bald head. "Katie moved them and swears she doesn't know what became of them."

"Was there . . . something in there about the spell?" Riley's mouth went dry.

"Aye. In fact, the priest quoted it. I copied the words into me notes, and now they're lost. I *think* I copied the lass's surname there as well, but I can't remember it now."

Stolen. The more Riley heard about this, the more he believed that Katie hadn't wanted Culley to know what her granddad's notes *really* said. She'd made up a pretty story in her head and used it to manipulate Culley into marriage.

But it hadn't worked. The curse had won.

Listen to yourself, Mulligan. He didn't want to, but he couldn't deny the facts. More and more, he believed a spell had caused the curse. The more Brady spoke of the old *cailleach*, the more sense it made. Of course the woman had wanted to avenge her niece's tragic death. Who could have blamed her for that?

"I do remember bits of the spell, though."

Jarred back to the present, Riley whipped his gaze around to Brady. "You do?"

"Aye." Brady looked up at the sky as if thinking very hard. "The crux of it was that those who were denied their love must wed before all would be well again."

"Whew." Riley rubbed the back of his neck, the tense, rigid cords there. "And how is that supposed to happen after they're all dead and gone?"

Brady's expression grew very solemn. "I have a theory."

"Theory" was the word Katie had used. "I'm listening."

Brady removed his glasses and narrowed his gaze at Riley. "It takes a powerful leap of faith to believe, lad."

Riley smiled, though he felt more like screaming. "I'm Irish, Brady."

"So you are, lad, but some of what I'm about to tell you will be considered blasphemy by Father O'Malley. And, I'm ashamed to say, by your dear mum."

"I suspected that," Riley admitted, deciding he had to trust this old man a bit. "I *need* to learn as much as I can."

Brady met and held his gaze for several seconds, then nodded. "We'd best go to confession after I'm finished. . . ."

"Lass, you look tired," Fiona said as she entered the kitchen on Wednesday morning.

Bridget nodded and yawned, bringing the glass of caffeine-laden soda pop to her lips. "I'm sorry."

Fiona puttered around the kitchen while Bridget sat and stared out the window at *Caisleán Dubh*. Today, the inspector and his crew would come. Once they had his approval, she wouldn't allow Riley to stop her. She'd find a way to convince them all.

"Riley's been lookin' a bit tired, too," Fiona said, joining Bridget at the table with her tea. "Can't imagine what would keep two young, healthy folks awake nights."

Bridget shot her mother-in-law a suspicious glance, but

the woman was sipping her tea in complete innocence. "I think I'm just nervous about the inspection."

"Ah." Fiona nodded. "I've been ponderin' this restaurant idea of yours, and I like it. I really do." She released a long sigh.

"But . . . ?"

Fiona offered a crooked smile and patted Bridget's hand. "Even if it can be restored enough for your restaurant, I'm not convinced it will be safe, Bridget. The curse."

"I have to try, Fiona." She squeezed her eyes closed for several moments. Then she met the older woman's gaze again and said, "The only way to prove to y'all that there is no curse is to use the castle."

Fiona chewed her lower lip thoughtfully. "What if there is a curse, lass?" Her expression and tone were solemn. "What if . . . harm came to someone? What about Jacob?"

"I wouldn't do this if I thought for a moment he was in danger. Besides, just last week Jacob and Riley entered and left the castle without harm." Bridget gripped the cold glass tightly. "It's hard to explain, but I feel sort of a . . . a kinship with the castle."

Fiona chuckled and shook her head. "Are you into this mystical stuff Maggie sometimes talks about?"

Bridget blinked. "Fiona, isn't a curse mystical?"

The older woman gasped. "Jaysus, Mary, and Joseph, but I've never thought of it that way." She looked around guiltily and crossed herself. "I guess you're right about that, lass, though I'm ashamed to admit it."

"I think God will forgive us both." Bridget squeezed her mother-in-law's hand. "I'll fix breakfast."

"No, you won't." Fiona rose and patted Bridget on the shoulder as she passed. "You look asleep on your feet, lass. I'll do it."

Sleepless nights combined with busy days to make Bridget a walking zombie. On those occasions when exhaustion had overtaken her and dragged her to sleep under protest, her dream lover—still faceless—had touched, caressed, kissed, but never satisfied the hunger. She always awakened craving more of his touch. More and more and more.

She couldn't go on like this night after night. At some point, something had to break the cycle. Maybe today's inspection would end it once and for all. Maybe . . .

"I've been meanin' to tell you about my trip," Fiona said over her shoulder.

"Trip?" Bridget turned in her chair to face Fiona.

"Aye. Me mum lives in a retirement home near Galway." Fiona dried her hands and leaned against the counter, facing Bridget. "I go every couple of months, and Maggie always goes along. 'Tis hard for Riley to get away, with the farm and all."

"Yes." Bridget stifled a yawn, trying to pay attention to Fiona. "Someone has to tend the stock."

"Aye." She took a few steps to the stove and stirred a pot, replacing the lid a moment later. "With your permission, lass, I'd like to take Jacob along to meet his great-*mamó*."

Just Jacob? Bridget chewed her lower lip, wondering why she wasn't included in this invitation. She glanced out the window at *Caisleán Dubh*. The thought of traveling far from it just now didn't set well with her. She needed to be here. At least for now.

"Yes, I think Jacob would enjoy it," she finally said.

And she would be left here alone with Riley. . . .

A hot flush crept over her as Fiona prattled on about how pleased she was, and so forth.

Alone with Riley . . .

The subject of her fantasy walked in the back door and washed his hands at the sink. Riley had already been out doing his morning chores, and when he turned toward Bridget, his gaze locked with hers.

Red rimmed both his eyes and dark circles smudged his high cheekbones. He wore a haunted look. A flame flared in the blue depths of his eyes and she amended that thought.

He wore a *hungry* look.

The passion she'd struggled so hard against flickered to life within her and a tremor trickled through her. He licked his lips and took a step toward her.

She licked her lips and waited.

"There you be, Riley," Fiona said, shattering the spell. *Thank God.*

"Mornin', Mum." He visibly reined himself in and kissed his momma's cheek. "Something smells good."

"Black puddin'."

"Ah, that'll stick to a man's ribs."

Bridget made a note to make Riley some kind of black pudding next time she cooked breakfast. She'd never heard of anyone eating chocolate pudding for breakfast before, but chocolate was chocolate, after all. Being black pudding, it would have to be very dark chocolate. *Yum.*

Granny had always said that a good brownie was better than sex. Glancing sideways at Riley, Bridget doubted that.

She was having naughty thoughts again. Riley fixed himself a cup of tea and lingered at the counter. She suspected he didn't want to be near her.

Remembering how much he'd wanted to be near her the other night made her squirm in her chair. Her breasts swelled and her nipples hardened. She didn't need a dream lover to frustrate her. Riley Mulligan did a fine job of it on his own.

Unless he is *my dream lover. . . .*

Her opinion of Riley had softened considerably since Maggie had told her the story of how Patrick Mulligan had died and been found. Plus, Riley adored Jacob. How could a woman not admire a man who was good with children and respectful and loving to his own momma?

And handsome enough to be in one of those cigarette ads, but without the nasty old cigarette. . . . Bridget could just picture Riley and his long, black hair in one of those ads. The wind would blow his hair and the sun would make him squint. Those little crinkles at the corners of his eyes would show.

Her breath snagged in her throat and she coughed.

"Are you all right, lass?" Fiona called over her shoulder. "Be a good lad and fetch her some water, Riley."

Bridget tried to protest, but that just made her cough more. Jacob was out gathering eggs with Maggie, so he couldn't come to her rescue just now.

Maybe that was just as well. As Riley set the glass of water on the table before her, his hand brushed against her and their gazes met. Bridget's pulse leapt into the final round of *Jeopardy*, and the rest of her was ready for *Let's Make a Deal*.

Who'd have ever thought that meek little Bridget would suffer from sexual anxiety? Or was it deprivation? What would Oprah or Rosie have called it? Granny had watched their shows loyally, and she surely would have been able to diagnose Bridget's condition.

Imagining Granny doing such a thing made Bridget giggle. The old woman would have called it what it was. She would have said, "Bridget, go out and get yourself a husband who can scratch that itch of yours."

"What's so funny?" Riley asked, his voice low and husky and *close*.

Bridget choked and reached for her water. She glanced at him as she sipped, which made her gasp and cough yet again.

"Give the lass a pat on the back, Riley," Fiona called.

Bridget's eyes widened, as did his. "No, don't," she whispered. "I don't think I could stand it."

Realization flared in his Mulligan blue eyes and his nostrils flared ever so slightly. Knowing he knew made her want him all the more. Why were they pussyfooting around this? They were both adults. Unmarried.

Definitely *willing*.

Shame oozed through her. There were a million reasons *not* to surrender to her desire for Riley. First and foremost, there was his momma. She looked over her shoulder and thought she saw Fiona wink at her. That must have been her imagination.

Another reason was Culley's memory and the accusations Riley had made when Bridget had first arrived. That thought made her blink and meet his gaze again. Why had he stopped slinging insults and accusations? For that matter, *when* had he stopped?

After that night at the castle. . . .

"Mercy," she said hoarsely, taking another sip of water and looking away from his smoldering eyes.

"At least the sun decided to shine today," Fiona said, carrying plates to the table. She pulled out the chair beside Bridget and told Riley to sit.

His usual place was *across* the table—not beside her. Frowning, she glanced over her shoulder at the woman, who was humming to herself as she carried more platters and bowls to the table.

Looking as confused as Bridget felt, Riley sat.

Why did he have to be so danged big? His muscular thigh brushed against Bridget's and his shoulder was hot against hers. *Mercy.* She reached for the water glass again.

"Fiona, let me help you with—"

"No, you sit." Fiona set a plate in front of Bridget just as the back door swung open, admitting Maggie and Jacob.

"Mornin', Momma." Jacob washed his hands, then bounced over to give her a hug and a kiss on the cheek.

Her son's presence might save her. She started to rise to give him her place, but he'd already plopped into his usual chair on the other side of the table. Maggie took the one normally occupied by Riley.

Just peachy.

Fiona took her seat and said grace, then started passing the bowls. The one containing the black pudding came to Bridget and she stared down at it. She leaned closer and took a sniff. *Definitely not chocolate.*

"It's good, Momma," Jacob said from across the table

as he shoveled eggs and bacon and . . . whatever this stuff was into his mouth.

"Aye, very good," Riley said, his deep voice rumbling through his shoulder and into Bridget's.

"Not everybody likes black puddin', Jacob," Fiona said diplomatically.

Remembering all the dishes Bridget had sprung on this family, she sighed and took a serving of the strange substance. Her instincts told her not to touch it.

Her sense of fairness demanded it.

Besides, concentrating on food instead of on the man beside her might be her salvation.

She tried not to think about the way Riley felt next to her, the way the muscles in his arm rippled when he moved even a little, the way her heart did the limbo with her windpipe when he looked at her from the corner of his eye with that "I want *you* for dessert" expression.

Oh, God. She took another sip of soda pop and started on her eggs. She'd save the black stuff for last, since pudding was a dessert.

Don't think about dessert.

What she wanted for dessert would be rated PG-13— not for a family breakfast. As she chewed, she felt something rub her ankle and gulped. It brushed its way around her ankle again to the inside of her bare foot.

Not wanting to alarm anyone, she glanced discreetly down at her foot, noticing Riley's big boot lying off to one side. His stockinged foot busied itself rubbing hers while his thigh pressed more intimately against her.

The heat of desire wafted through her and Bridget tried not to fidget. How could she make him stop without causing a scene? She hazarded a glance at his profile and found him watching her from the corner of his eye again.

All right, so what she wanted for breakfast would be rated R in American theaters. She pushed food around her plate, trying to ignore the tingling sensations snaking their way up from her foot to the rest of her.

Shamelessly, she lifted her foot just a bit and returned

some of his torture. His breath came out on a hiss as she dragged her big toe sensuously along the cuff of his sock, and found his bare leg.

Yes, skin. That was what she wanted. His skin. Her skin. Theirs. She wanted the full length of his nakedness against hers.

She wanted to feel his sleek muscles rubbing against her softness. She wanted his hot, hot mouth to suckle at her breasts until she couldn't stand it anymore.

She linked her big toes with his, mimicking what she wanted most—their ultimate joining, when he would fill her and make her his. It would be wonderful. Perfect.

Satisfying.

Oh, yes. Satisfaction was what she needed. The endless torture had to end. He slipped his toe between two of hers.

Filling her.

Bridget stiffened, imagining another type of fulfillment. More. So much more. She would scream if she—

"Momma, aren't you gonna taste your puddin'?"

Earth to Bridget. She drew a shaky breath and blinked several times, focusing on her son's sweet face.

Mercy. She'd almost had an orgasm at the breakfast table. A real one—not fake like the noisy one Meg Ryan had performed in *When Harry Met Sally.* Granny had loved that movie, and especially that scene.

Bridget was mortified. At least she was quieter than Meg Ryan. She cleared her throat and withdrew her foot from harm's way.

Oh, Lord. My dessert wish is X-rated, and I'm a bad, bad girl.

Properly chastised, she nodded and took a big bite of the odd pudding.

And froze.

"What . . . *is* . . . this?" she asked around the glob on her tongue.

"Black pudding," Fiona said, confused. "What did you think it was, lass?"

Bridget forced herself to swallow it and drained her

glass to wash it down. "I don't know, but pudding is supposed to be sweet. This is . . ."

"Sweet?" Maggie laughed. "I haven't been able to eat black pudding since I learned what it really is."

Bridget met her sister-in-law's gaze. "And what *is* it?"

"Black pudding is . . ." Maggie wrinkled her nose. "You don't want to know. Just don't eat it."

Fiona chuckled and Jacob looked around the table with confusion. "Is it somethin' bad?" he asked.

"No, lad." Fiona gave Maggie a stern look. "'Tis not bad. Your uncle Riley ate all of his. Look."

"Aye," Riley said, his voice rumbling through Bridget again.

Mercilessly.

He rested his toes near hers and said, "Black pudding will make a man tall, strong, handsome, and . . . virile."

Perfect. Bridget tried to edge away from the man with the talented toes, but he rested his hand on her thigh.

Have mercy. She held her breath.

"What's in it?" Jacob asked again.

"Blood," Riley said.

Bridget bolted for the bathroom.

Sixteen

Riley worked near the stable, watching for the inspector and his crew.

What the devil had come over him this morning?

And why had Mum manipulated him into sitting beside Bridget? He'd seen the twinkle in Fiona Mulligan's eyes. Mum was obviously bent on matchmaking, and that realization left Riley even more confused.

So Mum had noticed the attraction between Riley and Bridget. Had Maggie? Jacob was too young to pay attention to such things. At least, Riley hoped so.

He cleaned tack and rearranged it twice while he contemplated the most unusual—and deliciously stimulating—breakfast he'd ever experienced. A wicked smile tugged at his mouth.

Aye, he'd been near to bursting sitting there beside Bridget. Knowing she wanted him as much as he wanted her had made him lose every bit of sense. The look in her green eyes, the softness of her mouth as she'd licked her lips . . .

He groaned and leaned his head against the saddle. "Get yourself under control, Mulligan," he muttered. This was a big day. The inspection.

Aye, he would concentrate on that. Stepping outside, he gazed toward *Caisleán Dubh* and drew a deep breath. Since his meeting with Brady, he had resigned himself to this. The Mulligans had allowed this wretched curse or spell to rule far too long.

This Mulligan would end it—God help him.

He didn't know how yet, but he sensed it was his duty. His destiny? Aye, even that. There had to be a reason Bridget could hear the whispering. A reason Culley had. A reason Riley could now.

Whatever it was, whatever it would bring, the time had come for the Clan Mulligan to reclaim *Caisleán Dubh.*

He watched the truck stop near the castle, while a small car continued on toward the cottage. "Well, then. 'Tis time." He put away his tools and tried to ignore the whispering that greeted him as he started across the meadow toward *Caisleán Dubh.* Toward fate.

Let's not be getting dramatic about it now.

He kept a steady pace, suspecting Bridget would ride out to the castle with the inspector. *Oh, Da.* He sighed, but his step never faltered. *Tell me I'm doing the right thing. Tell me this isn't the biggest mistake of my life.*

A gentle breeze wafted in off the ocean and a dove came with it, sailing over Riley, then back toward *Caisleán Dubh.* A sign? Did Riley believe in such nonsense?

At this point, he'd believe almost anything. After all, he'd spent all his life believing in a curse, only to learn it could be a spell instead. Either way, it would end. He would see to it.

Brady was in Kilmurray looking for duplicates of missing parish records. At one time, the only priest in the area had been in Kilmurray. Brady was confident of finding at least some of the missing pieces of this very bizarre puzzle he'd uncovered. Once Riley had all the facts, he would share them with his family. Eventually.

First, he had to come to terms with his raging desire for Bridget. At least he'd stopped denying it to himself. Even more significant was the fact that he no longer believed his craving for Bridget was all curse-induced. No, his ache for her was about flesh and blood—man and woman. All right, so he had to allow there could be more to it, but still . . . it was *Bridget* he wanted.

Would he have wanted her if she'd come home on Culley's arm as his bride?

Now *there* was a question Riley didn't want to answer—not now or ever. Nor did it matter, since Culley was gone. "Boyo, you had good taste in women. Except for Katie," he added, shaking his head.

Enough about that. Riley lengthened his stride as he heard the small car returning from the cottage. After greeting the architects and inspectors milling about the massive doors waiting for their boss, he turned to watch the small, blue car roll to a stop beside the castle.

Bridget climbed out of the passenger side, but there was no sign of Mum. He was glad of that. *Caisleán Dubh* always upset her. Mum must have kept Jacob at home. For that, Riley was doubly glad.

Bridget approached him with a tentative step and a nervous expression. Since he'd practically seduced her at breakfast, he could easily imagine why she was tentative. He'd been a boor, then a brute, and now . . .

What, Mulligan? What do you want to be?

Lover. Aye, her lover.

He wanted to spread her out like a fine delicacy and savor every inch—

"Mr. Mulligan, I'm Brian Kelley from the Irish Trust."

The tall, thin man with a head full of wild red curls thrust his hand out and Riley shook it, struggling to control his lust for Bridget.

"Thank you for coming so soon," Bridget said.

"*Caisleán Dubh* is a site we've longed to explore. This is a treat." Smiling, he turned to face the tower. "My crew is ready when you are. Are you both very sure you want to be present during the inspection? It could be dangerous, depending on what we find."

Bridget's breath came out in a whoosh, and she said, "Yes, please." She looked at Riley and waited for him to say something. Anything.

Finally, he grunted and gave a curt nod. "Let's do it," he said, holding her gaze. "Then . . . we'll see."

Was that promise Bridget saw in his eyes? What had changed?

Everything.

They had silently acknowledged their mutual attraction—right or wrong—and now they were going *together* with the inspection team.

You're a glutton for punishment. That was what Granny would have said. Not that the time Bridget had spent in Riley's arms was punishment. On the contrary—those brief moments had been breathtaking. Unforgettable. Her cheeks warmed.

She looked up at him, reminding herself of what it must have been like to have been the little boy who had found his daddy inside this castle. Her knees felt like uncooked sausage that would collapse at any moment. She drew a deep breath and squared her shoulders.

This is what you wanted, Bridget. The inspection.

But be careful what you wish for.

For once, she wished she could silence her memories of Granny's endless clichés—wise or not. Right and wrong didn't matter when faced with destiny.

Yes, destiny. Crazy or not, Bridget knew she was facing just that with *Caisleán Dubh.*

And Riley.

After his game of footsie at breakfast, she could barely face him. What had come over the man? *Don't think about that now. Think about the inspection. About the castle. About Mulligan Stew.*

She faced the doors, relishing the wash of welcoming whispers that sighed over her. Yes, this was right.

Was she more nervous about being near Riley inside the castle again, or about the inspection itself? One thing was for danged certain—she would *not* touch that banister again. Remembering her crazed reaction to it, she wondered how she could avoid ever touching it again after she opened Mulligan Stew and worked there every day.

"Mr. Mulligan, why don't you and your wife wait over here until we get the doors open?"

Bridget's sharp gasp drew Riley's gaze. She didn't find the accusation and suspicion that she'd expected there. Instead, his blue eyes reflected confusion and the heat of desire. Well, Riley and Bridget were both feeling that, and neither of them bothered to correct Mr. Kelley.

Warmth insinuated itself between her legs and spread from there. The sight of him at this castle made her ache all over again. Yes, craving was the perfect word to describe what she felt for Riley.

"My crew will go in first with an industrial vacuum that will remove enough dust to allow us to examine surfaces more thoroughly," Mr. Kelley said, withdrawing a notepad and pencil, and jarring Bridget back to the present. He handed hard hats to both Riley and Bridget, and donned one himself. His wild hair poked out from beneath the sides and back. "We'll follow a few minutes later."

Riley grunted acknowledgment and Bridget merely nodded. Their lack of outward enthusiasm must have confused Mr. Kelley. Considering how important this day was to Bridget, she should have been jumping up and down with anticipation.

Oh, she was jumping up and down on the inside. With total confusion. How could she want Riley so much and not . . . love him? She'd loved Culley with all her heart, so the wanting had come naturally. In fact, Culley and Riley were the only men who had ever aroused her sexually.

Did that mean . . . ?

No. She couldn't be in love with Riley. The thought made her mouth go dry and her hands tremble as she watched the crew use crowbars to pry open the massive double doors. The iron hinges groaned and squeaked in protest, and Mr. Kelley jotted down some notes.

Her future was at stake, and maybe Jacob's as well. She needed money and some security, though at least her fear that Riley might steal her son had eased. Still, she was a single mother with a child to raise and no income. Even with the family farm, which Fiona insisted was part hers and Jacob's, Bridget still needed to pull her own weight.

She'd worked hard her whole life and it felt strange not to have a job to go to each day, and money of her own to spend on Jacob's new shoes. She loved keeping house alongside Fiona, but it just wasn't the same. Mulligan Stew would belong to *Bridget*. At least, for the most part. . . .

Besides, she needed this for herself. Not just the money, but the feeling of self-worth and accomplishment it could bring. She'd also learned through the years that independence was a very good thing. She didn't want to be beholden to the Mulligans or anyone.

Squaring her shoulders, she focused on that and forced thoughts of Riley and sex and love far to the back of her mind. She hoped.

Love. Forget that, Bridget. Just forget it. So she lied to herself and concentrated on the present. This was her castle. Her future. She smiled as the men filed inside with ladders and flashlights, ropes and various tools. The sound of the vacuum Mr. Kelley had mentioned roared to life, echoing from inside.

After what seemed like an hour, the noise ceased.

"Shall we?" Mr. Kelley asked, indicating that they could enter through the open doors.

Riley stood frozen, staring at the gaping chasm. Bridget sensed his fear and touched his arm. Touching him felt so good. So right. She had to fight against the urge to put her arms around him and pull him to her.

"It's all right, Riley," she said quietly. Mr. Kelley had gone on ahead. "Let's go."

He met her gaze and she saw his Adam's apple work up and down the length of his throat. Finally, he nodded and took a few steps toward the entrance. He stopped partway and looked over his shoulder, holding his hand out toward her.

Bridget's heart skipped a beat and she couldn't breathe, let alone walk, for several seconds. Wrestling her resolve into place, she joined Riley and slipped her small hand into his large one. She met his gaze and found intensity, heat, and confusion waging a fierce battle there as they must have been in her own eyes.

"Promise me something," she said, her voice shaky.

"What?"

"Don't touch anything while you're touching me."

He gave her a cock-eyed grin and a nod, but his eyes told her that he remembered every delicious and terrifying detail of what had transpired—and almost transpired—between them the other evening.

"We're standing on part of it now, Bridget," he reminded her, glancing down at their joined hands. "And I'm touching you."

Touching him—especially here—was dangerous. But it also seemed right. She drew comfort from the feel of his strong hand holding hers as they took a few more steps and entered *Caisleán Dubh*.

Like a song, the whispers swirled around them. They both stood still as the castle serenaded them. Welcomed them.

"Like a bloody doorbell," Riley whispered.

Confused, Bridget shook her head, then realized what he'd meant and laughed. Her laughter sounded nervous, but that made perfect sense, too. She met his gaze again and his crooked smile gave him a softer, more youthful appearance than the scowl he usually wore. His smile crawled inside her and lit a steady warm glow in her heart, far different from the fiery longing in her loins.

Mr. Kelley was talking and taking notes. "I suppose we should pay attention," Riley murmured.

Oh, she *was* paying attention, but to Riley. To how much he'd changed. Why?

"Don't you . . ." She bit her lower lip as Riley paused and leaned his head closer to hear her. "Don't you believe in the curse anymore?"

He stared at her for several silent seconds. "Aye. Or something."

Now *that* was definitely different.

"Let's have a look around now that there's some light," he said, surprising her again.

Bridget blinked and turned her attention to the main chamber she'd visited twice before, but in darkness. Sea air poured in from behind them, filling the room with its freshness. Dust motes danced in the daylight flooding the dark, once-forbidden room.

Mr. Kelley had paused several feet in front of them, and had his flashlight aimed at the huge portrait over the massive hearth. "There be magic here," the inspector said with complete sincerity.

"Aye," Riley said reverently.

"Oh, yes," Bridget agreed, amazed that Riley had agreed with Mr. Kelley. "There's magic here." She looked at Riley again. "Or something."

Just don't touch the doggoned banister.

Mr. Kelley followed his men around, taking notes and measurements, and giving orders. He was a man who was passionate about his work. That became increasingly evident by how careful and insistent he was to leave everything as they'd found it. Only the dust and the bats were disturbed, and the latter sought refuge high in the dark tower, away from the sunlight flooding the main chamber.

"It's . . . it's beautiful." Bridget paused before the hearth, again drawn to the portrait. Mr. Kelley had moved to the back of the chamber with his crew. Gazing up at the painting, she asked, "Who is he?"

Riley released her hand and stepped onto the hearth to examine the massive portrait more closely. "Aye, as I suspected," he said after wiping dust away from an engraved plate on the bottom center of the frame. "'Tis himself—Aidan Mulligan."

Aidan. Bridget remembered the story Maggie had told her. "The curse started with him," she said.

Riley looked at her sharply, his brows drawn together. "How would you be knowing that?"

"Uh . . ." Bridget lifted one shoulder. "Maggie told me, because I asked."

"Aye, she knows the tale, as all Mulligans do." He stood back and rubbed his chin, turning to admire the portrait again. "Who knows? Maybe the story will change before it's passed on to young Jacob."

Bridget's heart flip-flopped. Something had *definitely* changed. Something significant. Big. She swallowed hard, vowing to restrain her urge to ask him outright. Their relationship had been hostile at first, then barely polite, and now . . .

Almost friendly.

Well, except for them having the hots for each other. That was more than friendly. Much more . . .

Bridget's face flooded with liquid fire and she turned her attention back to Aidan's portrait. She barely made out his features through centuries of grime. "I wonder if it can be restored, too?"

"The portrait?" Riley stared up at his ancestor, his expression unfathomable. "We'll see."

At least he wasn't outright denying her the chance. She had hope. Mulligan Stew could become a reality yet. Hope insinuated itself in her heart and stayed there.

"I'd like to follow Mr. Kelley and his crew into the other rooms," she said, almost as a question. She didn't want to anger Riley now—not while she was so close. However, she would go with or without his permission.

"Aye." He sighed. "We're here, so we might as well see what we can."

The castle's whispering faded and increased haphazardly. The only times Bridget was certain it always grew louder were when she and Riley had first entered the castle, while they were near the portrait of Aidan Mulligan, and—especially—near the banister. Other times, it seemed to come and go.

"The structure seems sound," Riley admitted. "And solid."

"Oh, yes." Anticipation buzzed through her. The castle was even more perfect for her plans than she'd hoped. She heard the crew shouting information and measurements to Mr. Kelley. She no longer felt the need to shadow the crew. She knew *Caisleán Dubh* would pass its inspection.

"Tell me, Bridget," Riley said as they made their way toward the back of the main room, "how do you envision using this particular room?"

She bit her lower lip, afraid to think in much detail, but unable to prevent it. "At first, as a great dining room. The floor is marble, I think."

"Aye." Riley brushed some dust aside with his boot. "White, once upon a time. And I believe the columns are all marble, too."

"Picture it with massive tables, and vines growing around the columns. Very romantic." Bridget saw it all so clearly. "The tables will be of dark, gleaming wood. I'll use brocaded table runners to complement the heavy drapers that will hang at the tall, arched windows." She walked over to one of the windows, amazed to find it unbroken. Unfortunately, the same could not be said of them all.

She looked out at the sea, sparkling below the cliff. "On second thought, no curtains. None at all. And everything should be light, except the wood. Lace. I see lace. Irish lace, I think."

She felt Riley come up behind her, his warmth radiating through her and producing a shiver of anticipation. An image flashed through her mind unbidden. She saw herself standing before this very window with her dream lover at her back, his arms wrapped around her waist. She wore a thin white nightgown, and he wore . . . the usual.

"Oh, have mercy." She could almost feel his arms

around her waist now, but when she glanced down, there were no masculine hands splayed intimately across her abdomen just beneath her breasts.

She didn't want her dream lover's hands now.

She wanted Riley's.

A wave of dizziness washed over her and she dragged in a great breath of air and spun around. Riley stood so close she bumped against him, and she saw desire smoldering in his eyes again. Had he shared the thoughts she'd just experienced? Had he seen—and felt—as she had?

The thought took root and wouldn't budge, though she wasn't about to ask him if it was true. Not now.

"I'll need a kitchen," she whispered. "Maybe that room yonder, where Mr. Kelley's crew is working now."

"Let's go have a look."

Bridget walked alongside Riley, past the hearth and Aidan's portrait, past the staircase and that dangerous banister. She struggled against the urge to reach for his hand every step of the way. Despite that, it felt perfect to stroll across this massive room at his side.

Other images of being in her dream lover's arms flitted mercilessly across her mind as she passed through certain areas or pieces of furniture. A large window seat near the back of the room brought a particularly powerful jolt to her and she almost stumbled.

Her dream lover sat there, leaning against the window frame, with her astride him. They were both naked as he devoured her breasts. His erection brushed against her nakedness, seeking entrance.

Entrance she wanted more than anything to grant.

She tripped again and Riley reached out to grab her arm, steadying her. "Are you all right?" he asked quietly, his voice huskier than usual.

As she nodded and gazed into his eyes, she saw the truth she'd known yet had fought to deny.

Riley *was* her dream lover.

• • •

Several times as they drifted along behind the inspection team, Riley was assaulted by a powerful sense of déjà vu. Though he'd never ventured any farther into the castle than the main chamber, it all seemed familiar. He even recognized alcoves and carvings.

Was Brady's theory true? Was *he* Aidan? He glanced askance at Bridget. Or Bronagh . . . ?

Jaysus. Riley could no longer deny the possibility, though he certainly tried. As they passed by the window near the doorway to the room Bridget wanted to use as a kitchen, an image struck that nearly felled him on the spot. He saw himself there with a beautiful, naked woman. Her slender back was to him, and her hair tumbled about her shoulders in shining brown waves. She straddled him.

Jaysus, Mary, and Joseph!

His breath came in short, rapid pants and he actually felt her moist heat sliding against him. Teasing. Promising. Her breasts filled his hands and he sampled them with gusto. She was sweet. So sweet . . .

"Riley?" Bridget asked, touching his arm.

He jerked, forcing himself to focus on her face. On the present. On reality.

"I . . ." He adjusted the hard hat and cleared his throat, trying to ignore his sudden and powerful erection. *Shite.* He'd been hard more in the past few weeks than he had in his entire life.

And the cause of most of his pain stood right before him, an expression of concern in her dewy green eyes. Her moist lips were slightly parted, and the urge to pull her against him and cover her mouth nearly made him do so before he drew his next breath.

Down, Mulligan. Easy.

"Let's go see this room." She walked away from him.

Riley stood frozen, admiring the way her soft, familiar brown hair swept her shoulders. She wore a blue knit shirt tucked into her jeans, and her shoulders tapered neatly to her tiny waist.

Just like his dream woman. . . .

"Riley?" She stopped at the entrance to the other room and waited.

He shook himself and released his breath in a loud whoosh. With hurried steps, he passed the window seat and joined her beneath the archway.

Her expression as she gazed up at him stole his breath. She had a question in her eyes, and he sensed there was something she wanted to say or ask, but didn't.

"Interesting . . . window seat," she murmured, a strained quality to her voice.

He cleared his throat again. "Aye, you could say that."

Had she seen it? Felt it? Been there with him . . . ?

Oh, Brady—find the answers, man. His old teacher had planted the seeds to this madness, and Riley was suffering the consequences.

"Let's go on," he said, touching the small of her back to guide her into the other room.

He wanted to do so much more—to drag her hard against him, to taste every inch of her.

Stop that now.

The crew had opened the shutters covering the massive windows. The ceiling was lower in this room, but it all seemed solid and safe.

Mr. Kelley beamed as he joined them. "Isn't it amazing?" He shook his head, staring up at the ceiling and the massive columns. "I've never visited a site that's been vacant so long and is this well-preserved."

"Aye, it seems sound enough," Riley said, his heart slamming against his ribs.

"With electricity, cupboards, a stove here, a freezer and refrigerator there, it will be perfect," Bridget said, turning in a complete circle as she spoke. "My kitchen."

Mr. Kelley said, "The Irish Trust has grant monies available for certain types of renovation."

Bridget's eyes grew round. "Really?"

Riley kept his gob shut, though the part of him that had bullied everybody about staying out of *Caisleán Dubh* wanted to surface again with a vengeance. He had to get his mind around this entire notion of allowing Bridget to actually open and use the place.

But was it his right to forbid it? Somehow, the situation—the castle's future—seemed much bigger, much more important than either Riley or Bridget.

"What are your plans, Mrs. Mulligan?" Mr. Kelley asked.

"At first, I want to open a restaurant," Bridget explained. "Later, if the entire castle is found habitable, I'd like to open a bed-and-breakfast."

Mr. Kelley nodded, and made more notes. "As long as a historic site is open to the public at least thirty days each year—"

"Oh, I'm thinking more like five or six days a week," Bridget said, laughing.

"Good. In that case, there might very well be a way to renovate *Caisleán Dubh* through a grant."

"A grant? Oh, did you hear him, Riley?" Bridget clasped her hands together, but released them just as quickly to grab Riley by the shoulders and jump up and down a wee bit. "A grant."

Riley was rotten. While she jumped up and down with excitement about her restaurant, all he could do was stare at her nice, round breasts. The knit shirt boasted a University of Tennessee logo, but the pattern couldn't hide her taut nipples from his roving eyes.

Aye, you're rotten to the core, Mulligan.

"I have some information with me," Mr. Kelley said, interrupting Riley's musings. "I'll leave it and the applications with you."

"Thank you." Bridget released Riley and hugged Mr. Kelley.

Jealousy exploded through Riley, but he clenched his fists to prevent his urge to physically drag Bridget away from the man. She was just showing her gratitude, after all.

Couldn't he do with a bit more of her gratitude him-self?

They made their way back out to the main chamber and examined the other ground-floor rooms. Mr. Kelley for-bade them to accompany his crew up the stairs and into the tower. Amazingly, Bridget didn't argue with the man.

As they waited in the main chamber, Bridget went through more of her thoughts on renovation, and how the restaurant would look. Suddenly, she stopped and a look of tenderness filled her eyes.

"What is it?" he asked. "What's wrong?"

"I was just remembering what Maggie told me." She bit her lower lip. "I've been so excited and carrying on, that I forgot what you must be going through."

"Maggie *didn't.*" He dragged his fingers through his hair and squeezed his eyes closed, vowing not to kill his sister, no matter how much he wanted to do just that. Re-opening his eyes, he said, "I'd rather not talk about it."

She shook her head. "Sometimes a body has to talk about it, Riley."

"Not about this. Not now."

"All right, if not now, then when?" Bridget folded her arms and struck a challenging pose with her head tilted and her eyes blazing. "When, Riley?"

He swallowed hard, knowing the mental vault sealing his memories had already crumbled away too much. "I . . . I can't, Bridget." He rubbed the back of his neck, sud-denly remembering that dark day. His da's body stretched out right in the middle of this very room.

He couldn't draw a decent breath for several seconds, and the urge to run away clamored through him. "I just can't. Please, just don't."

She touched him again, and this time he *did* pull her against him. Hard. He kissed her mercilessly, tilting her head back and holding her with his fingers buried in her luxurious hair. Her hard hat fell to the marble floor, its sound echoing through the massive hall.

Their hearts thrummed together as one as their tongues

parried and withdrew, each seeking to drive the other mad with the lust licking through them.

He dragged his mouth away from hers, his breathing ragged in the dust-laden air. "I want you, Bridget," he whispered. "I want you naked. Now."

Bridget gazed up at him, her lips swollen from his kiss, her eyes snapping green flames of raw need. "I know."

He cupped her breast, brushing her nipple with his thumb, and she pressed her hips more firmly against his throbbing erection. Mingled with her passion, he also saw fear in her eyes, and he dropped his hand to her waist. She was as confused by all this as he.

Besides, he needed answers to all the mysteries of *Caisleán Dubh* before he could satisfy himself that some supernatural force wasn't pushing them toward what they both seemed to want so desperately.

But it *would* happen. He knew that without a question. He simply didn't know when.

A shudder rippled through him, and he whispered, "Soon, Bronagh."

Seventeen

Whoa! That was some kiss. Bridget stared up at Riley, still tingling all over from the kiss that could have performed a tonsillectomy. Awash with the afterglow and the desire for more, she started to reach for him again when he said that name.

"Soon, Bronagh."

Stunned, she pulled away and stared at him for several seconds while his internal battle played itself through in the depths of his eyes. For a few, fleeting moments, he had left her. Where had he gone?

And, more importantly, who in tarnation was Bronagh?

"You called me Bronagh again," she said, drawing strength from anywhere she could find it. She lifted her chin and waited for him to return to reality from wherever he'd gone. "Why did you call me Bronagh? Who was Bronagh?"

Riley frowned, drawing his brows together and shaking his head. He reached up to remove his hard hat, raking his fingers through his hair before replacing the helmet. "What?"

"Don't you know what you did?" Dear Lord, didn't he remember that humdinger of a smooch? She winced, hoping he hadn't kissed her without knowing why. Hoping he hadn't been kissing someone named Bronagh in his mind. "And what you said . . . ?"

"I kissed you, and you kissed me back." He cleared his throat. "I definitely remember *that.*" One corner of his mouth slanted upward.

"Yes, you did." Relief swept through her and she sighed. "And you said 'Bronagh' again."

He stroked his chin thoughtfully. "Did I say anything else?" He bent down to retrieve her hard hat and handed it to her.

"You don't remember?"

He clenched his jaw so tightly a muscle twitched in his cheek. "Do *you* remember taking off your clo—"

"No. I don't." Bridget looked around to ensure they were still alone. "Okay. So you're saying something . . . happened to you?"

"Something."

"That seems to be the word of the day." Bridget rolled her eyes and flashed him a grin that actually made him grin in return. Mercy, but she loved the man's smile. It sort of made her insides feel like they were filled with warm, peppery red-eye gravy. "You did say other things."

"What?" Concern etched itself across his handsome face.

She drew a deep breath and held his gaze, though she wanted to jump his bones. "You said, 'I want you,' and something about . . . naked."

Lust flared in his eyes again and he nodded. "Well, I *do* want you—preferably naked." He grinned again, but this one was devilish and filled with both threats and promises. "I don't think that's much of a secret anymore."

A volcano erupted inside Bridget. "Have mercy."

"*No* mercy." He reached out and stroked her cheek with the backs of his fingers. "I want you, Bridget, and you want me. There's no sense denying it."

"I . . . I reckon there's no sense in doing anything about

it, either." She bit her lower lip and looked away, but he cupped her chin in his hand and tilted her face upward.

"Look at me."

She blinked and brought her gaze back to his. What she found in the depths of his eyes ripped away every shred of reserve and made her want to tear off her clothes along with it. She wanted to throw herself wantonly at his feet and beg him to take her.

Now. Hard. Fast.

"There are things going on here we don't understand." He looked around the chamber, then back to her. "Yet."

Bridget nodded, pinned by his probing gaze.

"Like why I've called you Bronagh here more than once."

"It *is* a name," she said. "I just knew it. A woman named Sorrow."

Riley arched a brow, obviously surprised by her knowledge. "Maggie again?"

"Yes." Bridget drew a shaky breath. "And she also told me what happened to your daddy, because I asked. Don't be angry with her."

Riley's swift indrawn breath sounded like the recoil of someone who'd been stabbed. Guilt niggled at her, but she gathered her resolve and squared her shoulders.

"You can't go on the rest of your life pretending it didn't happen," she said firmly, though not unkindly. Granny had always said the best way to handle upsetting things was to just get it all out before it festered into an infection. Riley was way past that. "And you can't be positive your daddy didn't die just because it was his time."

Riley's scowl returned, but it was directed beyond Bridget—at something or someone only he could see. "I don't know. I just don't know."

Bridget shook her head, wanting desperately to help Riley heal. The little boy who'd been hurt so long ago needed to face this before the grown Riley could recover. She understood this so clearly it astounded her.

He would have to talk it through, and, sadly, relive that

dreadful day. That was the only way to put it in the past where it belonged—not his memories of his father, but of the man's tragic death.

What better way to do that than for Bridget to prove that the curse didn't exist? Yes, there was some kind of power or magic here, but she refused to believe it was evil. Empowered, she smiled and cupped Riley's cheek in her hand, brushing the pad of her thumb gently along the lower curve of the dark circles under his eyes.

Caisleán Dubh's whispering encircled them, seeming to urge Bridget to go farther, touch more, take more. Oh, she wanted to, but now wasn't the time. However, for the first time, she believed there might actually be a time for them to follow passion's lead. Someday.

Soon, Bronagh, he'd said.

There was a reason he'd called her by that name. The only way to find out was to learn who Bronagh was. Or had been . . . Bridget didn't believe in ghosts. But she believed in spirits, after a fashion. She'd gone to a couple of séances with Granny at Widow Harbaugh's farm back in Tennessee. The widow had summoned her late husband's spirit, then she'd proceeded to give him what-for about something he'd hidden before he died.

Bridget hadn't heard the old man talk to his widow, but the woman sure as heck had believed it. After she'd come out of the weird trance where she'd ranted and raved at her dead husband, Mrs. Harbaugh simply rose and walked to a bookcase where she opened an old Bible to a particular chapter and verse. Right there, she found the deed she'd accused her dead husband of hiding.

The other women had called it "amazing" or the "work of the Lord." Granny had called it "horse puckey," but Bridget didn't think so. She tended to agree with those who'd called it amazing. Of course, she'd only been about ten years old at the time.

"Well, I think we've seen enough," Mr. Kelley said as he and his crew came down the staircase.

Bridget dropped her hand to her side and paid particu-

lar attention to the man directly behind Mr. Kelley. He
trailed his hand along the banister all the way down. He
seemed fine. Whatever power lurked in that banister was
apparently reserved just for Bridget.

Lucky me.

"What's up there?" she asked, forcing her attention
back to the castle.

"Bedchambers on the next level, which is unusual, but
we've already seen that *Caisleán Dubh* is one of a kind."

Bedchambers. Bridget swallowed hard, remembering
her dreams.

"Higher in the tower, there are other bedchambers, sitting rooms, and places where they kept watch and even
shot arrows during times of war."

"Ireland has seen more than its share of that," Riley
said on a sigh.

"Aye." Mr. Kelley looked around the main hall again.

"And what do you think of *Caisleán Dubh* now?"
Riley asked, turning his attention to the inspector. "Is this
pile of rocks ready for demolition?"

"Hardly." Mr. Kelley seemed offended.

So was Bridget. Clenching her teeth, she prepared to
lambast Riley.

"Mr. Mulligan, *Caisleán Dubh* is a treasure." Mr. Kelley adjusted his glasses again and brushed dust off his
jacket. "Aye, it's definitely worthy of restoration and reg-
istration as an Irish historic landmark. And, I believe, for
a grant from the Irish Trust."

Bridget's heart sang. She grabbed Riley's hand and
made a sound that closely resembled a squeal of delight.
She didn't care that her behavior might seem childish.
This was just the news she'd wanted to hear.

"Mrs. Mulligan seems to understand the significance
of our findings."

"Aye. Bridget understands." Riley sighed and folded
his arms across his abdomen. "As do I."

Bridget mouthed a yes and crossed her fingers. The
men filed out with plans to have food and a pint or two at

Gilhooley's, leaving their boss behind to go over their findings with the Mulligans. Bridget invited Mr. Kelley up to the cottage for a late lunch.

She *would* have her restaurant, and if the grants Mr. Kelley had mentioned came through, she wouldn't have to beg or borrow to do it. She wanted to start *now*, but of course the construction would have to be done first.

Best of all, Riley was coming out of the shell he'd built around his heart all those years ago. He wasn't ready to admit it, but Bridget sensed it. He'd withdrawn again momentarily, but he would come around.

And she would find out who the devil Bronagh was, so she could decide how to deal with her dream lover.

Awake and asleep.

Riley climbed the stairs to his bedroom, so exhausted he could barely breathe. The decision had been made after hours of family discussion.

Hadn't he shocked them all by siding with Bridget? Jaysus, but no one was more shocked than he.

It was time. Past time. The Mulligans would reclaim *Caisleán Dubh*—their ancestral home. Their heritage. Jacob's birthright.

Aye, Bridget would have her Mulligan Stew—and hadn't they all been surprised by the name she'd chosen for her restaurant? Mr. Kelley had assured her the grants would be forthcoming, and the construction necessary to make the main level useable would be completed this summer. Reinforcements on the tower would commence simultaneously for safety's sake. By fall, she could open her restaurant.

Riley was running out of time. He could have stopped everything with one word, but he hadn't. He'd allowed the plans to commence, and now he had a curse to end or a mysterious spell to break.

He would see Brady tomorrow and learn what the old man had discovered in Kilmurray. The truth was all Riley

asked for. Nothing more. How could the spell—if there
was one—be broken? What was Bronagh's last name?

And *why* did Riley keep calling Bridget by that name?

Sleep, Mulligan. He was off his nut from lack of it.
Tonight, he would surrender to Morpheus. He managed to
miss the low beam on the stairs, for once, and staggered
into his room. He stripped to the skin and climbed beneath
the quilt.

Let the bloody dreams come. He was too tired to fight.
Too tired. . . .

*She came to him again, as he'd known she would. She
sneaked into his bedchamber and slid the bolt into place.
He watched through veiled lashes as she slipped off her
robe and left it in a puddle at her feet. Slowly, purpose-
fully, she walked toward him.*

*Her breasts were high and full, their tips drawn to tight
peaks to tempt a man. Her waist was slight enough for
him to encircle with his hands, flaring to nicely rounded
hips. His gaze rested at the dark, curling hair between her
creamy thighs, and he sighed.*

*He would keep her here in his bed until dawn, and she
would give him more than he'd ever dreamed. How could
he have known how much he would grow to love her? If
only he could make his da understand.*

*But he was promised to another. Bronagh knew the
truth, yet she still loved him. Still gave him her heart and
her body. He would marry a woman of his da's choosing.
Their families' lands would be joined from their union.
But his heart would forever belong to the woman who now
offered herself to him so sweetly. So completely.*

*He shoved back the covers and she slid in beside him,
her skin cool against his warmth. Without words, she covered his mouth with hers, burying her slender fingers in
his hair, pressing her silken flesh against his length. How
could a man want so much and not perish?*

And how could he turn her away to marry another?

"Bronagh," he whispered as she kissed her way down

his abdomen to the part of him that throbbed with a longing only she could fulfill. She took him with her mouth, making him shudder beneath her.

She reached between his legs, cupped him, and he groaned. A moment, later, he grabbed her forearms and pulled her away before he exploded too soon. He wanted to be deep inside her when that happened. He wanted to feel her tiny body stretch to take his. He wanted to make her beg for her own release, as she made him beg now.

She hovered over him and he filled his hands with her breasts, laving them with his tongue, savoring her unique flavor. He had never wanted a woman more—never loved a woman as he loved her. Aye, love. And he would soon be trapped in a loveless marriage. Bronagh would be lost to him forever.

He could ask her to be his mistress, but it seemed so wrong. She was so much more to him than that. For them, it had to be everything or nothing.

He banished the sadness and thought only of this night and the time they had left to them. She teased his engorged body with the hot, slick folds of her womanhood. Taking the tip of him inside her, she leaned forward to tempt his lips with her breasts. She'd been an innocent the first time they'd come together, but now she was a woman who knew how to please and be pleased.

He took her nipple into his mouth and drew deeply, arching his hips toward heaven.

Riley tore the quilt off his bed and growled. He'd dreamed of Aidan—that had to be it. It must have been from seeing the man's portrait today. It couldn't be anything else. Could it?

"Shite." He bolted out of bed and drained his water glass. The clock told him he'd been asleep for hours, so at least he'd slept some.

He glanced down at his erection. Well, some of him had rested.

He paced the room, knowing he would get no more rest this night. After pulling on his clothes, he slipped down the back steps and out the door. A fine mist fell, cooling his burning skin within seconds.

He'd likely catch a chill, but if it cooled him off a bit, it would be well worth it. Without thinking about his destination, he walked across the meadow. *Oíche* nickered as he passed the stable, but Riley kept going.

No moon lit the night—only clouds and mist and fog. The top of the tower was lost in the swirling dampness, but he didn't need to see it to find it.

Tomorrow, he would call on Brady. He would have his answers or lose what remained of his sanity. All his life, he'd lived on this farm without ever believing the curse of *Caisleán Dubh* was anything more or less than what his da had told him. Of course, his da had learned what his da and those who'd come before them all had shared. But the Mulligans had told only their side of the story, as Brady claimed. Bronagh's story brought another dimension to the tale.

And, perhaps, it brought hope.

Riley felt it in his gut—the shift to his thinking, his beliefs. He walked around the castle to the entrance and shoved his hands into his pockets. His hair and clothes were damp and he shivered. The night was cool for June.

The whispering circled him and he drew a deep breath. If only the castle could talk—what a tale it would tell. He shoved his fingers through his hair, feeling like a caged beast seeking freedom. *Aye, a horny one.*

He almost laughed at himself but couldn't. All he could do was pace and stare. And listen. "Talk to me," he whispered. "Tell me your bloody secrets. *Tell me.*"

But the whispering remained unintelligible. With a sigh, Riley approached the opening beside the double doors. The urge to enter the castle burned within him, but he froze, staring into the blackness as he had the day his da had died.

He would never forget, though he'd tried. Jaysus, how

he'd tried. Riley drew a deep breath and knew what he had to do.

He opened the vault door and set the past free.

"Da," he'd called, his small body trembling. He'd never ventured this close to *Caisleán Dubh*. The curse was a bad thing. A frightening thing.

Why had Da entered the forbidden castle?

Riley called again, hearing his own small voice echo back to him in desperation. "Where are you, Da?"

He heard nothing but the surf pounding the cliffs below. No sound came from inside, though he'd *seen* his da enter *Caisleán Dubh* with his own two eyes.

After several minutes of waiting, Riley squeezed his eyes closed in prayer. He had to disobey his da's orders never to set foot inside the castle. He had no choice.

"Da?" he tried once more, and heard no reply.

Holding his breath, he slid through the wide gap easily and stood within the forbidden tomblike structure. His heart battered his rib cage as if seeking freedom, and his knees quaked. "Da?"

The only light filtered in around the shuttered windows and through the opening at his back. The tower was sealed, allowing no light to filter down from there. All Riley could do was search this main room as best he could. If he didn't find Da, he'd have to go for help.

Fear clawed at him as he remembered the countless stories of Mulligan tragedies he'd been told since birth. Centuries of Mulligans had died, been maimed, had watched their loved ones die. One after another after another. Only after the family moved into the cottage did the tragedies cease. Hadn't Riley's own family been blessed with joy?

"Da?" He walked slowly across the blackness, scanning the floor for anything he might fall into or trip over. His eyes slowly adjusted to the darkness, and he made out large shapes. A staircase in the corner wound its way up into the castle.

He shuddered, praying his da hadn't gone up there. The

maiden had flung herself from the top of the tower. That was the tragedy that had started the curse. At least, that's what they'd told him, and being a good lad, Riley believed everything his da said.

Why had Da entered the cursed castle? Why?

"Da, it's Riley," he said. "I've come to fetch you home now."

Silence.

Riley's eyes burned, but he scrubbed them furiously. He wouldn't cry. Culley could cry, being younger than Riley, and Maggie cried all the time. Of course, she was a baby who still wore nappies.

As the eldest, it was Riley's duty to find his da. He squared his shoulders and made a circle about the entire room, then again. He slowly made his circle smaller, venturing toward the room's center, calling intermittently and praying almost constantly.

When his foot bumped against something solid and warm, he screamed and ran a few steps toward the exit. However, a sense of dread settled in his stomach and his heart flipped over in his chest. "Da?" he asked, his voice quivering.

He knew before he reached the object on the floor that he would find his da. What he didn't know—couldn't have known—was that his da was dead.

Riley shook him, but there was no response. He grabbed his tall, strapping Da beneath both arms and dragged him slowly toward the opening. The entire time, he spoke to him, begged him to wake up.

In the end, after he had Da outside in the sunlight, he wept, knowing there was no medicine powerful enough to bring Da back. He was dead. Riley cursed the castle, using words he knew he'd have to go to confession for using. It didn't help. Nothing did.

Riley sat there beside his da's still form, listening to the crashing waves for a long time before he could fully grasp his loss. Like the waves, his acceptance came in harsh curses, followed by quiet understanding.

Finally, exhausted and trembling, he knelt beside his da and prayed. "Dear Jaysus, help me do what needs doing. I'm small, but I'll grow. Help me make me . . . me da proud, and to do for my family what he always did." He removed Da's rosary from his pocket and put it in his own. It was his now, and so were all the responsibilities that had been Da's.

Including making sure no one ever entered the cursed castle again. No one . . .

"I'll make it right, Da," he'd promised. "I'll take care of them all."

Now Riley dragged in a breath and shook himself. He wiped the dampness from his cheeks. The memories he'd kept locked away in his heart and soul for so many years were free now. He was free to accept what had happened. Free to grieve.

Free to live.

Eighteen

Bridget was just passing by the front door when the knock sounded. It was early for visitors, so she peeked out the window. Seeing Brady with a bulging pouch, she immediately opened the door and showed him into the parlor.

"Here, Brady, let me help you." She reached for the pouch, but Brady clutched it close, shaking his head.

"No, but thank you kindly, lass." He looked around the room. "Would Riley be about, or is he off in the fields already this morn?"

"He's just finishing breakfast." She motioned Brady toward the kitchen. "The kettle's warm. I'll fix you a cup of—"

Brady shook his head. "If it's all the same to you, lass, I'll wait here." At least a day's growth of beard covered his face. "I have personal business with Riley."

Bewildered, Bridget made sure Brady was comfortable and went to the kitchen, where Riley lingered over his third cup of tea. She hadn't seen him this relaxed since her arrival. He looked younger, somehow. The sight of his unruly black hair falling across his forehead made her burn to push it back and kiss the newly exposed skin.

Mercy. She'd dreamed again last night. A flood of heat

rushed through her and she drew a shaky breath. However, her dream lover was no longer anonymous, and knowing his identity made her want him all the more.

But she wanted to be awake for *that*.

Mustering her self-control, she cleared her throat. Riley looked up from his woolgathering and smiled. He actually *smiled* without any coaxing. The sight left her speechless for a few seconds.

Finally, she said, "Riley, Brady is here to see you."

His smile vanished immediately and an anxious expression replaced it. "Thank you." He rose immediately, leaving his tea and his smile behind.

Guiltily, Bridget glanced around the room. She should be upstairs with Fiona and Jacob, packing for their visit to Galway.

Bridget should accompany them, but she couldn't bring herself to leave *Caisleán Dubh* just now. Besides, it would do Jacob good to spend some time alone with his aunt and new granny, so they could all get to know each other better.

Though all her rationalizations were true, Bridget couldn't deny her guilty secret. She wanted some time alone with Riley. Her feelings for him had escalated from lust to something terrifying.

Dare she even think it again? The thought had crossed her mind already, but she'd buried it. Denied it.

Do you love him?

"I wish Granny was here." Bridget drew a shaky breath, summoning Culley's smiling face. Was he looking down from heaven with a blessing, or disapproval? She shook her head. Somehow, she couldn't believe he would disapprove. The Culley she'd loved believed in love and happiness. He would want her to be happy. And he would want their son to be raised right here.

She would have a frank discussion with Riley, because they'd already admitted their mutual attraction.

Now there's *an understatement.*

At any rate, it was no longer her secret, although—

thank heavens—he didn't know about her dreams. She
fanned herself, remembering how close she'd come last
night to fulfillment. Right on the brink, she'd awakened
again, quivering with the powerful cravings spiraling
through her body. Knowing Riley was her dream lover
hadn't helped any, and she was ashamed to admit that the
thought of creeping downstairs to his room had crossed
her mind.

⸱ More than once.

Now that she and Jacob would definitely be staying in
Ireland—Bridget had to hug herself at the thought—the
need to come to some kind of understanding with Riley
became more urgent. She couldn't continue with these
sleepless nights, or the constant hunger pulsing through
her. She wanted him something fierce, and she knew he
shared her desire.

Somehow, the constant wanting had to end.

Or . . . they had to follow through to the logical conclusion.

The mere thought of sleeping with Riley made her
pulse quicken and her blood warm. She rubbed her arms
and gazed out the window at the tower. The sun broke
through the clouds, bathing the castle in light. The blackness of the stones appeared almost golden now.

Bridget touched the windowsill, her breath hitching.
She watched the play of light and shadow as the clouds
drifted between the sun and *Caisleán Dubh*. Soon, she
would have her restaurant.

She was here for a reason. How could she deny that
after all she'd experienced? The castle's whispering, the
dreams, the powerful response she'd had upon touching
the banister . . . Her destiny was here in County Clare.

Caisleán Dubh was part of it.

And, heaven help her, she couldn't deny that the other
part of her destiny might very well be a tall, dark-haired
Irishman with eyes of Mulligan blue.

Dragging herself away from the window and her musings, she cleared the table and did the breakfast dishes.

Once or twice, she thought of offering Riley and Brady tea, but she'd sensed their need for privacy and would respect it.

The dishes done, the table and counters wiped, Bridget climbed the back staircase to help Jacob finish packing. He was shoving items into his backpack she knew he wouldn't need on his short trip. With a smile, she helped him decide what he could and couldn't live without for three whole days, but drew the line when his toothbrush and toothpaste went into the "leave behind" pile.

"I'm going to miss you," she said, ruffling his hair.

He rewarded her with a hug that melted her heart. "I'm a big boy now, Momma," he said. "And an Irishman takes care of his kin, so I gotta go meet my great-*mamó*."

"My, but don't you sound grown up?" *And more than a little like your uncle Riley.* Bridget studied her son for several seconds while he sorted through his collection of coloring books and eliminated all but one.

"Do you miss Mr. and Mrs. Larabee?" she asked, remembering the frantic letter she'd mailed Mr. Larabee just a couple of weeks ago. It seemed like a lifetime ago. So much had changed during that short time.

"Yep." Jacob zipped his backpack closed and sat on his bed beside Bridget. "Maybe they'll come visit sometime."

"I reckon." Bridget smiled to herself, remembering. "I miss them, too, but . . ."

"What, Momma?"

She gave him a thoughtful look. "I think this feels like home now."

His smile glowed, and a second later he was in her arms. "Oh, boy," he said as he pulled away, the bud of his new tooth glowing against his gums right in front. "We're gonna stay forever."

She laughed and pulled him into another hug. "Yes, I reckon we are."

"Then General Lee can come live with us here?"

Bridget gasped and coughed, then cleared her throat. "Er, I think Ireland has laws that would make him stay in quarantine." she said diplomatically. "Besides, he's awfully old, and I'll bet the Larabees are spoiling him rotten."

Jacob nodded thoughtfully. "I'll bet he's sleeping on that red couch in their fancy living room."

Bridget had to laugh again at that.

"You about ready, boyo?" Maggie called from the base of the attic stairs.

"Yep." Jacob slung his backpack over his shoulder and said, "Time to go."

Bridget had herself one fine son. She hugged him again, then followed him down the steps, where Fiona and Maggie waited in the parlor. Riley and Brady had stopped talking.

"Let me help with the bags, Mum," Riley said, rising.

Brady pulled the books and papers they'd been reading into a neat pile right in front of him.

You'd think they were plotting to overthrow the government or something.

Though curious, Bridget wouldn't pry. Instead, she walked out to the car with her new family and made certain her son's seat belt was properly fastened, and that she had one more hug before he left. Maggie sat behind the wheel, and Bridget knew she was a good driver, despite her youth.

"Y'all have a good trip." Bridget walked around to Fiona's open window on the passenger side and gave her mother-in-law a peck on the cheek. "I'll go next time."

Fiona gave her a bright smile and patted her hand. "Maybe."

Bridget studied the older woman's expression, wondering again if she knew about the attraction between her son and daughter-in-law.

"You promise me to have fun while we're gone, lass." She patted Bridget's hand. "And forget about everythin' except followin' your heart. Just listen to that, and all will be as it should."

Bridget stood staring after the car as they drove down

the narrow lane. Jacob waved until they were too far away for her to see. She glanced to her side, where Riley stood watching the car, too.

"Well, then," he said, turning toward the cottage again. "I'd better get back to Brady."

"Yes." She stared at him as he climbed the steps and disappeared into the front door.

And forget about everythin' except followin' your heart. Just listen to that, and all will be as it should, Fiona had said.

But what had she *meant*?

And why hadn't her mother-in-law mentioned the impropriety of Bridget remaining here with Riley? Alone?

A powerful tremor raced through Bridget. It didn't matter. She and Riley weren't teenagers, though no adolescent's hormones could rival hers these days. Or theirs, now that she thought about it.

Once Brady left, she and Riley would be alone.

Completely alone. Her gaze drifted to the tower and the sea beyond.

Except for *Caisleán Dubh.*

Riley only performed the minimal chores—milking and tending the stock—and spent most of his day poring over Brady's research. The man was definitely onto something. The alleged spell cast by the *cailleach* had been recorded by the priest after Bronagh had plunged to her death from the tower.

Suppressing a shudder, Riley glanced out the window toward the tower now. The thought of the young woman climbing there to throw herself to the rocky shore below made his belly lurch.

Again, he returned to last night's disturbing dream. Now he knew for certain that his dreams were of Aidan Mulligan and his beautiful Bronagh. Insane though that sounded, there was no sense denying it. Bronagh was the woman who'd haunted Riley's dreams for years, and who'd come to life for him in these recent weeks.

Through Bridget.

He didn't have the proof yet, but his instincts insisted it was true. Hadn't his dreams returned with a vengeance after the first moment he'd seen Bridget?

She was a beautiful and appealing woman. Perhaps that was the only reason she'd triggered the dreams. However, Riley didn't believe it was that simple. Not at all.

Brady was looking for one more missing bit of information—the part with the girl's full name. After that, Riley might be able to piece together more of this conundrum. The records of Bronagh's death would help. Unfortunately, she had been buried in an unmarked grave, as peasants often were back then. Furthermore, suicide was a cardinal sin even now, so Bronagh wouldn't have been buried on hallowed ground. Still, there would be *something* somewhere.

And wasn't Brady just the man to find it?

He had to smile at that. His old teacher's enthusiasm was contagious. The man thrived on the research. If Bridget could uncover the missing pieces, Riley would be forever in the old man's debt.

He again picked up the page with the spell written upon it. The words were faded but legible.

A darksome curse on them that walke these halls
May they finde only death and miserie.
No joying be withstood within these walls—
Much daunted by sore sad despaire they be!
Until that cruell, disdayned destinie
Beguile them torne asunder with her power,
Rejoin the accurst for all eternity
with her so fierce bewronged within this tower
And ende this spelle, forever, in that blessed hour!

How was Riley to right a wrong committed centuries ago? He had to try. No, he had to succeed. Brady had admitted there were volumes he hadn't read yet in Riley's stack. Perhaps Riley would find the missing bits later. Just now, he needed a break.

His head ached from reading the faded scrawls for hours without a break. He stored the notes Brady had left with him on his desk in the corner of the parlor. No one in the family ever disturbed his desk, for he was the only one who knew how to order supplies and feed for the farm. The notes and diaries would be safe here.

His stomach growled and he remembered he hadn't eaten since breakfast. Riley glanced at the clock on the wall, shocked to discover the afternoon had passed to early evening without his notice. He'd missed lunch entirely.

Sniffing the air, he smiled. Bridget was cooking. Ah, and what man could resist anything that woman could cook?

What man could resist *her*?

Oh, and wasn't he tired of resisting? He rubbed the back of his aching neck and walked into the kitchen. The aromas wafting toward him were more than a bit of heaven.

The woman stirring something at the stove looked even better than the food smelled. Riley's appetite forgotten, he watched her for some time. Her hair was pulled up with a large clip in the back, probably to keep it away from the food. He liked her hair down, but seeing her long, slender neck exposed ignited his blood.

He ached to kiss the back of her neck, the slope of her shoulder. He wanted to slip up behind her and wrap his hands about her waist. He wanted to pull her back against him, to feel her softness against his hardness.

His breath stuttered in his throat and he had to blink several times to bring himself under control. Even that didn't help, though at least he could see straight now. Still, his blood sang with a primal hunger to make her his.

Aye, his.

Not Culley's widow. Not Jacob's mum.

Of course, she would always be all of those things, and

Jacob couldn't want for a better mum. And to think Riley had once thought her devious. Shame slithered through him, dampening his desire only slightly.

"Something smells better than a pint after Lent," he said quietly.

She gasped and whirled around to stare at him. She stammered for a few seconds, then said, "I hope you like it."

Just you. Not y'all.

He rather liked it that way. Alone here with Bridget. "Have you fixed anything yet that I haven't liked?" he asked with a smile.

She smiled back and that soft look he'd noticed yesterday entered her eyes again. It tugged at something deep inside him and gave him pause. What he felt for Bridget was more than simple lust.

Though the lust he'd been feeling was anything but simple.

He rubbed the kink in the back of his neck again. "I spent too much time with my head bent over Brady's research."

Bridget put a lid on the pot and set her spoon aside. She adjusted the flame, and walked toward him. "Why is that?"

"Why is what?" he asked, so mesmerized by her nearness he'd forgotten his own words. He breathed in the scent of her and wanted more. So much more.

"Why were you going over Brady's notes?" she asked, clasping her hands in front of her.

Riley turned his head and a pain speared through his neck into the base of his skull. "Ow."

"Here." She pulled a chair out at the table. "Sit. Granny used to get a stiff neck from playing too much bingo."

"What?" Riley didn't dare shake his head again. "Aye, I'll sit, but I don't understand what my stiff neck has to do with bingo."

"Never mind." She wiped her hands on her apron and pointed to the chair. "Sit."

"Aye." Riley obeyed, anticipation zinging through him. She would touch him now, and knowing that made him ache inside—but not only his neck.

Her hands were cool against the stiff cords in the back of his neck. She massaged gently with her thumbs, then with the heels of both hands, working her way slowly down to the base and across his shoulders. He rotated his head to one side, groaning with pleasure as she found a particularly tender spot and worked the knots away.

"Your hands are magic," he whispered, the image of Bronagh cupping Aidan in her hands flashing unbidden to his mind. His breathing grew labored as Bridget continued to work her magic, relieved she couldn't see how pronounced his physical response really was.

Jaysus, but he wanted her.

The thought of Bronagh and Aidan had augmented his desire for Bridget, but he was convinced now that he would burn for her even without the dreams. Her hands stilled after a few minutes, though they remained on his shoulders.

He reached up and captured one hand in his and brought it to his lips. Tenderly, he planted a kiss in her palm and felt her shiver behind him.

"Riley . . ." Her voice was barely more than a whisper.

"Hmm?" He kept his lips pressed to her palm and her other hand gripped his shoulder tighter.

"What . . . what are you doing to me?"

He half-turned and rose, keeping her hand in his. He brought his other hand to her cheek, caressing it with the backs of his fingers. "Why did you stay here?" he asked, realizing he hadn't paid much attention to that until now.

She looked down quickly, then lifted her chin and met his gaze. "To talk to you . . . about this."

"This?"

She nodded. "You're driving me crazy."

He had to chuckle at that. "And what do you think you've been doing to me?"

"Driving you crazy?" she asked, her smile tremulous.

"Aye." He slipped his arms around her waist very gently, and pressed his lips to hers. That wasn't nearly enough, and less than a breath later he brought her flush against him. Their kiss deepened, the softness of her mouth reminding him of another part of her body he wanted desperately to explore.

Reeling himself in with more strength than he'd believed he possessed, he released a long, shaky breath. "Bridget," he said, keeping his tone light, "you've set me on fire, lass."

"What are we going to do about that?" she repeated. "I . . . I . . ."

He swallowed hard and cupped her chin in his hand. "I'm listening." *And keeping my hands off you will be the death of me yet.*

"I want to . . . to make love with you," she said, her eyes wide and filled with a sincerity that stole his breath. "And . . . and . . ."

He could barely breathe. "And what?"

"You won't think I'm being silly?"

"Nothing about what I'm feeling right now could be called 'silly,' Bridget." He gave her a crooked grin. "I'd call it very serious indeed."

She blushed and returned his smile. After a moment, her expression grew solemn and she drew a deep breath. "Riley, I've been having dreams," she blurted.

Riley made a choking sound and bit the inside of his cheek. He brought his hands to her shoulders and stared into her eyes. "Dreams about what?" He kept his voice calm, though inside he was anything but calm. His hormones performed a jig while his pulse played a reel. The beat of a *bodhrán* pounded through another part of him, echoing the rhythm of the very act he'd thought about day and night for weeks. "Your dreams, Bridget. Tell me."

He held his breath and waited, watching the fluctuating expression in her eyes. "Tell me," he urged.

"About you," she said, exhaling in a loud whoosh.

"What about me?" His mouth went dry.

"Sex," she whispered. "I've been dreaming about *sex.*"

"And me?" Knowing they'd both been plagued with erotic dreams sent Riley's libido into a rage. He could barely speak. "Sex and me?" he repeated, his voice breaking.

She shook her head, holding his gaze, though her cheeks flamed crimson. "Sex *with* you."

Riley wanted to swing her into his arms and carry her up the stairs. No, to hell with that idea. He wanted to knock the pretty dishes off the table and take her there. Right there where she'd tortured him for weeks with her lovely breasts, sweet smile, and delicious food.

"Aren't you . . . aren't you going to say anything?" she asked, and her expression made it clear that her confession was one of the most difficult things she'd ever done. "Have I offended you?"

"*Offended* me, is it?" He almost laughed, but feared that might offend *her.* "Far from it, lass."

"I'm not a girl." She licked her lips. "I'm a woman."

"Aye." His gaze drifted down to her breasts and back to her eyes. "Aye, a woman in every way."

"I've never . . ." She bit her lower lip. "I've never wanted anyone since . . ."

Riley took a deep breath. "Since Culley."

"Yes." She shook her head. "I don't know what's come over me here. Maybe it's Ireland."

"Irishmen make the best lovers," he teased.

She smiled and lowered her lashes. He reached out and cradled her chin again, dying a little inside. He wanted desperately to tell her about his own dreams, but he couldn't. Not yet. Not until he understood the full magnitude of them.

But he wanted Bridget. Only Bridget. His dreams had nothing to do with that. But why was she dreaming about having sex with him?

The thought of it made the ache between his thighs intensify and his next breath was labored. "Bridget, you're killing me here."

The smile she gave him was filled with mischief. She reached down between them and pressed the heel of her hand against him. He throbbed against her and a groan erupted from deep in his chest.

"I'm glad I'm not the only one."

She walked away to finish cooking, leaving him there in a very bad way. Barely able to think, let alone walk, he called over his shoulder in an odd voice even to his own ears, "I'm off to take a shower, love. A bloody *cold* one."

Her giggle followed him up the stairs. Unable to see straight, he crashed his skull into that fecking beam again and cursed.

She giggled louder.

Well, she'd told him. Bridget finished preparing supper while Riley cooled off. The thought brought a smile to her lips and warmth to the rest of her.

He wanted her, too, and hadn't seemed totally shocked by her confession. Now what were they going to do about it? Neither of them had discussed *that*. In fact, they'd both skirted around the subject.

What was there to discuss? Either they would or they wouldn't.

Bridget's cheeks flamed and her hands trembled as she set the serving platters on the table. She went to the bottom of the steps and called to let Riley know supper was ready. As an afterthought, she reminded him to watch out for the beam on his way back.

He thanked her and started down the steps. Every step brought him closer to her. She would have to face him again after her confession. Of course, she'd known that, but it had to be done.

But now what?

Maybe that was all it would take. Her dreams would end and she'd turn her attention to opening Mulligan Stew. Problem solved.

He emerged from the stairway with his damp hair curling around his face. He'd shaved, too. The shirt he wore was a rich blue. She didn't remember seeing it before. It matched his eyes.

Problem not solved.

She'd opened a bottle of wine and was letting it breathe. Maggie had told her it was homemade from some kind of berries, though she didn't know which kind. She'd also told Bridget that Mum sometimes sipped it for her gout.

Bridget had to smile, wondering if she could make wine from cherries.

Riley saw the wine and the crystal and raised an eyebrow. "It looks good."

"It's nothing fancy—just fried chicken, and before you pick up your knife and fork, let me tell you that where I come from, fried chicken is finger food."

"I'm not a fancy kind of man," he said, pulling out a chair for her. He quirked an eyebrow. "And did you fetch the chicken from the yard yourself?"

She shook her head, grinning. "There are chickens at the market."

He smiled, watching her. Just having him look at her set her heart aflutter. The thought of having him touch her again set her on fire.

Problem definitely *not solved.*

Bridget made sure the stove was off and removed her apron. On knees made of rubber bands, she lowered herself into the chair. Riley brushed her shoulder with his hand after he'd pushed in her chair.

She sighed, but resisted the urge to grab his hand and put it on her breast. Wouldn't that have shocked him?

Looking across the table at him as he took his seat, she noted the gleam in his eyes had transformed them from blue to cobalt. There was an intensity about him this evening that stole her breath and had her libido doing the twist to an Elvis tune like she had with Granny as a little girl.

She uncovered the platter of crispy chicken and passed it to him. "Dark or white?" she asked.

His gaze left the platter and dropped to her chest. "I've always been a breast man."

"Oh, mercy." Bridget almost dropped the platter, but he reached out to help her ease it back to the table. "You're a dangerous man, Riley Mulligan."

He remained silent as he served himself a crispy chicken breast, a mound of mashed potatoes smothered in gravy, and some of the fried cabbage he loved. He added a biscuit to his plate and looked across the table at her.

"Not yet," he whispered.

"Not yet what?"

"Dangerous." He bit into the chicken breast, tearing the tender meat away from the bone, and chewed very slowly before swallowing. "I'm not promising anything, though."

"Promising?"

"You're starting to sound like a parrot, Bridget." He grinned again and served her since she hadn't bothered to fill her own plate. "Eat up now. You need to keep up your strength, love."

Love? She drew a deep breath to quell her trembling. "Promises, promises," she whispered, wondering where she'd found the nerve to say such a thing.

He threw back his head and laughed. The joyousness of it filled the kitchen and Bridget's heart. "Something about you has definitely changed," she said as his laughter subsided. "For the better."

He grew solemn and nodded, eating very slowly. Between his first and second breast—*mercy*—he told Bridget that he'd followed her advice about something.

"About what?" she asked, barely tasting her own food.

"The past." An expression of resignation settled across his handsome face. "I faced it. Accepted it."

Tears welled in her eyes, but she blinked them away. "I'm glad," she whispered. "Very glad."

They sipped their wine and he asked about the sourdough she'd used to prepare the breading on the chicken and for the biscuits. Bridget prattled on about the methods she'd used to prepare the food and why, realizing as he helped her clear the table that he'd done it to distract her. She was thankful for that.

But soon she knew they would discuss their dilemma again. Now that it was out in the open, they couldn't very well bury it again. Not comfortably anyway.

Nothing about this was the least bit comfortable. He insisted on washing the gigantic iron frying pan for her, so she wiped the table and stood staring out the kitchen window. The sun slowly sank beyond *Caisleán Dubh*, creating almost a halo around the tower.

"Riley, look."

He came to stand beside her, drying his hands on a towel. "Jaysus. I've never seen it look like *that*."

She took his hand. "Let's go down there. It's a lovely evening, and I want to see it again."

He winced, blinked several times. "Aye, get your jumper while I fetch the flashlight."

"No, not the flashlight," she said, grabbing what was left of the wine and two glasses. "Candles."

Riley sucked in a breath. "That could be dangerous."

"I thought you said you weren't dangerous."

"Yet."

"Well . . . I wasn't thinking about that," she said, though she probably had been, at least subconsciously. "I made tarts for dessert. We can be the very first customers in Mulligan Stew's dining room."

"I'm still a bit uncomfortable there," he admitted. "But I'd better get used to it."

"Yes." She looked out the window again. "I feel a powerful sense of . . . belonging there. It's very strange."

His voice sounded very odd. "Then I say let's do it."

Bridget whirled around to stare at his face. Which "it" did he mean?

There's only one way to find out. . . .

Nineteen

Caisleán Dubh had never looked more beautiful. Considering Riley had once thought it the most terrifying of places, thinking of it as beautiful was a concept that would take some time to get his mind around.

The woman walking at his side, on the other hand, would outshine any castle. He wanted to hold her hand, but he was loaded down with wine and a blanket. She carried a basket with the candles, dishes, and their dessert.

This was madness. He chewed on that thought in silence, then had to wonder if it was, really. After all, Bridget would be opening a restaurant in *Caisleán Dubh.* Folks would be eating more than tarts there, and probably by candlelight. What was wrong with a bit of pretending if it made her happy?

Aye, and wasn't she glowing with happiness just now? The closer they came to *Caisleán Dubh,* the happier Bridget grew. She was the most perplexing woman, and the most desirable.

What was he to do about her? She'd dreamed about him. About *him.* It was bloody vexing, to say the least.

And the highest form of flattery.

It had taken more courage than *he* would ever have for

her to make such a confession. After all, he hadn't told her about his dreams of Aidan and Bronagh.

A thought took root in his mind and refused to budge. Were they sharing their dreams? Did she believe her dreams were of him, when they were really of Aidan? The thought that he wasn't the man of her dreams grated on him. *Shite.* Was such a thing even possible? It sounded completely mad.

Of course, believing in a curse or spell didn't sound exactly sane. Despite his hope that the spell could be broken, the nagging questions about why and how his da had died continued to plague him. If only he knew for sure what had killed Da. If only . . .

"Isn't it amazing?" Bridget paused before the entrance.

"Aye, I'll grant you that." He watched her from the corner of his eye. "As are you."

"I think you've kissed the Blarney stone," she said, heading toward the opening. "It's a pity we can't open the door ourselves."

"Not without some heavy equipment, I'm afraid." Though Riley was hard enough now to possibly manage it on his own. *Ouch.*

She edged sideways through the opening with far more ease than he would, but she was much smaller. "I'm thinking maybe a wall of leaded windows and French doors should replace these monsters. They'll have to complement the historical integrity of the whole place, though."

"Aye, that sounds like a good plan," he said, following her inside, and wondering why the whispers hadn't greeted them. The silence was odd. Disconcerting. Bridget didn't seem to have noticed. Perhaps she still heard them.

After spreading the blanket out near the hearth, he lit the candles she'd placed in the small alcoves that flanked Aidan's portrait, far enough away to prevent any accidents, yet close enough to offer a cheery glow.

You've lost it, Mulligan—a "cheery glow" in this place?

Aye, but it was. He raked his fingers through his hair, watching Bridget set out plates and wineglasses. She perched herself on a corner of the blanket and held her hand out to display her work. "Dessert is served, sir."

His gasp echoed off the walls and she laughed at him. *Laughed!* How often had he thought of her as dessert? "Why are you laughing?" he asked, positioning himself as comfortably as possible, and wishing he'd left his belt in his closet. It pinched something awful.

"I don't have to answer that question," she whispered in a sultry tone that rippled through him. She passed him a plate bearing a tart. "It could prove incriminating."

He held his breath, watching her work while bathed in candlelight. After pouring them each a glass of wine, she nibbled at her tart in silence. After a few bites, she licked her fingers.

Which almost killed him.

He wanted to lick her fingers. Her neck. Her breasts. Her navel. Her—

Jaysus.

"What's wrong, Riley?" she asked. "You aren't eating. I expect all the customers in my restaurant to leave happy and fulfilled. Eat."

Fulfilled? Aye, just what he had in mind, but only she could provide the sort of fulfillment he craved.

Ignoring his fork, he picked up the tart with his fingers and took a huge bite, chewing as he stared at her sipping her wine. The tart was cheese and filled his mouth with creamy sweetness. He popped the last bit into his mouth and stacked their plates and forks, dropping them into the basket while still chewing.

"What are you doing?"

"Getting these out of the way," he said, his voice husky.

"Oh." She giggled. "Don't put the wine away yet."

He moved to sit beside her, leaning against the wall behind them. Knowing Aidan's portrait hung nearby, just over the hearth, he swallowed hard. He had to make certain his feelings weren't part of any stupid spell. "Are you getting tipsy, Bridget Colleen?" he asked.

"Mmm." She fell silent for a moment and held her glass out for him to refill. "I don't think so. I've only had champagne once in my life. No wine."

"No other alcohol at all?" He watched her take the refilled glass to her lips for a generous sip.

"None."

"Best go easy, then." He took a sip himself. As a rule, Riley wasn't much of a wine drinker. He'd have preferred a Guinness.

She giggled again. The sound circled him like music— like the whispering he *didn't* hear tonight normally would. Why was tonight different?

Was it because he'd finally faced the worst of his own personal demons and set them free? The thought gnawed at him as he sipped the wine and stared at Bridget.

"Penny for your thoughts," she said, her voice taking on that sultry note again.

"You think they're worth a penny?" he teased.

"Riley, everything about you is worth much, much more."

He held his breath as she scooted closer until her shoulder pressed against his. The candlelight flickered and a cool breeze sifted through the opening and beneath the double doors. The wind didn't normally carry such a chill in June.

"I think it's going to storm," he said.

"Is it?" She leaned her head against his shoulder. "Let it."

"We should go back."

"I like it here. Right here." She looked up at him and he smelled the sweet wine on her breath. "With you."

Riley flinched. "Lass, you're torturing me again."

She turned slightly, her breast pressing against his arm. "I'm still waiting for dangerous."

He was in serious trouble here. "You're tempting fate," he whispered.

"You haven't objected so far. . . ."

A tremor rippled through him and he put his arm around her, drawing her against him. The softness of her breast seared him. He wanted her naked in the candle-light—right here in *Caisleán Dubh*. Especially tonight, when the whispers were blessedly absent.

She stroked his thigh through denim, sending shock waves of pleasure through his entire body. With a trembling hand, he reached down and grabbed her wrist.

"How much wine did you drink?" he asked, needing to assure himself that she was sober.

"Half a glass at supper, and a whole one plus a little here."

"You're not drunk, then." He released her wrist.

"Of course not." She resumed stroking his leg.

"You're sure?"

"Not drunk," she said on a sigh. "Did you notice the quiet?"

"Aye."

"What do you think it means?" Her fingers traced their way higher up his thigh, leaving a trail of fire in their wake.

"I . . . I'm not sure." He shifted, trying to find a comfortable position, but he was so engorged and his jeans were so snug, there was no such thing as comfortable. "Maybe the castle is getting used to us."

She giggled again and stopped tormenting his thigh. Instead, she turned sideways and lifted her delectable bottom onto his lap.

"Jaysus, Mary, and Joseph!" Riley's head hit the wall behind him with a thud that echoed through the chamber. "I was right all along—you *are* trying to kill me."

At least she didn't giggle this time. Her wine-scented breath fanned his face and he breathed in her essence. Meeting her lips halfway, he tasted her, drank from her, hungered for her.

With nimble fingers she released the buttons at the front of his shirt and pulled it from his waistband. If she didn't stop squirming on his lap, he would explode before they ever reached any point more intimate.

And intimate was exactly what he had in mind.

Now. Tonight.

He dragged his lips from hers, needing to ask her one more time. "Do you know what you're doing, Bridget? Where this will lead?"

"To a dream come true."

Bridget moaned as he rose off the blanket and lowered her onto her back. The candlelight flowed around him, reminding her of her dream, when he'd stood before the hearth with the fire's glow outlining his magnificent body.

His shirt gaped open and she satisfied her need to touch him. She pressed her palms flat against his chest, stroking the hair, loving the feel of his bare skin. *Yes, skin.*

She'd never been as ready in her life as she was now. Culley had been a tender lover, but she'd been young and inexperienced. Now she knew what she wanted.

Riley kissed her again, releasing the clip holding her hair. He spread the tresses out around her face like a fan. Her heart hammered in her chest, and her most private place clenched the emptiness he would fill. "Hurry," she whispered, reaching for his belt buckle.

"This isn't to be rushed," he said, his voice sounding strained. "No matter how eager we both are."

"Eager is an understatement." She gave a throaty chuckle. "I feel as if we've been waiting *centuries* for this."

He stilled over her, gazing down through the darkness, and making her wonder what she'd done wrong. "What is it, Riley?" she asked. "What's wrong?"

"Not you," he said, kissing her again. "I just remembered something. That's all."

He trailed kisses along the side of her throat while his fingers released the buttons down the front of her blouse. The cool air flowed over her as he rose high enough to ease her blouse from her shoulder, freeing her arms.

She shivered until he covered her again. The wind

howled outside and the surf crashed against the cliff below. "A storm," she whispered.

"Aye." His voice rumbled through her and straight into her bone marrow. "A storm here, too."

"Be dangerous, Riley," she invited, her voice falling to a husky whisper. "Very dangerous."

Molten lava rushed through her as he cupped her breasts in his large hands. "Sweet." He drew on her nipple right through her bra. After a moment, he reached behind her and unhooked it, tossing it aside.

Again, he took her breasts, but this time free of barriers. Bridget arched upward against him, weaving her fingers through his hair, holding him to her. She loved the way he made her feel, the burning deep in her loins and in her heart.

She loved *him.*

A whimper slipped from her lips at the thought, and he rose over her. The wind caressed her damp nipples and she shivered.

"Did I hurt you?" he asked.

"No."

"You made a wee sound, and I thought . . ."

"You could never hurt me, Riley," she said, believing it. "Unless you don't finish this before I die from the wanting."

He chuckled and circled her nipples with his tongue, cradling her breasts in both hands. She wanted him naked. Both of them.

She reached for his belt again, and this time he didn't stop her. She released his belt buckle, followed by the snap and zipper at his fly. Her hand trembled and he left her breasts to push himself higher above her. She felt each of the five buttons at the front of her jeans pop open, bringing her closer and closer to Riley.

She pushed his zipper lower, hoping she wouldn't catch anything vital in its teeth, which made her giggle again.

"I've never known a woman to giggle so much during lovemaking," Riley said.

She stopped lowering his zipper, stricken. "Is that bad? I'm sorry. I'll try not—"

"Don't you dare," he whispered, kissing her again before he resumed lowering her jeans. "Don't ever stop laughing. Don't ever stop being yourself, Bridget. 'Tis you I want. You I need. Only you."

She ached to tell him she loved him, but instead she would show him. The telling could come later. She reached for his zipper again, lowering it a little at a time. His heat radiated through the fabric. He would be hot to the touch, and her hands itched to do just that. In last night's dream, she had taken him with her mouth. She wasn't quite ready for that, but perhaps later. . . .

"I want to see you. All of you," he whispered, his breathing labored. "Let's be rid of these bloody barriers once and for all." He rose onto his knees, easing his jeans down his slim hips. "You, too. I won't be naked alone."

"No," she whispered, following his lead. "You won't be."

She watched him roll onto his hips to shed his jeans. A moment later, they knelt before one another completely naked. Bridget could scarcely breathe. She leaned toward him, felt his erection brush against her belly. "Oh, God."

He cupped her breasts in his hands, brushing his thumbs across her nipples. "You're so beautiful."

She looked down between them and followed her urge to touch him. Groaning as her fingers encircled him, she hissed an indrawn breath in anticipation of having him inside her.

"Aye, love. I feel it, too. The hunger . . ."

She stroked his length, amazed that something so hard could be covered with such soft skin. The more she touched him, the more she wanted him. "I . . . I can't wait, Riley."

He pressed her down to the blanket again and kissed her breasts, drawing the sensitive peaks inward, driving her mad with the want of more. After torturing her to a trembling mass, he moved lower, tickling her navel with his tongue. He cradled her bottom in his hands, tilting her hips.

Bridget held her breath—afraid he would and afraid he wouldn't. Just like her dream . . . Her legs trembled and he held her bottom more firmly.

His breath scorched the tender flesh between her legs as he said, "Open for me."

And she did. Shockingly. Wantonly. Shamelessly.

He teased her with his tongue, stroking and tasting at leisure. Bridget moaned as he covered the sensitive nub with his mouth and drew gently. She clawed at the blanket, filling her hands, fighting the urge to grab his head and hold him against her. She wasn't *that* far gone.

He slid his fingers inside her as he drew against the deliciously tingling nucleus. That did it. She released the blanket and buried her fingers in his hair, gently urging him not to stop.

She moaned, whimpered, climbed higher and higher as he tortured her. An explosion built within her, pushing her closer and closer to a steep precipice. She would fall. She wanted to fall.

A scream tore from her throat as she plunged into a pit of ecstasy. Within seconds, he was over her again. As if in a daze, she reached between them and drew him closer.

"Fill me," she whispered, bringing her knees up to angle herself better. "I want you inside me. *Now*."

Riley growled and eased himself inside her. "Jaysus," he muttered. "You're so tight. So hot."

"So are you." She wrapped her legs around his waist and pulled him closer. "More."

Riley answered her plea, burying himself to the hilt. For a moment, he froze, waiting for the urge to burst to ease some before he dared move. Like millions of tiny fingers, her muscles gripped him, drawing him ever inward.

He'd known it would be this way with Bridget. From

the first moment he'd seen her, he'd known. "Ah, but you feel so good."

She reached up to caress his nipples and he gasped. No woman had ever done that before, and he didn't realize it would feel so good.

He withdrew his full length—all but the very tip—and returned again and again. She clung to him now, riding along with him toward journey's end, her nipples brushing against his chest hair. She linked her ankles behind his waist, drawing him even deeper into her tightness.

She clenched him in a vise of pure pleasure; over and over as he drove into her, she demanded more. The wind howled louder, and lightning crashed nearby. He'd never known lightning to light the sky this time of year, but he shoved the thought aside as he climbed higher.

She was a merciless lover—the best kind. She took and gave and took some more. He'd never known such a wild ride. Bridget was a woman who would always give and take. Always want him. As he would always want her.

The knowing made this even better. No more denials. He knew the truth now. He loved her. Only her.

Always her.

He loved her smile, her laughter, her beauty, her generous nature, and her cooking. Most of all, he loved her heart. Her tender, giving heart.

The explosion came. He plowed his seed deep, gave his love freely, pledged himself to her through action, if not word.

She shouted a single word that echoed from the high ceiling: "Bingo!"

With the storm raging outside, he slumped against her and whispered. *"A ghrá mo chroí."*

Their hearts thudded in unison as their breathing returned to normal. Riley slid to his side to avoid crushing her, pulling her snug to keep her from catching a chill. She sighed and curled against him.

"That was nice."

"Nice, is it?" He chuckled. "Only nice?"

"It was . . . spectacular."

"Better. My ego can handle spectacular."

"Riley?" she asked in the semidarkness. "What did that mean?"

"What we did?" He pulled her closer, though he doubted he could ever be close enough to her.

"No, what you said."

"Bingo?"

"No, silly. That was me." She gave a throaty chuckle. "What *you* said."

He thought back, remembering. *"A ghrá mo chroí?"*

"Yes, that." She rose up on her elbow to stare at him through the candlelight. "What does it mean?"

He caressed her cheek. "Are you sure you want to know?"

"Yes, and if you don't tell me, I'm letting Maggie do all the cooking after she gets back."

He shuddered against her. "You don't fight fair, lass. All right, I'll tell you if you promise not to let Maggie poison us all."

"I promise."

"A ghrá mo chroí means . . . love of my heart."

As the rain eased, they strolled from the castle to the cottage, where they spent the night in Bridget's bed. They made love again and again—each time more magnificent than the previous one.

Bridget stared at the window as the first streaks of drawn fanned across the sky. Riley slept at her side, his arms about her waist and his cheek pressed to her back. She smiled, remembering.

Love of my heart.

Her heart fluttered and she bit her lower lip, praying it was true, and hadn't been merely the heat of passion talking. She loved Riley Mulligan with all her heart. After Culley, she'd never believed she would love another.

She loved Riley's strength, his passion, his tenderness.

She loved his sense of honor, his gentleness, and the way he treated her son.

He shifted, and the pattern of his breathing told her he was awake. She rolled onto her back and gazed into his eyes. "Good morning," she said.

"The best." He kissed her and propped himself on his elbow to gaze down at her. "Did I tell you I love you?"

Tears welled in the corners of her eyes. "I love you, too." Relief and joy soared through her and she reached up to brush his hair away from his strong forehead. "So much."

"Bridget . . ." He sighed and she watched the internal struggle play itself out in his eyes. "I want to marry you, to make you my wife, to raise our children with you, to spend my life at your side."

She gasped and fought the urge to immediately agree. She had to use her brain—this was too important. "I . . . I want to say yes," she said.

"Want to?" He smiled. "Then say it, lass."

"Let me think about it today, and I'll give you my answer this evening." She caressed his morning stubble with the palm of her hand. "I want us both to have time to consider our future before we commit our lives to each other forever." Releasing a long, slow breath, she added, "Especially you, Riley. I want you to think this over very carefully before you decide."

"I've already decided, Bridget." His voice was husky with emotion. "I can't imagine living my life without you in my arms. I want to start every day of my life just like this."

She giggled, acutely aware of his erection pressing against her. "Hmm. Well, I rather like it myself, but just take this one day to make sure. Please?"

"Aye." He kissed her again, pressing her back against the feather bed. "I'm giving you something to carry with you the rest of the day, though."

She sighed as his mouth found her breast. Entwining

her fingers through his hair, she held him against her. "Yes. Oh, yes."

Later—much later—they had a light breakfast before Riley left to fetch a cumbersome part he'd ordered for the tractor. Bridget waved from the front porch as he drove away in his truck. He blew her a kiss as he turned onto the road.

She loved that man, and hugged herself as he rounded the curve beyond *Caisleán Dubh*, heading toward the village. Maybe she should have agreed immediately to his proposal, because she wanted to marry him more than anything. She just wanted to make sure *he* wanted it as much. If she gave him time to ponder it and he still wanted it, then she would have her answer.

And she would become Mrs. Mulligan again. The thought brought a smile to her face as she watched the sun rise higher in the sky. After last night's storm, seeing the sunshine today made it even more perfect.

She closed the front door and headed toward the kitchen to clean up the breakfast mess, but a piece of folded, yellowed paper on the floor caught her eye. She stooped down and retrieved it from beneath Riley's desk, intending to lay it on top of the stack of Brady's research material, but curiosity prompted her to stand there, staring at it.

She unfolded it carefully, as it had grown brittle with age. She shouldn't read it, but it wasn't as if she were prying into Riley's personal papers. This was research material on the Mulligans and *Caisleán Dubh*, and she definitely had a vested interest in the castle's history.

The paper was a record of death, signed at the bottom by a priest. A powerful premonition swept through Bridget and her hands trembled as she read the deceased's name.

Bronagh Erienne.

Was Erienne her last name? It sounded like a middle name to Bridget. She kept reading and came to the full name near the bottom of the page. A sob erupted from her very soul.

"Oh, my God." She clawed at her throat with one hand, and a burning sensation washed through her. "Frye . . . like me." A lump formed in her throat and she struggled to breathe, rereading the entire document again. And again.

Bridget had always known her Frye roots were Irish, but she had no knowledge of what part of Ireland. She knew nothing at all about her family tree beyond Granny and Grandpa. Could she be a descendant of the same family?

She dropped into Riley's desk chair, confused. Was that why he'd called her Bronagh more than once? He hadn't last night, though, and she was glad. Their love-making had involved only them—she was certain of that. Even the castle's whispers had been absent.

Why? What had been different about last night?

She was spying, but this was *her* business, too. With trembling hands, she lifted the diary on the top of Riley's stack, finding a verse of some kind. The following pages described it as a spell cast by Bronagh's elderly aunt—a witch. The rest of her family had disowned the old crone, according to the priest's accounting. However, Bronagh had been kind to her aunt. Apparently, the old witch had cast a spell on *Caisleán Dubh* after Bronagh had plunged to her death from the tower. The aunt had also revealed that Bronagh had been with child at the time of her death.

The word "suicide" didn't appear in the documents, but it was certainly suggested. Bridget kept reading, then returned to the verse—the spell.

The cause of the alleged curse of *Caisleán Dubh*?

"It all makes a sick sort of sense." She held the diary open to the spell and looked at the record of Bronagh's death again. The date leapt off the stiff parchment, stealing Bridget's breath.

Yesterday had been the anniversary of Bronagh Erienne Frye's suicide. And Aidan's wedding day, if the stories Bridget had heard were true.

The evidence made tears spill from Bridget's eyes. She had to add up the facts and use her brain. That was what Granny would have done, though sometimes the old woman's "facts" hadn't quite added up.

Shoving memories aside, Bridget scrubbed her eyes and focused on the evidence staring her in the face. The burning questions inside her would have to be asked.

And they would have to be answered.

Had Riley known about all this before he'd made love to Bridget in *Caisleán Dubh*?

She looked at the witch's spell again, her heart thundering.

> *A darksome curse on them that walke these halls*
> *May they finde only death and miserie.*
> *No joying be withstood within these walls—*
> *Much daunted by sore sad despaire they be!*
> *Until that cruell, disdayned destinie*
> *Beguile them torne asunder with her power,*
> *Rejoin the accurst for all eternity*
> *with her so fierce bewronged within this tower*
> *And ende this spelle, forever, in that blessed hour!*

Bridget was a Frye. Riley was a direct descendant of Aidan Mulligan. Riley had seemed so relieved and happier these last few days. Was the reason because he'd discovered a way to remove the curse on his family? On *Caisleán Dubh*?

And ende this spelle, forever, in that blessed hour!

Did that mean the spell could only be broken on that date? She covered her face with her hands. If he'd known the words of the spell and the significance of the date . . .

"That son of a bitch!"

Riley had *used* Bridget to break the spell.

Twenty

Riley stopped at Harrigan's to pick up the part, only to find an Out to Lunch sign in the bloody window. He shoved his fists into his pockets and decided to pay Brady a visit now. His old teacher had planned to phone the parish in Kilmurray this morning. Maybe he'd learned something more.

He walked the two blocks to the Rearden's cottage and knocked on the door. Katie answered.

I'm the one who's fecking cursed.

"Riley," she said, obviously surprised. Her eyes were red-rimmed and her nose swollen.

She'd been crying. "Is something wrong?" he asked gently. "Are your parents and granddad well?"

"Aye." She opened the door and stepped aside. "She's won."

"Who?"

"Bridget."

Riley winced. His Bridget. "I don't think we need to talk about—"

"I don't care what you think, Riley Mulligan." Katie flounced into the house, leaving Riley to show himself in.

He looked around, wondering where Brady was. Katie

was in a snit, and Riley didn't want to deal with it alone. "I came by to speak with your granddad," he said, hoping to steer her away from whatever had upset her.

"Ha!"

"Is he here?" Riley drew a deep breath and counted to ten. He wanted to hurry his business and get back home to Bridget and her answer to his proposal. *Jaysus, please let it be yes.*

"Aye, he's here all right." Her lower lip trembled and she spun around to march back through the kitchen, leaving Riley no choice but to follow.

"Graddad, Riley is here," she said in a surly tone, shoving open the door to a cluttered room off the kitchen that Brady used as a study. "I'm sure you'll both enjoy ruining my reputation."

"I haven't the vaguest notion . . ." Riley shook his head, feeling helpless. He looked at Brady. The older man's face was flushed and his eyes snapped with anger.

"Katie, if we were both a lot younger, I wouldn't hesitate to put you over me knee." He rose from his chair, and though his height didn't quite equal Katie's, his expression and tone reminded Riley of his school days when a student had been caught breaking a serious rule. "You'll be about fetching me missing notes now."

So she had taken them.

Katie stomped her foot and shouted something unintelligible, slamming the door behind her.

"Well, then . . ." Riley cleared his throat, relieved to be rid of the lass. "That was a bit ugly."

"Aye. Sit, lad. Sit."

Riley flopped into the chair across from Brady, and asked, "Have you learned anything more?"

"Aye and no." Brady scratched his head. "The parish secretary in Kilmurray insists there was a paper documentin' Bronagh's death tucked inside one of the diaries."

"Loose?" Riley looked around the chaos. "It could be lost."

"Aye, or still in the papers I left with you." Brady appeared hopeful. "I'll keep lookin' here, and you have a look when you get home."

"Aye." Riley stood. "Thanks for all your help, Brady."

"Think nothin' of it, but don't be runnin' off just yet, lad." Brady stood and winked. "I've spent a good part of my adult life researchin' *Caisleán Dubh*, and I distinctly remember recording Bronagh's full name. Wait for the notes Katie's fetchin'."

A soft knock sounded on Brady's study door, and since Riley was standing there, he answered it. Katie stood there with a pained look on her face. She had a small box clutched in her hands.

"Since you think more of your research than of your granddaughter, here are your precious notes." Katie tossed a small box onto the top of the desk. "I'll be packing now."

Brady stopped his grab for the box and stared at his granddaughter. "'Tis sorry I am you feel that way, lass."

"The only reason I stayed here was because . . ."

"Go on, lass," he said. "I'm listenin'."

She glanced nervously at Riley, though he tried not to notice.

"Because I thought *Caisleán Dubh* was . . . my destiny. A silly romantic notion." She sniffled and a tear trickled down her cheek. "Way back when you first started your research, I would sneak in here to read your notes. It all sounded so romantic, and I thought it would make you proud if I . . . I . . ."

"Ah, lass," Brady said, his voice gentle.

"Aren't I being punished enough to suit you both?" she asked, her eyes flashing angrily again. Resentment radiated from her.

Riley tried to sink lower in his chair. He didn't want any part of this.

"Punished?" Brady asked. "You mean for stealin' me notes?"

"Culley married that other woman and shamed me,"

she said, her voice rising with every syllable. "Then he had to go and *die*."

"Jaysus." Riley covered his face. The woman was mad.

"Now his widow is flauntin' herself around Ballybron-agh with her son—Culley's son."

"She is his widow, and Jacob is Culley's son. 'Tis her right, lass." Brady sighed.

"Because of your research, I believed it should have been *my* right."

Riley faced her again now, curious. "What madness is this?" He'd never figured it out, even after her earlier visit to the farm.

"Granddad's research mentions Aidan Mulligan's lover by name." Her voice grew quieter now. "When I saw it, I remembered my great-*mamó*'s maiden name was the same."

Brady appeared as confused as Riley felt. "Aye, but—"

"I know." She heaved a huge sigh. "All my romantic dreams are shattered now. Thanks to your stupid notes."

"Ah, lass . . ." Brady smiled at her, but she continued to glower. "All you had to do was ask, and the truth would've been yours."

"It's too late now." She drew a shaky breath and squared her shoulders. "I was wrong. *Caisleán Dubh* isn't for me. It never was. I've spent my life believing a ro-mantic lie—a fairy tale." She released a long sigh. "I'm going to Aunt Mary's in the States."

She turned and left the room, closing the door quietly behind her.

Brady sighed and shook his head. "That was unfortu-nate. The lass read something into me notes that was never there." He rubbed his bald pate and cleared his throat.

"She told me her soul-mate theory," Riley said, certain now they would find Bronagh's last name in that box. "Obviously something happened to change her mind."

"Oh, aye." Brady untied the ribbon holding the box closed. "Her mum's *mamó* died years ago. No one ever tried to keep her past a secret, but Katie wasn't old enough to understand then. After the woman was gone from this earth, it never seemed necessary to mention. "

"Mention what?"

"Katie's *mamó* was an orphan, lad." Brady shook his head. "The name Katie found was of the family who took her in."

Riley groaned. "All this time, she believed—"

"That she could break the spell by marryin' a Mulligan."

"Poor lass." Riley shook his head. "I think the States will do her good—help her put all this behind her."

"Aye. I hope you're right, lad." Brady sounded tired. He scrubbed his face with both hands, and turned his attention back to the box. "I didn't have any original documents here, but I had notes. *My* notes."

"Let's have a look."

Both men took their seats and Brady opened the box. They both sifted through his words. Riley soon discovered that reading someone else's notes was like trying to read their mind. He found a page with Bronagh's name scribbled across the top. There were dates and place names beneath that. "What's this?" He held it out to Brady, who took it and adjusted his glasses.

"Woo-hoo! This is it." Brady pointed to the page. "*This* is what I should've remembered when I met her."

"What?" Riley shook his head. "Met who?"

Brady's eyes twinkled. "When I met Bridget and young Jacob on the plane."

Riley's breath caught in his throat and he leaned forward, scanning the words again. "For a teacher, you have lousy handwriting."

Brady grinned and took a pencil from behind his ear to use as a pointer. "See here? This be her name. Bronagh's *full* name."

"I recognize Bronagh, but not the rest." Riley squinted, trying to make sense of it all.

"Bronagh Erienne *Frye*, lad. Frye, it is."

"Jaysus!" Riley bolted to his feet, his mouth dry, and a fine film of perspiration coating his skin. He took the page from Brady again. "Aye, I see it now. Frye."

"Like your Bridget." Brady narrowed his gaze. "But wouldn't marryin' Culley have fulfilled the requirements to break the spell?"

"But he died." Riley sobered, his palms growing sweaty. "Did anyone ever tell you about the whispering?"

"No. What whispering?"

Riley cleared his throat and released a long sigh. "Culley heard it all his life. It's a faint whispering or sighing that comes from *Caisleán Dubh*. I never heard it until . . ."

"Until after Culley died." Brady pulled his rosary beads from his pocket and clutched them in his fist. "I'm feelin' blasphemous again, lad."

Riley had to smile. "We weren't the evil person who put a spell on the castle."

"True." Brady relaxed somewhat. "So *you* now hear the sounds from *Caisleán Dubh*?"

"Aye, but only since Culley's death."

"And . . ." Brady shrugged and gave Riley a sheepish grin. "I have to ask, lad."

"About Bridget?"

"And you."

Riley couldn't prevent himself from telling his old teacher and friend that he'd found the love of his heart. "She hears the castle, too," he said very carefully, not wanting Brady or anyone to believe the curse had *made* him fall in love with Bridget. "I asked her to marry me this morning, but not because of the whispers or curse or *Caisleán Dubh*. I asked her, because I love her."

Brady sighed and stood, reaching for Riley's hand. "Well, now, and doesn't it speak well of you to know you asked before you learned Bronagh's last name?"

"I hope so," Riley said, holding the page in his hand. "May I keep this? I want to show it to Bridget."

"Aye, of course." Brady waved Riley away. "You're

dismissed, lad," his old teacher said with a grin. "I've research to do."

"Thank you, Brady." Riley stood staring at the document for a few seconds, hoping Bridget would understand.

He made his way back to Harrigan's with Brady's note
in his pocket. He'd learned so much so fast. Riley would
have to tell Bridget everything. He didn't want any secrets
between them as they began their life together.

Most of all, he didn't want her to think he'd known
about this before last night. That would cheapen what
they'd shared, and Riley couldn't bear that. Bridget was
too precious to hurt.

By the time Harrigan finished with another customer
and helped Riley load the cumbersome part into the back
of his lorry, the day was more than half spent. Riley was
so eager to get back to Bridget he could barely stand it.
His day had started late—but with good reason—and now
he was hours behind schedule.

He stopped at the barn and dropped off the part. Most
of the afternoon had waned by the time Riley parked his
lorry in front of the cottage.

He climbed out of the cab and stretched, deciding a
shower was definitely in order. He paused, wondering if
he could convince Bridget to wash his back. No, he
wouldn't coax her into any more intimacy until he'd told
her everything. Anything less would be dishonest. He
couldn't spring this news on her smelling like this,
though.

"To the shower with you, Mulligan," he muttered,
trudging around to the back door. He stepped inside and
stopped, listening to the eerie silence. Where was Bridget? He glanced at the stove, surprised to find nothing
simmering or baking.

Maybe she was taking a nap. They both had every reason to be exhausted after last night, though Riley was particularly enthusiastic about seeing her again. Holding her.
Kissing her.

And getting an answer to his proposal.

He patted the pocket with Brady's notes, then headed up the stairs and to his room. After gathering clean clothes, he showered and shaved, transferring the paper into the pocket of his clean shirt. Eager to see Bridget, he bounded down the stairs—missing the low beam—only to find the kitchen still silent. Still empty.

He ventured into the parlor, down to the cellar, then up to Bridget's attic room. Everything looked fine, except that there was no sign of Bridget.

He returned to the kitchen, thinking she might have left a note, but he found nothing. At the window, he gazed out at the gathering darkness and worried.

Caisleán Dubh had a glow about it this evening. Riley blinked, and looked again. No, *Caisleán Dubh* had a glow coming from *inside* it. "Bridget." She was waiting for him there—waiting to give him her answer. Of course. It made perfect sense that she'd want to meet him there.

He ran across the meadow, slowing his pace once he reached the castle's foundation. Eager to see Bridget, he didn't even hesitate to slip through the opening as he had in the past.

The whispering was back, circling and beckoning him. Riley swallowed hard. Aye, he was Aidan's descendant, and it had fallen to him—both the responsibility and the love. He hadn't asked for it, but there it was. Now he would simply have to deal with it. But first, he wanted to see Bridget's smiling face.

"Bridget?" he called, scanning the main chamber. She'd placed the candles beside Aidan's portrait again. He looked around, but didn't see her. "Where are you, lass?"

"Behind you."

Riley spun around at the sound of her voice, spying her standing at the base of the steps. "There you are," he said, approaching her. "I was worried. You could've left a note, Bridget."

Something white came flying toward him. He ducked and the plate shattered on the marble floor. "Jaysus." He continued toward her, dodging flying saucers of the earthly kind all the way. "Stop, Bridget!"

"Don't you mean *Bronagh*?" she asked, her voice icy.

He stopped a few feet away, gazing up into her face. She'd been crying, and she held a flashlight in one hand and a plate in the other. "No," he said quietly. "I said Bridget and that's what I meant."

"Why didn't you tell me?" She stood there on the steps, a plate clutched in her hand.

He shook his head. "You'll have to be more specific, lass. Tell you about what?"

"About Bronagh Erienne *Frye*."

"How did you—" Riley stopped and drew a deep breath. "Who told you? I just found out my—"

"I found her death certificate, or whatever they called it back then." She dropped her arms to her sides, still holding the plate.

A basket of plates sat on the step at her feet. She'd come well armed.

"I saw the date, Riley. The *date*." She flung the plate, barely missing his head.

Now he was really confused. "What date, lass?" He shrugged. "I just saw Brady this afternoon, and he showed me his notes." He withdrew the paper from his shirt pocket and unfolded it. "Aye, it says Frye."

"You expect me to believe you didn't *know*?" Her voice trembled and she bit her lower lip. "That you didn't sleep with me just to stop your silly old curse?"

He took a step toward her, but she retreated a step, steadying herself with her hand on the wall—not the banister. "Bridget, it wasn't like that." He reached toward her. "Come down here and let's talk about it, love."

"Don't call me that."

"All right." Riley couldn't lose her now, and he didn't deserve to lose her. "Bridget, it's the truth. I didn't know her last name until today. Brady will vouch for me."

"You . . . you didn't see the death certificate before . . . ?"

"No. I did *not*."

"Well . . ."

"Come, lass." He held his hand out to her and thunder shook the ground beneath them. "I came here to tell you what I learned today, because I don't want to begin our marriage with secrets. We're meant to be together, but we knew it before we saw the bloody name."

"I want to believe you," she whispered as lightning flashed, illuminating the chamber.

He took another step, slowly closing the gap that separated them—physically and emotionally. "I love *you*, Bridget. I wouldn't care if your name was Bridget Elizabeth Francesca Martini instead of Frye."

She smiled.

"Ah, there's me lass." He was at the bottom step now, reaching for her. "Come with me. Let's talk about our marriage. Our future together."

"I . . ." She retreated another step. "I'm not sure."

"Don't go up the stairs, Bridget," he said. "It's dark. You could fall."

"Like Bronagh?"

"You aren't Bronagh."

"I . . . I'm not so sure."

"What?" Riley climbed up one step. "Even if the spell the witch cast is true, it doesn't matter. You've proven we can enter *Caisleán Dubh* without dropping dead."

"Yes." Her voice sounded vague and distant. "But the dreams, Riley."

Aye, the dreams. He exhaled very slowly, deciding to tell her everything. "I had dreams, too." She gasped and he added, "About Aidan and Bronagh."

"Not yourself?"

"I . . . I'm not sure."

"And Bronagh? Not . . . me?"

He swallowed hard, trying to find the words to explain it all. "I can't deny there's something special—even powerful—between us, Bridget." He shrugged. "Maybe we're soul mates. Maybe you were Bronagh and I was Aidan.

Who knows? Does it really matter, since we love each other?"

"I do love you," she said. "But . . ."

"But what?" He took another step, but she retreated two more. She still had the flashlight, but all the circular artillery sat safely on a lower step.

"The dreams. I need to understand them. I think they took place here in the castle."

"Aye," he said. "I felt it, too."

"When we were here with the inspector, I had . . . images flashing through my mind of myself with my dream lover." She gave him that sad smile again. "With you."

Riley's throat went dry and he could barely swallow. "Aye. I know." He reached again. "Come down here so we can kiss and make up proper."

"What about the date, Riley?" she asked. "Did you know that yesterday was the anniversary of Bronagh's death?"

Taken aback, Riley narrowed his gaze. "The devil, you say?" He raked his fingers through his hair. "No. I didn't know. Are you very sure about this?"

"Yes." Her voice was calmer now, but she made no effort to halt her slow but steady retreat up the stairs. "I want to believe you," she repeated. "I need to understand all this. I need to know the whole truth."

The wind outside whipped through the opening. The doors behind him groaned and shuddered. He looked over his shoulder as thunder again reverberated through the castle. Lightning flashed overhead. Had it been inside the castle? No, of course not.

He turned to Bridget again.

But she was gone.

Twenty-one

Bridget's heart hammered as she raced up the steps, being careful not to touch the banister. She needed to see more of *Caisleán Dubh*. She *had* to know if she was Bronagh. It sounded crazy, yet in a way it all made sense.

She was a Frye, like Bronagh. She'd fallen in love with not one, but too Mulligan men. She heard the castle's whispering, especially now as it seemed to urge her up the circular stairs.

What was happening to her? Was she *becoming* Bronagh? No, that was ridiculous. She was Bridget and she wasn't about to fling herself to her death from the top of the tower.

But she needed to see the room where her dreams had taken place. Aidan's bedchamber. It had to be. Somehow, she knew exactly where she would find it. She didn't pause to wonder why now, but she would later. How could she not?

She ventured through an archway at the next floor, rather than continuing up the stairs. Mr. Kelley had said the master bedchamber was on this floor. Hadn't he?

Riley called her name, and guilt niggled at her. "I'm here, Riley," she said. "I'm all right. I just have to see."

"I'm coming, too."

"Be careful." She couldn't bear for anything to happen to him because of her impulsiveness. After all, *she* had the flashlight.

Another thunderclap shook the castle as Bridget shoved on a heavy planked door. It squealed in protest, and the shutters covering the windows inside burst open, admitting a fierce gust of wind that almost slammed the door in her face.

Bridget screamed, taking several seconds to recover her ability to breathe. The gale stirred the dust in the room and she sneezed.

Riley came in behind her and placed his hand on her shoulder. "You scared me out of my wits."

"I . . . I'm sorry. I had to see." Only a little twilight remained outside, as she aimed her flashlight at the huge object in the corner. A bed. "Aidan's?"

"I . . . I think so," Riley whispered.

A flash of lightning illuminated the room, followed by another, and another. "Yes," she said. "I've seen it before." A shudder rippled through her and she walked slowly toward it, knowing Riley was right behind her. "They made love here. They made a child here—a child who never took his first breath." A sob choked free from her throat and she bit down on her knuckles to silence herself.

"Aye." Riley's voice sounded odd. Respectful.

"You know it's true," Bridget said. "Their spirits live on inside us. Riley, it's *true!*" She turned in a slow circle, noticing the huge hearth across from the window. "They made love in front of the fire, too."

"Aye." Riley exhaled very slowly, sliding his arms around her from behind.

Though the dreams had worried her, now that she knew the truth, a sense of peace washed over her. She leaned back against his broad chest, feeling his love and his strength. "Thank you."

"For what?" he asked.

"Loving me."

He turned her slowly in his arms as another blast of wind made the shutters close and open again and again. "I *do* love you, no matter when or if our spirits ever lived or loved before." He kissed her and she returned the kiss with a passion that left him weak in the knees.

She came up for air. "I love you, too."

The wind died. The thunder and lightning ceased.

He took Bridget's hand in his and led her to the window. A full moon broke through the clouds, bathing the farm and the sea below them in silver.

"It's beautiful," she whispered.

"Aye." He slid behind her again with his arms about her waist and his chin resting on her shoulder. "I'm thinking that when we renovate the castle, we shouldn't stop with the ground floor."

"No?" Her pulse quickened. "For the bed-and-breakfast?"

"Aye."

"I'd like that."

"Would you . . . ?" He kissed the side of her neck.

Bridget melted into him, remembering the image she'd had of him holding her just this way. "Bronagh wanted to live here," she said. "And so do I."

"Then you shall." He held her close. "*We* shall."

"Yes." Bridget smiled to herself, feeling at peace for the first time in a very long time. "Bronagh loved Aidan with all her heart."

Riley sighed. "I know she did. And he loved her."

Bridget nodded. "It was awful for them both."

He nodded against her. "It's over now."

Bridget turned in his embrace and gazed into his handsome, moonlit face. "No, it's not over."

He flashed her that crooked grin that made her dizzy with desire.

She reached up to caress his cheek. "I will marry you, Riley Francis Mulligan," she said, and the whispering of *Caisleán Dubh* embraced them with joyous song.

"Thank the Blessed Virgin and all the saints." Riley

spun her in a circle, then set her back on her feet as the whispering ended. "We'll make this old castle a real home, Bridget. For us, for Jacob, for all the brothers and sisters we'll create for him. . . ."

"Oh, yes," she breathed, closing her eyes and seeing Aidan and Bronagh as they had been before the tragedy. In her heart, she bid them farewell, but it wasn't the end—not for any of them.

"It's time to come home."

Epilogue

Riley stood in the main chamber of *Caisleán Dubh*, gazing up at the restored portrait of his ancestor, Aidan Mulligan. After the grime and damage from moisture, salt, and age had been repaired, it became clear that Riley definitely resembled Aidan.

However, staring into Aidan's eyes was more like staring into the eyes of Patrick Mulligan so long ago. It comforted Riley to see the resemblance—and to know that the dreams he'd had of Aidan had truly been of himself. With Bridget—not Bronagh.

He turned to survey the room, decorated with Irish lace and a profusion of vines and flowers. Chairs filled with guests sat theater fashion, and a white carpet stretched its entire length from the wall of windows and open French doors where the old double doors had been, to the bottom of the curving staircase. An altar of white roses and violets adorned the bottom step, where Father O'Malley waited.

All the renovations respected the historical integrity of the castle. Bridget and the Irish Trust wouldn't have it any other way. Riley smiled to himself.

Since the night Bridget accepted his proposal, the curse

or spell seemed to have vanished. Since then, there had been no whispers, no aphrodisiac banister—not that they needed one.

"Uncle Riley?" Jacob asked from his side. "I'm glad you and Momma are getting married."

"I'm glad, too." A smile curved Riley's lips as he gazed down at his nephew and best man. Culley's son. Nothing could be more perfect.

Harp music came from an area beneath the stairs, the crisp notes echoing off the high ceiling. Mr. and Mrs. Larabee came over to pump Riley's hand again, declaring their joy about the marriage. Bridget and Jacob had been thrilled that they'd made the trip, though General Lee had, thankfully, remained in Tennessee.

The tone of the music shifted, and the Larabees took their seats. Riley and Jacob walked quietly to the altar, where Father O'Malley beamed at them both. Riley turned his attention to the French doors, watching his old friend Sean Collins escort Mum up the aisle. Tears of joy streamed down her face and she blew Riley a kiss before taking her seat.

Kevin Gilhooley and Maggie came next. Riley's baby sister looked dazzling in a gown of violet lace. Her smile for Riley reflected his own joy as she took her position as maid of honor.

The music grew louder and Riley's breath stuttered. All eyes turned toward the wall of windows overlooking the sea. Brady appeared first, holding his elbow out for the bride.

A vision in Irish lace, Bridget appeared beside Brady and took his arm. Her face was covered by a veil, and the train trailed several yards behind her as they made their way toward the altar.

Riley swallowed a lump in his throat and blinked rapidly as his love for this woman billowed through him. By the time Brady placed her hand in his, he was dizzy with it.

"You're beautiful," he whispered, gazing through the lace at her lovely face.

"I could eat you with a spoon," she whispered, smiling.

The ceremony was long and there wasn't a dry eye in the place. They all must have felt it, too—the powerful joining of two hearts, two lives.

And two souls for eternity.

"You may kiss the bride," Father O'Malley finally said.

Riley tenderly lifted the lace covering Bridget's smile and embraced her. Their kiss was gentle and sweet, yet filled with promise.

A faint, magical whirlwind encircled the bride and groom. Riley sensed that the whispers had returned to say good-bye.

Bridget smiled up at him with joy glittering in her eyes. Applause and cheers echoed through the castle from behind them, but he distinctly heard his bride's fervent whisper.

"Bingo, Granny. Bingo."

Dear Readers:

This opportunity to know Ireland through the Mulligans has been one of the most exciting and rewarding experiences of my career. I hope to write many more novels set in Ireland, as I am now madly in love with that lovely emerald isle. I hope you enjoy sharing Bridget and Riley's adventure.

I love to hear from readers. You can write to me at P.O. Box 274, Marylhurst, OR 97036. I'm easy to find online at www.debstover.com, or e-mail deb@debstover.com.

"The Irish Blessing"
Author Unknown

May the road rise up to meet you.
May the wind be always at your back.
May the sun shine warm upon your face;
the rains fall soft upon your fields and until we
      meet again,
may God hold you in the palm of His hand.

Go n'éirí an bothar leat
Go raibh an ghaoth go brách ag do chúl
Go lonraí an ghrian go te ar d'aghaidh
Go dtite an bháisteach go mín ar do pháirceanna
Agus go mbuailimid le chéile arís,
Go gcoinní Dia i mbos A láimhe thú